Shadows of War

Book 2
The King's Frog Hunter

Books by Ken Young

The King's Frog Hunter

Shadows of War

Shadows of War

Book 2

The King's Frog Hunter

Ken Young

North Point Publishing
California, U.S.A.

Requests for permission to make copies of any part of the work should be
mailed to the following address:
Permissions Department
North Point Publishing Company
P.O. Box 157, Paradise, CA 95967

For more information about the book and the author contact:
www.kingsfroghunter.com

ISBN-13: 978-0-9903488-3-2

Library of Congress Control Number: 2018903395

Maps by Ken Young,
Cover and Map Illustrations by Steve Ferchaud
Cover and Interior Design by C. Young

Printed in the United States of America

First edition

For my remarkable wife, Cindy,
without whom, I'd be lost.
And for our amazing daughter, Heather.

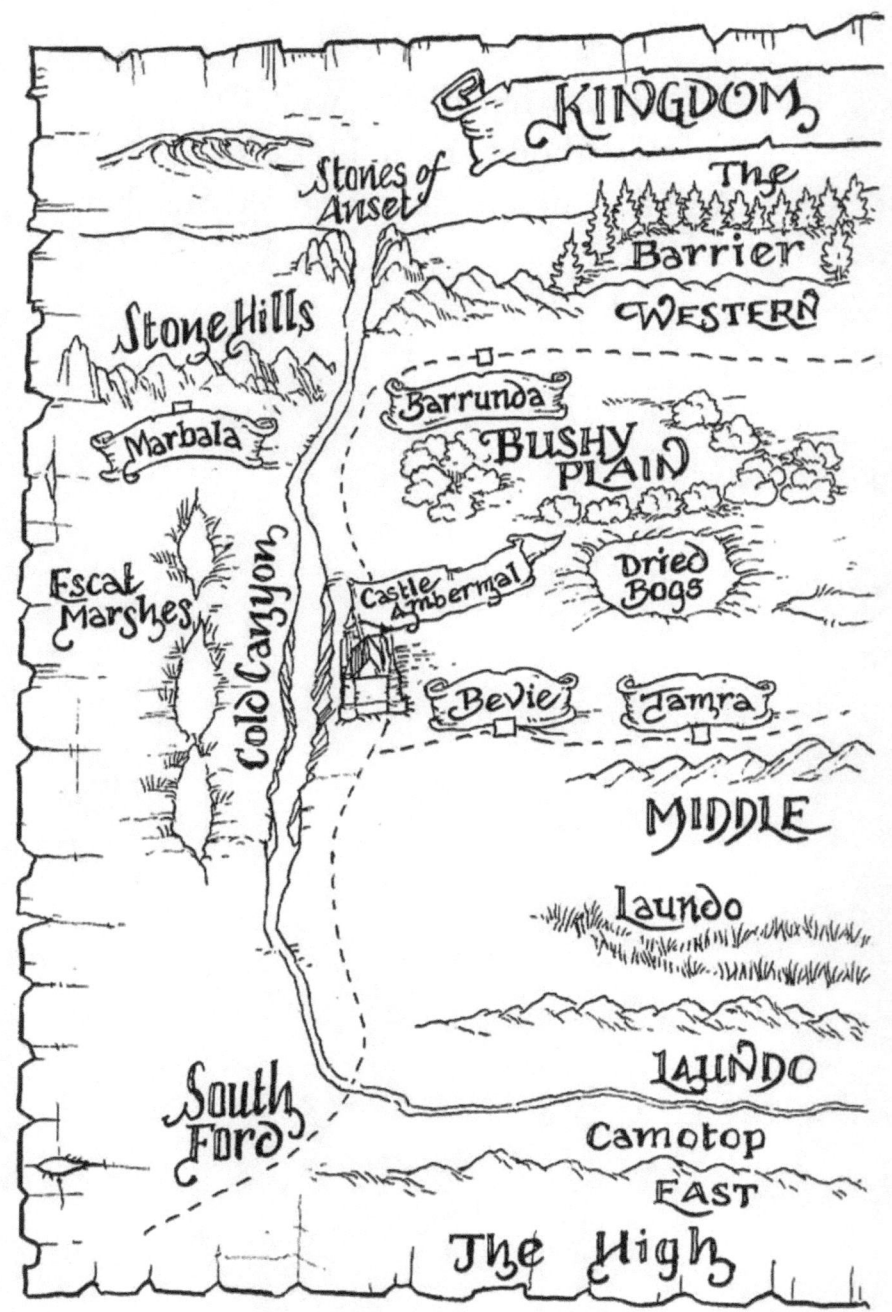

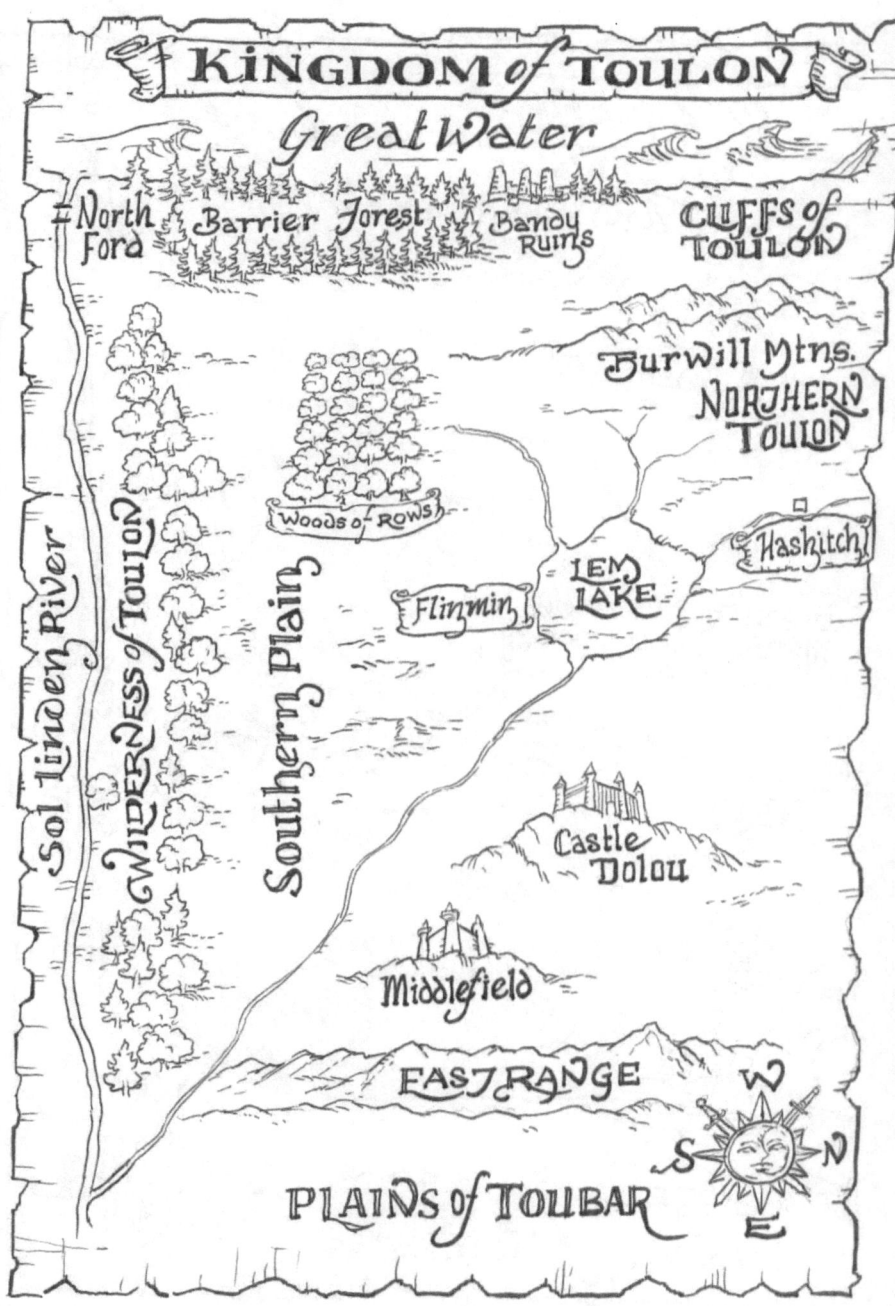

Author's Note

This story is a continuation of The King's Frog Hunter. It begins where the epilogue of the first book left us: leaving Thalmus' serene meadow in the hopeful glow of a new future for the Kingdom of Ameram. Thus begins, *The Shadows of War*.

At the back of the book are profiles of the characters, animals, and locations in the story. I hope this will help you with pronunciation of the names, and provide additional information about the people, creatures, and places in the Kingdom of Ameram. The maps, in the front of the book, should be a good visual aide as you follow the events taking place in the narrative. Please note the maps have been oriented with West on top, North is to the right. My wish is that you will heed the messages and thoroughly enjoy the adventure.

Table of Contents

Maps		*viii*
I	*Dudoon*	15
II	*The Message & Commission*	27
III	*Befuddlement*	38
IV	*A Strange New Friend*	47
V	*Faithful*	60
VI	*The Broken Stone*	72
VII	*The North Ford*	82
VIII	*A Dangerous Decision.*	96
IX	*Veracitas & Thoe*	108
X	*The Beast*	121
XI	*Lord Glasrauss*	131
XII	*Discovery*	142
XIII	*The Woods of Rows*	151
XIV	*The Heart of the Woods*	162
XV	*Arborina and the Kairtaykars*	174
XVI	*Swords at the South Ford*	185
XVII	*Ekala's Awakening*	195

XVIII	*The Gulley*	203
XIX	*Betrayal*	212
XX	*Into the Wilderness*	223
XXI	*Kali's Frustration*	233
XXII	*Ahmautahmin*	241
XXIII	*Surprise at the River*	253
XXIV	*Barges on the Water*	263
XXV	*Battle at the North Ford*	272
XXVI	*It is Not Finished*	284
XXVII	*Masquerade*	294
XXVIII	*Ello*	309
XXIX	*Message Delivered*	320
XXX	*Surprise in the Torchlight*	332
XXXI	*Duty Fulfilled*	345
XXXII	*The Lords of Barrunda*	358
XXXIII	*Lord Rundall & the Message*	369
Profiles		384
Acknowledgements/About Author		398

One must learn to grasp the messages of truth we hear, see and feel. Whether they stare us in the face, ring warning in our ears, prickle our skin or pass by us unnoticed like a stranger in a crowd. For it is by the understanding of these signals that we act, and choose the paths we travel. To be ignorant of, or to ignore the messages, will spiral one down a trail that can only end in ruin.

-- Lord Rundall

Chapter One
Dudoon

Larma stood on the precipice of the southern waterfall as the creek poured smoothly over the edge of Table Top Mountain and spilled into a chaotic pond far below. Swirling, damp spray rose up from the water's turmoil. It was driven by wind hitting the mountain's stone wall and then pushing upward to the flat top, tugging at the mystic's loose pants and blouse, and flipping her long silver hair as she balanced straight and firm on the edge of the cliff. The circling mist was cool on her skin, a refreshing respite from the morning sun.

The crashing noise of the waterfall filled the air; yet, she could hear the wind's complaints, its teasing banter, and something more. Buried deep in its chatter were clashing messages she could not quite understand—one that spoke of change, another of joy, and something else…something wicked. *What was it?* Larma lifted her ancient eyes to watch formations of white clouds tumbling and pushing south through the blue sky over the Great Plain. She saw worry and heard mumbled tales of trouble in the wayward clouds. Despite the pleasant picture of normality, all was not right. *What were the clouds and wind trying to tell her?*

Looking down, she followed the waterfall's long decent to the foot of Table Top. From there, the water flowed into a run that snaked across the Great Plain all the way to the Dudoon Bog and Bufon Marsh, an isolated and mysterious region.

The Kingdom of Ameram's Middle Road began near Castle Ambermal and ended at the village of Dudoon. However, the main road turned before the village, squeezed between the marsh and bog and crossed the north end of the Bushy Plain to the Western Hills Road. North of Dudoon was the road-less expanse of the Great Plain. Thus, few people ventured into the remote town unless for business. Though the villagers of Dudoon had prospered as farmers, growing fruit trees in the Middle Hills and grain along the river, the constant danger from the marsh and ponds of the bog lay at their doorstep. Only Thalmus, the King's Frog Hunter, knew the marsh and bog, its creatures and secrets well enough to survive its grip.

Larma smiled as his image came to mind. Thalmus, the man who had helped Ekala save the kingdom from Metro and fulfill her prophecy; the man who was always ready, always present when called. He had been a Guardian almost as long as she had. There were so few left of the old order—so few. Sighing, she wondered how much longer they could survive. Who would take their place? Who had the ancient knowledge and strength to rise up and combat the evil? Veracitas, the Stone Cutter, perhaps? His daughter, Boschina, could she learn? *She has the heart*, Larma thought. *I must spend more time with her, try to teach her.*

Larma took one last look at the wayward clouds, felt the wind pressing her, the spray from the falls on her face, and then turned away from the cliff and walked to her horse. Eidolon was waiting for her alongside the lazy creek, just a short six meters from the edge where it disappeared from the Top. Larma swung onto Eidolon's back with the agility of a young girl. The majestic gray horse bobbed her head, crossed the water, and trotted along the Top's southern rim.

They came to a stop at a promontory with sheer cliffs on three sides. The wind had followed and now she could hear and understand one of the messages. The other two had blown away with the clouds. She sat quietly atop Eidolon, waiting and studying the plain. In the distance, she could just now make out two riders coming toward Table Top. The dust from their horses' hooves barely rose behind them, but she could tell the color of the riders' clothing—maroon and gray. They were Oleen soldiers, scouts for the column that was still out of sight behind them. One of the wind's messages was confirmed: Queen Ekala Oleen was on her way to Table Top.

Turning Eidolon, they started toward home across the open, undulating terrain of the flat top mountain. Joy replaced concern as Larma rode over the hard-creased ground, stopping twice to admire a new bloom of tiny purple flowers blanketing a swale and popping up through brown, craggy rock formations. She had not seen Ekala since the coronation and was thrilled that her royal student was returning to the hollow. The mystic was also looking forward to hearing how Ekala was faring in her new role. Larma rode under the stone archway into the hollow that bore her name, passing the water wheel, flume, and terraced gardens where workers tended rows of various sizes and colors of plants.

"I have good news," she announced to the women. "Ekala Oleen will be here tonight."

The women burst into cheers as Larma rode on through the cave that came out onto the wide, flat shelf of her mountain fortress. She dismounted, stroked Eidolon's nose, and released her to go to the stable on her own. She then walked to the eating tables and cooking area, where the head cook was evaluating the condition of their pots and pans.

"Good morning, Larma. Did you enjoy your ride?"

"Yes, Saylan, I did. I received good news. We will have an additional twenty or more to feed over the next several days. Can you prepare food for that many more?"

"Of course. As you wish, Larma. May I ask: who are these people?"

"Someone you know well. Our queen, Ekala Oleen, and her escort."

A broad smile spread on the woman's face. "What a delight." Then her expression changed to concern. She looked at the wooden tables, benches, and cooking fire. "Oh, I must get busy; there is much to be done. We have to harvest more crops, fire up the other oven, get all the bowls cleaned, bring in feed for the horses…." She glanced around the perimeter of the shelf at the caves and huts that were built into and along the stone cliffs. "And rooms to prepare."

* * *

When Queen Ekala Oleen and her entourage left the serene meadows and hospitality of Thalmus' home, she was refreshed and looking forward to an enjoyable tour of the kingdom, especially returning to Table Top Mountain and spending time with Larma. Accompanying the Queen of Ameram was the Stone Cutter's Daughter, Boschina; the exiled Crown Prince of Toulon, Prince Bolimaz; his companion and guardian soldier, Camp; and a force of Oleen soldiers under the command of Captain Ritzs. They had spent two restful days with the King's Frog Hunter, his animal companions, and the families from the Village of Tamra. Riding north on the Middle Road, they traveled for two long dusty days, past the turn-off to the Western Hills Road, and finally stopped to rest and visit with the villagers of Dudoon.

The people were thrilled to see the queen. As a princess, she had visited their town many times on her way to and from the castle. She had always treated them as equals, purchasing supplies and fruit for the community on Table Top. But now, she was the ruler of the land and they honored her with a banquet and presented her with gifts of wood bowls and goblets made from the trunks of their olive trees. The party lasted late into the night. Ekala spoke of her plans for the kingdom, Boschina answered questions about her father and his famous statue of the king, and Prince Bolimaz—known to them as Maz—announced his complete support for the Queen of Ameram and a new relationship with his country, Toulon (once he regained control, of course).

Finally, when the three honored guests, tired and full of delicious food, left the noisy, warm glow of the hall and stepped into the night, they were met by a quiet, murky darkness. The odor of wet earth and decaying plants wafted up from the bog. A frog croaked in the distance, answered by another frog's deep and throaty response. And then came a sound they had never heard before, a vicious growl that turned into a wailing howl that rang in their ears and hung on the cold air.

"What was that?" Boschina asked, her heartbeat quickening.

Maz shivered, more from the sudden change of warmth and light than from fear of the howl. "It sounded like...I'm not sure," Maz said. "I can't see a thing out here."

"Whatever it is, I sure don't want to meet it in this darkness," Ekala said, glancing around. "Where are Camp and Ritzs?"

Suddenly, the door to the hall swung open and a square of light shone on them. Captain Ritzs and Camp stepped out with a torch in each hand.

"Sorry, Oleen," Captain Ritzs said. "We were trying to get these torches lit from the kitchen fire."

"Thank you, Ritzs," Ekala said, taking one of the torches. "Where is Lander?"

"I don't know. She must be making the rounds, checking the posts."

"Are the horses safe?"

"Oh, yes. Fed, watered, and guarded."

The leader of the village, a bulbous man with graying, curly hair and beard, had followed Ritzs and was standing in the doorway, listening. "Did you hear the creature's howl?" he asked.

"What is it?" Boschina asked, staring into the night.

"Don't know. No one has seen it." He glanced back into the room. "People are scared to go out at night. Some sheep and cattle have gone missing; we're sure it's that beast out there 'cause the frogs rarely venture out of their ponds." He paused, looking into the darkness. "You'll be alright, Your Majesty. You have the torches now and the protection of your guards."

Ekala felt the heat on her face from the torch in her hand. *Guards.* She still wasn't used to this blanket of security. No one had paid attention to her traveling alone before becoming queen. Now, she couldn't go anywhere without her overly protective force of Oleens. "How long has the creature been there?" she asked.

The man thought for a moment. "Oh, two...maybe three full moons."

"If it's a problem, we will hunt it for you," Ekala said.

"Thank you, Your Majesty. I would not venture into that place. It's a trap."

Ekala studied the man, half lit by the light from the room and the flare of a torch. His name was Onus—Lord Onus of Dudoon. He had once been one of her father's advisers on the Council of Learned Men, which she disbanded upon becoming queen. To Ekala, they were an unnecessary gaggle of political men who had failed to support her father in his desperate time of need. There was no way she would take advice from such a lot.

"That is to say," Lord Onus added, his eyes looking toward the marsh. "I would not go there, but you are a warrior and you have your soldiers."

She did not like the way he spoke the words, how he avoided looking directly at her. Lord Onus had been friendly to her when she was just the king's daughter, a rambunctious princess. Now that she was ruler, there was an underlying tension in his demeanor. Along with some of the other Learned Men, he had publicly protested their dismissal and warned of disaster without their guidance. She had disregarded their statements as embarrassment, hurt feelings, and the loss of influence. Not trusting the wisdom of these men was one thing, but suspecting their loyalty to the Kingdom of Ameram was entirely different.

"We will see you in the morning before we leave, yes?" she said.

Lord Onus nodded and watched the group walk to their camp on the outskirts of town with a torchbearer at the front, in back, and one on each side. They didn't speak much. The crunching of their boots, the memory of the howl, and then the comfort of their blankets was enough. Despite her exhaustion, Ekala could not feel at ease. Even with her guards nearby, she woke several times to listen, thinking she had heard howls and screams far off in the night.

* * *

In the gloom of the Dudoon Bog a lone rider weaved carefully between stagnant ponds, searching for a safe trail. Drifting clouds smeared any moonlight that might have shone on his path. The horse's wide eyes searched the shifting, dark shadows. Her nostrils flared, inhaling smells that struck fear. She snorted, chomped at the bit between her teeth, and pulled at the tight reins controlling her head.

"Whoa, steady now," the man on her back said. "We'll be out of here soon."

Entering the bog at this hour had not been his choice. But it was part of the agreement and he knew that his secret could not stand the light of day. So here he was, against all caution, riding into this dangerous place. *Was the reward worth the risk?* he wondered.

The rider pulled his horse to a halt. Peering into the night, he looked for something that he could recognize—something that would tell him which direction to go. A mist drifting from the nearby water surrounded him with a cold embrace and obscured the path ahead. The man tightened his coat, adjusted his hat, and tugged at his gloves. The horse was fidgeting, stepping, and shuffling. "Shhh—shh," he whispered, trying to calm her.

Something ran across the trail behind him, kicking up bits of mud. He turned quickly, but the creature was gone before he could tell what it was. A sudden splash in the water to his right spun him in that direction. He couldn't see anything—it was too dark. The man urged the horse slowly forward. The horse sniffed and snorted, bobbing her head. Another splash, this time to his left; he was deeper into the bog than he had wanted to be. "I'll be alright if I stay on the trail," the man told himself. A squeal in the mist, then a deep croak of a frog; the horse stopped and tried to back up. He pulled the reins tighter and reached for his sword.

"That's far enough," a voice announced from the darkness. "Drop the bags and go."

The rider lifted two canvas bags that had been strung across the horse's shoulders, one hanging on each side. He dropped them to the ground and waited.

"I said go," the voice said.

"What about my pay?"

"Your reward is your life," the voice declared.

The rider hesitated. "You owe me."

"I owe you nothing. If you want to give your life too, then stay."

The rider stared into the darkness. A splash to his left—closer than before. The horse jerked. "I'll be back in the daylight," he said.

"Good," the voice replied. "The frogs can see you better then."

The rider took several quick breaths. "If you don't pay me, I'll report you."

The unseen man laughed. "No one dares come in here. They're all afraid."

"The frog hunter isn't," the rider replied, gripping his sword. "He'd find you."

"You're a fool," the voice said angrily. "Do you think Thalmus would protect you after what you have done? No, he would not. You are alone."

A chill suddenly struck the rider. He heard a hideous growl and he shivered with panic. The horse reared and he almost slid off her back. Hanging on, he pulled himself onto the saddle. "Run, run," he screamed at the horse. He heard claws digging at the dirt, saw a hairy creature leaping out of the darkness, and felt its yellow fangs puncture his neck. Its weight knocked him from the charging horse to the ground, where he lay broken and bleeding under the beast.

* * *

In the morning, the Oleen soldiers rolled up their blankets and pup-tents, shared a morning meal, put out the cook fires, and loaded fresh supplies onto the pack horses. Camp, Prince Bolimaz's friend and protector since they had escaped from Toulon, had risen early and rode along the outskirts of the bog looking for the creature's tracks. Before eating, Boschina bound her blankets and strapped them along with her clothing bag onto her horse, Radise. The roan nickered, bumped, and then rubbed Boschina with her head. She was happy that they were preparing to leave. Maz crawled out of his small tent, stretching his muscular torso from side to side. In the cool mornings, he could still feel the blade that had cut through his ribs. He sighed, feeling the ache of the healing wound; a brief memory of Metro's spell and the swordfight with Corsair lingered in his mind.

Ekala noticed his discomfort as she tied her bedding and prepared her things for packing. "That's not the look of a man who is fully healed," she said, searching her bag.

"A 'good morning, Prince' would have made this man feel better," he responded.

Ekala smiled. "Good morning, Prince Bolimaz."

"And a good morning to you, Queen Ekala Oleen," he replied with a smile. "What are you looking for? Did you lose something?"

"I'm missing my blue shirt," Ekala answered, closing the bag.

"Soapy must have taken it to clean," Boschina said as she picked up Ekala's things to take to the horses. "I think she took my old pants yesterday."

Ekala shook her head. "She needs to check with me. I was going to wear it today."

"I wouldn't complain," Maz said, "when you've got someone willing to wash your clothes."

Ekala grunted. "I suppose. Let's get on the road. I'm anxious to get to the Top."

Captain Ritzs and her force sat on their horses in formation as Queen Ekala Oleen, Prince Bolimaz, and Boschina said goodbye to the elders and people of the village. The curly-bearded Lord Onus bowed his head briefly. "Did you have a good night's sleep, Your Majesty? No troublesome worries?"

What an odd question to ask me, Ekala thought. She decided to ignore it. "We are all thankful for your village's kind hospitality," she replied.

Lord Onus was looking directly at her now with a grin on his face. "Well, thank you for stopping in our little village, Your Majesty. In case we don't meet again, give my regards to King Ahmbin, your father. Please tell him that...that we miss him."

His intention was clear; he preferred her father over her as a ruler. He had just confirmed her suspicion of his loyalty. His words of affection for her father were false.

"I will tell him," Ekala responded. "And don't be so sure we will not meet again."

"You..." Lord Onus started and then stopped. The smile dropped from his face as he bowed his head. "Goodbye, Your Majesty."

Ekala turned to her waiting soldiers.

"Are we ready, Captain Ritzs?" Ekala asked after she had settled onto an impatient Shadahn. The shiny black warhorse was ready to run.

"Yes, Oleen," Captain Ritzs answered. "Lander is ready to scout ahead with Karl when you're ready."

Ekala looked over at Lander, a strong woman with short black hair and piercing blue eyes; an archer of reputation and a dedicated follower of hers for some time. Lander had led a force in the fight for control of the North Gate at Table Top. She then came to the Battle for Ambermal in Larma's force and fought tirelessly, shooting her arrows with pinpoint accuracy to counter Metro's archers. As always, Lander sat upright, with a large knife belted on her hip. A bow that she had made herself protruded from a cover tied to the saddle; a quiver of arrows was strapped to her back and two more on the horse's sides. She was a formidable warrior.

"You look ready, Lander," Ekala said, complementing the archer.

"I'm always ready," she replied with a smile.

"Then go."

Lander and Karl, another archer, trotted away as the Queen of Ameram waved to the crowd and led the column of Oleen soldiers along the Dudoon Run and onto the Great Plain. She knew this area of the plain better than anyone, having traveled it many times to and from the Oleen stronghold on Table Top. Ekala guided them away from the river on a more direct line toward the flat mountain. Boschina rode on one side of her and Maz on the other as she pointed out landmarks: a series of unusual earth mounds, outcroppings of red boulders, a confluence of three dry ravines; all of which she used as trail markers, possible hiding places, or escape routes if she was pursued. After a long day of riding, their direction brought the column alongside the meandering river once again, where they camped for the night. The Oleen soldiers knew their duties and routine: gathering fuel for the cooking fires, making sure the horses were watered and secured, cooking, eating together, and rotating guard duty. Everyone was responsible and took part in the chores, including the queen and prince.

After his watch, Camp removed his sword and plopped down next to Maz and Ekala sitting at one of the fires. "Maybe I'm just tired. It's been a long day," he said. "But something's causing my skin to crawl. I can't grasp why. Didn't hear anything out there, just a bad feeling."

"You're getting old," Maz chided.

Ekala poked the fire with a stick. "I had an odd sense of something strange when I was checking Shadahn and the other horses. I didn't feel it after I came back to the fire."

"You two let that howl last night get into your heads," Maz said.

"Where's Boschina?" Ekala asked.

"She's on watch with Ritzs," Camp said.

"Good, she's not alone," Ekala said. "And Lander?"

"She's on the other side. If there's anything out there, she'll stick it full of arrows."

"That's for sure," Maz said. "She never misses a target, even a moving one."

Ekala agreed. "You can count on her."

By late afternoon of the second day, they approached the entrance trail to the East Gate of Table Top and Larma Hollow. Looking up at the cliff far above, Ekala saw her teacher and old friend standing on the edge, watching. A feeling of joy and calm swept through her like a gentle breeze.

"There's Larma!" Boschina waved.

The scouts, Lander and Karl were waiting at the trailhead with the Oleen guards at the gate. As Ekala rode up, leading the column of soldiers, the guards raised their right arms high over their heads with open hands and chanted, "Oleen, Oleen, Oleen."

Queen Ekala Oleen responded with a smile, raising her open hand and then swinging it down to pat Shadahn, who charged up the narrow dusty route to the open shelf of the mountain fortress, where hundreds stood waiting and cheering as the queen appeared.

* * *

Out on the Plain, in a shallow cave hidden behind boulders on the side of a ravine, snored a beast. The animal was restless in its sleep because the cave was not dark enough for its comfort. The hiding spot was the only place it could find before the sun rose that day. Still, when darkness returned, the beast would rise to do what its blood and its training demanded—follow the scent inhaled into its senses until it found the thing and killed it.

Chapter Two
The Message and Commission

Ekala's return to Larma Hollow was a joy, not only for herself and Larma, but for the entire community. This is where she had first come as a child with her mother and the mystic Larma to be free from the constraints of royalty—of name—and grow into the stone truth of who she was. This is where she developed as a leader, raised and trained an army of dedicated warriors of life, and learned to believe in her prophecy: that she would be the first woman ruler of Ameram. It was here, at Table Top, where as a young girl she had taken the ancient name of Oleen to honor Larma's sister who had been a teacher and spiritual leader. More recently, it was here where Ekala met the mysterious Maz and his friend Camp, who joined Larma and the Oleens to win the battle to secure the Top. Then the army marched to Castle Ambermal, joining their namesake, Ekala Oleen, to defeat Metro and save her father, the king, and the kingdom. And it was here at Larma Hollow, carved into the cliffs and ravines of Table Top Mountain, where Ekala Oleen felt at home.

For four days the royal party enjoyed the camaraderie and atmosphere of a very large family reunion. There were horse races with Boschina on Radise and Ekala on Shadahn, galloping down ravines and splashing through creeks, and then over the flat Top with Maz on his horse, Mendu, and some of the Oleen riders in pursuit—

dust and smiles on their faces. They dug and channeled water in the muddy flumes and harvested vegetables from furrows of the gardens; reveled in boisterous cooking and crowded tables at meals; sang songs and told stories. Maz and Camp taught enthusiastic students sword lessons in the style practiced by the Toulons. In exchange, Maz and Camp learned new methods of gardening and cooking from the proud, stalwart workers of the Oleens. And of course, archery competition, with Lander giving lessons and taking on all comers who challenged her. To Lander's surprise, it was Boschina who came close to matching her in judging distance and the quick fluid movement of continuous accurate shooting. In a final contest, a small wooden box the size of a rabbit was pulled behind a horse and they were each given three arrows to try to hit it as it bounced across the field forty meters away. Boschina shot, pulled an arrow from her quiver, nocked, aimed in front of the moving target and released. She nocked the third arrow and shot again, hitting the mark two out of three times to the cheers of the onlookers. However, Lander stuck all three of her arrows in the target.

"That was good shooting, you two," Ekala said, slapping them both on the shoulder. "I know I've got the best archers in the kingdom right here."

"That goes for Toulon, too," Maz added as they went to examine the target.

"You have improved much since I first saw you shoot at the Battle for Ambermal," Lander said.

"I practice whenever I can," Boschina replied. "But I doubt I will ever match you."

Lander looked at the target where it had been placed on a knoll for all to see. The five arrows with each archer's personal mark protruded from the battered wood surface. Returning her gaze to Boschina, she said, "You're good, Stone Cutter's Daughter. You have a natural feel for movement and timing. Keep practicing and one day you'll best me."

The archer held her gaze on Boschina for a moment, studying the younger woman, and then picked up her bow and quivers and walked away. Boschina watched Lander go. She suddenly sensed a mystery to the archer that felt dangerous, but she dismissed it as admiration for the warrior's strength and skill.

It wasn't all fun and games. Even though there had not been a threat since Ekala became queen and Metro's soldiers were defeated, Larma insisted they remain vigilant, cautious, and prepared. So, guard duty continued through the days and nights at both gates to the Top, as it had been since the Oleens took control. Table Top was Larma's Keep and many people felt it was more secure than Castle Ambermal.

Early on the morning of the fifth day, Ekala rode Shadahn to the lookout—her favorite spot along the cliffs. She dismounted and sat on the rocks. There was no one in sight; the countryside stretched as far as she could see. Closing her eyes, she let her mind drift, remembering when her mother was here with her and then Larma. They had told her this was her place—this secluded, secure place—where she could retreat and think about whatever she wanted or needed to resolve her concerns. She could speak openly here, let her words loose into the vastness of the land and listen for the wisdom returned to her by voices of the past, as well as her own. And so, she asked for guidance as the new ruler of this kingdom, just as she had asked for advice many times over the years

The sound of approaching hooves brought her attention back. Shadahn snorted softly. Glancing over her shoulder, Ekala saw Prince Bolimaz riding toward them. He stopped his horse, swung off to the ground, and walked up to her.

"May I?" he asked, motioning at the nearby ground.

"Of course."

He sat down and looked at the view. They did not speak for a while as both of them delved into their own thoughts. Finally, Ekala asked, "Where are you?"

"I was thinking about my father," Maz said, tossing a rock over the cliff. "I wonder what's become of him and what my brothers have done."

"You must miss him," Ekala said.

"I worry about him, and my country. I don't know what to do. But I have to do something."

Ekala nodded. "I was thinking about my father, too, and this land and my people that are entrusted to my care. He did well and was strong for so long, until he began to crumble. And now it's my turn to be strong, to build on his legacy, to keep Ameram safe and prosperous."

Maz turned toward her. "When I first came to the Top, before I knew who you were, I'd see you out here and wonder what you were thinking; what burdens you carried to this edge to throw off the cliff."

Ekala smiled at him. "Did you really? Sounds like you have some of your own to drop off."

"Oh, you know I have much to resolve. You and your father have made the exchange of power. Mine, not so, and I fear that it will not be without bloodshed. I'm glad to be going with you to the North Ford so I can at least find out something of my country."

She put her hand on his shoulder. "I'm glad you're with me, too, Maz."

They looked at one another, appreciating the moment and the affection growing between them. And then the queen of Ameram stood up. "Well, Prince Bolimaz of Toulon, I think we need to go see what's happening at the ford." She extended her hand. He smiled, grasped it, and she pulled him to his feet.

They rode back to Larma Hollow and the queen announced that it was time to depart and continue the tour of Northern Ameram. However, Boschina wished to stay longer. She had found with Larma the comfort of a mother she had never known.

"Larma," she said respectfully. "May I stay here for a while?"

From the first day of the visit, Larma had observed Boschina and saw the natural gifts in the young woman she had hoped to develop. But this was not her decision alone.

When Larma hesitated, Boschina turned to Ekala, who had adopted her as a sister.

"Would you mind, Oleen? I want to learn, as you did, from Larma."

Queen Ekala Oleen smiled. "I can think of no better place for you to be—except with me, of course." She tapped Boschina on the shoulder. "Not for too long, mind you. Who will I have to confide in?"

"You've got Maz," Boschina replied with a mischievous smile.

Ekala poked her. "It's not the same as a sister. Besides, I'm sure your father is hoping you will work with him soon. He has numerous projects in front of him."

"Yes, but after I learn from Larma."

"You may be here a very long time then," Larma said.

Ekala glanced at Larma. "If she becomes a nuisance, kick her out."

Larma put a hand on each of their shoulders. "Time can be as quick as a bolt of lightning or as slow as a seed waiting for a drop of moisture to sprout. Neither one of you can stop the motion. It's there and gone or acting without notice. One day you part and what seems like the next, you meet again."

The queen looked around the shelf, the large open gathering area of the Oleens' home, and then at the wide view of the Great Plain beyond the cliffs. "You will learn much here, as I did." She turned back to Boschina. "Captain Ritzs will stay as well. She will see that you return safely when you leave."

With much fanfare and sadness, goodbyes were expressed with wishes for a safe journey. Soon after, Queen Ekala and Prince Bolimaz led the queen's force of Oleens and pack horses through the gate of Table Top and down the trail onto the Great Plain.

* * *

In the growing light of morning, three men walked into a muddy ravine that still held mist from the night before. Six large cages made of thick hardwood bars were built into the bank along one side of the ravine. At the back of each cage a cave had been dug into the earth.

The cages appeared to be empty, but as the men approached, growls echoed from the darkness of the caves. A foul odor of death hung in the damp air.

Two of the men wore dirty work trousers, long-sleeved shirts, knit caps, and mud-stained boots. One of them walked with a limp and carried a staff, while the other man wore gloves and held a bucket in each hand. They were large, broad-shouldered men accustomed to heavy, hard labor. The third man, though wearing similar clothing that blended with the earth and grass around them, was thinner and cleaner with an authoritative posture.

The men stopped at the third cage. "Three has almost chewed through the branches again," one of the thick men said, pointing at a crossed-hatched section of the cage. "Twice we've replaced these branches. They've all been digging to get under. We keep putting rocks along the bottom."

"This is all normal," the thin man said. "They want to hunt. When we've let them out, they've always come back here—to their den."

"Then where's Six? The one that killed the villager?" the man with the limp said. "We haven't seen him for days."

"He must have gotten a scent off that man and he's following it—still hunting. That's what we trained them to do."

"If they get too free, we'll never control them and you won't be able to use them as you wish. That's what happened in the Toulon Wilderness. They got away from us."

"Don't worry," the thin man said. "The time is near to release them to hunt their prey. Then we can leave this stinking mud hole. Where are the bags from that villager?"

"Still closed in a wood box."

"Good. Now I must go meet Onus," the thin man said and smirked. "He's too afraid to ride in here. I always have to meet him outside the bog."

"Doesn't he know the Chorgens killed and chased the frogs out of this area?"

"I told him, but it's not just the frogs. It's these Chorgens he's afraid of."

"I would be too if we hadn't raised them from pups," the man with the buckets said as he set one down by a cage.

"It doesn't matter," the man with a limp said. "When they reach a certain age, they can't be trusted. They'll kill anything or anybody for any reason."

"Not these beasts," the thin man said. "The way we've trained them is different. They'll obey us."

The man with a limp laughed. "That's what every Chorgen breeder has said and most of them got eaten by their pets. I let down my guard once and a tame one almost took off my leg."

"You know we're in this for the money," the bucket man said to the thin man. "We don't care a wit about who rules who, what country, or what man or woman—your Lord Glasrauss included. As long as he keeps paying, we'll keep doing our job. Besides, there ain't nobody better than us."

"And I'm telling you these beasts are different," the thin man said. "You don't believe that, but it doesn't matter because in a short time we'll be letting them run to do what we trained them to do—kill the leaders of this kingdom. And you *will* declare your loyalty to the new king."

* * *

Larma and Boschina stood on the ledge in front of the mystic's cave at Table Top Mountain, gazing at the Great Plain spread out before them. A soft breeze headed south across the rolling hills, gently bending the vast carpet of grass in shimmering shades of green. Clusters of white clouds drifted slowly across the blue sky on their journey toward Ambermal. All appeared serene and peaceful.

"What do you hear?" the silver-haired mystic asked.

"The wind," Boschina answered.

"Can you hear the clouds?"

Boschina concentrated. "No, I see them, and the sky beyond. Do they make a sound? I only hear the wind."

"Clouds are like people, Boschina. And just like us, each one has its own way of knowing and expressing itself. They complain and grumble, gossip, cry, play, and shout with their companions. Always traveling, watching from high above, they see a lot more than they reveal. Though, they like to talk about it. What else do they have to do all day but to observe and talk while being pushed around by the wind? If you know how to listen, you can hear their conversation. Occasionally, the clouds, just like the wind, will speak the truth we need to hear. But if you don't know how to listen, you'll miss the message."

"How do I learn to listen?"

"Watch the clouds moving by—do not try to listen or think about them—just watch and feel."

Boschina looked up and followed a cluster of clouds sailing overhead. She tried to drop all thoughts and do nothing but feel, as Larma had said; tried to sense only the sun, wind, and clouds. But her mind would not quiet. Sounds, voices, and images—good and bad—boiled like a stew. Boschina shook her head. "I can't understand them. Are they speaking?"

"They are saying where they have been and what they have seen. One is calling your name."

"Truly? I wish I could hear that," Boschina said, pulling her long brown hair away from her ears and holding it in a ponytail behind her head.

"Listen," Larma whispered. "It is calling you, Stone Daughter...Stone Daughter."

Boschina closed her eyes and listened. She felt the breeze push against her, the sun on her skin and Larma at her side. Still, the voices of memories in her head would not be quiet. "I can't hear it," she finally said, frustrated.

Larma smiled at her. "Each one of us has different gifts. This may not be one of yours."

Larma focused her attention on the distant views of the landscape before her. Many days' ride to the west was Ello, one of the few gateways through the Barrier Forrest to the Great Water. The people had returned to the village and life was back to normal. To the southeast, beyond the Middle Hills, were the dangerous Laundo Ponds. As always, a sense of warning emanated from there. Further east, stretching to the border of Ameram, was the depressing, gray Rainland. The mystery and confusion of that realm continued and, for now, was best left alone. Closer to the Top, she could see the slithering slice in the plain that was the insidious Barranca. Trial, defeat, or inspiration awaited the unsuspecting traveler in its confused, sunken world.

"Boschina, do you see and hear the Barranca?"

"Yes, I see it," Boschina replied, and shivered. "I'm hearing the Gauks—those vicious, giant lizards and the voice in the black tunnel. Maybe not coming from there, but they are in my head."

Larma nodded. "You must learn to discern the difference between what is old and what is new; what is vital and what is not."

Straight ahead in the distance, almost out of sight, they could see the northern end of the Dudoon Bog, which was fed by a run with the same name that flowed from the eastern fall of Table Top. The bog and the nearby village had always been a forlorn place. But the people were industrious, friendly to travelers and loyal to the royal family. Larma started to look away, and then hesitated. She now sensed an odd vibration coming to her from that region. Something different was happening there. *Is this what the wind had tried to tell her?* Closing her eyes, she drifted with the breeze and listened; listened to what was there to be heard. It was not clear: a muffled haze surrounded the messages. Still, she had learned enough.

"Boschina," Larma said in a different, more serious voice, "find Captain Ritzs and meet me on the shelf."

Surprised by the change, Boschina glanced up at the statuesque woman. "As you wish, Larma," she said and hurried along the cliff trail toward the open gathering place of Larma Hollow.

Larma went into her rooms in the cave, opened a roll of fiber-woven writing paper, and cut off a small piece. She took down two bottles of ink from a niche and held them to the flame of a candle. After examining their contents, she mixed the two together, took a quill, dipped the tip in the combined ink, and wrote a message in ancient script on the fiber. She held the sheet up to the candle to dry the ink, reviewed her words through the flame, and then carefully folded the material and walked out to the gathering shelf where the women were finishing with the breakfast meal and cleaning up. Others were walking through the tunnel to work in the growing fields for the day, while a dozen more were feeding the horses and mucking out the stables. The changing of the guards at the gate to the plain below was in process.

Captain Ritzs had been organizing a force of newcomers for sword-training when Boschina found her. When Larma appeared, the trainees nodded and deferred to the tall, silver-haired woman, and then stepped away as she motioned to Boschina and Captain Ritzs.

"Yes, Larma?" they responded.

"I want you to take a force, find Thalmus, and give him this," Larma said calmly, though her demeanor was serious. She did not reach out with the item. Instead, the cloth rested in her open palm close to her body, as if she were protecting a precious object too valuable to expose.

Boschina carefully lifted the folded message and immediately felt its weight. She looked up into Larma's eyes and was struck by a sense of importance. Tightening her grasp on the cloth, Boschina tucked it into the inner breast pocket of her vest, where she felt it begin to throb in rhythm with her heart.

Larma gently placed a hand on Boschina's shoulder. "You must deliver this to Thalmus. It is of utmost importance. He should be at the Great Water. Do you remember the route?"

"Yes, I can find the way," Boschina replied and glanced at Ritzs. Feeling the urgency of the message, she apologetically added, "It will take a number of days to get there."

Ritzs agreed. "It is a long ride."

Larma smiled. "This time you won't have our great tortoise, Thunder, to slow you down. Still, be cautious—not only of frogs at the river, but other dangers as well. There are still those who are lawless and uncivil. Take experienced warriors with you."

"They have been split up between the Castle Guard, me, Kali, and Ekala Oleen," Ritzs answered. "We felt it necessary that our queen have a fully trained force," she explained. "So, most of my force will be new and not fully trained."

Larma nodded. "I will send riders to Oleen to inform her of your journey." She looked into Ritzs' eyes. "I am glad you stayed when Oleen left. You are a leader, Ritzs. And you, Boschina, have the gift of strength in your heart and mind. I can think of no one better for this mission. I trust in you both."

Ritzs and Boschina smiled and felt an overwhelming confidence fill their bodies and minds. "It will be done," Captain Ritzs said and hurried to assemble her force, supplies, and horses for the journey.

Just before they were ready to depart, Larma spoke quietly to Ritzs. "Watch over Boschina. Keep her close. This journey will place her in the treacherous path of another's destiny."

"As you wish," Captain Ritzs replied, feeling honored to be given such a task. "I will watch over her."

Chapter Three
Befuddlement

The Sol Linden River flowed from Rainland to the Great Water and created a natural barrier between the kingdoms of Ameram and Toulon. The broad, swift river was north of Table Top. There was only one ford where the water was shallow enough to cross without the use of a boat or a dangerous swim. This lone crossing was at the river's western end before it dropped into the canyon that funneled the raging current into the Great Water. Over time, the ford had become a major route of commerce and travel between Ameram and the northern kingdoms of Toulon, Banyon, and beyond. This vital portal, known as the Crossing of Sol Linden or the North Ford, was on Queen Ekala Oleen's itinerary to visit before turning south for the return trip to Ambermal. She had not been to the ford since she was a teenager and accompanied her father on a tour of the north. Now, she wanted to see for herself the impassability of the river, the condition of the crossing, the amount of traffic, and the sort of goods being transported to and from Ameram.

Ekala, Maz, Camp, and the Oleen force had enjoyed their return to Table Top. They had been reluctant to leave and would rather have stayed longer with Larma and the people of the Top, but duty and responsibility had called them back to the saddle and their journey.

The day after leaving the flat mountain, Ekala and her entourage crossed the small Table Run that flowed parallel with the Sol Linden

River, and continued for another day over the rolling hills of the Great Plain until coming to the banks of the big river.

"We'll camp here and continue west in the morning," Ekala announced.

Maz looked at the sun's height in the sky, and then west at the land along the river. "There's a lot of daylight left," he said. "We could get a ways down the river before stopping."

"I'm ready to stop," Ekala replied, getting down from Shadahn.

"Then we're camping," Maz said with a smile. He patted Mendu's neck and dismounted.

"I'm glad you agree, Prince." Ekala smiled back at him. "Captain Susa, get some fires going. It will be colder tonight. Post guards along the river, as well as the flanks."

Captain Susa had fought and served as second-in-command with Ritzs, moving up in rank when Captain Ritzs stayed at Table Top with Larma. She was a smart and agile warrior.

"As you wish, Oleen," the captain replied, for this informal title was acceptable to the queen.

Maz and Camp walked to the edge of the riverbank that dropped two meters to the flowing water. The river was fifty meters across. On the other side was the ragged dark forest known as the Wilderness of Toulon.

Ekala joined them. She watched the speed of the muddy river's current. "This is much too fast for frogs—and for anyone to cross safely."

"Why are you posting guards then?" Camp asked.

"I'm not taking any chances," she replied and began scanning the dense foliage on the opposite side. "It does not look inviting."

"It's not," Camp said. "You can get lost and never find your way out if you're not careful. Our people have always stayed clear of that forest."

"It has a strange aura that befuddles your thoughts," Maz said, turning to Ekala. "No one goes there willingly. There are wild people and creatures living in its confines. We had to travel through its grasp on our escape from my brothers."

"It is ugly-looking," Ekala replied. "But that doesn't scare me."

Maz gave her a sideways glance. "You haven't been in there. I can tell you: I hope to never go through that maze again."

Ekala studied Maz for a moment, and then bumped his shoulder with her forearm. "Let's start cooking. I'm getting hungry."

Maz laughed. "Hungry?" He shook his head and walked away with Ekala. But Camp hesitated at the riverbank, staring across at the foreboding forest.

* * *

Boschina, along with Captain Ritzs and her force of ten, galloped across the Great Plain, stopping briefly to rest the horses, eat, sleep, and move on again. At night, Boschina's sleep was restless. Sounds in the dark scratched at her attention, waking her from dreams of something chasing her—something she could not see. She could hear it though, snarling and huffing in the night. Radise neighed nearby, letting Boschina know that she was watching so her mistress could try to sleep again. Throughout the journey, Boschina felt the message in her pocket against her chest, throbbing slowly, constantly, like a small living thing waiting to be born. It drove her forward and she pushed the Oleen soldiers onward. Over the long hours of riding, Boschina began to think of her father, Veracitas, in his shop in Ello carving a new statue from a stone that she had not seen or laid hands upon. This would be the first statue since she was a small child with which she had not helped him, except for the ones he carved when he was in hiding from the king. The sound of hammer on chisel and stone chips flying flooded her memory, bringing a smile to her face; she missed her father. She would see him again soon and the anticipated joy of that meeting also pushed her to keep moving.

In the afternoon of the third day, they rode tired and thirsty into Ello. Stopping in the plaza, the Oleens bucketed water from the stone well and emptied the wooden vessels into a trough to quench their horses' thirst, and then their own. The townspeople were pleased to see a gathering of Oleen soldiers in their village. From their booths around the plaza, merchants brought out items to give or sell to the weary troops. The last time Captain Ritzs and Boschina had been in this plaza, it was deserted: the villagers were held captive at Safedor and Metro's soldiers and renegade troops roamed the country.

Now, the town was a bustling marketplace.

"Where is Veracitas working?" Boschina asked several of the merchants surrounding them.

"Veracitas?" a man questioned. He was holding onions and carrots in his hands that looked as if he had just dug them from the ground.

"You're the Stone Cutter's Daughter," another man said respectfully. He had a booth with shirts and trousers. "I didn't recognize you dressed as an Oleen soldier."

"I am an Oleen," Boschina replied. "Do you know where my father's working?"

"He left," the man answered.

Boschina looked at him in disbelief. "He's gone?" She glanced around the plaza.

"What about Captain Kali and the Oleen soldiers?"

"They went with him."

"Did he finish the statue of the queen?"

The farmer shook his head. "No. It broke," he said sadly. "They went to get another stone."

Surprised, Boschina questioned the man. "Broke into pieces?"

"Yes. Three or four, I'd say."

She looked at Ritzs. "How very strange that a second statue should break."

"Well," the farmer said, "the first one was deliberately broken. This one just cracked—right across the middle. That's the way it is with marble; you can't trust it. Don't you agree?"

Boschina did not answer him. She was thinking about the queen's statue and the oddity of it breaking. Her father was a careful, skilled artist. He was fastidious about the stone that he chose for his statues.

Had he missed a flaw?

Could he have made a mistake? Not likely.

"You look like you've been riding for some time," the farmer continued, looking at the Oleens stretching and caring for their horses. "Will you be resting here for a few days?"

Ritzs focused on him. "No, we cannot delay. However, we will buy some of your vegetables."

Boschina wanted to find her father's studio, to see the broken statue, but felt the message throbbing in her pocket and knew the note must come first—it must be delivered.

After filling all the water bags and purchasing food to supplement their supplies, the force of Oleens walked their horses out of town and onto the dry trail to the Great Water. What they did not see was the clothing merchant standing by the corner of the last building, watching them.

The Oleens rode into the dusty hills at a steady but careful pace, remembering to conserve water for this barren portion of the route. Not having Thunder slowing them down this time, Boschina and Captain Ritzs thought the journey would take at least half the time as before. Keeping the column moving until dusk, they finally stopped and made camp. Weariness settled in. They unsaddled the horses and watered them from the bags. Ritzs posted guards at each end of the camp. Drawing from their supplies, they ate the raw vegetables and bread for the evening meal and settled down to sleep.

Halfway through the night, Boschina was awakened by Ritzs for her turn at guard duty. She picked up her sword and bow, and then replaced the Oleen soldier at the rear of the camp, nodding to her as they passed one another. She sat and listened, hoping not to hear anything approaching them in the darkness, but found herself wanting to hear some sort of life in this desolate place. It was dead quiet except for the stirring of the horses and her fellow soldiers sleeping just fifteen meters away. The minutes passed slowly. As she struggled to stay awake, a scratching sound brought her to full attention. The noise came from the direction of the trail they had just traveled. Boschina turned her head, trying to hear, trying to determine what it was: something scratching—no, clawing the ground, was more like it. She could hear faint sniffing, an animal inhaling and exhaling as it searched for a scent.

Her sword vibrated on her hip.

Boschina stood up, pulled an arrow from the quiver, and nocked it on the bow's string. She started backing toward the slumbering Oleens. Radise snorted softly. The mare had heard something as well and was trying to catch a smell of whatever it was, but the breeze blew in the wrong direction.

Silence again.

Boschina stopped and listened. Maybe it had gone away. *What if it's a Gauk?* She suddenly thought, remembering the Barranca. *Could it be?* She listened intently and heard nothing. Letting the bow string relax, she took a deep breath. Then to her left she heard a grunt and clawing again. It was closer this time.

"Awake, awake!" Boschina readied the arrow once more; pointing it into the darkness. "Wake up, grab your weapons!"

Ritzs was at Boschina's side instantly, a sword in her hand as the other Oleens shook away the sleep and gathered their bows and swords.

"Encircle the horses," the captain yelled to her troops. "What's out there?" she demanded from Boschina.

"I don't know, some sort of animal."

"How big is it?"

"I couldn't see it," Boschina said. "It sounded large. It kept moving in closer...clawing at the ground."

For a long time they waited and listened, not ready to relax. The horses, disturbed by the hustle of the Oleens suddenly moving around them, shuffled uneasily; the camp was no longer quiet. Finally, Boschina spoke. "Whatever it was must be gone." She looked at Ritzs. "Sorry, Captain. I guess I panicked—but my sword hummed."

"It's alright," Captain Ritzs said. "Let's assume the thing is dangerous. We'll pull in tighter; double the guards and stay alert."

In the light of the morning sun, Boschina and Ritzs searched the ground for tracks while the Oleens saddled the horses and prepared to move on. There were claw marks in the hard soil five meters to their left and fifteen meters on the old trail to the rear.

Nothing else was visible in the dry ground.

"It had to be a large creature with claws," Ritzs said, examining the marks. "Look at the width and length of the grooves it made. I've never seen a track like this before."

Boschina shook her head slowly. "I thought it might be a Gauk. But this is not like the tracks I saw in the Barranca. I hope we can see it in the daylight."

Ritzs looked around at the desolate terrain. "Let's move. We might be able to reach the forest by tonight."

The column mounted up with Boschina and Ritzs in the lead and they hurried on toward the Great Water. They watched for animals throughout the day, but saw nothing beyond the barren land, and smelled only the constant foul odors borne from the stagnant ponds. By nightfall, they had reached the edge of the forest and the first creek, where they stopped. The evening mist hung in the trees and the fading light obscured the way.

"Let's camp here," Captain Ritzs said. "We'll enter the forest in the morning."

"Good," Boschina agreed. "I'm tired."

Gathering wood from the base of the trees, the Oleens started the first fire they'd had in three nights. After eating a hot meal and posting guards, they laid down hoping for a quiet night. Boschina was exhausted. Still, she tossed and turned, trying to get comfortable and empty her mind of images that danced through her thoughts. She was drifting in and out of sleep when she heard someone whisper, "Stone Daughter…Stone Daughter."

She opened her eyes. Had she dreamt someone called out to her? She looked around. The fire still burned. Everyone was asleep in various positions around the fire, except for the guards at the edge of camp. She closed her eyes and tried to sleep.

"Stone Daughter…Stone Daughter," the voice called again.

Boschina sat up.

This time, she knew someone was calling her.

She grabbed her sword and walked to one of the guards.

"Did you hear someone calling me?" she asked the soldier.

"I haven't heard anything," the woman replied. "Just the rustling of those tree leaves."

Boschina looked toward the forest. The glow from the fire fluttered fingers of light on the trees. Was that someone in the shadows pointing to her? Motioning in the darkness? Or fluttering leaves and branches? Boschina shook her head and had started walking back to her blanket when she heard the sniffing. The sword began to vibrate in her hand. A foul odor of death struck her nostrils and the sound of claws scraped the earth in the darkness before her.

"You're back," Boschina whispered, then shouted, "Captain, it's back!"

She saw silhouettes in the fire's light rush from the forest. A flash of silver spear points. A scream and howl erupted, and then thundering feet pounded away in the dark.

Ritzs jerked up, pulled her sword, and rushed to Boschina's side. "Everyone up! Grab your weapons! Guard the horses! Where is it, Boschina?"

"It was close; I could smell it. But something happened. I think it moved into the forest."

A sudden howl startled them. Then thrashing of brush and trees mixed with screams and growls tumbled from the woods.

"Put more wood on the fire," Ritzs commanded. "Are the horses okay?"

"We've got them," a soldier reported from the darkness.

"Something's killing that beast," Boschina said. "Let's get a torch and go in there."

"No, we're staying right here," Ritzs said.

The battle in the forest ended and quiet returned. However, sleep was not possible. The Oleens stayed awake the rest of the night. In the morning, they ventured into the forest where the fight had taken place. Small trees and brush had been trampled and blood was splattered throughout the foliage.

There was no body.

"Whatever it was got carried away," Ritzs said, "But by what?"

"It must have been big to smash everything like this," Boschina said.

The message in her pocket began to throb. Boschina put her hand over it. "We need to find Thalmus."

Once again, the Oleens packed up after a sleepless night, formed into a column, and rode into the Barrier Forest. Ritzs found the trail, crossing numerous creeks and finally the slow-moving river, where they stopped to rest and eat at the statues of Veracitas and Currad. Ritzs and Boschina made sure to keep everyone away from the river's edge, where the giant frogs lay in wait. It was here that one of the creatures had almost taken Ekala Oleen with its quick tongue.

While she ate, Boschina walked around her father's carvings of himself and Currad. The two statues were not polished, as Veracitas normally completed a carving. Instead, the stone's surface was left rough, unfinished, with chisel marks depicting the rugged character of each man. The effect suited the image of the actual men. Boschina also noticed how they had been placed. Though they stood apart, and looked in opposite directions, she saw how they supported one another—protected one another. It gave her a feeling of combined strength. But she also sensed a tremble, a warning of danger, from the stone faces. She remembered that it was these statues that guided them the first time to the Great Water. And, more importantly, they revealed the man who had helped Veracitas escape from the castle's prison cell and Metro's torture.

The weary Oleens mounted up, and shortly after leaving the sculptures, they entered what Boschina had been dreading—the cold fog—and were soon lost within its dense vapor.

Chapter Four
A Strange New Friend

For days, a thick, damp fog had covered the sea and its opposing land, lying on the earth like a lumpy, gray blanket. Through this murk, Boschina led Ritzs and the Oleen riders as they followed one another in a single file. They were moving slowly, cautiously. The wetness muffled the sounds of their horses' hooves and the metallic clinking of the swords and cooking gear. The horses trailed so close to one another that their noses touched the tail of the horse in front of them. The riders did not speak as they strained to hear above the roar of ocean waves rumbling in their ears and to see anything of their surroundings. Piney trees and mossy green boulders appeared ghost-like, emerging into view and then fading away in the enveloping mist. Yet, they still did not know how close they were to the water—or for that matter, to the edge of a precipice that might drop hundreds of meters to the rocks below. Undaunted, they continued on, determined to complete their mission no matter where it led them.

Boschina suddenly jerked Radise to a stop and looked up.

"What's wrong," Ritzs asked.

"Did you feel that?" Boschina whispered.

"Feel what?"

"That rush of air."

"No."

"It was right over our heads."

"I can't feel much," Ritzs replied. "I'm too numb."

"Something sailed right over our heads," Boschina said, peering into the fog.

Ritzs looked around. "I can't see a thing, and it is getting darker. We should stop for the night."

"Not yet, we're almost there," Boschina pleaded.

"Alright, but go slow," Captain Ritzs answered.

Urging their nervous horses forward, they started again. But within a few steps a deep and resonate call, clearly heard over the waves, sounded in front of them. "Whoo-Whoooo." The horses stopped before the riders could react, and then stood alert, their heads up.

"I heard that," Ritzs said.

Boschina leaned forward and patted Radise's neck. "Okay, Lady. Okay, we'll stop." She sat up, stared into the fog and smiled.

Ritzs turned to the column behind her and shouted, "We'll camp here, stay close."

* * *

Just up the coast, not too far from where the riders had stopped, was a narrow valley that opened to the sea. A meandering river flowed down from the hills through this bushy, green valley, and then cut through sand dunes to meet the waves and enter the ocean. Strong winds, often pushing damp fog, blew up this little valley more often than not. But, on pleasant days, it was one of the most serene places one could imagine. Just inland from the ocean, and about halfway up the south slope of the valley, was a granite formation with a half-domed room on a shelf recessed into the hillside. The rock at the western edge of this shelf stuck out like a hand and deflected the sea wind away from the room behind it. The room was not deep enough to be a cave. It was more like a protected hollow in the rock-face with a view of the valley. There, in that recess, a small campfire burned. Behind the fire laid a man. His eyes were closed, but he was not asleep.

A Great Horned owl sailed in from the fog and landed on a ledge near the opening. The bird shook and settled its wings before turning its yellow gaze on the man. The owl chortled and softly hooted. The man did not respond. Again, the bird talked to him, hooting and bobbing his head. There was still no movement from the prone man. Frustrated, the owl clawed at the ledge and hooted again. Then, turning its head away from the man, the owl stared into the fog, into the darkening day, watching and listening.

A soft breeze entered the hollow. It brightened the embers of the fire and began to push the fog toward the sea. The man's eyes opened, but he did not move. He had the look of someone returning from a distant place, a traveler reluctant to return to a world he must inhabit. Slowly, he sat up, gazed at the flames of the fire, and then turned to the owl.

"You brought the wind with you—an east wind."

He stood and stretched. The man was short, muscular, with sandy brown hair. "I had hoped for more time. It is so restful here." He bent over at the waist, touching his toes. "But it is not about me, is it?"

He walked to where the bird was perched, reached up, and stroked its breast feathers. "Unlike me, my loyal friend, you are always ready."

The owl's head swiveled and the yellow discs looked down at the man.

"Yes, I know, Bubo. We are fortunate to be chosen."

Taking some bread from a pack, the man broke off a piece and offered it to the owl. The bird nodded and then quickly grabbed the bread in his beak and ate it. Taking a piece for himself, the man held it in his hand a moment before placing it in his mouth. Removing a flask from the pack, he poured a little of its content in his cupped hand and held it up to the owl. The yellow eyes examined the liquid. Bubo bobbed his head, bent, and then drank. The man waited for Bubo to finish and tilt his head back to swallow. He then poured some more in his hand, placed it to his lips, and sucked it in.

He put the bread and flask into the pack before walking to the edge and looking into the fog. The wind pushed the dense mist toward the ocean. "It will be clear tomorrow," he said softly and turned to the owl. "Then we shall see Boschina and these soldiers you found and learn of our mission."

* * *

It was a long and uncomfortable night for the ten soldiers. They weren't sure of their surroundings or what creatures might be lurking in the fog. Stories of wild water beasts coming out of the waves to devour lost souls had long been the lore of this land. Not to mention the Insurphs, the mysterious native people of the Great Water. Double guards were posted at both ends of their group and changed frequently throughout the night. The horses were kept in close and the saddles remained on their backs. But Ritzs, after giving orders for the night watch, seemed content to snuggle into her blanket and sleep. The other soldiers admired her confidence and trusted her leadership. She was strong and one of the originals. They knew that she had chosen them for this mission and did not want to disappoint her.

As the light of morning began to chase the darkness, the fog was pushed out over the water by the wind and the land shined clear and bright. The soldiers rose, surprised at the clarity, and looked at where they had camped. They were on a narrow headland protruding into the sea. Crashing waves pounded the cliffs on three sides of them. They had stopped just five meters short of the end of the land. Looking at this beautifully dangerous view, they smiled nervously at one another.

"The owl kept us from the edge," one soldier said.

Boschina smiled. "He certainly did."

She looked up and down the ragged coastline, and then back at the lush forest on the hillside from where they had come. "He must be near. Let's continue our search."

"The owl hides well. We won't find it," a soldier said.

"I know. I am not speaking of the bird," Boschina replied.

Packing their blankets and mounting the horses, they rode back to find a trail along the shore. The day was warming as the sun rose in a clear sky and the sea calmed to gently rolling swells. The column of soldiers moved more quickly now as they rode confidently along the bluffs. Most of them had never seen the Great Water, so they were impressed and taken by the beauty and power of the place. Slowly, the land sloped down to sand dunes sifting onto the beach. They rode through the wet sand at the edge of the surf to a river cutting through the dunes and roiling into the waves of the Great Water.

Boschina felt the message in her vest pocket beat more strongly against her chest. "Ritzs, stop," she called.

The captain threw up an open hand to halt the column and turned to look at her. "What is it?"

Boschina held her hand over the pulsating package. "We must be close," she whispered and looked across the river to where the land rose up again to high bluffs that extended as far as one could see. At this point, the river was shallow enough to ford. *We could cross and continue on,* she thought. Then turning to follow the course of the river, she looked up the narrowing green meadow. This was more promising, but where would it lead—away from the Great Water? "Where are you, Thalmus?" she said softly. "You know we're here." Boschina scanned the trees on the hillside. "Come on, Bubo, give me a clue."

Radise sniffed the wind coming from the valley, and then snorted and bobbed her head. Boschina patted the roan's neck. "Yes, I think so, too, Lady."

Ritzs and the Oleens were watching her, waiting for directions. "We'll go up this valley," she told them. "Go slow. Watch for prints or signs."

The riders spread out and started working their way into the meadow. Three of them crossed the river to explore the north side of the valley.

It wasn't long before one of the Oleens called Ritzs to look at a track she had found. Ritzs and Boschina examined the print in the soft soil of a bare area in the tall grass. They knew right away what made it.

"It looks like a shell creature's mark," the Oleen soldier said.

"Yes," Boschina replied, looking around for more tracks. "It is Thunder's—and here are hoof prints. We're in the right place."

A sharp *thunk, thunk* was heard in the distance. They all turned quickly and peered up the little valley.

Thunk, thunk: the noise persisted.

"Someone's chopping wood," Ritzs said.

Boschina started for Radise. "Let's find out who."

The force of warriors swung onto their horses and began to ride slowly through the foliage along the river toward the noise. Captain Ritzs repeatedly held up her hand to stop their advance in order to listen, and then continue with a change of course. Finally, rounding a bend, the horses and riders pushed through some tall, thick shrubbery into a clearing to find Thalmus swinging an axe against a small tree. A dozen tree branches about twelve centimeters thick and five meters long were settled in a crosshatch pattern on the ground. The small logs were strapped together at the joints, creating a framework like a raft. Thalmus kept chopping as the Oleens approached, pulled their horses to a stop, and watched him with curiosity.

Finally, Thalmus cut through the trunk and the tree tipped over onto the ground. He looked up at the riders. "Good morning, Stone Daughter and Captain Ritzs. It is good to see you again."

Boschina dropped from Radise and hugged Thalmus. "I'm so glad to see you, even though you didn't help me find you."

Thalmus smiled. "I knew that you would get here."

"Bubo saved us at the cliffs last night, so I knew you were near."

"He told me. You should be more careful."

Boschina gestured at his pattern of logs. "What are you doing?"

"I am building a carrier sled for Thunder. It appears that you have come to get me and that time is of the essence. Is that true?"

"It is. We've been looking for you." She looked at the unfinished frame of branches.

"Where's Thunder?"

"He is in the water behind you."

The Oleens all turned in their saddles to see the great shell creature nestled in an eddy of the river. Just the top ridge of his shell, looking somewhat like a boulder, showed at the surface as the water swirled over him. His head barely rose above the current while his black eyes stared at them. The Oleens had been so focused on the vegetation and on finding Thalmus that they had not seen Thunder in the water.

"Where's Dallion?" Boschina asked. "I found his tracks."

"He got bored and went for a run several days ago. Bubo went to get him."

Thalmus noticed the Oleens looked soiled and weathered. The horses were mud-splattered and weary.

"What has happened? Why have you come for me?"

Thalmus watched as Boschina reached into the pocket of her vest and removed the folded cloth. He knew immediately it was from Larma. The power of the words reached him as they waited in Boschina's hand.

"Larma directed me to find you." She extended the message. "It is urgent." Holding the cloth in her outstretched hand, she looked at the web of tree branches on the ground. "I don't know why I'm telling you this, Thalmus. You already know." The message throbbed in her palm.

Thalmus carefully lifted the message, taking the weight from her. "You look tired, Boschina. You all do."

He unfolded the cloth and interpreted the old language. The script rose off the page, filling him with purpose. His expression did not change, but his posture did as he folded the leaves of the sheet together and looked at Thunder, who had been watching him and now rose out of the water. "Do you know what this says, Boschina?"

"No. It's in Larma's language. She only told me to deliver it to your hand."

He nodded. "I am sorry to tell you that you will not have time to rest. We must finish this sled and leave as soon as possible."

* * *

In the middle of the night, Ekala was awakened by Captain Susa.

"Oleen, Oleen," the captain whispered urgently.

"What is it?" Ekala asked in the dark, her hand instinctively grasping the handle of the sword on the ground beside her.

"There are strange sounds coming from the river," Susa replied.

Ekala heard the nervousness of the horses as they snorted and paced along their rope line. They sensed danger. Queen Ekala threw off the blankets and felt the cold surround her. She pulled on her boots and a coat held by Susa. The moon and stars were hidden by clouds, darkening the earth. Carrying her sword sheathed in its scabbard, she followed the captain and another guard to the river's edge. Two other Oleen guards knelt there.

Ekala expected to hear splashing noises or something in the water. Instead, over the hiss of the streaming current, she could hear mournful cries, and scratching—like claws on bark. She was surprised the creature sounded so close; yet, she knew it had to be in the Wilderness across the river.

"Wake up Maz and Camp," Ekala told the guard.

"We're here."

She heard Maz's voice in the dark. He came closer so they could see one another.

"That is what we heard every night we were in the Wilderness," he said. "We were attacked twice by a beast that was so quick we could not tell what it was. It moved through the darkness of the forest faster than we could keep track. It was as big as a man, but it was not a man. It growled and moaned like a dog and hissed like a snake. Despite our attempts, we could not hit it with a sword."

Ekala listened to the animal sounds for a moment, and then slowly shook her head. "Hopefully, the river will keep it from us.

Still, stay alert, Captain, and calm the horses. I'm going back to sleep."

"Aren't you worried?" Camp asked.

"No, not until whatever that thing is gets over here."

In the morning, the queen was up with the cooks and the changing of the guards. She shook off the cold and walked the river's bank with Shadahn trailing her, checking for tracks and scanning the land on the other side. The terrain on the southern side of the river was a treeless, rolling plain; whereas, the northern shore was a forested, mysteriously obscure landscape. The contrast, separated by the murky river, was disturbing. The earth itself seemed to cry out that something was wrong.

"Oh, Thunder," she said, with a deep breath. "I wish you were here to warn me of the dangers of this place. Bubo, you could fly in and out of that wilderness so silently they'd never know you were there."

Shadahn bumped Ekala with her head.

"Well, tell me what you think, Girl," Ekala said in response.

The sleek, black war horse snorted and stomped once with her front hoof.

"I agree. This place doesn't feel right at all, does it?"

She thought of Thalmus and his companions enjoying the peacefulness at the Great Water. Maybe she could go there on their way back to Ambermal. That would be enjoyable, except for the terrible trail through the Barrier Forest. No, a side excursion was not possible. There was too much to be done; although this journey was important, it was delaying necessary work back in the court of Ambermal. As they returned to camp for the morning meal, Ekala patted Shadahn's neck and rubbed her nose.

When the force mounted up and started west along the river, Camp dropped back to be the rear guard and Maz joined Queen Ekala riding in front of the column. The forward scouts were already out.

"You slept in," Ekala said. "Haven't seen you miss a meal since your recovery from the wound."

"I was up all night patrolling the river bank."

She looked at him curiously. "Was that necessary? We had double guards posted all night."

"I know," he said. "It's not that I don't trust your soldiers; I don't trust this place."

"Truly, you think whatever is over there can get across that wild river and attack without us knowing about it?" she asked.

"What's over there is evil. And I don't know what it can't do."

Ekala studied him. "You worry me, Maz. Something's got hold of you."

Maz did not respond. He just stared ahead or across the river at the Wilderness.

She noticed the exposed handle of the Corsair sword strapped to his horse. It was usually covered by its wrap. Now, it showed—menacing metal gray, ready for use.

"Maz," she said, getting his attention. "Why do you carry the blade that almost killed you?"

He shrugged. "To remind me of the power of evil." He reached down and fastened the flap of the sleeve over the sword's handle.

Ekala watched him cover the sword. She felt a sudden coolness and glanced across the river at the Toulon Wilderness. The branches swayed in a breeze, tilting toward them. She looked back at her force of Oleens riding behind them in two tight rows. "We'd best pick it up and get on to the North Ford as fast as we can."

She urged Shadahn into a fast trot and the whole column increased their pace. They rode all morning without speaking further until stopping to rest and eat at midday. Maz and Camp were quite hungry by then from missing breakfast. Getting their portion of bread, tomatoes, and cheese, they sat with the Oleens to eat—letting the horses loose to drink at the river and graze. Maz tried to avoid looking in the direction of the river. Eventually, he could not help himself. The Prince of Toulon stood and gazed across the water at his homeland. Ekala noticed him and decided to leave him alone. She motioned to Captain Susa to join her.

"I want you and Maz, along with Camp, at the head of the force. I'm going to drop back as the rear guard."

Captain Susa was concerned. "Are you sure you want to do that?"

"Yes, Captain, I will be alright. Veer the column away from the river, but keep it in sight. Continue the quick pace until the horses need water and rest. Then come back to the river. I will catch up with you."

Captain Susa nodded, but was not happy about leaving her queen behind. "As you wish, it will be done."

The force mounted up and moved on as the Oleens looked back with surprise upon seeing their leader acting as the rear guard. She was Ekala Oleen. And they knew she could take care of herself. Still, their job was to take care of her and this did not seem right.

Ekala let the column ride away as she sat on Shadahn. "Well, Girl, it's just the two of us, just like it used to be."

Shadahn neighed and bobbed her head.

"Let's go up to that knoll where we can get a better view."

Shadahn trotted onto the rise, stopping at the peak, sniffing and surveying the surroundings. From the higher ground, Ekala could see her force moving west. The terrain to the south was empty, just the rolling open plain. It was the same to the east, except for the river that appeared as a continuous ruddy stripe; and on the north of the stripe, the strange wilderness. There wasn't a soul in sight anywhere.

Ekala breathed deep the smell of the grassy plain. A sense of freedom filled her. She had not been alone like this since before the prophecy's journey began. Meeting Thalmus and Boschina on the road to Table Top, as they were traveling to Ambermal to see her father, should have been a clue. Thinking back on it now, she realized how blind she had been; how she had not recognized the events taking place that would change her destiny. That story seemed so long ago; yet, it played in her mind still, as if it had happened yesterday. Smiling, she heard Larma's voice: "Be aware, time can be a fickle jester and a cruel teacher."

Ekala patted her horse's neck. "Looks like we've got the country to ourselves. Let's go down to the river."

Shadahn reacted immediately and carried Ekala quickly to the water's edge. They stopped and looked across to the opposite side. It was a strange-looking forest. Many of the trees were stunted and gnarled. The underbrush beneath the trees was thick, obscuring any view into the depths of the wilderness.

Ekala shrugged. "It doesn't look so bad, does it?"

Shadahn lifted her head and sniffed the air. She snorted and pawed the bank with her hoof.

"Easy, Girl, what do you smell?"

When Ekala looked again at the woods, she saw a huge animal edging out of the trees, glaring at her. The animal was more than half the size of a horse with a broad chest, large head, a black snout with yellow fangs, and tangled black and brown curly hair. The beast's head was up, nose in the air sniffing, trying to get her scent.

"Where did you come from?" She asked casually. "What are you?"

Even though it was a great distance, and the turbulent river stood between them, she could see the creature's large eyes stared at her.

"Whatever you are, you don't look friendly," Ekala said. "Why don't you go back to where you came from?" She turned Shadahn and started trotting along the river.

The creature began loping along the tree line, stretching its long legs and staying even with Ekala while watching her. Ekala stopped and started again. Each time, the animal followed.

"You want to race?" Ekala shouted and urged Shadahn into a full gallop. They rode hard for six hundred meters. When Ekala glanced at the other side, the creature was keeping pace with them and had moved down along the edge of the river. Its eyes were now ablaze and its mouth hung open, revealing more jagged teeth.

Stopping Shadahn again, she saw the creature stop directly across the river. It was panting, its tongue hanging out. It watched her for a moment, and then splashed into the shallow edge of the river and drank.

"Are you getting tired?" Ekala called to the beast, and then she slapped Shadahn's shoulder. "Go!"

Bolting away, Shadahn raced along the bank with Ekala bent forward, riding smoothly. The beast jerked its head up, howled, and ran after them with long, bounding strides. They ran hard until Ekala looked up over Shadahn's head and saw a rider coming toward her. It was Maz on Mendu. She pulled Shadahn to a stop just as Maz reached her. She looked across the river to point out the animal to Maz, but it was gone. Glancing up and down the shore and tree-line, the beast was nowhere to be seen.

"What are you doing?" Maz asked. "Was something chasing you or are you two just having fun?"

"When you rode up, did you see anything on the other side?" Ekala asked.

"No, did you?"

Ekala scanned the empty ground between the river and the tree line. "Yes, but it's gone."

Maz looked across at the trees, and then at Ekala for a moment. "What was it?"

"I don't know. It wasn't friendly, that's for sure."

"Man or animal?" Maz asked.

"Some sort of beast I've never seen before. It was large and ran fast."

"It was out in the open?"

Ekala nodded. "It was following me, running along the river's edge."

"So I'm not crazy after all," Maz said, smiling.

Ekala looked at the grinning prince. "Apparently not," she answered. "Why are you looking for me?"

"I came back to get you. There's a camp of people up ahead— refugees from Toulon."

Chapter Five
Faithful

At Castle Ambermal, Currad was looking for King Ahmbin. The burly soldier had left the king in the courtyard by the pond and gone to Culinary's kitchen to get him a snack. When he returned with a sandwich, the king was gone. He was not in his chambers, nor at the Great Hall where Currad had found him before: standing alone in front of the large, rosewood chair of the throne, staring in blank silence. Thinking the king must be with Lord Rundall, his uncle and trusted advisor, Currad went to Lord Rundall's room only to find the ailing counselor lying in bed and being attended to by a nurse.

"Pardon me, Lord Rundall," Currad said, standing in the doorway.

Lord Rundall rolled his head slowly on the pillow and focused on Currad. "Honored Soldier, come in."

It was not a large room with elegant furnishings. Though it did have several intricate tapestries hanging on the walls, a high, beamed ceiling and a window opening with a view of the castle's western parapet. The room was a fitting expression of the man who lived there.

Currad approached the bed across a worn wood floor "Are you feeling better today, Lord?"

"I cannot say how I feel today over yesterday or the day before that," Lord Rundall replied with a dry, raspy voice. "Though, seeing your hairy face brings a smile."

Currad grinned. "I'm glad my appearance brings you some joy. I don't usually have that effect on people."

"You bring much more than that, faithful soldier," Lord Rundall said, his voice cracking and the words coming slower. "You bring me peace of mind because I know you are with our king."

The nurse gently lifted the old man's head from the pillow and tipped a chalice of water to his lips. He swallowed hard several times before she let him rest his head again. He smiled at her and she smiled back at him before looking at Currad with a face that said, "You should go now."

Intimidated by the nurse's glare, the seasoned warrior shifted his weight and leaned over the sick man. "You need to rest," he said. "When I return, I expect to see you much improved."

Currad turned to go, but Rundall stopped him, grasping his wrist with a surprisingly strong grip.

"Take care of him, Currad," Lord Rundall whispered. "I will not be here much longer. With Ekala away..." He swallowed several times, trying to bring moisture to his throat. "Trouble is coming. I can feel it."

Currad put his hand over the old counselor's hand on his wrist. "I will watch over him, Lord Rundall. I am a soldier and I will die before I allow any harm to come to King Ahmbin. You can rest in that."

Lord Rundall released his grip on Currad and smiled at him. "Thank you."

Leaving the dying man's room, Currad was now more concerned than before. He moved quickly through the hallways and passages, checking with staff and workers. No one had seen the king. Back in Culinary's kitchen, hoping the king had wandered there to eat, he confronted the cook.

"Was the king here?" the soldier asked, glancing around at the wooden tables and fireplaces.

Culinary was mixing something in a pot over one of the fire pits. The aroma was delicious. He turned to Currad with a wooden spoon in his hand and a puzzled look on his face. "No. Didn't he like the sandwich?"

Currad shook his head. "He didn't eat it."

"What? That's one of his favorites. Is he ill?"

"He never saw it."

The pudgy cook suddenly understood the situation. "You can't find him."

"I've looked in all of the usual places." Currad rubbed the back of his neck. "I hope the queen returns soon. She will perk him up."

The red-faced chef had an idea. He pointed the spoon at Currad. "Did you look on the wall? He might be up there looking for his daughter."

"I'll check," Currad responded and started for the door. "What are you cooking? It smells wonderful."

"What? Oh," the cook said, turning back to the pot. "I haven't named it yet, so I won't say what's in it. I hope it will please the king and bring health to Lord Rundall."

"I'm sure it will," Currad said as he went out through the heavy wooden door that led to the cobbled street.

He hurried down the canyon-like, narrow street that had three-story stone buildings standing on each side until it opened into the main plaza. Climbing the steps to the Great Hall, he stood on the portico and looked out at the plaza. People scurried here and there; others were standing and talking while some laid about the fringes, napping in the warmth of the sun. At the far side, merchant booths and eateries with tables and chairs set out in the plaza were spread along the buildings on either side of a fountain that spilled into a shallow pool. It was mid-day and the businesses were busy selling their wares and serving customers. The various smells of food mixed with the sounds of voices bartering, laughing, and singing, filling the air of the plaza. This was where the king first saw the statue that drove him further into Metro's grasp. And after Ekala's victory, where the image of the stone truth freed him from the magician's control. On this portico, between these massive stone columns, was where Ekala Oleen was crowned Queen of Ameram, the first woman ruler, by her proud father, King Ahmbin.

Currad remembered it all: the terrible journey that had seemed doomed; the kingdom in the grasp of Metro. But hope survived in Ekala's Prophecy and it was guided to fulfillment by Larma and the quiet man, Thalmus, and his animal companions. Circling the columns with carvings of the royal history and exploits, he saw no sign of the king. He hurried along the balustrade to the stairs leading up to the castle's walls. At the top, guards nodded to him and stepped aside.

"Have you seen the king?" Currad asked.

"Yes," one replied, pointing toward the parapets and tower of the east wall. "He is there."

Currad looked that direction, and then back at the guard. "Did he climb the steps by himself?"

"We helped him, Currad. But he was halfway up before we saw him."

"You did right," Currad told the man. He turned and walked calmly along the stone way atop the massive wall that encircled the city and castle. He saw the king standing with one leg forward and both hands on his hips, gazing across the plain toward the Middle Hills and Laundo Ponds. Currad, the King's Honored Soldier, stopped and stood quietly three meters from him and waited.

After several minutes, the king spoke, but kept his eyes on the plain and the trail of people coming from the South Ford of the Camotop River. "Have you ever ventured into the Laundo Ponds?"

Currad nodded. "Dysaan and I passed through there in search of Veracitas after he had escaped."

"Did the frogs come after you?"

"No. We stayed on the higher ground along the edge of the Middle Hills. We saw them and they watched us. They were certainly interested, but we kept a wide distance."

The king shifted his weight to the other leg. "When I was a young prince, I hunted the ponds once with Thalmus. It was in the high-water season. There was very little dry ground like you describe. With Thalmus' guidance, we got one frog and were after another one when two others attacked us. Two of our hunters were killed and I barely escaped. If it had not been for Thalmus stepping in with his spears, I never would have lived to become king."

"I didn't know you had hunted frogs," Currad said, impressed by the old monarch.

The king looked at Currad now for the first time. "That's why I wouldn't let Ekala hunt. I never told her that story. She thought I had no faith in her ability or strength. I just wanted to make sure she would live to rule our people. And now she is."

"She certainly is," Currad replied.

Turning back to the view, the king said, "I hope she returns soon. I miss her—and I'm worried about her."

"She can take care of herself," Currad said. "Besides, she's got the best force of Oleens, plus Maz and Camp with her."

"That's good, but they are not Thalmus, are they?"

"No, Your Majesty, no one can match the frog hunter."

They stood in silence for a while before the king spoke again. "Lord Rundall is failing."

"Yes, I know."

"What will I do without him, Currad?"

"You have your daughter, Your Majesty."

"Yes. That is comforting. Still, she will be busy. There is much for her to do."

"Well, Your Majesty," Currad said. "Looks like you'll just have to put up with me."

✕ ✳ ✳

Thunder was not happy. His jaws were clamped onto the top branch of the sled Thalmus had built and he was bouncing on the make-shift frame as two Oleen horses pulled it over the rough ground. Thalmus knew he had to get to the Dudoon Bog as soon as possible. And this was the only way to bring the giant shell creature along with him. He would be needed, as he always was.

"Sorry for the rough ride, Thunder," Thalmus said.

They had stopped at a creek along the trail from the Great Water. Thunder released his grip on the frame and slowly stepped off the sled. He eyed Thalmus and grunted.

Boschina stroked his head. "Are you alright?"

Thunder pressed his head against her belly, and then plodded into the water.

"I do not like rushing him like this," Thalmus said. "It is not good for him." He turned and walked up the trail. He was wearing his sword and carrying one spear.

That is unusual, Boschina thought. Thalmus rarely carried a spear when traveling.

Boschina looked around, inspecting the area. The Oleens were watering the horses and themselves. The creek was narrow, perhaps four meters wide and shin deep; not large enough for frogs. Still, one never knew. Her left hand rested on the handle of her sword hanging from her belt. The tool gave her a feeling of comfort. Her arrows and bow were on Radise, who was watching her from the creek. They were still in the Barrier Forest, but away from the river and not yet to the barren part of the trail. Radise suddenly lifted her head, listening––and then the other horses did the same. The Oleen soldiers, reacting to the horses, grasped their weapons. The roan whinnied as Dallion emerged through the trees, trotting toward them. The Paint stallion's stark-white patches gleamed in the sunrays filtering through the overhead branches. Excitement filled the horses as they nickered and whinnied at Dallion's presence.

The stallion threw his head upon seeing Boschina and came directly to her. He pushed his head into her and she rubbed his nose and hugged him. "Where have you been, Dal, out exploring?"

Dallion nickered.

"Yes, I missed you too," Boschina replied. She looked toward Thalmus to tell him of Dallion's arrival and was surprised to see Bubo perched on his shoulder. "Bubo's here!"

While Boschina was turned, Dallion grabbed her ponytail in his teeth and gently pulled her head back.

"Hey," Boschina shouted, grasping at her hair, and then turning to playfully slap at Dallion.

He jumped away with a rolling snort.

Thalmus was talking quietly with Bubo as the owl stared at him; his head turned sidewise.

"What are they up to?" Boschina asked Dallion. They walked together to Thalmus as Bubo's head pivoted and his eyes focused on her.

"Thank you, Bubo, for stopping us at the cliffs," Boschina said, looking straight at the owl on Thalmus' shoulder. "If you had not been there...well, I might not be here now."

The Great Horned owl chortled and bobbed his head once.

"It's so good to see you—and Dal and Thunder. I've missed all of you." Boschina looked at Thalmus. "What have you two been talking about? And why are you carrying a spear?"

Bubo's head swung to Thalmus, who was smiling at Boschina. "We were just saying how much we have missed you, Boschina."

She looked at Bubo and then back at Thalmus. "You were not," she said firmly. "Something's happening. Is Ekala alright?"

"Yes, she is," Thalmus replied. "She will soon need our help, but we have time." He turned and called to Captain Ritzs. "Captain, we need to continue."

Captain Ritzs immediately ordered her force to mount up. Bubo spread his wings, pushed off from Thalmus' shoulder, and flew above the trees. Thunder climbed onto the sled and tried to get comfortable. Radise came alongside Boschina and Thalmus jumped onto Dallion's back. The frog hunter and Dallion led with Boschina on Radise, followed by the two Oleens pulling Thunder on the springy frame, and then Captain Ritzs and the rest of the Oleen force.

As they rode, Boschina told Thalmus about their ride across the Great Plain, the nightmares of something chasing her, the feeling of being watched, the second broken statue of Ekala in Ello, the mysterious animal she heard in the night, and the voice that woke her. Thalmus was quiet; he listened to her story and asked few questions. When they reached the dry barren trail, he stopped the column at the edge of the forest.

"Show me the animal's tracks," Thalmus said to Boschina.

Boschina and Ritzs led Thalmus into the woods to the dried blood and broken brush. The hunter knelt, smelled the dark blotches and gooey pools, and searched the area. He uncovered a blood-stained broken spear and a piece of torn green clothing. Then he followed tracks out of the foliage onto the hard, dry ground and found claw marks.

"These are like the marks farther down the trail where I first heard the beast," Boschina said.

Thalmus knelt and examined the tracks, running his fingertips in the grooves made by the animal's claws. He continued to search the ground, finding faint paw impressions so shallow they were unnoticeable to most eyes. Thunder sniffed the tracks and eyed the impressions before grunting and snapping his jaws several times. Thalmus patted the giant tortoise's shell.

"Do you and Thunder know what it is, Thalmus?" Boschina asked.

Thalmus nodded. "You were right to be scared, Boschina. That blood in the woods and these tracks are from a Chorgen." He stuck the spear tip into one of the claw grooves. "No other animal has the strength or claws large enough to scratch that wide and deep in this hardpan."

"I've never heard of a Chorgen," Boschina replied.

"Nor have I," Ritzs added.

"It is an animal that I have not seen in Ameram for generations," Thalmus said, standing the spear up and holding it at his side. "Their home is in the Kingdom of Banyon, where they were raised for hunting and game-fighting."

"Banyon?" Ritzs questioned. "That's north of Toulon, a long ways away."

"Indeed, it is," Thalmus said.

"What's it doing here?" Boschina asked.

"Good question," Thalmus said, looking at the desolate terrain they were about to cross. "This is not the sort of land they like, nor do they like the daylight. Something has drawn it here." He looked at Boschina and thought of the message from Larma that she had carried—and that he now held within his pocket.

Had it attracted the beast? He wondered.

"What about the voice I heard calling me?"

"It was the Insurphs, trying to warn you."

"I thought I saw someone," Boschina said, "standing there in the trees, and then running, but I wasn't sure. It was dark."

"The Chorgen must have gone after them and they killed it and carried it away. The broken spear is an Insurph tool. Some of them may have been hurt, but they probably saved your life, Boschina."

"How did they know about us or the beast?"

"The Insurphs know and like Veracitas. They saw you when we came here to find him. They do not miss anything that goes on in their land. How they knew you were coming and the Chorgen was following is a mystery. We need to stay alert and ride on to Ello."

"I'm all for that," Boschina replied as she headed for Radise.

* * *

Queen Ekala Oleen sat atop Shadahn, watching an encampment of people huddled down the slope near the river. As near as she could tell there were about 200 men, women, and children moving around cooking fires and makeshift lean-to tents. Maz and Camp, still dressed in their worn Toulon uniforms—green shirts with gray-green trousers—sat on horses to her right. Captain Susa and three of the Oleens were riding toward them from the camp.

"I can tell from here they are not organized," Camp said.

"You have not been to see them?" Ekala asked Maz.

"I held him back," Camp said, gesturing at Maz. "I wanted to find out who they were before revealing ourselves."

The queen looked at them. "You're under my protection."

"I know," Maz said. "But I don't want to cause you trouble."

"Trouble," she laughed. "You two have been nothing but trouble since I met you."

Captain Susa and her soldiers trotted up and stopped their horses before Ekala.

"They're Toulons," the captain said. "Been gathering here for several weeks, say they're fleeing the strife."

"What about weapons?" Ekala asked.

"Some common swords and bows—nothing military," the captain replied.

"How many men of fighting age?" Maz asked.

Captain Susa thought for a moment. "Only a few, many of the men are too old or too young. It's mostly women and children. We could bypass them, if you wish. The North Ford is a short ride ahead."

"No," Maz said. "I must talk with them, find out what's happening." He looked at Ekala. "You can go on if you want. We'll catch up with you."

"I'd like to join you," Ekala answered. "I want to hear their story." She turned to Captain Susa. "I'll go with Maz and Camp. Take the force around; we'll meet you on the other side of the settlement."

Captain Susa hesitated. "I'd feel better if these three soldiers went with you."

Queen Ekala Oleen smiled at her captain. "Thank you, but those are the prince's people down there. He won't need guards."

"I meant as protection for you," Susa said quickly.

"I know, Captain. Don't worry, we'll be fine," she replied and urged Shadahn forward.

Ekala, Maz and Camp rode to the edge of the desperate settlement. There, they dismounted and walked their horses into the camp. Tents made of old canvas and scrap wood were erected in a haphazard manner along a central path through the settlement. Cooking fires were burning in various shallow pits. Wagons, some with goods still strapped in the beds, stood with their tongues and yokes lying on the ground. Horses, hobbled or tied with a rope, grazed behind the tents. When the people saw the green uniformed men, they cautiously moved away, watching them closely. Maz and Camp were surprised by the people's wariness and fear.

"Not a very warm greeting," Ekala said to her two companions.

"They act like we're going to attack 'em," Camp said.

"Look at their faces," Maz said. "They're afraid of us. What is wrong here? I must speak with them."

Maz approached a group of men repairing a wagon wheel. Upon seeing him, the men quickly stood, shoulder to shoulder, and stared at the three strangers.

"Why have you left Toulon?" Maz asked the men.

The men looked back at him with silent questions in their eyes. Only one of them wore a sword. They glanced at Ekala, standing with one hand resting on the handle of her sword, and at the large black horse glaring at them—and then back at Maz and Camp. The man with the sword spoke. "I'll answer that when you tell me why Toulon soldiers are on this side of the river."

"Fair question," Maz replied. "We're not here to harass you. We left Toulon long ago; chased out, it appears, like you."

"Why should we believe you?" He pointed at Maz's chest. "The men that forced us to leave wore that uniform."

"The King's Guard?" Camp asked.

"The King's Henchmen, you mean," the man replied.

"Wearing this uniform is a sign of honor," Camp said.

"Not anymore," another man said.

Camp started at the man, but Maz restrained him. The men stepped back and the one with the sword grabbed the handle.

"Steady," Maz said. "We are not here to fight. I want to know if Souma is still king?"

"You *have* been gone," the swordsman said. "His sons rule now. Old Souma hasn't been seen for a long time."

Maz looked at Camp. "Tamar."

"That's right," the man said. "Tamar and Sharpna. Do you know them?"

"Long ago," Maz replied and quickly held up an open hand. "But I am not with them now."

"So you say," the swordsman said.

Ekala felt her sword begin to vibrate. She glanced around, but saw no threat. Then she heard the tense creak of a bow as the string was stretched taut with an arrow. She jumped forward, pushing Maz and Camp. "Get down!"

They stumbled forward just as an arrow zipped passed where Maz had been standing.

Ekala turned, drawing her sword and searching the huts for the bowman. Maz recovered, quickly pulled his sword, and backed up Ekala. Camp was already bounding toward the swordsman, thrusting then slashing. The man deflected Camp's sword and backed away. Another arrow cut the air, just missing Camp. Some of the other men had picked up burning branches from the fire and one had a spear.

"Stop your archers! We are not here to fight," Maz shouted. "We are not a threat to you!"

"We don't know that, nor what you want," the swordsman replied. "Only that you are wearing those uniforms."

A third arrow zipped between them and stuck in the plank holding up the wagon wheel. That was enough for Ekala. She had to stop this before blood was shed.

"Call off the archers," Ekala demanded, stepping toward the group of men with her sword pointing at them. "Don't you know who he is?" she shouted, gesturing at Maz.

The men moved back, surprised at her audacity and question. The swordsman raised his arm and waved. "Alright, the arrows are stopped—for now," he said. "Who are *you*? You're not a Toulon."

"I certainly am not," Ekala replied. "I don't know what's going on in your country. But I do know that this man can help you. You truly don't recognize him?"

The men studied Maz, shaking their heads.

"I know him," said an old woman standing by one of the tents. Then her eyes focused on Ekala. "And I know who you are."

Chapter Six
The Broken Stone

W ho are they, Nattie?" the swordsman asked the old woman.

The woman stepped closer. She looked frail but stood erect—her shoulders and head held up with an air of confidence. Her graying hair was short and her face creased with age. She wore a dirty skirt and worn blouse that had once been elegant attire. Studying Maz, she said, "He is Prince Bolimaz."

"Bolimaz is dead," one of the men said.

"I can assure you he's not," Ekala replied. "He's standing before you right now."

Unsure of her sight, the old woman walked up to Bolimaz and examined his face. She smiled and pointed at the scar on his cheek. "You have the scar. I see it clearly now—where Tamar cut you. You are Prince Bolimaz." She bowed before Maz for a moment and then asked, "Do you remember me?"

"Nattie?" Maz said, looking at her, trying to recall the face and name. "Nattie," he repeated. Then he suddenly remembered. "You are Nateen Nadar. You served in my father's household. Why are you here?"

"I left when your brothers took control."

"You didn't leave," one of the men said. "They threw you out because you wouldn't swear loyalty to them."

"That was bold of you," Ekala said.

The men looked at Ekala, still holding the engraved sword in her hand and ready to use it. She was dressed as usual in brown pants and a shirt with a maroon vest and brimmed hat.

Nattie turned to Ekala. "You may not remember me. It has been many years. I waited on you and your father when you came to Castle Dolou."

"Waited on them?" the swordsman said roughly. "Why?"

"Because Benton, her father is King Ahmbin."

Stunned, the men looked at Ekala with new appreciation. The swordsman, Benton, stammered, "You're…you are…Ekala Oleen, the…"

"Queen, is that what you're trying to say?" Ekala said.

"The first woman ruler," Benton answered softly, reality striking him square in the forehead. "You are the Queen of Ameram, ruler of the ground we stand upon."

"Yes, I am," Ekala replied.

Maz sheathed his sword. "I suggest you men stand down. Not that she needs them, but the queen's soldiers are waiting just outside this camp."

Benton slid his sword into its sheath at his side and knelt on one knee. The other men dropped their weapons and did the same. "I have heard of your fierceness in battle and the kindness that you show to your people," Benton said. "I hope you will extend that grace to us as well."

"Your deadly greeting did not impress me favorably," Ekala replied. "You almost killed your crown prince."

"You truly are Prince Bolimaz?" Benton asked Maz.

"Yes, he is," Nattie said firmly to the men. She turned to Maz and Ekala. "I am glad you're alive, Prince Bolimaz, for our country is suffering under your brothers. We need your help." She bowed her head to Ekala. "It is an honor to have the great Ekala Oleen, Ruler of Ameram, in our presence."

"Thank you, Nattie, but I am not great, as you can see for yourself," Ekala replied and remembered hearing Thalmus say those exact words about himself.

* * *

Thalmus scanned the trail ahead as he rode Dallion alongside Thunder, who was sprawled on the bouncing sled. The giant tortoise's jaws were still clamped onto the cross branch at the top of the frame. His eyelids were closed, but Thalmus could tell that he was not asleep. The hunter vowed to free his friend from this humiliation as soon as he could. They had left the tracks of the beast behind and were continuing across the dry, desolate region. Boschina scouted forward with two of the Oleen soldiers. Captain Ritzs led the rest of the column. Thalmus had lashed his spear with the other tools onto the frame of Thunder's sled. Now, he was thinking about the future, preparing for what lay ahead. His thoughts kept coming back to the message.

Larma's message was disturbing. She had called him to action. Her words were clear about a threat, but as always, questions lay in the choice of words and what was not expressed. *Had Larma intended that mystery? Perhaps not willing to be explicit in a written message, even though it was in an ancient language that very few could understand?* Thalmus wondered. *Was she still searching for the truth?* He had no doubt that forces were moving against Ekala Oleen. It was a matter of determining who they were, how deep they had penetrated the kingdom, where their strength was hiding, and how to confront it. Not an easy task. From the beginning, Larma and Thalmus had expected opposition, subversion, and outright attack from other countries, as well as from within, to Ekala's rule of Ameram. It was a matter of time as to where and when, and which wicked characters would rise against her. It was beginning sooner than he had thought.

Once again, Thalmus was to be the hunter.

And the prey was as dangerous as ever.

Horses and humans alike were thirsty and tired when the desolate terrain ended and they rode into Ello. Ritzs led the column while Thalmus stopped outside of the village to let the giant tortoise step off and walk into the square. Thunder flexed his legs and stretched his neck before moving forward. Thalmus stroked Thunder's head and patted his shell as he walked beside him.

The people were excited to see Thalmus, Thunder, and Dallion, for it was good fortune that the frog hunter and his companions were in their village. The people were thankful for their rescue from captivity at Safedor. Most of them had taken part in the march through the dust storm to fight in the battle for Ambermal. Happy villagers of all ages crowded around the visitors, welcoming and honoring them. Dallion snorted and huffed warnings not to come too close to him. He did not like crowds confining him, but wanted to be part of the celebration with his friends. Thunder did not mind the many hands touching his shell or the children Thalmus lifted onto his back for a short ride. He was just glad to be off the torturous contraption he had been bouncing on for two days. When they reached the central market plaza and joined the Oleens at the well, Boschina was waiting for them with buckets of water. The village elder, Porter, was also there, beaming and greeting the travelers.

"How good it is to see you, Thalmus, and the great Thunder and Dallion," he said. "Welcome, welcome."

Thalmus looked around at the bustling square. He was pleased to see the people so happy and that the village appeared industrious and healthy again. The hunter was used to inquisitive and curious faces and he still enjoyed the happiness of children riding on Thunder. However, he had never become comfortable with the admiration and praise he and his companions received. He was also keenly aware of the not-so-friendly eyes that watched him, and he felt such attention now. A clothing merchant, standing by his booth, stared at Boschina and Thalmus. Thalmus met the man's eyes and smiled at him. The merchant hesitated, caught by Thalmus' gaze; he cracked a weak smile and turned away.

Thalmus returned his attentions back to the crowd. However, what he and Boschina really wanted to see was Veracitas' studio and the queen's statue. "Will you show us the broken statue of the queen?" Thalmus asked Porter.

"Of course, follow me."

Porter led Thalmus and Boschina down a narrow street that curved into another cobbled lane. They followed it to a street on the western edge of the village, where he finally stopped in front of a rugged barn door. "Veracitas' workshop," Porter said, grasping the handle and sliding the door partially open. "Veracitas was very upset when he left with the Oleens. It's been closed ever since. I'll return to the plaza now to arrange food for you."

"Thank you," Thalmus and Boschina said together.

"Of course, it is our pleasure," Porter said. He then smiled and walked away.

They stepped inside the dusty room and looked around. The half-carved statue lay in three pieces on one side of the room, where it had been pushed out of the way. Boschina knelt and ran her fingertips over the stone, feeling the surface and the rough edge of the breaks. "I know I'm young, and do not have the knowledge of my father, but I have never seen a natural break like this."

"How so?" Thalmus asked.

Boschina cupped her hands and scooped water from a nearby bucket and poured it on the unfinished statue. The crystals in the stone glistened. She turned her head sideways to see the sun's light glare on the surface. There were no bubbles or signs of water seeping into a crack. "You see, Thalmus, there's no apparent fault, no warning of weakness. Father must have been shocked when it broke."

Thalmus examined the three pieces. "Could someone have fractured it without Veracitas knowing?"

"I don't see how."

Thalmus stood up and looked around the workshop: at the benches with chisels, hammers, and mallets lying at rest. "Who is with Veracitas besides Captain Kali?"

"Father left the castle before we did. Captain Kali and a force of Oleens were with him."

"Did he go to Marbala?" Thalmus asked, fingering a blunt chisel on the workbench.

"He said that he was going to cut a stone, and then take it to Ello. He wanted to work on the statue here," Boschina replied, watching Thalmus. "Besides, Ekala wanted Captain Kali and some Oleens to make sure the village was secure."

Thalmus laid the chisel on the bench. "Then why are they not here?"

"I guess they thought it was safe. It certainly looks like it. So they went with Father to get another stone?"

"So it appears," Thalmus said, looking out the window at the hills rising toward the Barrier Forest. The Stone Cutter's shop was among some scattered barns and stone warehouses on the last lane of the village. Light filled the room through windows on the north and west walls. A large, crosshatched wooden entry door was on the east wall, where it opened to the cobbled lane.

Thalmus turned to Boschina. "How long has it been since you were at the quarry in Marbala?"

She thought for a moment. "When we chose the marble block for the king's statue," she answered. "Father rarely buys from a stone merchant. He likes to choose his block right from the pit or caverns."

"That has always been the way of his family," Thalmus said. "Choosing and cutting the stone for themselves."

"I like the whole process," Boschina said. "The examining, marking, sawing and cutting, wedging, and then sliding and rolling; it's all very noisy and dangerous. In the caverns, where some of the stone is removed, it's dark and smoky from torches. Stories are told of people disappearing and about wild hungry creatures living in the depths. When we were in the mines, I always felt like something was watching me."

"I heard those stories," Thalmus said. "The village had me hunt the caverns once."

"What did you find?"

"Bubo and Thunder spent three days with me searching the tunnels. We found some old bones, but nothing else."

"I did not hear about that. When were you there?"

"It was before your time, Boschina."

She looked at him and wondered, once again, how old he was. For all the things Thalmus had done, the people he knew who no longer lived, the many places he had been and battles he'd fought, why did he not look old?

Thalmus smiled at her. "I know what you are thinking, Boschina. You have asked before—the answer is the same." He turned and left the shop.

The Stone Cutter's Daughter was left alone with the broken statue in her father's workshop to remember what Thalmus had told her. She looked at the partially carved stone and thought of Thalmus' answer, "much older than I appear and much younger than I am." She shook her head. "I still don't understand it."

She picked up a chisel and hammer, feeling their weight in her hands and arms. Laying the wide point of the chisel on a ridge of the partially chipped stone, she tipped the shaft of the instrument at a steep angle and struck the end with the hammer. A chunk flew off as the ring of the hammer filled the room. She adjusted the angle of the chisel and struck it again. It felt good, the vibration tingling her hand and arm. Boschina began working in rhythmic motion, striking the chisel and chipping the stone—exposing new angles and crystalline colors. Her mind settled into a comfortable sense of feel: sound and vision locked with the response of the marble.

Thunder had been waiting for Thalmus outside the door.

"What do you think, Thunder?" Thalmus asked the giant tortoise. "What do you sense? Is the village clear of trouble?"

Thunder snapped his jaws twice.

"I am not sure either," Thalmus replied.

They walked together back through the village, visiting with the people. Thalmus stood beside Thunder at the edge of the plaza and watched the busy activity. Dallion, uncomfortable amongst so many strangers, had already left. Thalmus patted the tortoise's shell. "It is time for us to go." He told Captain Ritzs where to find them, jumped onto Thunder's shell, and they plodded out of town.

Ritzs and the Oleens were gathering food and supplies when Boschina returned to the central square. The plaza was crowded with people shopping and passing through in both directions. She could not find Thalmus, Thunder, or Dallion.

"Where's Thalmus?" she asked the captain.

"He said they'd wait for us on the hill outside the village," Captain Ritzs replied. She motioned at Boschina's horse. "We packed some bags of food on Radise for you."

"Thank you, Captain." Boschina patted Radise, who was glad to see her. The roan nibbled Boschina's hand when she fed her a carrot. Boschina wanted to join Thalmus, but knew his behavior. He needed to be alone to think about the journey. She had no idea where they were going or what the danger was before them, but she felt safe with him and the Oleens. The engraved sword sheathed on her belt added to her confidence. She had no doubt about its authority. Wherever they were headed, the Stone Cutter's Daughter was ready.

Thalmus sat down on a rise overlooking the road into Ello. Thunder stood beside him. Dallion waited on higher ground. Upon seeing his friends settle down, he trotted to them. He sniffed, rubbing his nose on Thalmus' shoulder and snorting softly.

"I am deciding," Thalmus said to the stallion.

Dallion bobbed his head and nickered to Thunder. The tortoise clicked his jaws.

"Bubo will not be back for a while," Thalmus told them.

They were at the crossroads of Ello. Behind them was a continuous line of rose trees that stretched north as far as one could see. In that direction, the road crossed Table Run and continued until it entered the North Ford of the Sol Linden River, which was the border between Ameram and Toulon. Queen Ekala Oleen and her force were somewhere along that wide river. In the opposite direction from where he sat, the road south snaked through the Bushy Plain to Barrunda and, eventually, Ambermal. Beyond Castle Ambermal lay the Escat Marshes and Marbala, as well as the entrance to the Stone Hills, where Veracitas was looking for new blocks of marble. Down this road also, just north of Safedor, was the turn-off for the trail that crossed the plain to the east and eased between the

Bufon Marsh and the Dudoon Bog to the village of Dudoon. The Dudoon Bog: something wicked grew in its muck.

What is more important? he wondered. *Where is he needed first?* Reaching into his chest pocket, Thalmus removed Larma's cloth and unfolded the message to read it again. He studied the odd-looking letters, interpreting the old language he often thought too vague for his liking. There was no mistaking the danger expressed in Larma's words. But it was not specific. He read the message again, this time touching each letter with his fingertips. As he did so, the figures suddenly began to move and change shape. New characters appeared in place of the others, sending a tingle through his fingers and Larma's voice to his ears. "Treachery from the Dudoon Bog now waits in the Toulon Wilderness. It must be destroyed."

Slowly removing his fingers from the cloth, the words faded and returned to the original characters. Thalmus smiled at Larma's hidden message within the message. He carefully folded the cloth and returned it to his pocket.

Boschina and Captain Ritzs led the column of Oleens out of Ello to where Thalmus sat with Thunder and Dallion. The riders stopped and waited for Thalmus to speak.

Having decided which path to take, the hunter stood. "Captain Ritzs, send two riders to Table Top and tell Larma that we are going to the North Ford to join the queen. It is important that Larma receives this message."

"As you wish, Thalmus."

"I want you and the rest of your force to ride north to find Queen Ekala and join her. She should be along the Sol Linden River or at the North Ford. Tell her that I said she should *not* cross the river for any reason. She is in danger of an attack."

Captain Ritzs was suddenly concerned. "Ekala Oleen is in danger?"

"Yes, but do not wear out your horses getting there. Boschina, Thunder, Dallion, and I will be coming behind you."

"Do you want the sled for Thunder?" the captain asked, motioning at the frame still being pulled behind the two Oleen riders.

"No. I have removed the tools. You may leave it in Ello," Thalmus replied. "I believe we have time to walk."

"As you wish, Thalmus," Captain Ritzs said. She directed the two Oleens with the sled to take it back to the village and then ride with Thalmus' message to Larma.

When the captain turned back, Thunder was already plodding north on the road and Dallion was trotting ahead of him. Thalmus, though, was waiting to talk with her.

"Tell the queen that we are on our way. We *will* be there," he said in a reassuring voice.

"I will tell Oleen what you said," Ritzs replied and looked at Boschina, who Larma had told her to protect. The frog hunter would watch her now. She had no doubt of that. Still, she had promised Larma.

"We'll see you at the ford," Boschina said to her, smiling confidently.

Captain Ritzs nodded. "Yes, we'll see you all at the ford." She motioned her soldiers forward. The riders and horses settled into a trot, passing Thunder, and kicking up dust as they moved quickly up the road.

Chapter Seven
The North Ford

The tall, broad-shouldered Benton was still kneeling on one knee before Queen Ekala Oleen. "I apologize for threatening you and Lord Bolimaz, Your Majesty. Our survival has become dependent upon fear of strangers, and even of our own people."

"Stand up," Ekala replied. "I understand, but you could have learned who we were before you started shooting arrows at us. It was lucky for us that your archer wasn't skilled or he would have hit one of us."

"It was your uniforms," Benton said to Maz as he stood up. "Only your brothers' soldiers wear that color and they are hated in my region of the north."

People were beginning to gather around them as word spread of the strangers' identities. Weary faces of all ages stared at Prince Bolimaz and Queen Ekala Oleen.

"You won't make us go back across the river, will you?" an anxious woman asked Ekala.

Ekala saw worry in the woman's face. Two children, five or six years old, stood closely behind her—their fearful eyes locked on Ekala.

"You may stay, if it is safer for you here," Ekala answered. "Is your husband with you?"

"Thank you, Your Majesty," the woman said, clearly relieved, and then bowed.

Ekala reached out and gently touched the woman's shoulder. "You don't need to bow to me."

The woman was confused. "You are a queen," she said respectfully.

"Yes, I am the Ruler of Ameram," Ekala replied. "I require respect, but not bowing. And where is your husband? I see few men of fighting age. You are mostly women, children, and old men."

"My husband was taken by soldiers on our way here. I don't know if they killed him or if he's now in their army."

"Queen Ekala Oleen, Prince Bolimaz," Nattie interjected. "Please excuse our rude behavior. I'm afraid that we have become distrustful people. We have stew in the pot. Will you sit and eat with us?"

Maz glanced at Camp and Ekala, who still held their swords. He knew the people could not possibly have extra food to give away; yet the gesture was important and should not be refused.

"Thank you, Nateen Nadar," he said. "It would be our honor to join you."

Ekala realized the value of such a gesture for Bolimaz and that the tension had been broken. She had questions to be answered as well. Sheathing her sword, she turned to Camp. "Would you ride out and tell Captain Susa of our intentions?"

"As you wish, Oleen," Camp said, glancing at Maz and the people around them before sheathing his sword and going to his horse.

Ekala and Maz led their horses and followed Nattie and Benton to a small campfire encircled with stones. Several blackened pots full of simmering liquid hung over the fire. A lanky woman in a long peasant dress stood over the pots, stirring the contents. Two young girls with straggly hair sat on the ground behind her. She told them to stand up when Ekala and Maz approached. All of their eyes were wary and watchful.

"This is my wife, Helene," Benton said, touching her shoulder. "And these are our daughters, Celeste and Elaine." The three of them bowed to Ekala and Maz.

"Thank you for including us at your fire," Prince Bolimaz said.

Helene told the girls to get chairs for their guests. The two hurried away and returned with short, rough-hewn three-legged wooden stools for Ekala and Maz to sit upon.

Ekala observed the girls and mother and their meager, tattered belongings. The entire population of the camp appeared the same. What could be worse than to be poor and homeless in a foreign land? She saw no threat among them.

The men who had been with Benton, along with most of the people, trailed after them and stood outside of the inner circle at the cooking fire. A tall, lanky boy moved through the crowd and stood behind Benton. He carried a long bow and had a quiver of arrows hanging on his back.

Ekala saw the resemblance between the boy and Benton; she knew that they were father and son. "This is the archer?" Ekala asked.

"This is Neb, my eldest."

"How old are you, Neb?" Maz asked.

"I'm fourteen, Sire."

"You're tall for your age," Maz said. "Who's been teaching you how to shoot?"

"That would be me," Benton said. "I never was much with a bow; the sword is my weapon."

"Maybe we can help with your training," Ekala said. "I have excellent archers in my force."

Camp returned, trotting quickly through the camp and dismounting from his horse near the gathering. The people moved out of his way as he weaved through the crowd with one hand on the handle of his sheathed sword. He stood behind Maz.

Nattie Nadar tore apart a small loaf of bread and handed a piece to Ekala and Maz. Helene leaned over the fire and carefully spooned the watery brown stew into small wooden bowls and handed them to Celeste and Elaine, who delivered the meal to the queen and prince.

"This is a mix of what was gathered last night and this morning," Nattie said. She smiled. "Sometimes, it can be quite tasty."

Ekala didn't want to ask what was in the soup while she and Maz waited for Nattie, Benton, and the family to get their share before eating. Dipping the chunk of bread into the soup and then drinking from the bowl, they finished before conversation began again.

"That *was* tasty," Maz said, handing the bowl to Celeste, who was collecting them from everyone.

"That is polite of you to say, Lord Bolimaz," Nattie said. "This has been our main food here."

"How long have you been here?" Maz asked.

"I've been here thirty-three days now with my family," Benton said. "We were some of the first ones. As you can see, more have been coming. Some have continued on south."

"I met Benton on the way here," Nattie explained. "I joined them for protection and crossed the river with his family."

Frustrated by what he was hearing, Maz asked, "What is happening to my country?"

"Your brothers are raising an army and all that goes along with that," Benton said. "The families of the north region have refused to be part of it because the king made an alliance with Banyon; a country with whom we have always battled."

Maz shook his head. "Banyon has never been our friend. They poisoned my grandfather when I was a child. I can't believe my father would agree to such an alliance."

"What's wrong with an alliance between old enemies if it's for peace?" Ekala asked.

"Nothing," Maz replied. "If the enemy changes and can be trusted, and it's truly for peace, then it's good. But I doubt this agreement has anything to do with peace. It's about control and power." He pointed at Benton. "Your people, opinionated as you are, have always been loyal."

"We *are* prideful," Benton said, smiling. "It was your brothers who made the agreement with our enemies, not your father. Our region was not considered in this treaty. When our lords objected, they were run out of the throne room. Now, the Banyons raid our homes and the Toulon army forces the people into its service. Many women and children have been abandoned. Some have fled here."

Maz eyed the swordsman. "How did you and these other men escape?"

"We gathered our families and left. It wasn't easy. We couldn't go north, so Ameram became our destination. We had to fight several times before they chased us across the river."

Ekala was getting irritated. "Did the Toulon soldiers cross the ford into Ameram?"

"Not at first," Nattie answered. "It is an open border and you have no guards here. Once they realized that, small groups started attacking us."

"We've been able to fend them off so far," Benton said. "If they came with more than six, we could not stop them."

"Is there a full army encampment?" Maz asked.

"No, it's a small force staying somewhere north of the river," Benton answered. "Beyond the high ground or in the wilderness where they can't be seen."

Queen Ekala stood up and looked at Maz and Camp. "We must get to the ford and stop this. Toulon soldiers raiding into my country and chasing after their own defenseless people—I cannot allow this!"

Benton, Nattie, and Helene stood up when Ekala did and were now watching her along with the rest of the crowd.

Ekala turned to Nattie and Helene. "Thank you for sharing your food with us. It was…generous of you. I'm sure we will see you again." She looked at the crowd of people looking at her. "We are going to stop the soldiers from crossing the river into Ameram," she told them. Then she turned to Shadahn, patted her on the shoulder, and started to walk out of the camp.

Maz thanked Benton, Helene, and Nattie and looked at the people gathered around. "I promise you that I will do something to change what has happened to our country."

"I hope you can, Prince Bolimaz," Neb said.

Looking at Neb, Maz saw a confidence in the boy's face, just like his father's. "We're going to need your help, Neb," Maz said. "We're going to need all of you and more to save our country." He focused on the swordsman. "We'll be at the ford, Benton. I'd like you to join me there when you can. I need to learn more about what's been happening in my country."

"I will come, Prince Bolimaz," Benton said. "I want to help save our country so we can all return home."

***

The North Ford was a short twenty-minute ride from the refugee camp. At this point, the water was only knee deep across the entire width of the river. It was here that a granite formation rose up from the bottom, blocking the flow of the river like a dam, causing it to spill over the hard surface for ten meters before dropping again. This was the only safe place to cross the Sol Linden River. The road on the north side climbed a long hill, and then disappeared over the ridge. The route on the south side ambled up a gradual slope and then curved between the Western Hills and the undulations of the Great Plain on its way to the village of Ello. On each side of the river crossing, people rested, watered horses, or worked at repairing wagons. Broken-down, derelict carts and wagons—some with rotting produce, others that had been plundered for parts—were abandoned on either side of the road. Trash and debris was strewn about and washed onto shore from the river.

When Queen Ekala's force approached the ford, a wagon with its heavy load, covered by canvas and drawn by stout horses, was plowing through the shallow water toward Ameram. Another wagon waited at the water's edge to cross into Toulon.

"What a mess," Ekala said. "We'll have to get this cleaned up."

"We need to position here and start patrolling this ford," Maz said. "I want to catch those raiders from Toulon."

"As do I," Ekala replied. She turned to look at the column of Oleen soldiers behind them. "Captain Susa," Ekala called.

The captain rode up beside Ekala. "Yes, Oleen?"

"We will be staying here for two days or more. Find a place to settle."

Camp had been surveying the landscape, twisting in his saddle from side to side. "You want us to set up camp in that low area below the knoll?" he asked Ekala, pointing at a swale seventy-five meters up from the river. "It'll give some protection from the wind. We can still see the ford and the road from there; guards can be posted on the higher ground."

Ekala Oleen searched the terrain and agreed.

"That spot looks like the best we can do."

"We'll help get set up," Maz said to Camp. "As soon as we do, I think we should change out of these uniforms."

"I agree with that," Camp replied. "I don't want to get shot at again."

Ekala smiled. "That's a good idea. While you're getting us settled, Susa and I will talk with those wagon drivers. I want to know what's moving in and out of Ameram."

Susa ordered Lander and three riders to join them and the other soldiers to go with Camp and Maz. Ekala, Captain Susa, and the four Oleens trotted to the water's edge at the ford. Lander withdrew the bow from its cover strapped alongside the saddle, tightened the string, and held it casually in her left hand. When the wagon coming from Toulon pulled up onto the bank, the Oleens moved their horses along each side of the harnessed horses and the drivers holding the reins, who sat side by side on a bench seat in front of the tall box of the bed.

Ekala and Susa were on opposite sides of the wagon.

"Welcome to Ameram," Ekala said to the two men. One held the reins. The other one held a long staff for prodding the horses.

At his side, the handle of a sword stuck out from between planks of the wagon.

The men—burly, bearded and suspicious of the Oleens—glanced from side to side at them. "What you want?" the driver asked.

"We are soldiers of Ameram," Captain Susa replied calmly. "I have orders to inspect your load."

"Oh yeah, whose orders?" the driver asked defiantly.

"Queen Ekala Oleen's orders," Susa said. "We want to see what you're bringing into our country."

"The queen?" the driver questioned.

"We heard about your woman *roooler*," the other man said mockingly.

"Whatta she want? Steal my merchandise?" the driver grumbled. "Who do she think she is?"

Lander pulled an arrow from her quiver and nocked it in the bow string, but kept it pointing down. Captain Susa glared at the driver. Her voice tightened. "You can ask her yourself," she said, motioning toward Ekala.

The men followed Susa's direction, turning to look at Ekala sitting on the black horse with its head up, its ears perked, and angry eyes intent on theirs. The woman wore no crown, gown, or fancy colors. A large knife was on her hip and a sword was sheathed on the shoulder of the big horse. There was no mistaking the sense of power emanating from her dark brown eyes and solid body. The men had heard that the queen of Ameram was not the typical genteel princess—and now they knew for themselves that the stories were true.

"Do you have something to say to me?" Queen Ekala asked and waited for their response.

The men stared at her, not knowing what to say.

"Are you expecting to be robbed?" Ekala asked, trying to make it easy on them. "We're not here to take anything from you. I am not a thief." She paused. "Do you think I am a thief?"

"No, no…Your Majesty," both men stammered, glancing at the Oleen archer.

"I want to know the trade that is coming in and out of our kingdom," Ekala said. "Can you understand that?"

The men nodded. "We didn' kno'…" The driver started to say more but stopped.

"You're from the north, yes?"

"Tha's right, transportin' goods from Banyon…Your Majesty," the man with the staff said.

"Banyon?" Ekala questioned. "And where are you headed?"

The men glanced at one another before the driver answered. "Barrunda, we carryin' a load of blankets an' quilted clothin' t'sell in Barrunda, an' maybe Ambermal."

"Barrunda?" Susa said. "They make clothes and blankets there. They sell them everywhere. Why would they want yours?"

"Um…don' kno'," the driver said. "We jus' drivin'."

"Your wagon looks awfully loaded down for blankets and clothes," Ekala said. "Looks like you've added taller sides, front and back."

"It's an ol' thing," the man with the shaft said, "built with heavy wood, good Banyon wood. We jus' wantta move on t'sell our goods."

The men sat still, making no move to uncover their load.

"Are you hiding something?" Ekala asked, becoming irritated.

"No, Your Majesty. It's jus clothin'."

"Then untie the ropes and pull the cover back or Captain Susa will cut the ropes."

The men hesitated. One started to reach for the sword handle. Lander immediately brought her bow and arrow up to aim at the man.

"Don't touch that sword," Ekala said, calmly. "Lander is an excellent archer and will not miss at this distance. Get down and untie the ropes."

The two men jumped down. They nervously worked the knots and loosened the ropes, and then stepped away. "We didn' load this wagon," the driver said.

"Tha's right," the other man said. "We only kno' wat they tol' us, full of blankets an' clothin'."

Captain Susa and the two Oleens pulled the tarp forward, revealing stacks of various colored blankets.

"See," the driver said, pointing at his wagon, "blankets."

"That's what I see so far," Ekala replied.

Susa began lifting and separating the layers of material. Under the first layer, she felt something solid: she reached in and touched a familiar metal shape. Grasping hold of the object, Susa pulled it out from between the blankets and held it up—a shiny new sword.

"That's an awfully big needle for sewing blankets," Ekala said, staring at the men.

The men looked at the queen, and then at the archer bending the bow with a drawn arrow—its sharp metal tip pointing at them. "I didn' kno' that was in there," the driver said.

Susa reached in and pulled out another sword, and then another. Two Oleens climbed onto the wagon and began throwing off the blankets, revealing layers of swords and shields.

Ekala watched calmly; inside, anger rose as the weapons were exposed and piled upon the ground. "How often do you bring *these goods* into my country?" she asked.

"I didn' kno' thos' weapons were in there," the driver said again.

"We was jus' told t'deliver this wagon," the second man said.

"Do I look like a fool?" Ekala asked the man. "You knew what was in this wagon or you would not have reached for your sword. How many of these wagons have come into Ameram and where did they go?"

The men lowered their heads and did not speak.

Queen Ekala Oleen glared at the men for a moment, waiting for a response, and then dismounted. Shadahn snorted and followed her to the men. She drew her sword, gleaming in the afternoon light, and pointed at the current of the river crossing. "Turn around and look at the ford," she told them.

The two men looked at her sword with the engraving of the horse, shell creature, and owl. They had heard the stories about this blade and of its power. Now it was before them, with the metal eyes of the animals glaring into their own. They did what she wanted, shuffling their feet to face the river.

"Since you don't seem to know anything about these weapons in your wagon, I'm letting you go...back across the river—on foot," Ekala said. "Have you ever walked through the ford? The stone at the bottom is slippery. If you were to fall, the current would sweep you over the edge and into the trough to the falls below—never to be seen again."

The men stared at the downstream edge of the ford where the water started dropping, picking up speed, and then farther down where the surface boiled and gushed away.

"Go ahead," Ekala said. "We'll help you." She motioned to the mounted Oleens, who started prodding and pushing the men forward with their horses.

When they stepped into the mud at the river's edge, where the wagon wheels had turned the ground to a slimy mush, the men hesitated. "You goin' t'push us over?" one said.

"It's a dangerous crossing," Ekala replied. "People disappear here all the time." She waited a moment, and then said, "You have a choice: answer my questions and live or try to cross the ford. Even if you make it to the other side, the people you work for won't be happy about losing their merchandise, will they?"

Staring at the water flowing at their feet, the man said, "I don't wanna drown."

The driver looked back at the queen. "You let us live?"

"Yes, though you will be prisoners."

"Alright," he said, nodding at the other man for agreement. "We was tol' that someone would meet us on the road t'Barrunda and tell us where t'deliver this load."

"We don't kno' where it's endin' up," the other man added.

Why Barrunda? Ekala wondered. The town was Ameram's industrial community; it made a wide variety of merchandise, including all the weapons and armaments for the army. Why would these Banyon weapons be going there? Who would want them? The community's lords, elders, and merchants were wealthy and politically powerful. Half of the men in her father's Council of Learned Men had been from Barrunda. She'd had a strained relationship with the counselors since becoming queen and stripping them of their influence upon the crown and the court. Despite her belief that they were selfish, and therefore did not have her trust, she had not dismissed their loyalty to the kingdom. She also knew that because of Barrunda's success as a center for wealth and opportunity, it attracted a seamy and morally corrupt element.

"What does this person look like?" Ekala asked.

"Don' kno'," the driver said. "We was tol' he'd show us the sign of a lizard."

"Lizard?" Ekala mouthed the word. Images rushed from her memory: a black lizard with vicious eyes on the soldiers' red uniforms and shields, and then the clinging creature on the ceiling in Metro's ghastly room where her unconscious father was tied to a platform. Her hand gripped tighter on the sword handle. "That's all that they told you, no name or description?"

"Only tha' he'd show us the sign of a lizard," the man answered.

Anger rose in Ekala's chest. She saw Metro's penetrating green eyes and hideous laughing face as he crouched in the castle window, Maz sprawled bleeding on the floor, and a grinning Corsair holding up his bloody sword.

Shaking the vision, she asked, "Where have you taken other loads?"

"This is our first delivery to Ameram. That man with the lizard sign suppos' t'pay us when we get there."

"I don't think your pay is going to be what you expect," Ekala said. "Do you know of other loads coming here?"

"Some, but we only been deliverin' t' the Toulon army."

Ekala turned to Susa. "Wait until Maz hears this."

Captain Susa pointed at the two men. "What do you want to do with them?"

"Bind them, gag them, and put them in the wagon with the weapons. Drive the wagon to our camp and guard it constantly."

"As you wish, Oleen," the captain replied and started giving orders to the Oleen soldiers.

Maz and Camp rode down from the Oleens' new encampment on the hillside. Having changed from their uniforms to the worn clothes of common folk, but still with a soldierly bearing, they were ready to engage.

"What have you got here?" Maz asked, looking at the wagon and the two men being tied up by the Oleens.

"Look at this," Ekala said and withdrew a sword from the wagon. "These men, from Banyon, are delivering this load of weapons to someone here in Ameram."

Camp joined Maz in looking at the sword, and then lifted the blankets in the wagon and pulled out one of the shields. "The wagon is filled to the brim," he said.

Maz pointed at the "S" on the blade of the sword. "Look at this mark, Oleen."

"I saw it."

"Who's getting these weapons?" Maz asked.

"They claim they don't know, but the man that's going to meet them will show the sign of a lizard."

"Let me talk to 'em for a few minutes,' Camp said. "I'll find out."

"No, Camp, I promised I wouldn't hurt them if they told me what they know."

"Well," Camp said, "it wouldn't be *you* hurting 'em."

"A lizard? This is not good, Oleen," Maz said. "What *did* they know?"

"That these weapons have been going to the Toulon Army. This was their first trip into Ameram, supposedly."

Maz watched the two men being taken away by the Oleens. "You sure you don't want to let Camp handle them?"

Ekala smiled. "I'm sure. They might be worth something alive and healthy."

"This ford…" Maz said shaking his head. "We've got to do something to stop this."

"I've been thinking about that," Ekala said, and then called to Captains Susa and Lander.

The captains left the others and came back to her. "Yes, Oleen?"

"I want every wagon, cart, and piece of luggage inspected going and coming. All traffic through the ford will stop at dusk. It will open again after sunrise. No night crossings, even on a full moon. We must be vigilant. In the morning, we'll send word of this to Larma and Currad. They must be warned about these wagons full of weapons."

"As you wish, Oleen," Susa and Lander said together.

"And let's get this debris and junk around here cleaned up. Maybe the refugees can use it at their camp. Also, if there are any merchants we buy food from, get extra for the refugees. And, take all of the blankets to them, too."

"Yes, Oleen," the captains replied.

When Ekala Oleen turned to look for the prince, Maz was still gazing across the river at his country.

Chapter Eight
A Dangerous Decision

Benton and Neb, the father and son from the settlement, rode up slowly, dismounted, and approached the Crown Prince of Toulon and the Queen of Ameram.

"Your Majesties," Benton said, bowing his head to Ekala and then to Maz.

The young man, Neb, bowed and nodded, and then bowed again. He was definitely shy and unsure about being in the presence of royalty.

"Thank you for coming," Ekala said to Benton. She looked at Neb, who held his long bow in front of him like a staff. "I'm glad you're here, Neb. You remind me a little of my sister."

Neb nodded and smiled, not knowing what to say about being compared to a girl.

"It's good that you're learning from your father," Maz told the boy. "My father spent little time with me, though he expected much of me. I was taught by other men, such as Camp." He motioned to the tall, rugged soldier. "It was from others that I learned how to be a leader, to be truthful, dependable, and strong."

Again, Neb nodded, and then motioned to his father. "I just want to be with him."

That brought a smile to Benton's face. "We have much to learn from each other, don't we?" the big swordsman said to his son. The boy, who was almost as tall as his father, smiled shyly.

Maz handed Benton one of the swords from the confiscated wagon. "The queen just caught those men with a wagonload of swords and shields. Have you seen any weapons like this?"

"These are definitely from Banyon forges," the swordsman said. "Weak steel and poorly made. The Banyons have always been crooks and deceivers. What have you done with the wagon drivers? Can I take them off your hands?"

"I already asked," Camp said. "The queen's not ready to give 'em up."

Ekala smiled at the two men. "I promised to spare them in exchange for talking to me."

"They don't deserve your generosity," Benton replied.

"I'm more concerned about how long these weapons have been coming into Ameram and who's getting them," Ekala said.

"There's no telling," Maz said. "This has probably been going on since Metro."

"But he's dead and gone. Bubo saw to that," Ekala replied. "And they're still coming? Who's behind all of this? That wagon carried enough swords to supply a medium-sized force."

Benton held up the sword. "This blade is shaped differently than Banyon's usual swords. And it has a new emblem, this odd looking 'S.' I saw some of these swords being used by Toulon soldiers."

Ekala grasped the sword. "You tell me of raiders coming across the ford and now we find weapons used by the Toulon army being smuggled into Ameram. Is it lawless over there or are they preparing to attack us?" She looked across the river and shook her head.

"I know what you're thinking," Maz said. "You cannot cross the river. That would not only put you in danger, but my brothers would see that as an act of aggression. It would give them an excuse to declare war. Besides, what could you possibly do over there?"

Ekala nodded her agreement. "We'll have to set a permanent post here to check for contraband, stop the raids, and help your people who are fleeing across the ford."

"We'll need more soldiers for that," Camp said.

"I'm sending word to Table Top for two more forces to take over for us here, and a message to Currad at Ambermal to put two companies of soldiers on the road right away. In the meantime, we'll stay here and do what we can."

"Thank you for helping us, Your Majesty," Benton said to Ekala. "We'll stay prepared and watchful at our camp. And I'll try to train the few men we have."

"Good. We have some extra swords you can use," Ekala said as she climbed onto Shadahn. "Keep practicing, Neb."

"I will, Your Majesty," Neb said firmly.

Maz joined Ekala riding toward the ford. They were both quiet, thinking about the situation. Finally, Maz spoke. "We need more information. Camp and I can cross over and see what we can find out."

Ekala looked at him. "If it's dangerous for me, it's doubly so for you—there's a price on *your* head. I know you're upset about what's happening to your people, Maz, but it's too soon for you to attempt going there."

"We know the country and the people. We can get around, see what's happening and return."

Ekala knew what he was going through: the feeling of helplessness and frustration. She understood his desire to do something. "I can't tell you what to do, Maz, but I do know that your people are going to need you. If you get captured, how can you help them? Besides, until more forces arrive, I need you here."

* * *

An arrow whistled through the air in a long arch and thumped into an old tree stump at the side of the road. The arrow's wooden shaft hummed, vibrating from the sudden stop.

"Good shot," Thalmus said, impressed. "That was a long distance in this breeze. Your accuracy is excellent."

"I was practicing at Table Top," Boschina replied. "The wind there is a challenge and a good teacher for judging targets at long range." She smiled. "Of course, moving targets are much harder to hit than that stump."

"Still, one hundred meters or so and you struck the target."

Walking along the road they had been choosing objects in the distance as targets, and then shooting arrows at them. Boschina was surprising Thalmus with her improved ability. Dallion was out scouting. Radise trailed behind Boschina and Thalmus as they walked beside or ahead of Thunder, releasing arrows and retrieving them.

"You have become a skilled archer," Thalmus told her. "That will serve you well. How is your sword technique?"

Boschina groaned. "Not so good. I have not practiced much."

Thunder grunted and clicked his jaws.

"I know, Thunder, but it's a different training, a different understanding," Boschina replied. "It's in-your-face fighting. And I have never liked that, even with you by my side."

Thalmus nodded. "It *is* different and difficult, but this tool," he tapped the sword on his hip, "is what you will use to defend yourself most of the time when the bow is not practical—up close and deadly, as you already know."

"Yes. I guess this means we'll be practicing tonight?"

"Being skilled with all of the tools, knowing when and how to use them, is critical," Thalmus answered.

"Like knowing how to use the right tool and where to strike, and with how much impact, when carving stone," Boschina said. "Or the blacksmith knowing how much heat is needed to shape a tool in a certain way and instill strength into its body."

"That is a good comparison," Thalmus said. "It is very similar. Knowledge of tools and how to use them takes one from being a user to a craftsman and artist, like your father."

"Or a hunter and warrior, like you," Boschina replied.

Thalmus looked at Boschina walking near him, her horse dutifully following behind her. She had learned much since she first appeared in his meadow in search of Veracitas. Through the struggles and battles, never losing hope, standing strong for her father and for Ekala, she had grown in confidence, knowledge, and physical strength. Still, she possessed the charming naiveté of her youthful age. He knew that her destiny was intertwined with Ekala Oleen's and the powerful draw of her father's artistic heritage. At this moment in her life, she was not aware of the important role she would play once again for the queen and their kingdom. Even though Metro had been destroyed, she was aware that not all was peaceful in their country. What she did not know was the depth of the evil that still existed, and its passion to regain power. Although her courage appeared undaunted, Thalmus knew Boschina would be tested, more than once, and must stand firm on her ability and commitment to truth in order to be victorious; hence, the continued training and knowledge of the tools.

"Which do you prefer," Thalmus asked, "the weapon tools or the carving tools?"

"I like both," Boschina replied. "Each has its own purpose. I know I have a lot to learn yet, but one day I hope to be a master of them all."

Thalmus smiled. "I think you will be master of the tools one day. For me, I would like to learn the use of new tools. Perhaps, you could teach me how to carve stone."

Surprised, Boschina said, "That would be fun. Do you really want to? My father is the master and he's a wonderful teacher. He can show you so much."

"I want *you* to teach me," Thalmus replied.

Boschina smiled broadly. "Fair exchange then," she said. "Schooling in weapon tools for schooling in carving tools."

"Alright, it's a deal," Thalmus said.

They continued on the road.

Boschina turned to Thalmus again and said, "Let's shake hands on it."

He extended his hand and she grasped it with hers.

"We start when we find some carving tools," she said, thinking about it, "wherever that might be, Ello or maybe all the way to Marbala. I'm going to hold you to it, Thalmus. I bet you're a natural. We'll have to choose a small, soft stone to start with—don't want you to get discouraged. I want you to be thinking of an image that we can discover in stone." She paused and said, almost to herself, "This is going to be fun."

* * *

Captain Susa rode in from the night, dismounted, tied her horse to the rope line with the other horses, and walked to the fire where the queen sat. "The guards are posted," she reported. "All crossing at the ford has stopped for the night."

Ekala looked up at Susa. "Where are Camp and the prince?"

"Patrolling along the river," Susa answered.

Ekala nodded. "They are determined to stop any invaders attacking their people in the settlement. The prince is quite upset at what's happening to his country." She paused before adding: "It's wearing on him."

Susa heard the concern for Maz in Ekala Oleen's voice and was unsure what to say. She stretched and warmed her hands at the fire. "Well, I'm glad to have their help. Their experience and fighting ability bolsters our strength."

"Oh yes, they know how to fight," Ekala said. "And I have a feeling *that* fighting ability could be on display soon. How are the wagon drivers doing?"

"Our two captives are complaining about food and being tied up still," Susa said. "You should've let Maz and Camp throw 'em in the river."

Ekala smiled. "Yeah, Camp would have liked that, Benton as well. But I think those drivers might serve a purpose yet," Ekala replied, standing up. "I'm going to bed down. Wake me if there's any trouble."

"As you wish, Oleen."

Ekala moved away from the fire to where her bed of straw had been arranged on the ground. She removed her sword and laid it down beside the bed, and then covered herself with two blankets. As always, the queen was in the center of the camp with the soldiers spread out in a large circle sleeping around her.

A new moon rising in the east did little to penetrate the darkness. The night was surprisingly quiet. The horses were relaxed and the Oleen soldiers moved about carefully as they changed guards and tended to the fire. Between shifts, after the fifth hour, when no one stirred, Ekala awoke with a feeling of something near. There had been no noise, just a sense of something in the dark.

She remained still and listened.

Had that been one of the guards passing by? She heard a faint sound: was that a footstep? There was a foul odor in the air. Wet fur and—something dead? A sniffing sound close by; it was an animal inhaling with short breaths, ever so quietly. Ekala grasped the handle of her sword.

It was vibrating.

Now she heard claws on the ground. *Where are the guards? Was everyone asleep?* Ekala threw off the blankets and in one motion jumped to her feet while drawing her sword from its scabbard. There was an ugly snort and more clawing in front of her. Suddenly, to her right, a blur in the night, silent wings in the air sailed past Ekala and were quickly lost in the darkness. Then, a startling roar broke the stillness. Ekala crouched, ready for an attack. Instead, she realized the roar was a scream of pain, and the agony of it pitched higher as the animal suffered. She heard claws on the earth again and then thumping paws fading as the animal ran away.

Awakened by the screams, the camp burst with activity as the soldiers gathered to Ekala and into defensive positions by the horses that huffed and pulled at their tethers. Now there were sounds of splashing and galloping horses, shouts from the guards at the river, and then Maz and Camp yelling.

"They need help," Ekala shouted as she ran to Shadahn. Swinging up onto the horse, the two of them bolted toward the melee in the darkness.

Captain Susa hurried to catch up, yelling orders for some of the Oleens to follow and others to guard the camp. By the time they were mounted and moving, the queen was gone.

Shadahn galloped, chasing the sounds of the stomping horses and clashing swords. Ekala held tight to the reins with her left hand and gripped her sword in her right hand, ready to engage.

Hooves splashed in the water ahead of them and Ekala heard her name being called, "Oleen, Oleen!" It was the guards at the river. She could barely see them in the darkness, waving at her to stop. She pulled Shadahn to a halt and the guards gathered on each side of Shadahn, looking up at her.

"Riders from Toulon came across," the guards yelled. "Prince Bolimaz and Camp attacked them. We fought until they turned and rode back across the ford. The prince and Camp chased after them."

"How many were there?" Ekala asked.

"Hard to tell, six, maybe eight," one guard said. "Couldn't see them much in the dark."

"Are any of you wounded?"

"No. They were surprised we were here."

"Did you hit any of them?"

"Several of them may have gone into the river; we heard some big splashes."

"We were afraid to shoot much—didn't want to hit our own," another guard said.

"And the prince was not injured?" Ekala asked anxiously.

"Not that we could see. He and Camp ordered them to stop and when they didn't, he charged into them."

Ekala slapped her thigh and peered into the night, listening. Distant hooves pounded the earth. Shadahn perked her ears and started forward into the river. Ekala hesitated, wanting to let her go—to ride on after Maz—but knew she had to stop Shadahn. It was foolish in this darkness. She patted her horse's neck. "Not now, Girl. We have to wait."

Captain Susa and Lander rode up with four soldiers. "What are your orders?" she asked immediately. They were ready to plunge into a chase across the ford.

Ekala took a deep breath before answering. "At first light, search the river for the dead or wounded. I want to know if these were Toulon soldiers crossing our border. Be careful not to wander off the ford."

"We could use torches to look now," Susa said.

"That would make you a target for archers," Lander said.

"Lander's right," Ekala said. "We don't know who's out there. We'll wait till morning."

"What about Prince Bolimaz and Camp?" Susa asked.

The queen did not hesitate with her answer. "If they're not back by morning, we'll cross the river to look for them."

Ekala rode back to the camp wondering about the animal that woke her. Did it come with the men crossing the river? Was it the same creature that had followed her the day before? And the wings in the darkness: was that Bubo? If so, had Bubo tried to warn her of the danger? The rest of the night passed slowly as they stayed alert, listening and waiting to hear the return of Maz and Camp.

By morning, there was no sign of them and Ekala's concern rose to another level. She walked the ground around her bed until she found the tracks of an animal. Claw marks in the earth were just four meters from where she had slept. Grass chunks were churned up where a fight had occurred—hence the screaming roar. Spots of dried, black blood speckled the ground. A white and tan flutter in the green of the grass caught her eye. She bent and picked up a small feather—a chest feather from a Great Horned owl. "Bubo," she whispered, looking around for the owl. "Thank you." Then she thought: *If you're here, Thalmus must have sent you, which means he knows something's wrong and he's on his way.* She suddenly realized that the strange creatures, the refugee camp, hidden weapons, and raids across the border were all related.

But she wasn't sure how.

She returned her attention to the creature. From where she had found the feather, the tracks were difficult to see in the grass, but she was able to locate depressions where the animal had stepped, crushing the blades as it ran. *It must have been large to leave such an impression,* she thought. Ekala followed the trail until the prints faded out. Oddly enough, the tracks did not go toward the river, but west to the hills and the Barrier Forest. Maybe it wasn't the creature from the Toulon Wilderness. Whatever it was, the animal had passed through the outer circle of sleeping Oleen soldiers to get to her. It had followed her scent. That was the sniffing she had heard in the dark. Ekala shivered. "Big but quiet," she said to herself. She scanned the hills. "You were looking for me, weren't you? Now, I'll be looking for you."

The Oleen soldiers searched the crossing from shore to shore for signs of the fight from the night before. If there had been any casualties, the river had washed them away into the trough of falls. Finally, an Oleen walking carefully back through the ford stepped on something that slid under her foot. She reached down into the shallow water and pulled up a sword. Its handle had caught in a crevice of the stone bottom.

"It's just like the ones from the wagon," Captain Susa said, examining the blade and handle. "It has the same marking here by the hilt." She pointed at the engraving as she handed it to Ekala.

The insignia on the sword was a single line in an "S" curve with a circle at one end and two cross-hatches in the middle of the curve. *Were those intended to be legs? Was this a simple emblem of a lizard?* she wondered.

Ekala shook her head slowly. "Someone is making a lot of these." She looked across the river, hoping to see Maz riding toward them. There was only a wagon coming slowly down the grade to the ford. It was not a merchant's wagon. Smaller, more like a cart, it was pulled by an old horse with children riding and parents walking alongside. More people escaping Toulon? She had hoped Maz and Camp had stopped somewhere in the night after chasing the invaders and waited to return with the daylight. They had either gone on or were in trouble.

"Where are you, Maz?" Ekala said to herself.

Prince Bolimaz and Camp had fought with her and Thalmus through the battle for Castle Ambermal to overthrow Metro and save her father. The prince had almost died defending her from the wicked Corsair, but was saved by the power of Bubo so that he might live to regain the throne of Toulon that was his birthright. She owed him the same unbridled support that he had given her. Besides, she had known for some time now how important he had become to her. Their feelings for one another had grown into something more than friendship. Ekala knew the danger of crossing into Toulon, not only for herself, but for her country. She also knew that she could not abandon Maz; she could not sit and wait, hoping he would return unscathed. That was simply not in her nature.

Ekala Oleen handed the sword back to Captain Susa. "I want three volunteers to cross the ford with me. Have them change out of their uniforms so they can't be identified as Ameram soldiers."

Captain Susa looked at her queen for a moment and decided it was her duty to object. "This is dangerous, Oleen. I don't think you should go."

"I know you don't," Ekala replied. "But I can't sit here."

"Let me go instead of you. If I am caught or killed, it means nothing."

"Thank you, Susa. But you're wrong; your life means something to me. I have to do this."

"Then take more soldiers with you."

"No. A small force will be less likely to be noticed, but will be enough to help Maz and Camp. And you need enough to guard the ford. Have the volunteers get some food from the cook and meet me here at the river."

Captain Susa started to speak and stopped. She knew Oleen had made up her mind and there was nothing to gain in arguing about it any further. "As you wish," she said and turned to call the soldiers together at their camp.

The queen sat on Shadahn in the shallows of the ford, hoping to see Maz and Camp appear over the crest of the hill on the other side. Captain Susa joined her on horseback with the three hand-picked Oleen warriors. Lander, Ricken, and Karl: each one had fought with her in the great Battle for Ambermal.

"We're crossing the border into Toulon to find and help Prince Bolimaz and Camp," she told them. "I don't know how far we have to go, how long it will take, or what we will encounter. If any of you wish not to go with me, I will understand."

The Oleen soldiers looked at her as if she were talking nonsense. Lander—fully armed with a bow, three quivers of arrows, a short sword on one hip, and a long blade on the other—said, "We go where you go, Oleen. We're ready."

Ekala Oleen smiled at them. "Good. Captain Susa, you're in command of the ford. Make sure Larma gets the message requesting two forces to bolster our position until Currad's troops get here. Do not tell her that I have crossed the ford, though she will know it anyway."

"As you wish," Captain Susa replied. She watched her queen on the black war horse and the three Oleens dressed in peasant clothes ride their horses through the shallow water of the ford, examine tracks on the other side, move slowly up the hill searching the ground, and then disappear over the ridge.

Chapter Nine
Veracitas and Thoe

Boschina held onto Dallion's mane as he galloped smoothly over the hills of the plain. She sat comfortably on his back, bouncing with the rhythm of his strides, her bow and quiver slung over her shoulders because there was no place to tie them on the bareback stallion. The two had been exploring the northwest area between the Barrier Forest and the straight road to the ford. The big Paint was enjoying the run with his friend. They had not played together in a long time, not since she had gotten the steady and protective Radise as her horse. Thalmus and Boschina were the only humans the powerful and independent stallion had ever trusted enough to let ride him. He slowed to a trot and came to a stop under the shady canopy of a cluster of rose trees where they could look over the landscape. Boschina let go of his mane and stretched. Dallion snorted, clearing his nostrils, and then turned his head and nickered at her.

"What?" Boschina said. "No, I don't think you've lost a step, Dal. You're still pretty fast."

He snorted at her, blowing air through his lips, and shook his head. Boschina laughed. She rubbed his neck, and then leaned back and patted his flanks. Down the hill to their right was the bare dirt road running from Ello to the North Ford. Several wagons rolled along the rutted track, churning up a small brown cloud. Looking back toward Ello, Boschina saw Thalmus, Thunder, and Radise on the trail far behind them, walking at a steady pace. It was a clear, blue-sky day and Boschina felt like there were no worries in the world. "This reminds me of the first time you let me ride you," she said thoughtfully. She leaned forward and wrapped her arms around Dallion's neck, resting her head on the back of his. He neighed softly, and then suddenly lifted his head, his ears perked up—listening.

Alarmed, Boschina sat up, knowing that Dallion had heard a troubling sound. "What is it, Dal?" She looked at the hills and then farther up to the forest, expecting to see something coming out of the trees. But it appeared void of any danger. Turning to the road, she saw a lone Oleen soldier riding hard from the north. Boschina immediately knew that it had to be a messenger from Ritzs or Oleen looking for Thalmus; and at the pace the rider was moving, it had to be bad news.

"This doesn't look good," Boschina said as Dallion started trotting down the slope. He made a wide circle, watching for other riders who might be chasing after the Oleen soldier. Satisfied there were none, he came in from behind and ran up alongside the Oleen rider's galloping horse. Boschina knew her. It was Renca, a member of Captain Ritzs' force. Upon seeing them, the soldier smiled and waved at Boschina. Her horse quickly fell into stride with Dallion.

"Are you looking for Thalmus?" Boschina yelled over the pounding hooves of the horses.

"I have a message for him from Ritzs," Renca hollered back.

"Follow us," Boschina yelled and Dallion sped up, moving out in front, leading the other horse.

Thunder had clicked his jaws in warning long before Thalmus heard or saw the approaching riders. When they came into sight, he recognized Dallion with Boschina and then the uniform on the other horseman. Radise threw her head and whinnied at seeing Boschina and Dallion racing toward them. Upon reaching Thalmus, Dallion slowed but ran on by, circling and coming back to face the Oleen pulling her horse to a stop in front of Thunder. The dust settled as the horse, sweating and breathing hard, shuffled and snorted.

Renca slid off her horse and stepped in front of Thalmus. She took several deep breaths, swallowing and clearing her throat before speaking. "Captain Ritzs sent me. She wants you to know that the queen has crossed the ford into Toulon." The soldier coughed and swallowed, trying to bring moisture to her mouth. "And she wants to know what you want her to do. Should we go after her?"

Thalmus quietly took in the news and the question. His expression did not change, even when Thunder grunted. The queen's actions did not surprise him, but the reason for it would. Boschina jumped down from Dallion, greeted Radise with a pat, and stood next to Thalmus.

"Did you get there before she crossed the river?" Thalmus asked.

Renca shook her head. "The queen was already gone. She went across with three Oleens looking for Prince Bolimaz and Camp."

"What do you mean, *looking for*?" Thalmus asked.

"They had a night fight with some raiders from Toulon," Renca said, her voice dry and cracking. "The prince and Camp chased after them; when they did not return, the queen went looking for them."

Boschina was stunned. "You don't know where Oleen is...or Maz...or Camp?"

"No," Renca said. "Captain Susa was left to guard the ford. She is very upset."

Thalmus untied a water pouch from the pack on Thunder and handed it to the dusty, thirsty Renca. She took it, smiling, and drank from it, paused, and then drank again before handing the pouch back to Thalmus. "Thank you," she said. "I left in such a hurry that I forgot to take water."

"A lesson to be learned," Thalmus said. He reached out to Renca's horse, stroking her sweaty neck and shoulders. "She needs water as well. There is a spring ahead in the hills. Dallion can take you there on your return. Tell Captain Ritzs to wait. We will be there in the morning."

"Waiting will be hard for her to do," Renca said as she got back on her horse.

"Waiting is never easy," Thalmus replied. "But sometimes it is the wise course of action." He turned to Boschina. "Take Radise, I am sure she is thirsty, and go with them to the spring. Thunder and I will meet you there."

Thunder's head was turned, looking at Boschina. She stroked his head and wanted to tell him to hurry, to walk faster, but knew that the big tortoise understood what was at stake and would do his best. Smiling, she said, "We'll see you there, Thunder."

Thunder answered with a click of his jaws.

Boschina swung up onto Radise, feeling her sword sheathed there on the horse's shoulder. She joined Renca as the horses started trotting after Dallion, heading north again. Watching their friends ride away, Thalmus and Thunder started walking after them.

Bubo had been gone since Thalmus sent him to check on Ekala. The owl had not returned and now he knew why. Bubo must be following Ekala. Thalmus was glad the Great Horned owl was with her, for she was in more danger now than before. Bubo's presence would help to keep her safe and guide her through peril.

Maz was another matter. His country was in turmoil, and he along with it. Ekala knew that and the possible consequences for her and Ameram by crossing the border. Still, she chose to go after him. Her feelings for the prince were deeper than Thalmus realized. He remembered Larma's prediction in the candle's flame; the images of Maz and Ekala, side by side, fighting their enemies in a burning battle. He had thought it was the battle for Castle Ambermal, but he was wrong. The burning battle was yet to come.

Thunder had sped up. He was walking more quickly than he normally did, which was highly unusual. Thalmus, who had been lost in thought, suddenly became aware of the pace. He watched the giant tortoise take longer strides, firmly planting his feet on the ground in a steady rhythm. *He senses something.*

"At this speed we will be at the ford by nightfall," he said, smiling at Thunder.

Thunder just grunted and kept moving.

"Are you ready for a hunt in the Toulon Wilderness?" Thalmus asked the giant tortoise.

Thunder snapped his jaws.

"I thought so," Thalmus replied. "It has been quite a while since we were there. This time, we will be fighting different creatures."

* * *

King Ahmbin stepped out of Lord Rundall's room, quietly closed the door, and leaned against the hallway wall. He rested for a moment, laying his head back against the cold stone, and then walked slowly through the dim corridors and out into the courtyard to the fishpond. There he stood, watching the fish swim in circles, wiping the tears from his eyes.

Currad was returning from the barracks where he had been re-organizing the various companies of troops: Castle Guards, the Ameram Army, and Forces of Oleen. They all, almost to a man and woman, wanted to be designated as Oleen soldiers, which to his traditional military style of thinking was not possible. Each group required different duties and responsibilities. The Castle Guard was just that: they guarded the castle and throne. The Ameram Army, which used to be the King's Troops, were to be in the field, guarding important places and ready to go to war to defend the kingdom. To be a member of the Forces of Oleen was considered elite and demanded certain skills and dedication.

Currad shook his head.

How could they all be Oleens? Only the queen had the power to decide who would be an Oleen. As he walked through the narrow cobbled streets, he glanced up, looking beyond the high stone walls of the surrounding buildings, to the sky. The clear blue morning was gone, replaced by afternoon gray clouds. The burly soldier thought about going to Culinary's kitchen for a snack and a chat, but decided to check in with the king. At this hour, the elder monarch was usually sitting by his pond. Currad climbed the narrow steps to the elevated courtyard, checked with the guards at the top, and passed through the arched iron gate of the wall into the serene Garden of the King.

"Currad," the king said as his honored soldier followed the gravel path to his chair by the pond.

"Yes, Sire."

"It is time to call Ekala back."

"Sire?"

"Lord Rundall will not live much longer. She must return before he...while he still lives."

"Your Majesty, the last report was that she was at Table Top and would be heading to the North Ford. That is a ride of many days. She could be anywhere by the time our messengers get there."

The king did not look up. He did not want the soldier to see he had been crying.

"Send troops to find her, Currad. The queen—the ruler of Ameram—should be here when Lord Rundall..." He stopped and rubbed his face. "Is Dysaan back?"

"He just returned from Toubar," Currad said. "I wanted him to continue organizing our army."

"Dysaan is dependable," the king said. "Send him. He will find her."

Disappointed that he was going to lose Dysaan's help, Currad hesitated. He started to object, but then reluctantly bowed. "As you wish, Sire. I will see it is done." He turned to go, but the king stopped him.

"Send a messenger to let Larma know. And find Thalmus, too. He will want to be here. He and Lord Rundall share a special bond with the old faith."

"Yes, Thalmus told us of it when we were about to enter the tunnel in the Barranca," Currad said. "There were characters drawn on the rock above the entrance. He said it meant that if one is not strong in faith, his spirit would fly away at the first test. That once lost, he cannot regain it—and without faith, he is dead. But, I disagree that you can't regain your faith."

Surprised, the king looked up at his soldier.

"I have been reading the writings in the library," Currad said. "The Ancient Order of Servants believe in what they call 'endless hope in the constant struggle.' To me, that means the door is left open for those who stepped into the darkness and want to return.

This life *can be* a 'constant struggle.' But then, there's the 'endless hope.'"

"You *have* been studying," the king said, seeing Currad in a new way. "That is good. The old faith needs to be carried on and you just might be the one to do that."

Currad smiled. Then, he turned and headed back to the barracks.

* * *

In the quarry of Marbala, Veracitas stood on top of a large block of blue-white marble. The block was not yet fully severed from the mountain of stone. Workers were swinging large sledgehammers, pounding wedges into a cut that had been partially sawn into the stone to break it loose. He jumped across a small crevice to the next block, where he crouched and swept the dust away with his hand to examine the surface. Then, he leaned over the side and looked at the flat front of the block. His fingers brushed over line after line of little horizontal ridges that had been made by the wire saw. Thick ropes that had been fastened to the rock higher up the mountain hung down across the blocks. The workers used these heavy ropes to move around on the blocks and to lower the slabs down when they had been wedged free. Made to hold the weight of the massive stone blocks, the ropes were woven with hundreds of fiber strands, making them too large for a normal man's hands.

Veracitas grabbed one of the ropes, gripped it tightly, and carefully backed off the edge of the block—lowering himself over the side where he could examine the veins and variations of colors in the marble. Hanging from the rope with his legs pushing off the stone, he shuffled left and then right, moving across the flat face of the block while he looked closely at its surface.

Something caught his eye.

He stopped and stared at a singular crystal shape in the marble. It was familiar. Where had he seen it before? Suddenly, he was struck by a wave of fear that caused him to shiver. A memory flashed before his eyes: an angular stone of white crystal dangling on a leather string.

Veracitas felt the cold castle cell around him; he saw the magician's emerald eyes glaring at him in the dark and the glinting crystal hanging from his neck. He heard Metro laugh and then hiss, "You will never speak in stone again!" The sculptor shook and looked away, trying to clear the vision before him.

"Are you alright?" Kali called from the ground below.

Veracitas' hands were sweating, his heart pounding. He slowed his breathing and took deep breaths. The last image he'd had of Metro was of Bubo and the magician tangled up in the air over Cold Canyon. Now, the torture of his imprisonment in the castle cell came flooding back from the depths of his memory: the constant beatings, whippings, and thrashings, Metro's mocking voice, buckets of foul garbage water splashed on his head and body, sleeplessness and shaking—always shaking.

He was shaking now.

His hands were slipping. He looked up the rope line at the mountain above.

Why is this happening? he wondered.

"Veracitas," Captain Kali called from below. "Are you coming down?"

He glanced over his shoulder and saw the red-headed, frizzy-haired Kali watching him, waiting for him. He tightened his grip. "I'm done," he hollered and started sliding his feet downward on the stone and alternating his hands on the rope, slowly lowering himself to the ground.

"You look confused," Kali said.

"What? No, I was just…thinking about the stone."

Kali watched him as they walked away from the pounding hammer noise and dust from the workers. "Do you like any of them? Will one of the blocks work?"

"They're not right," Veracitas replied. "Wrong veins and color."

"Do you want to look at another section or the stone in the caves?"

"Not today," Veracitas said.

Kali shook her head. "I don't understand. You were so anxious to choose a new stone and get it cut. We have a lot of daylight left."

"I'm tired. I just need to rest," he mumbled.

She put her hand on his arm and turned him toward her.

"What happened up there? You're different."

He looked at the tall, freckle-faced woman: the strong-shouldered Oleen captain in her worn uniform and sword at her side; the woman he had met long ago when Boschina was a small child. Only to meet again years later and fight by her side through the battle for Ambermal to save the king and put Ekala on the throne. Kali and her force had traveled with him to Marbala to choose the stone for Ekala's statue, and then on to Ello, where the marble broke; then back again to the Stone Hills of Marbala to find another block. She believed in him, in his work and skill. How could he tell her of his weakness? How could he explain what he had seen—and worse, of the paralyzing fear that had suddenly returned?

He didn't have to tell her.

She saw it in his eyes and felt the tremble in his arm.

"Oh, Veracitas, you need more than rest. Let us go from this place that troubles you so. We will find Boschina and then ride to Table Top where Larma can heal you."

Veracitas shook his head. "I have work to do. And you...you have duties for the queen."

Captain Kali gripped his arm. "You are my duty. Oleen told me to guard you, wherever you go. And that's what I'm doing."

"Guard me?" Veracitas questioned.

"Don't you remember? Oleen was worried that her enemies would hurt you—try to stop you from carving. You didn't think it was necessary, but agreed that a force of Oleens and I could travel with you." Kali paused, and then said, "You were happy to have me with you."

"I still am," Veracitas said. "But I don't need to go to Table Top. What I need is to carve, to work, to have the tools in my hands—and then I will feel better."

"Alright," she replied. "Let's go to your family studio in Marbala so you can work and get better."

Veracitas nodded. "Yes, it is a safe place, a good place to carve."

* * *

Larma stood next to the creek that dropped over the edge of Table Top to become the western waterfall. A rumbling mist rolled up from the gushing water and cooled the air around her. Looking out over the plain, the silver-haired mystic saw a lone rider heading toward the trail that led up to the West Gate of the Top. She had been listening to the clouds drifting eastward from the Great Water and had learned from their chatter that there was trouble at the North Ford. This rider would confirm for Larma what the clouds had told her about the strange encampment: the sounds of fighting in the night and the silent wings over Ekala Oleen.

* * *

The Oleen soldier called Thoe carried the message to Currad and the king at Castle Ambermal from the queen at the North Ford. The short, joyful woman was from the village of Dudoon, where she met Ekala when the princess passed through on her trips to Table Top. Thoe and her husband were olive growers, had two sons, worked hard for their living, and felt blessed every day for a good life—until their youngest boy, just nine years old, died of fever. Three months later, a bad crop forced her husband to seek other income. Frog legs would not only feed them, he told her, but they could sell the excess at the market. He took his eldest son, thirteen, with him to hunt frogs in the Bufon Marsh.

They never returned.

Heartbroken and alone, Thoe followed Ekala to Table Top Mountain, to Larma Hollow, where she found community and purpose once again. She was one of the few on the Top who knew Ekala Oleen's true identity before the princess announced it. Trained in the tools of war by Ekala and Lander, she became a solid soldier. Thoe was wounded in a skirmish with renegade troops at the East Gate. She recovered and fought in the Battle for the North Gate, and then again at the Battle for Castle Ambermal. She was an experienced warrior and a true Oleen.

Now, Thoe rode south across the Great Plain with important information and warnings for Currad about the smuggled weapons they had found, and the order for more troops to be sent to the North Ford. She had crossed Table Run with the Oleen messenger going to Table Top. There, they had split up, their destinations taking them in opposite directions. Stopping in Ello to water and rest her horse, Thoe found herself warmly greeted by the villagers and was asked to answer questions about the queen. Especially from one inquisitive man who wanted to know why she was traveling alone.

"Don't Oleens always ride in small forces?" he asked her. "Are you on a mission?"

Thoe told him she was going to visit her mother, and then mounted up and rode out. He had distracted her and it wasn't until she was well down the road that she realized she'd left her old scarf on the water trough. She stopped and considered going back. But it was getting late and she wanted to get to the junction to the Middle Hills Road before stopping for the night. Tomorrow, she could cross between the marsh and Dudoon Bog in the daylight.

Too much time would be lost if she went back. Her first responsibility was to get this message to the Castle. It was just an old scarf. One she had worn or carried with her since leaving Dudoon. She removed her hat and wiped her forehead with her hand. The scarf was the last thing her husband had given her. She sighed, made a waving gesture toward Ello, and urged the horse south.

The darkness of night surrounded Thoe long before the day's destination loomed on the horizon. Knowing the route well from transporting carts of produce to the villages, she rode on. All the other travelers had stopped to camp for the night. The road was deserted. Thoe slowed the horse to a walk when she thought they were approaching the crossroad. It would be easy to miss in the night and she was ready to stop.

Finally, she did stop.

"I must have passed it," she said to herself.

Sniffing and scraping claws drew her attention. Turning toward the sounds, she saw a beast jumping out of the darkness at her. She threw up her left arm in front of her face and reached for her sword with her right hand just as the animal slammed into her, crunching her arm in its jaws and knocking her off the horse to the ground. The horse bolted and ran into the night.

Thoe could hardly breathe.

The animal had rolled over her, but its teeth were still clamped onto her arm. It was growling and shaking, dragging her and tearing her apart. With all her might, Thoe stabbed and beat at the animal with her sword as it whipped her around. Again and again she tried to hit it, but couldn't. The animal was flipping her about like a rag doll. Suddenly, the beast let go of her, backed away into the darkness, and howled.

Thoe struggled to her feet. Her left arm hung limp, dangling at her side. Her lungs and body felt smashed. She was exhausted from the exertion of the fight. Holding her sword ready, she slowly turned around and tried to listen for the beast over her own deep breaths.

"Where'd you go? I'm not done with you," she said defiantly.

Then, for some reason, she remembered what Camp had taught them at Table Top: how Toulon soldiers held their sword at the ready. She swung the blade up and rested it against her shoulder, holding the handle near her waist. From this resting position, he had shown them how you could quickly thrust or swing the sword with power in all directions. *Might as well give it a try*, she thought.

"Are you Toulon?" a voice said from the darkness.

Surprised at hearing a human voice, Thoe hesitated. "Who are you?"

"I asked if you are Toulon." The voice was stern, impatient.

"What happened to the animal?" Thoe asked. "I didn't kill it."

"No," the voice said. "It's waiting to kill you. Answer me. Are you Toulon?"

"What makes you think I am?" Thoe replied.

"You know, the way you hold your sword is Toulon training. No matter. You are a soldier of the Oleens now, a follower of the woman ruler. So, there can be no mercy. I must congratulate you on surviving the Chorgen's attack. That is rare. However, if I had not called him off, you'd be dead now."

"Maybe," Thoe said. "Or maybe your beast would be dead."

The voice laughed in the darkness. "You're carrying a message. I want it."

Now it was Thoe's turn to laugh. But her lungs hurt and she started coughing.

"You're not going to live, unless I help you," the voice said. "I will show you mercy. Tell me the message and you can live."

Thoe closed her eyes and took short breaths in through her mouth. The pain in her arm and chest was overwhelming. She felt the blood pulsating out through the torn veins in her shredded arm—her life draining into the soil.

"That's a lie," she said, opening her eyes. "You can't save me and you have no mercy in you."

"Tell me the message from your ruler," the voice demanded, "or I'll let the Chorgen tear you apart."

Thoe's knees were buckling. She was losing the strength to stand. Dropping on her knees, she swung the sword tip to the ground and leaned against the handle for support.

"You want to know the message?" she said, her voice fading.

"Yes, tell me."

Her breath almost gone, Thoe said, "You must live in the Stone Truth with all your heart, no matter what happens…or you will fall into the darkness…like you."

Thoe closed her eyes and toppled over.

As the sun rose in the morning, warming the land and bringing the road to life, travelers found Thoe sprawled in the dust. Her sword was stuck in the ground beside her—an old worn scarf tied to the handle.

Chapter Ten
The Beast

Boschina lay on her back, sleeping next to a small pond. The water's surface rippled gently from the flow of a spring bubbling up from the bottom. Dallion and Radise grazed nearby, lifting their heads occasionally to check on her. She had learned to be patient when traveling with Thunder and Thalmus. The giant tortoise may be slow, but he was steady, dependable, and fearless. Thalmus knew Thunder's limits and rarely pushed him, even though his friend would have tried anything Thalmus asked. Having the shell creature carried on the bouncing thatched sled had been pushing the edge of endurance and dignity for both of them.

The spring's pool was on the fringe of a large grove of rose trees. Over time, the space between the trees had filled in with a thick underbrush that had meandered down like a river from the Barrier Forest and provided protection for the animals traveling to the water hole. Despite its close proximity to the road, the spring was hidden in the foothills and few travelers were aware of its refreshing water. The Oleen soldier, Renca, had spent little time here watering her horse and filling the pouch Boschina loaned her before mounting up again and hurrying back to the ford with Thalmus' response.

Waiting with the horses for Thunder reminded Boschina of the first day she had traveled with Thalmus, leaving his cabin in the meadow ringed with rose trees and riding to a creek where they stopped to wait for the tortoise to catch up. She was surprised and frustrated that Thalmus casually took a nap while Dallion grazed. She had paced impatiently waiting for Thunder to arrive, wanting Thalmus to get to the castle as quickly as possible to talk with the king about her father, and then onward to find him. Now, she was anxious to get to the ford and find Ekala. Radise could have her there in a short time while the three companions continued at Thunder's pace. However, she knew Thalmus had a reason for everything he did, that there were mysterious influences and a larger picture she often could not see or understand.

With Dallion and Radise watching over her, and the bow and quiver beside her, Boschina closed her eyes and slumbered comfortably—until the sound of a sniffing animal entered her sleep. It was unusual breathing, she thought dreamily, but familiar: short, quick intakes of air through a wet nostril, just like the beast in the night on the trail to the Great Water. She opened her eyes, waking from fitful sleep, and rolled to her side to look at the horses. They had moved farther away. Their heads were down as they nibbled on the grass.

Had she been dreaming? No.

There was the sniffing again; this time, it was closer. Two quick snorts, and then quiet. Something was in the bushes between the trees, smelling her scent. Dallion and Radise were still eating. Boschina quietly stood, picked up her bow and strung it, setting the string tight. She pulled an arrow from the quiver and nocked it in the string. She scanned the dense forest, not seeing anything. Then, branches cracked and shook, claws scratched the ground. Dal and Radise picked up their heads, staring at the forest. The big Paint caught a scent, threw his head, and whinnied. Bushes broke and fell aside as the creature pushed through the tangle of green foliage. A large brown head suddenly burst out of the brush. It was covered in wild, dirty fur and had a black snout with long fangs protruding from its mouth.

Boschina drew the arrow back and aimed. The beast stood as tall as she did, with long hairy legs and a broad chest heaving as it breathed through an open mouth, revealing rows of teeth behind the pointed fangs. It snorted at her; growling now, drool hung from its mouth. Boschina expected it to charge at any moment, but the creature hesitated, turning its head slightly and sniffing; its claws pawed at the ground.

Where should she shoot, at its head or its chest? Where would the arrow penetrate to kill this thing? It was just four meters in front of her. She would only have time for one shot before it was upon her. Then what? Her sword still hung on Radise who was too far away. Boschina slowly stepped back, ready to release the arrow at any second. She heard Radise and Dallion running toward her. The beast followed her, sniffing. Stepping clear of the branches, it turned its head to listen as it crouched on its large hind legs.

Suddenly, Thalmus was beside her, his sword drawn, gleaming in the sunlight.

"Iech ma ta!" he shouted.

The beast jerked at hearing the words, and then clawed at the ground. Lowering its head and turning, it snorted and sniffed at Thalmus. The hunter stepped forward, his sword ready, his eyes searching for the creature's eyes. He saw only blood-matted fur where its large eyes should have been. Thunder scampered up to Boschina's other side, snapped his jaws, and hissed. Dallion reared and stomped the earth. Radise ran to stand behind Boschina with her sword.

Tilting its head from side to side, the creature seemed confused by the different sounds. It began sniffing again, redirecting its attention on Boschina. It growled and crouched.

Thalmus jumped in front of Boschina, shouting: "Iech ma ta!"

The beast hesitated, snorted, and then leapt at him. Thalmus dove forward, ducking under the creature before it reached him, and drove his sword up into its belly as it came down. The animal roared and rolled with Thalmus hanging on, driving the blade deeper. The beast kicked and turned, trying to get at the hunter, but he dodged its slashing claws and snapping mouth. Boschina followed the animal's twisting, writhing body, timed her release, and shot the arrow into its neck. The beast howled. Choking and kicking, it finally stilled; its head flopped to the ground and the long legs fell to the side.

Thalmus put a foot on the animal and pulled his sword from its body. The tool had done its work. He washed the engraved blade in the pond before sheathing it at his side. Thunder and Dallion sniffed at the dead animal with curiosity. It had a foul odor, like an animal long dead. Dallion snorted and shook his head, trying to clear his nostrils of the stench, and then looked at Boschina. Thunder clicked his jaws, confirming the strange animal was no longer a threat.

"You can relax," Thalmus said, watching Boschina.

She had nocked another arrow and was ready to shoot the creature again. Slowly, she let her arm forward, releasing tension from the bowstring, and gripped the loose arrow in her hand. Her eyes stayed fixed on the creature. Thalmus knelt, examining the animal's paws.

"It was after me, wasn't it?" Boschina asked, still trembling.

"Yes, it was," Thalmus replied. "It had your scent and was determined to get you."

"Why? Why is it stalking me?" Boschina asked, staring at the yellow fangs in its gaping mouth.

"This is not the same animal that followed you to the Great Water," Thalmus said, looking at the paws. "There is a cut, a crease in the back pad of this one. It is different than the tracks we saw on the trail."

"There are two of them after me?"

"Yes, and maybe more. There is something wrong with this one, though," Thalmus said. "These are night creatures. They do not hunt by day. But this one has been blinded. Did you see its eyes?"

Boschina shook her head. She had been so mesmerized by the snout and teeth that she had not noticed the beast's eyes were obscured by hair and blood. "What happened to it?"

"Its eyes have been clawed," Thalmus said. "I think it has been wandering, confused; must have been searching for the water, and then smelled you."

"Why are they after me?" Boschina asked angrily.

"These animals are trained to hunt or to fight to the death. Someone has given them your scent and ordered them to hunt you, and probably Ekala as well."

"Both of us? We must find Ekala. She may not know...she could be riding into their teeth."

"I think Ekala is aware of them now," Thalmus replied. "These creatures are vicious and fearless knowing they have the cover of darkness, but they do not know about another night predator, about the silent wings and deadly claws of the owl."

"You mean Bubo attacked this beast?"

"I think this one got close to Ekala and Bubo hit it; like knives dropping out of the night, cutting its sight to blindness."

Thunder gently pushed his big head into Boschina. She put her hand up on his head. "I'm glad you're here, Thunder." He clicked his jaws, bumped her with his shell, and started plodding north. Dallion snorted and went with him.

Thalmus was looking at the beast. He stuck his short blade between its jaws and spread them farther apart, examining the teeth. "This is a young one. He is big for his age. Or someone is breeding the creatures larger now."

"Why does it smell so bad?" Boschina asked, covering her nose.

"It is the foulness of the innards and skin. Usually, you cannot smell them until it is too late. Their instinct is to approach their prey from downwind." Thalmus looked at Boschina standing with her bow. "Their skin is very tough, especially when it comes at you head-on. You would not have stopped him with one arrow."

"I realized that just before you came," Boschina said. "So you have to kill these things as you did?"

"Remember the Gauks in the Barranca?" Thalmus said. "How they dodged and snapped, high and low, getting in close to clamp onto a part of your body and pull you down?"

"How can I forget? The big one almost bit my head."

"These Chorgens have a different approach. They do not banter with their prey. They are very quick for their size, but they keep a distance until they decide to attack. Then they leap, using their weight to knock you to the ground, and they pin you there with their claws and rip into you with these fangs. Hunting at night, this method is very effective because their prey cannot see them until the last moment when they suddenly appear out of the darkness. You must have the courage to charge forward, right into its attack, duck under and thrust the sword up into the soft spot at its heart, using its own weight to kill it. Do you think you can do that?"

Boschina stared at the dead creature, its blood staining the ground where she had laid minutes earlier. Taking a deep breath, she said, "I hope so."

"Hesitation would be fatal," Thalmus said.

Boschina met Thalmus' eyes. "Then I better not hesitate."

He smiled at her. "I suggest you wear your sword from here on. And perhaps, we should stay closer."

Radise nudged her and Boschina untied the tool from the horse and strapped it on her waist.

"Trust in the blade and let it do its work," Thalmus told her. He looked again at the dead beast and then for Thunder, who was already gone. "We need to catch up with Thunder."

As they walked, Boschina asked, "What were those words you shouted at the Chorgen?"

"It is difficult to explain," Thalmus said. "Words from an old language that are used to train animals like Chorgens do not translate well."

"The Chorgen understood what you said. It stopped and looked your way. What do the words mean? In case I have to use them."

Thalmus thought for a moment. "It depends on how you speak the words. It can mean, 'halt your death,' but it can also mean, 'your death be mine with mine.'"

"Oh," Boschina said. "That's a bit confusing. I don't think I'll try those words."

They traveled the rest of the day and into the night before stopping to sleep. Dallion, Thunder, and Thalmus shared guard shifts until just before dawn when they started again, rejoining the dirt road.

As the sun rose in the east, the group crested the last hill and headed down the slight slope to the North Ford.

The Oleen scouts saw them approaching and sent word to Ritzs and Susa, who rode swiftly out to meet them. The two anxious Oleen captains pulled their horses to a halt in front of Thalmus and dismounted, but hung onto the reins. Dallion whinnied, snorted at the other horses, and trotted to the river. Thunder also continued to the water, where he splashed in and dunked his head.

"I'm glad you're here, Thalmus," Ritzs said. "We've had no word from Oleen."

"Our soldiers are worried and want to cross the ford to find her," Susa said.

Thalmus turned from their gaze to the river where Thunder was soaking in the shallow ford while the Oleen guards watched. "How long ago did she cross?" he asked.

"Two days. She's been gone two days now," Susa said. "I tried to convince her not to go, but she was determined. I don't know what else I could have done."

"You did what you could, you spoke your mind," Thalmus said, trying to make her feel better. "How many went with her?"

"Three. Three of our best; Lander was one of them," Susa said proudly. "That's all Oleen wanted. I tried to get her to take more, but she wouldn't do it."

Overhead, the high white clouds had turned gray and were thickening. The air was cooler, the light tarnished. On the breeze was the smell of damp earth, burnt wood, and something unfamiliar: an oddly sweet odor from a distant place. Thunder raised his head, stepped out of the water, and stood still; he looked across the ford.

Thalmus watched Thunder for a moment, and then turned back to the captains. "Show me where the night creature came near the queen."

Susa was surprised. "What? How do you know about that?"

"We killed one yesterday," Thalmus replied. "I think it had been here, stalking the queen."

"It was over there, near the fire pit," Susa said.

She led them to the site where the animal's blood still stained the grass. Thalmus examined the tracks and followed them for a short distance.

"Look, Boschina," Thalmus said, pointing at an imprint. "Do you see the line across the pad?"

"It looks like our Chorgen's paw," she answered. "It must be the same one."

"Oleen said Bubo attacked the creature...ran it off," Susa explained. "Nobody saw it or heard the animal until it screamed and ran. That happened the same night as the fight at the ford when Prince Bolimaz and Camp chased after the raiders. When they didn't come back, Oleen decided to look for them."

"We're going after them, right?" Ritzs asked.

Thalmus was scanning the distant Barrier Forest where the beast had run after being mauled by Bubo. *If more Chorgens were hiding there, they would have ravaged the blinded one,* Thalmus thought. *No, it came across the ford or up from the south. And what happened to the one following Boschina? Hopefully, the Insurphs killed it.* He looked across the river at the edge of the Toulon Wilderness. He knew other wild creatures roamed in that tangled mess, and now, perhaps, Chorgens too. And Bubo? He must still be following Ekala.

"Are we going after Oleen?" Ritzs asked impatiently. "I have a force ready to go."

Two riders were approaching from the east along the river bank. Half a dozen people were walking down the hill from Toulon toward the ford. The clouds continued to darken.

Thalmus surveyed the Oleen encampment and a foreign wagon parked nearby.

"Who are those men tied to the merchant wagon?"

Ritzs and Susa were surprised again by his question. At the moment, the smugglers seemed less important to them than saving the queen. However, Boschina knew how Thalmus observed and gathered knowledge before acting.

"They're not our people, are they?" Boschina asked.

Susa glanced at the men. "No, we caught 'em hiding weapons in the blankets and clothes in that wagon. They claimed to be heading to Barrunda to sell blankets. They're from Banyon and say they were supposed to give the weapons to a man who would give 'em a sign of the lizard."

"The lizard?" Boschina turned to Thalmus. "I thought we killed that evil."

"Metro's dead, right?" Ritzs said. "And we destroyed his army."

Thalmus felt Larma's message begin to vibrate in his pocket. Thunder had left the water and was plodding toward them. "Metro is gone," Thalmus replied. "But the evil that consumed him still lives. It has not given up. Show me the weapons, Susa."

"Swords and shields," Susa said. "They're in the wagon." She went to the back end of the wagon, lifted the tarp, and removed a sword and shield to show Thalmus.

Thalmus waited for Thunder before walking to the wagon where the two men sat, leaning against the wheels. The men's hands were tied behind their backs and lashed to the large wooden axels. The wagon driver and his partner had been watching Thalmus and the Oleen officers. The men could tell something had changed with the arrival of the short man. Now they fidgeted and their eyes widened as the man and giant shell creature thumped toward them. Since childhood they had heard stories of the mysterious and deadly shell creatures, but thought the tales had been nothing more than myth, for they had never seen one. Now they stared in horror and cowered on the ground as Thunder approached and stood over them. They heard the man say, "What do you think of them, Thunder?"

The driver pressed himself back against the wood wheel, turned his head to the side, and held his breath as Thunder extended his snout right into his scrunched face. The tortoise's black eyes glared; he sniffed, and then snorted on him. He pulled back a little and clicked his jaws twice at the frightened man.

"That's what I thought," Thalmus said. He took the sword that Susa was handing him and examined it carefully. The mark of an "S" etched in the blade caught his eye. Like the lizard, it was another emblem of the wicked—of a power brewing below the serene surface, waiting to rise and take control. The ancient vice of greed inhabited Toulon and had spread into Ameram.

Metro's masters still lived.

Thalmus handed the sword back to Susa. "No matter what these men tell you, do not trust them," he told her. "They are harbingers of something much bigger."

They walked away from the men and into the camp. At the fire, an Oleen cook gave Boschina and Thalmus bowls of soup.

"When do you want to look for Oleen?" Ritzs asked.

"Now," Thalmus replied, eating from the bowl.

"We're ready," Captain Ritzs said.

Thalmus looked at the captains. "You will need every man and woman here to guard the ford. It is likely you will be attacked, possibly from within our own land. Stay alert and prepared. Boschina and I will cross the river and find the queen."

"Just the two of you?" Ritzs asked.

"And Dallion and Thunder," Thalmus answered.

The captains glanced at one another. They did not like the idea of being left behind, let alone the danger Boschina would be in. Larma and Oleen both would not be happy if something happened to the Stone Cutter's Daughter.

Thalmus knew what they were thinking. "Boschina," he said. "Do you want to stay here? If so, I will go by myself to find Oleen."

Boschina stopped eating. "Absolutely not. I'm going with you and Thunder across that river to find Oleen."

Thalmus smiled. "I thought so. You had better change into some peasant clothes. Captains, you must hold the ford so we can get back across. That is your task. I do not know how long it will take us, but we *will* be back with the queen."

Chapter Eleven
Lord Glasrauss

Thunder stepped into the shallow water of the river and began splashing his way across the ford. Boschina sat on Radise, with a few extra bags of food strapped on the horse's flanks. She had changed out of her Oleen uniform and was wearing the work clothes she wore when helping her father carve stone. Hanging from her belt was the engraved sword. Her bow was sheathed alongside the saddle, a quiver full of arrows strapped on her back. A broad-brimmed felt hat shaded her face. Boschina patted Radise's neck while the two waited at the river's edge for Thalmus, who was talking with Ritzs and Susa up the bank near the camp.

Nearby, a tall boy carrying a bow watched Thunder plow through the river. Then he looked Boschina over, admiring the weapons she carried and the way she sat on her horse. The Stone Cutter's Daughter noticed the boy watching her. He had a handsome face. His frame was a bit thin, but he was taller than most men. She caught how he held his bow—thoughtfully, proudly. Their eyes met for a moment and neither one looked away.

"Is that the frog hunter with the Oleen captains?" he asked, pointing at Thalmus.

"It is," Boschina replied.

"And that's his shell creature?" he said, nodding toward the giant tortoise climbing out of the water on the other side of the river.

"That's Thunder. He belongs to no one," Boschina answered. "They are the best of friends, as am I."

He was quiet, not sure what to say next.

"Your accent sounds northern," Boschina said. "You're not from Ameram, are you?"

"No. I'm from Toulon. My family's camped down the river with others who've left our country."

"Like Prince Bolimaz and Camp?" Boschina asked.

The boy brightened. "Yes. I met the prince and talked with him before he left. Are you goin' looking for 'em?"

"Mainly for the queen, but we'll help them, too, if we find them."

"I wish I could go with you," he said. "The prince could use my help."

Boschina doubted that. He didn't appear to have experience in combat. But who was she to judge? People underestimated her ability all the time, except for Thalmus, who perhaps placed too much confidence in her.

"Are you good with the bow?" she asked.

"Oh, I'm good," he said quickly. Then, feeling embarrassed, he added, "Well, truthfully, I'm learning. My father is a swordsman, not an archer. He's not any better than I am. Your queen said there was an Oleen who could teach me."

"That would be Lander," Boschina said. "She is the best. She's with the queen now."

"Oh," he said, disappointed. "You must be good or the frog hunter wouldn't be takin' you with him."

Boschina hesitated. She hadn't thought about whether it was a question of skill or not. "I do alright," she said.

Radise turned her head to look at the boy, her brown eyes curious. After a moment, she snorted and turned away. Dallion trotted up with Thalmus on his back. Radise whinnied and bobbed her head at Dallion. The Paint stallion glared at the boy.

"Are you ready to cross the ford?" Thalmus asked Boschina.

"Ready," she responded.

Dallion stepped forward into the water and started across. Radise began to follow when the boy spoke again to Boschina.

"My name's Neb," he said quickly.

Boschina looked back at him—at his hopeful, waiting eyes. "I'm Boschina of Marbala," she said.

The boy with the bow in one hand smiled and waved with his free hand.

When they reached the other side of the ford and stepped onto Toulon soil, Boschina pulled Radise to a stop and looked back. Neb was still there, watching; so were the Oleen soldiers, lined up along the river's edge. She raised her arm in an Oleen salute and they all saluted back. Boschina realized that each one of them wanted to be in her place: going to save the queen, instead of waiting helplessly. Suddenly, she felt a weight of importance—of responsibility—settle on her shoulders and on her conscience. Her friends, fellow soldiers, and her country were putting their hopes in her and Thalmus to find the queen and bring her back.

Radise whinnied and Boschina turned to see that Thalmus and Dallion had not stopped. They had caught up with Thunder and were almost at the top of the hill.

"Let's go, Lady," she said to Radise.

The roan happily trotted up the slope, reaching Dallion and Thalmus, and then Thunder as they crested the hill and started down the other side. To their right was the strange forest of the Wilderness of Toulon, to the left was the coastal forest, and straight ahead was open land to a line of trees in the distance. Thalmus was moving quickly. He looked briefly at the many tracks in the soil, found what he wanted, and kept moving out in front of Thunder as the tortoise plodded along. The hunter was fully focused now on the hunt. Boschina responded, concentrating on the task at hand.

"What are you seeing in these tracks?" she asked. "There are so many; twenty horses must have passed this way."

"I am looking for certain hoofmarks," he answered, watching the ground. "Shadahn has an unusual left front hoof. It is flat on the inside edge. She also runs hard, leaving a deeper mark. There, that one." He halted Dallion and pointed at an imprint. "You see?"

Boschina leaned to the side of Radise, looking for the one Thalmus pointed at.

"Yes, it is different."

Dallion sniffed the track and then started a quick walk again.

"How can you move so quickly and see the one track you're looking for?"

"These tracks are going in the same direction, and Shadahn, with Ekala, is among them," Thalmus said. "I think they are heading to those trees. We can follow the whole lot unless they split." He glanced at the clouds. "We need to cover as much ground as we can. It could be raining soon. Then it will be more difficult."

Boschina looked around the open terrain. "I'm surprised there's no one out here. I expected Toulon soldiers."

"No need to be disappointed; they will find us soon enough. Thunder will let us know when they do."

Following the trail of tracks across the plain, they approached a large expanse of trees that grew in rows, like an orchard. The tops of the trees were five times the height of a man. Their branches and thick foliage overlapped one another, creating a massive canopy. Underneath, the branches hung down two to three meters above the ground. It looked cool and calm in the shade under the crown of branches and dark green leaves. Here and there thin shafts of light penetrated the cover, illuminating the twisted gray bark of the trunks. Thalmus slowed Dallion to let Thunder catch up. Radise followed and they both stopped outside of the tree line.

"This looks serene," Boschina said, indicating the orderly rows of trees. "But I'll bet you're going to tell me it's not."

Thalmus smiled. "It does look inviting. I am glad to see that you have learned to not trust appearances."

"After all the things we've been through, how could I not be suspicious?"

"This beautiful forest grove is called the Woods of Rows. It is a deceptive maze," Thalmus told her. "Directions can become confusing quite quickly in there. Every tree, every row looks the same. Sounds are muffled and difficult to discern. The air is sweet, but stifling. I would prefer to avoid this place; unfortunately, all of the tracks lead into it."

Thunder had just about reached them when he began to click his jaws. Two steps, two clicks; two more steps, two snaps of the jaw: click—click. He kept coming, snapping, and sending out the warning, his eyes fixed on Thalmus. Humans and horses turned, looking for the danger. Boschina's first response was toward the Woods of Rows, but Thalmus' was to search the terrain along the tree line. Thunder stopped clicking and Boschina turned to see him looking east, down the edge of the Rows.

At the same time, Thalmus and Dallion heard the rumble of horses' hooves. Dallion whinnied. Thalmus glanced at the trail of tracks they had been following, and then toward the approaching sound. He could tell that it was a large number of horses, many more than they were looking for. *These riders will not be our friends,* Thalmus thought. *Surely this enemy will see the tracks and know what we are doing.*

"Boschina, move into the trees," he said calmly. "Several rows back, where you can still see me, and wait there."

Boschina did not hesitate. She knew better than to question Thalmus at this moment.

"Let's go, Lady," she said.

Radise stepped quickly through the first row of trees and then passed the next row, and a third, before Boschina turned her to a stop. Through the lower branches she could see Thalmus sitting on Dallion and Thunder beside them, but she was surprised at how far away they seemed to be. She had only gone three rows into the grove, and yet the distance appeared to be much farther than it actually was. Boschina looked over her shoulder, down the alleyway of endless lines of trees behind her that narrowed to a blurred vision of miniature trees in the distance. Thalmus was right: perception was distorted and sight confused in the simple order of the rows. Breathing in the moist, thick air, she felt a change in temperature and a sense of foreboding. Radise pawed the ground and snorted lightly, letting Boschina know she was uncomfortable in this place. Boschina patted Radise's neck with one hand and grasped the handle of her sword with the other.

A column of riders appeared along the tree line—galloping right at Thalmus. He counted fifty soldiers, all wearing the green and gray uniforms of the Toulon army. Half of the men carried long spears pointing straight up as they rode, one of the staves brandished a flapping black flag with vertical white, wavy stripes. As the troops approached, the lead riders drew their swords and held them in front, ready to attack. Dallion's eyes flared; he whinnied and reared. The soldiers' horses began throwing their heads, bucking and bolting away from Dallion, causing their riders to grasp wildly at the reins in an effort to regain control.

Thalmus watched as the neat column jumbled into a boil of confusion, trampling the tracks he had been following. All attempts at aggression toward him ceased while the riders shouted and battled with their horses. Some men dropped their weapons, others were thrown from their saddles. Finally, a man dressed in black with green trim forced his horse toward Thalmus, shouting, "Make him stop! We will not attack you!"

Thalmus knew him. He was Lord Glasrauss of Middle Fields, a member of a powerful family of Toulon and one of King Souma's advisors. The black flag with the three Ss was his family crest.

Dallion was stomping and snorting. Thalmus patted his neck. "Shh – shh," he whispered, calming the stallion. The big Paint tossed his head one last time and then stood still, though he kept breathing noisily as a warning.

The tumultuous mounts of the soldiers slowly calmed down, allowing their riders to take control, but they continued to shy away from Dallion. The soldiers picked up their strewn gear and began reforming. Lord Glasrauss and a half dozen men rode their fidgeting horses to Thalmus. In the trees, Boschina felt Radise tense. Her head rose slightly. "Easy, Lady," she whispered

Lord Glasrauss' face was not friendly. His skin was rough and creased like weathered wood; brown eyes flicked nervously under thick brows. His head hair was short, cheeks and neck shaved. He sat erect, chin up, with an air of superiority.

Thunder hissed at him and the lord's horse took a step back.

"Lord Glasrauss," Thalmus said, acting as if nothing had happened. "I have not seen you in a long time. How is your father and family?"

Glasrauss' eyes blinked. His horse stepped back again from the hissing tortoise and he pulled the reins tighter. "What are you doing in Toulon?" he asked abruptly.

"Doing what I usually do, hunt," Thalmus replied.

"There are no ponds in this region."

"I am not hunting frogs," Thalmus said. "You act as though I am a threat. Have I not always been granted the right to hunt in this country?"

Lord Glasrauss ignored the question. "Why did you unleash the Paint to scare our horses?"

"That was not *my* doing, Lord. Dallion has a mind of his own," Thalmus responded. "You should know that."

Dallion's blue eyes had not moved off Lord Glasrauss. The stallion remembered the cruelty of this man to animals from a previous excursion into Toulon with Thalmus. Then, as now, Dallion had caused a disruption, helping horses and dogs to flee.

"Perhaps you should not have come at us so aggressively," Thalmus continued. "He thought you were going to attack us."

Glasrauss blinked, looking from Dallion to Thunder, and then to Thalmus. "I didn't recognize you in time to warn my men," he said. "We've been hunting invaders from Ameram. It seems your new ruler is harboring traitors and is helping them to overthrow our king. Her soldiers, what are they called, Oleens, are raiding across our border. She's amassing an army at Table Top."

Thalmus knew who he meant; still, he wanted to hear the lord say it, to confirm his allegiance. "Are you speaking of Prince Bolimaz and Camp?"

"I am," Glasrauss snapped, his eyelids blinking rapidly, "And everyone else running to join him. Your woman ruler has made a big mistake."

"You do not know Queen Ekala Oleen, do you?" Thalmus asked.

"Never seen her—just know she's doomed. And so is Ameram, under her rule."

Thalmus smiled and thought, *He will be surprised when he meets Ekala.* "You have a new crest?" Thalmus said, pointing at the black flag. "Is that three wavy white lines?"

"Those are *S*s," Lord Glasrauss said sternly, "for the three *S*s in my name. Can't you tell that?" He motioned to the flagbearer and the man grabbed the edge of the flag and held it out straight. The *S*s were the same design and shape as the "S" engraved on the swords Ekala confiscated at the ford.

Thalmus nodded. "Oh, yes, I see it now. Does King Souma like your new crest?"

"King Souma is ill; he's quite ill," Glasrauss answered. "His son, Prince Sharpna, now rules, with the aid of his brother."

"You are friends with him and the youngest brother, Tamar, yes?"

Glasrauss' brown eyes glared at Thalmus. "They are not afraid or weak, like their father or older brother. They are strong and rule with power, making our kingdom powerful."

Drops of rain began falling, spotting their clothes.

Neither man paid attention to the wetness.

"I am not here to overthrow your kingdom," Thalmus said, "merely to hunt."

Lord Glasrauss nodded toward the woods. "In there? What are you hunting in there?"

Thalmus paused, meeting Glasrauss' stare before answering, "Chorgens."

Lord Glasrauss stiffened. Hesitating, he blinked rapidly and finally said, "There are no Chorgens, haven't been for years. If there were such creatures in these parts, I would know."

"I killed one two days ago, south of the Sol Linden River, on the road to Ello," Thalmus said. "It was the first one I have seen in Ameram. You know that they come from the north? Did your family once breed them, Lord Glasrauss?"

Glasrauss was stunned. "You killed a Chorgen?"

Thalmus nodded. "That is why I am hunting here."

"You killed a Chorgen," Glasrauss repeated. "How?"

"With this blade," Thalmus replied, tapping the handle of his sword.

Looking at Thalmus' hand on the sword, Lord Glasrauss blinked. He looked up at the woods, knowing the dangers of the mysterious rows and scented air. Boschina could see Glasrauss through the wet leaves, searching the rows, and thought she might be discovered, but his face turned away and back to Thalmus.

"The royal family has allowed you to hunt. I cannot change that without talking to Prince Sharpna. Therefore, you are free to go."

"As it should be," Thalmus replied.

Glasrauss continued. "My orders are to find these Oleens, and the rebels who join them, and then publicly kill them to discourage others."

"Who determines whether someone is a rebel or just people wanting to leave your country?"

Glasrauss smiled at Thalmus. "I do. As for you and your friends, good luck on your hunt for Chorgens. I suggest that you not sleep at night."

Thalmus smiled back. "I recommend the same for you."

Lord Glasrauss blinked. "I hope we do not meet again, Thalmus. I would hate to think what would happen to you and your animal friends." He quickly turned his horse and trotted off, the soldiers falling in behind him.

Thalmus watched the column of green uniforms until the black flag with the snaky white *S*s was out of sight in the mist of the rain; he waved to Boschina to come out of the trees. Dallion snorted as Thalmus slid off his back to the ground. Thunder clicked his jaws once and hissed. Thalmus rubbed the big tortoise's head. "Yes, he is full of himself," Thalmus said, agreeing with his friend. He untied and removed one of the spears from Thunder's back and opened one of the bags strapped over the shell, pulling out two frog-skin coats. The frog hunter handed one of the coats to Boschina as she dismounted from Radise.

"What? You made new coats?" she said, surprised.

"Well, we both needed new ones," Thalmus said. "Mine was shredded in Rainland and you wore yours out."

Boschina removed her quiver and quickly slipped into the frog skin.

"When did you make them?"

"At the Great Water; Thunder and I hunted at the river, where the statues of Currad and Veracitas stand."

Boschina looked up from buttoning her coat. "Where Ekala was almost eaten—is this the frog?" she asked, looking at the sleeves and feeling the texture of the skin with her hands.

"No. But it was similar to that one, very aggressive. That was its downfall."

"Why didn't you give it to me sooner?"

Thalmus smiled at her. "I saved it until you needed it."

"Thank you, Thalmus," she said, flipping the hood over her head. "This reminds me of when we entered Rainland. Oh, that was wet and cold. I just hope we're not heading into creatures like we met there."

Thalmus buttoned up his coat and then handed Boschina's quiver to her. "Don't wear this on your back; it might get caught in the tree branches."

Radise bumped Boschina with her nose, smelling the frog skin as she tied the quiver on the roan. "That Lord Glasrauss knew of the Chorgens, didn't he?"

"Yes, he knew," Thalmus said, picking up the spear. "He knows the Chorgens are hunting."

Boschina grabbed her bow. "We must find Ekala and Maz before they do."

"We are two days behind Ekala," Thalmus said, looking into the Woods of Rows. "They should not still be in this maze, but we have to follow the tracks. Hopefully, they will come out the other side."

"Will the soldiers come back? Will they follow us in there?"

Thunder started walking into the grove, between rows of trees. Dallion followed him as Radise stayed by Boschina.

"The soldiers *will* come back, looking for us," Thalmus replied. "They will not come in this wood, though, unless they are desperate."

"I wish Bubo was with us," Boschina said, her eyes searching the trees.

Thalmus nodded. "I do, too."

He examined the tracks inside the first row of trees and slowly shook his head. Rain was dripping off the trees, splattering on them and the ground, turning the Woods of Rows into a blurry tableau. Looking at Boschina, he said, "Question everything you see or feel in here, and stay close."

Boschina took a deep breath and let it out. "Alright, I'm ready, Thalmus."

He pointed at the sword sheathed on her hip. "Trust in what the blade tells you."

She nodded. "I have learned to do that."

"Good." He patted her on the shoulder. "Now, let us see what tracks we can find."

Chapter Twelve
Discovery

Dysaan shaded his eyes from the bright sun with his large hand. There was no sign of anyone on the road ahead, not even a dust cloud. The king's tall, rugged soldier was hoping to meet up with the queen and her force on their way home before he had to ride too far north. He had left Ambermal with fifteen soldiers of the Castle Guard the day before and headed north on the Middle Hills Road to the village of Bevie, where they had spent the night. Currad had told him Queen Ekala Oleen should be returning from Table Top by way of Dudoon along this road. In case she had changed route, troops were also sent to Barrunda to watch the road from Ello. They all carried a message from the king that his daughter, the queen, should return promptly to Castle Ambermal.

Now, Dysaan and his small force were approaching Thalmus' home in the sunny, green meadow on the outskirts of the village Tamra. The last he had heard, the frog hunter was at the Great Water with his companions. The king's soldier was disappointed he would not see Thalmus on this trip. The rosewood cabin would be empty, Thunder would not be swimming in the ponds, nor the Paint stallion grazing in the tall grass. Bubo would not be quietly watching from the trees.

It seemed so long ago since he and Currad had come to Thalmus looking for Veracitas and found the Stone Cutter's Daughter there. Little did Dysaan realize then that the quest for the ancient prophecy had begun, and that he would be swept into its dangerous journey. His duties since the Great Battle for Ambermal had been boringly routine and he found himself wishing for the excitement of a quest or a good fight.

As soon as the soldiers entered the meadow, Dysaan could tell something was wrong. The birds were silent; there weren't any horses grazing or children from the village playing in the creeks. An eerie hollowness permeated the meadow. When they reached the hunter's cabin, they were shocked to see the door was busted in. It was hanging sideways by the bottom strap hinge. Large claw marks engraved the wooden jambs and door.

Dysaan motioned for three of the men to dismount with him and for the others to stay on horseback. They drew their swords and Dysaan led them slowly into the cabin. Everything was thrown about; blankets and clothes, table and chairs, and the chest and bed were broken and askew in the room and in the little creek that flowed through one side of the cabin. The inside walls were scared with claw marks and it reeked of death.

Dysaan searched through the mess, trying to find something that would tell him who or what did this. He could not find anything but the deep scratches on the walls. He ran his hand over the marks, feeling the size and viciousness of the claws that made them. "I don't know of any animal that could leave such marks," he said.

"It had to have been huge," a soldier said, "to knock down the door and claw this high on the wall."

"More than one beast did this," Dysaan said. "I'm guessing two, maybe three."

"It smells bad in here," the soldier said. "Like something dead, but I don't see anything."

"Must be the animals," Dysaan said, putting his arm up to his nose. "They left their scent."

They hurried out and Dysaan stopped to examine the door and outside walls, and then he looked around the meadow. "This wasn't just wild beasts," he said. "Something wicked is guiding them—someone tried to kill Thalmus."

"Maybe they're still around, waiting for him," a soldier said. "We could hide and kill 'em."

"I would like that," Dysaan replied, sheathing his sword. "I would *really* like that. But I have orders to find the queen. We have to move on to Dudoon." He climbed onto his horse. "Then we'll come back and hunt these beasts."

* * *

The village of Dudoon nestled the low slopes at the north end of the Middle Hills and looked out over a large frog-infested bog that gave the community its name. The people had tried numerous times to change the name of their town, but were never successful because of the proximity to the dangerous bog. Anyone from the vicinity of the bog was known as a Dooner and looked upon with sorrow for having to live in such a place. However, the inhabitants of the village and surrounding farms did not feel the same. They relished their remoteness: the hills were abundant with plentiful game and the wide open Great Plain to the north was farmable, especially along the Dudoon Run, the small river that flowed from a waterfall at Table Top into the murky ponds of the bog. As long as they stayed clear of the ponds, all was well and life was good. Not easy perhaps, but good.

In recent days, however, mysterious incidents had happened that had the community confused and fearful. There were new animal sounds in the night, carcasses of deer and cattle had been found slaughtered and half-eaten, strange new tracks were discovered, and strangers had been seen riding into or out of the bogs. Fear of the giant frogs had always kept people away. Now, the nightly croaking of the frogs was diminished and new calls were heard—deep chilling howls that pierced the darkness.

* * *

When Dysaan and his men reached the junction of the road to the western trail that led to Ello, they stopped to rest the horses. The trail, known as the Dudoon Fork, squeezed between the Bufon Marsh and Dudoon Bog and went straight across the southern end of the Great Plain to meet the Western Road. The Dudoon Fork had long been used by merchants and travelers to reach the villages along the Middle Hills and, conversely, by people going to the towns in the Western Hills or to the North Ford and beyond. At each end of the trail were wells supplied by ancient aqueducts that brought water from springs in the high hills down to the trailheads. Except for the passage between the marsh and bog, it was a safe route and well-traveled. The community of Dudoon was at the northernmost end of the road. It was the last village along the Middle Hills before entering the expanse of the Great Plain. Very few people went beyond this point, except those going to Table Top; and since Ekala Oleen's success, more of her followers had been finding their way to the flat-topped mountain.

While the soldiers and horses refreshed themselves, Dysaan questioned travelers coming from the west about whether they had seen the queen in Ello or along the way. Much to his disappointment, and to theirs as well, no one had seen her; although, one man said that he saw the frog hunter, Dallion, the giant tortoise, and Oleen soldiers passing through Ello on their way to the North Ford.

"The North Ford?" Dysaan questioned. "Are you sure?"

"Can't mistake the hunter and his friends," the man replied. "They were headin' north on the road when I last saw 'em."

Why would Thalmus be heading toward Toulon with an Oleen force? Dysaan wondered. *Unless the queen was there...and needed help?* The experienced soldier felt his heart beat more quickly with the feeling that something was wrong: first was the destruction at Thalmus' cabin, and now this. It may be nothing, just Thalmus traveling to meet with Queen Ekala, but his gut told him otherwise and he felt a distant danger coiling to strike. He recalled Currad telling him about reports of Toulon's treaty with Banyon and the growing size of their combined armies. Looking at his men, he wished he had brought a full company instead of this small contingent. He wanted to send a messenger back to Ambermal for more troops, but he had no evidence the queen was in danger. He looked up the road that led to Dudoon. If Queen Ekala was coming from Table Top, she would use this route because he knew she preferred the open plain. However, if she was at the North Ford, they would surely return by Ello and the Western Road. As for the possibility of an attack from Toulon, that would have to happen at the North Ford; there was no other place for an army to cross the Sol Linden River. Dysaan felt the pull of urgency to the river and decided to take the Dudoon Fork that would lead him to the western trail and more quickly to the ford. He ordered two men to ride into the village and wait for the queen in case she came that way. The other soldiers mounted up and followed Dysaan onto the fork trail.

* * *

Veracitas arose from his bed with a new vision. For days he had suffered through nightmares, depression, and a total loss of any desire to move. He had lost his grasp on hope and in his ability to carve, to create statues. Then, early in the morning, before daylight, he heard the ping of a hammer hitting chisel and chipping stone. He rolled to his side to see his daughter, Boschina, rhythmically swinging a hammer, carving the broken carcass of the statue he had left in Ello. She looked sad, yet determined, as she tapped, tapped, tapped on the chisel; her eyes focused on the lines the bit was creating in the rough stone. With the repetitive sound of the hammer and its tip scraping marble, Veracitas felt calmness come over him, a clearing of his mind, as he watched his daughter working on the very piece he had abandoned. The large broken chunks of the unfinished statue took on a new form in his eyes, a melding together in a combination of images of Queen Ekala Oleen he had never before imagined. He saw the shape of the new statue clearly and how the parts would fit together creating a stunning depiction of Ekala Oleen, the first woman ruler of Ameram.

His daughter had shown him the way.

"Boschina," he called softly.

The Stone Cutter's Daughter stopped, lifted her eyes from the marble, and looked around the shop. She took a deep breath and admired the tools in her hands, and then she placed them carefully on the workbench along with the other worn hammers and chisels. Gripping her hands together, her fingers interlocking, she looked down at her work on the stone and smiled.

The dream disappeared and Veracitas' eyes opened. He remained still for a moment, worried that the dream would fade from memory. As the room lightened with the first rays of sunrise, he realized the images were emblazoned in his mind to such a depth that he would never forget. He threw off the blanket and swung his legs over the edge of the bed.

"Kali!" Veracitas called as he slipped on his boots. He pulled on a long-sleeved shirt and searched the room for his travel bags. "Kali!"

The door swung open and the red-haired Oleen Captain stepped in with a worried look.

"Gather your troops. We're riding back to Ello," he told her.

She looked at him in disbelief. "Ello? What about a new stone?"

"I won't need it," he said, smiling at her. "The old one is going to work just fine."

Kali watched him gathering his things. "It's broken. That's why we came back here: to get another one, right?"

"Right, but I don't want another stone."

Confused, she brushed her hair back. "What got into you? You wouldn't eat or get out of bed for days and now you're all fired up to go work on a broken statue you said was ruined."

"I am hungry," Veracitas said. "We should eat, and then we'll get on the road." He grasped her shoulder. "It's not ruined, Kali. I thought it was, but it's not. Boschina showed me the stone's value, even in its brokenness."

"Boschina?" Kali questioned. "When did—"

"I'll tell you over some food," he replied, going out the door. "Gather the Oleens. We have a long ride and I have a lot of work to do."

Captain Kali looked at him and shook her head. "I don't know what happened to you or what flipped you around, but I'm glad you're back."

* * *

Currad was training troops along the tail end of the Laundo Hills, where the ridges flattened into a long slope to the South Ford of the Camotop River. The army had reoccupied and was rebuilding the old fortification set on the high ground above the river that overlooked the road from Castle Ambermal to the ford. Beyond the Camotop was the East Range of Ameram that separated the river basin from the High Plains of Toubar. The location of the fort had been chosen by King Ahmbin's grandfather, Ahmbin the First, during the long period of battles with the Pawndors. However, in recent peaceful years, the king and his advisors decided it was not necessary to keep troops there on a constant watch. The soldiers pulled out and the buildings were left deserted and at the mercy of the weather and scavengers.

Before leaving on her tour of the kingdom, Queen Ekala Oleen had ridden with her father, Currad, and an entourage of Oleens to the South Ford and along the hills to the abandoned fort above the busy crossing. The fort was more barracks and stock pens than a walled defensive position. It had never been intended to withstand a siege—that's what the castle was for. The structures were built to house enough soldiers and supplies to stop or, at the very least, slow an army attempting to cross the nearby ford. Over time, without maintenance, the roofs of the stone buildings had caved in; the wood fencing had rotted and fallen apart.

"You see the view from here," her father had said, as they sat on their horses and looked out over the ford, "how far you can see across the river. An approaching army can be seen a day's march away."

"I used to play in these empty buildings," Queen Ekala Oleen said. "I pretended to command an army rushing to battle in the shallows of the river."

King Ahmbin smiled at his daughter. "Now, here you are, grown up, victorious in battle, and commanding all the forces of Ameram."

Shadahn snorted and lifted her head. Ekala leaned forward and patted her horse's neck. "And I have learned the brutal, bloody reality of battle. It is not safe and clean like my childhood games."

"There is always sacrifice, in one way or another," her father said, "whether it is in fighting or everyday living. As a leader, you cannot let your feelings of loss influence your decisions for the overall good of the people."

Ekala turned in the saddle to look at her father.

"That sounds like something Larma would say."

He nodded. "It does." He reached over and put his hand on hers. "You are strong; that is why I named you Ekala. I saw it from the day you were born. You have faced every challenge in your path and won. But it does not get easier. Now that you are queen, you must be prepared for challenges from directions you would never expect."

Ekala looked around at the dilapidated buildings and pen fences, and then at the ford and beyond—as far as she could see in the distant haze. "You think I should revitalize this fort and post a garrison to guard the ford. That's why you brought me out here."

"Yes," the old king replied. "We have not been invaded from the south since my father was king. Now I fear that with the change of power, it is a possibility."

"Because I am a woman?" Ekala snapped.

"You have to admit, Ekala, that other countries see that as a weakness."

"I understand that," the queen replied. "But I don't like it."

Currad, who had been quiet, suddenly spoke. "Others don't know you like we do."

She turned to him. "You think this a good idea, Currad?"

"I do, Your Majesty," the King's Honored Soldier answered. "Showing strength here may discourage those who think we are weak and sleeping."

"Do you think I'm sleeping, Currad?"

"No, Your Majesty. I know your mettle, but many do not and they will foolishly challenge you, causing suffering, our people's lives—and the peace that we now enjoy."

"Well spoken, Currad," Ekala said. "You're sounding like Larma, too."

Ekala looked back at the ford, at the people crossing from both sides through the shallow water. She took a breath and exhaled, frustrated. "I don't want to make Ameram a fortified kingdom, constantly flinching at shadows and barking dogs. Though, I understand the reasoning to protect our people, especially because of who I am." Turning to her father and the loyal Currad, she said, "Go ahead, Currad, rebuild this fort, supply and arm it with enough soldiers to defend the southern approach to Ambermal."

"As you wish, Ekala Oleen," Currad said and bowed his head slightly. "I will tell the King's Builder to start on it immediately. Oh...I guess we need to change his title to the Queen's Builder."

The queen sighed and looked at her father.

"No, Currad, for now, leave his title as it is."

Old King Ahmbin had smiled at her. Then, they rode together back to the castle.

Chapter Thirteen
The Woods of Rows

The ancient grove in which Thalmus and Boschina now traveled had existed for so long that no one remembered how it began. It was generally agreed that someone must have planted the trees because they grew in such perfect lines and were spaced an exact distance apart from one another. The trees were lined up diagonally, as well as horizontally, and were the same size: trunk, branches, and height. Their arching, stretching limbs laced together at the top, completing a canopy that covered the spaces between the trees and created the feel of an enclosed world. It was a feeling of both comfort and danger, causing a strange prickly sensation on the skin. The humid air was thick with the sweet aroma of the leaves and pretty white flowers that bloomed amongst the green foliage. The ground in the grove was flat and soft from layers of decaying leaves; creating a home for little burrowing, crawling critters. Here and there, patches of weedy sprouts grew wherever the sun filtered through the leafy cover. At first glance, the grove appeared as a simplistic and pleasant diversion; but upon entering its depth, the rows became confusing, never-ending, and threatening. It was believed mysterious creatures roamed amongst the trees. Some people who had gone too deep into these woods were never seen again; others who emerged were changed, and not for the better. The people of Toulon had learned to steer clear of the Woods of Rows.

Thalmus, with a long spear in hand, walked in front of Thunder, following the tracks between the rows of trees. Boschina, with the frog-coat hood pulled over her head, rode on Radise alongside the tortoise. Dallion, who normally did not stay close, was content to walk at Thunder's pace and watch Thalmus reading the tracks. Large drops of rain dripped from the trees, splattering on the travelers and the ground. The storm's wind rumbled over the tree tops; yet, beneath the canopy, the lower branches swayed little and the air was barely disturbed.

"How can you see the tracks in these leaves?" Boschina asked, looking out from under her hood.

"The leaf bed has been disturbed, flattened, or pushed aside by the horses' hooves," he replied. "When a horse walks, it might drag a hoof and leave a scrape in the surface. When it is running, it will kick up large chunks of debris, especially when it turns, like this here," he said pointing at a churned roll of leaves.

Motioning to his right, Thalmus continued after the tracks, stepping through the next row of trees, and then the next and the next before turning left again. The others followed him as he crisscrossed through rows of trees, and then back again as the rain fell. Despite her concentration, Boschina was becoming confused. She had been trying to maintain a sense of direction by counting how many rows they had crossed to the east and then to the north. But they had changed direction and gone back and forth across the rows she had counted, subtracted, and then counted again, so she wasn't sure how many they had crossed in either direction. As for knowing north from south, or east from west, she now had no clue. The hunter was not counting; he just continued, tracing the trail before finally coming to a stop when Thunder clicked his jaws. Thalmus glanced at the tortoise before looking around at the trees.

"What is it?" Boschina asked.

"There was a fight here," Thalmus said. "Blood on the

ground...see?" He pointed. "The rain has almost washed it clear. Look over there."

Boschina followed his eyes to a nearby tree, where an arrow stuck in a branch.

"That's Lander's arrow. I can tell by the feathers."

"That one missed its mark," Thalmus said.

Boschina tensed. "I hope the others didn't miss."

"There may not have been more arrows," Thalmus replied. "From the amount of blood on the ground, it was more of a sword fight."

"But the arrow proves Ekala was here."

"It proves that Lander was here. It is hard to tell whether the queen was with her; the tracks are a mess." Thalmus walked around examining the ground. "It was a fight on horseback. I see no human marks, only hooves. Three of them came in from this direction," he said following tracks in the mulch, "and two from over there. At least four more were here where they fought."

"Four? That could be Ekala with the three Oleens," Boschina said.

"Yes, but I do not see Shadahn's hoofmark; the tracks are too trampled."

"Then they all rode on?" Boschina said, pointing at tumbled leaves.

"This way," Thalmus said and walked through to another row.

Thunder and Boschina followed while Dallion went to the next row and walked parallel to his friends with one line of trees separating them. Again, the trail led them haphazardly back and forth through the grove until Thalmus stopped. Thunder clicked and then began hissing. Boschina saw Thalmus staring down the row. In the distance, she saw a lone rider on a motionless horse staring back at them through the rain. When Thalmus raised his hand and waved, the horse and rider bolted away into the trees.

"Could you tell who it was, Thalmus?"

"No, but Thunder does not like him," Thalmus answered and rubbed the tortoise's head.

Dallion suddenly took off in a full gallop after the rider.

Radise jerked, but stayed steady.

"Dallion!" Boschina shouted.

Thalmus hurried to the row where Dallion had run, but the big Paint had already crossed into the next row. Thalmus continued through that row of trees and then to another, only to see rain and deserted space between the trees.

Dallion was gone.

Thalmus shook his head. He knew Dallion had keen senses, but the horse had never been in a place like this; he could get confused easily and wander aimlessly. Thalmus took a deep breath and started back to Boschina when the shaft of the spear began to hum in his hand. He immediately dropped into a crouch and glanced around. He thought he would see Thunder and Boschina past the trunks of the trees just several rows over. But, they weren't there. The spear continued humming. After looking around again, and seeing no danger, he carefully started through the rows, knowing something was wrong.

* * *

When Thalmus ran off after Dallion, Boschina heard someone call her name. She looked down the long row and saw Ekala standing by a tree, waving at her—waving at her to come as she turned and went into the next row.

"Ekala! We've come to help you." She turned to look for Thalmus. "Thalmus! Thalmus! Ekala's here." She patted Radise. "Let's go, Lady."

Radise hesitated, pulling her head back, not wanting to move. Still, Boschina urged her forward until the horse gave in and started into a trot, passing through the next row and beyond. Thunder clicked his jaws and snorted. He couldn't let her go by herself, so he hurried after her.

Boschina and Radise went through the first line of trees and headed up the clearing between the rows. "Where'd you go? Ekala!"

They trotted along, looking between the trees. Rain continued to drip through the leaves. The ground was becoming soggy like a sponge. Radise splatted along, trying to get a feel for the mushy ground and an understanding of the constant rows and lines of trees. Thunder tried to keep an eye on Radise with Boschina in the distance as he followed behind. Despite the soft soil, he could still feel the thumping of the horse's hooves and, beyond them, more vibrations. He became aware of an odor in his nostrils he did not like. It was an aroma he knew humans thought of as sweet.

However, *he* knew it as deadly.

* * *

Thalmus returned to the place where he had left the others and searched the ground for their tracks. He found the marks left by one horse through the trees; he followed it for twelve meters and saw imprints he knew well, the giant tortoise's feet. The long spear in his hand still hummed; he moved cautiously in the direction of the tracks, keeping his eyes wide.

With each line of trees crossed, they had moved deeper into the grove, much deeper than Thalmus had wanted to go. He had hoped to stay in the outer rows, following around the edges to find the tracks coming out the other side. However, the trail had led them farther and in such a confused tangle, especially with the evidence of a fight, that he had to surrender to the knowledge that the queen was still somewhere in the labyrinth of trees. Someone, or something, was in there. Still, despite its steady, mesmerizing pull, Thalmus knew they had not yet crossed the center line, nor come close to the heart of the grove.

That could be fatal.

The hunter stopped when the tracks made a sharp turn to the east, toward the center. He searched the area for signs of others, and for the first time found footprints. Then he heard a new sound, almost obscured by the rain—a shaking branch in the tree behind him. The point of the spear turned, pulling him around to see a creature swinging down at him from the tree. Thalmus twirled the staff of his spear and slapped the creature to the ground. It howled and rolled up to its feet to glare at him.

It was a Kairtaykar.

The shape of a man, it stood about one and a half meters tall with weathered gray-green skin. Its feet were the same as its hands with long fingers hanging loosely from lanky arms; its round brown eyes were more curious than threatening. The creatures lived in the trees and had the ability to change their looks to blend into the foliage or imitate another form. At this moment, it looked like a small man wearing a mottled green shirt and trousers like the Toulon soldiers.

Thalmus stood calmly with the spear turned away from the creature to show he was neither afraid nor wanted to hurt it. Without warning, the Kairtaykar suddenly leapt at Thalmus. He stepped aside and batted it down again with the spear. Arms and legs sprawled in the leaves, and then it flopped over and stood again to face Thalmus with an angry, surprised look.

"You do not have to die," the hunter told the creature. "Leave me be."

They stared at one another for a moment, and then the Kairtaykar suddenly grunted, scampered to the nearest tree trunk, climbed up into the branches, stopped to look down at him, and promptly disappeared into the canopy. Thalmus searched the surrounding trees for more of the creatures and noticed the changing light. The day had been long, gray, and wet; now, the light was dimming. He had to find Boschina before darkness engulfed the grove.

* * *

"Ekala! Ekala Oleen!" Boschina called. "Where are you?" She turned back and forth, peering through the trees, searching for her adopted sister, the queen. Twice she thought she had seen Ekala in the distance, waving at her. Both times, when they reached the spot, nobody was there.

Why would she hide from me? Boschina wondered. *Why is she running?*

Boschina heard hooves thumping, horses running in the distance—first to the left and then on the right. Then she heard the dull clink of swords.

But from where? What direction?

Radise snorted and began stepping slowly along, twisting her head side to side, glancing in between the rows. Thalmus' warning before they had entered the Woods of Rows came back to Boschina: "Question everything you see or feel in here, and stay close." She had done neither and now she and Radise were alone in these perplexing woods. Hearing something behind her, Boschina spun around and saw only long lines of wet trees stretching as far as she could see and the arching branches covering the rows like a never-ending tent.

Were the trees getting closer? The grove darker?

She shook her head. The sword at her side was still.

"Come on, Lady, let's retrace our steps and find Thalmus."

Radise agreed with a short whinny and turned back. They moved along slowly with Boschina searching the ground, trying to see her horse's imprints just as Thalmus had shown her. Here and there, she found divots in the thick leaves from hooves and they followed them until there were no more. They had wandered into a row that looked undisturbed.

Boschina was trying to decide which direction to go when she heard a faint moan. Radise heard it as well and perked her ears. Both stood motionless, listening. Then they heard it again, a low painful moan of agony. Boschina looked carefully down the row at the branches and at each trunk until she spotted something out of place at the base of a tree twenty meters away—a flesh-colored object flipping back and forth. Boschina quietly slipped the bow from its cover, pulled the string tight, drew an arrow from the quiver, and nocked it in the string. Radise cautiously stepped toward the thing, sniffing, trying to get a scent, but the rain and perfume of the wet decaying leaves filled her nostrils. Moving closer, Boschina could see the back of someone sitting against the tree, facing the next row.

She glanced around, checking for others.

By the pressure of her knee, Boschina directed Radise to cross into the next row as she kept her bow up, ready to shoot. Turning into the opening of the row, she saw a bloody soldier slumped against the tree. A sword lay near him. His bare hand was slowly flopping, trying to reach the handle. The man's eyes were closed; his head down and his chin on his chest.

There was a sudden scrambling in the tree overhead and she quickly pointed up, drawing the bowstring back. Something large and brown disappeared into the branches. Radise stopped well short of the man as Boschina returned her attention to him. He wore no uniform or insignias; yet, he appeared to be a soldier. He was broad-shouldered with short hair and a beard. His stomach and left arm were covered in blood. She relaxed the bow, but noted how close his hand was to the sword. Then she saw the mark on the blade just below the handle, a snaking "S."

"Soldier," she said softly.

The man did not respond.

A rutted trail in the leaves showed where the man had crawled to the trunk. "Soldier," she said louder. His hand jerked toward the sword and his head bobbed, but his eyes stayed closed. Boschina watched him for a moment, glanced around, and then replaced the arrow in the quiver; she hooked the bow onto the saddle and swung down from Radise.

She drew her sword as Radise grunted with concern.

Boschina approached the man from the side, reached out, stuck the tip of her sword under his sword on the ground, and flipped it away. Picking it up, she examined the mark. The blade was just like the ones Captain Susa had seized at the ford. This was surely a Toulon soldier. Boschina tapped his boot with her sword.

He didn't move.

Rain continued to drain his blood into the leaves. She had seen similar wounds at the Battle for Ambermal and knew that he would not live; he was almost gone now. If he could speak, she might learn something of Ekala.

"Soldier," she shouted. "Wake up!"

He stirred, blinked, and muttered.

Boschina stepped forward and shook his shoulder.

"Who did you fight? Who cut you?"

The man groaned in pain. His head rolled back, eyes opening— glazed and confused.

"Who cut you? Have you seen women warriors?"

The man stared and mumbled, "Fight…chased…lost…can't find…"

"Who can't you find?" Boschina asked, holding his head up. "Who'd you chase?"

"Out…can't find way out." His eyes closed.

"Who stabbed you?" Boschina asked.

The man's voice was weak, barely heard. "Bad place…can't get out."

And then he was gone.

Boschina took a deep breath and gently let his head down. Insects of various sizes with many legs and twitching feelers emerged from the leaves and crawled over the man's legs, and then up his arms. Boschina brushed them away with the back of her hand. She stood and stuck his sword into the ground next to him and placed his hand against it.

"You've got a long road ahead of you, Soldier." She looked up at Radise. "Well, Lady, *we're* going to get out of here." She looked up and down the row. It was getting darker. "Which way?"

Radise snorted and nodded straight ahead.

"Okay. We don't have much more daylight," Boschina said, climbing back onto the saddle. "Let's go."

Following tracks in the leaves, they passed through numerous tree lines before stopping in another identical row. "I think I see an opening down there—at least it looks lighter," Boschina said, patting Radise's neck. The roan mare started trotting that way.

Boschina felt good. "We'll wait for Thalmus, Dal, and Thunder on the outskirts. They'll know how to get out."

Minutes passed, but the glow at what she thought was the end of the row was not any closer. "Come on Lady," Boschina urged. "Faster."

Radise kicked into a gallop, charging toward the fading light. It was no use, they did not gain on the glow and now darkness surrounded them. The long rows of trees were no longer visible, but Boschina felt their branches brush against her as she rode on. Radise breathed heavily and kicked up mucky clumps of leaves that splattered onto her sides and Boschina's legs.

They were running blind.

When a branch almost knocked her from the saddle, Boschina pulled Radise to a halt.

"It's too dangerous, Lady. The light's gone."

Boschina's good feeling was also gone. The rain continued to drip on them. The frog-skin coat had kept her head and upper body dry, but from the waist down she was soaked and mud-splattered. It was so dark that she could barely see her hand in front of her face. The soldier's last words rang in her head: "Can't get out." She suddenly felt exhausted, cold, and confused.

What was she to do?

Leaning forward, she hugged her horse's neck.

"I got us into trouble again, didn't I?" she said. "I shouldn't have left Thalmus. He told me to stay close." She sat up. "Okay, I've got to think like Thalmus. We're spending the night here—but where? Not on the muddy ground with those crawling things, that's for sure. So it's in the saddle or...in the trees?" She glanced up, trying to see the trees in the darkness. "It's worth a try." She rubbed Radise's neck and shoulder. "Move this way, Lady, slowly. Let's find a trunk and lower branches."

Radise stepped carefully while Boschina held her hands out in the dark to feel for a tree. Branches brushed by her before she was able to grab onto one and guide Radise forward to the trunk of a tree. "Stay right there," she said while her hands felt their way up the bark to the first thick branches. Boschina pulled her legs up onto the saddle and lifted herself into the tree. Groping through the leaves and branches, she found a spot that securely supported her. She took several deep breaths. "These leaves and flowers smell so sweet." She shook her head. "Are you alright, Lady?"

Radise neighed. But she didn't feel safe. She sensed danger all around them.

"Good. Don't go away. In the morning, we'll find Thalmus and get out of here."

Boschina shivered as she wiggled into a more comfortable position, pushing twigs and leaves away from her face. She was hungry, wet, and worn out. Closing her eyes, she quickly fell asleep, so deeply that she didn't feel the first vibrations of her sword or the fingers that began to grasp her arms.

Chapter Fourteen
The Heart of the Woods

Boschina felt fingers and hands sliding over the slippery frog-skin coat, grasping at her arms and pulling her through branches and wet leaves. Blinded in the dark, groggy and confused, she reacted slowly. She finally realized what was happening: somebody was moving her. She reached for the vibrating sword on her hip. Hands slapped and shoved her fingers from the handle, and then pulled the sword away from her. The sweet aroma of the leaves filled her nostrils making her sleepy, dulling her senses. Still, she tried to resist by pushing back, grasping a branch or prying at the hands.

Nothing worked. She was too weak to fight.

Radise heard the commotion and Boschina's grunts above her. The horse knew something was wrong—that her mistress was in trouble. She reared in the dark and whinnied, calling to Boschina.

Boschina heard Radise as if she were far away.

"Lady...Lady?"

Radise reared again and again, pounding the tree with flailing hooves.

Boschina heard her horse's panic and thought she was in trouble. "Lady!" Boschina called. "I'm coming to help you." With new vigor, she squeezed her arm free from a grip and grabbed at the handle of her short blade. The hands pushed her against a branch and she rolled enough to pull the knife from its scabbard and lash out. The creature screamed in pain and slapped at her head and face. Boschina tried to duck and slash at the hands and those holding her feet. She whipped the blade back and forth in the dark, banging her arm on branches. Now something was kicking at her—pounding on her legs, hips, and side. She rolled again, the branch broke beneath her and she dropped, slamming her head and side as she landed on another branch.

Radise snorted and shuffled under the tree, trying to see into its darkness. Suddenly, fingers grabbed at her shoulder and she spun, kicking and spinning, knocking them away. The fingers returned, grabbing at her head and then the saddle. She reared, stomped, and pulled her head away. The experienced warhorse had learned long ago how to keep an enemy from controlling her.

Still, the hands kept pawing at her.

She could run, get away, but that would mean leaving Boschina to whatever it was in the trees. No, Radise would not desert her friend; she would stay and fight. Now, more fingers tried to grasp her mane. She felt something trying to climb onto her. Spinning again and kicking, she tried to throw the body, but it had grabbed hold and was hanging on, its fingers squeezing her neck. Then she heard a snap and a horrific scream. The fingers let go and the creature fell away. There was another snap and more painful screams, and then scurrying, splashing feet fading into the darkness. Radise heard hissing and then two clicks from snapping jaws. It was Thunder. He had found her in the night and chased away the attackers.

In the tree, Boschina grimaced and tried to raise her head when the creature pounced on her, grabbing at her arm with the knife and slapping at her head. "Get...off me," she grunted and brought her knee up to hit it. Their bodies shifted and they broke through smaller branches, falling free until thudding onto the wet spongy ground.

Both Radise and Thunder hurried to her. The creature climbed back onto Boschina, and then saw the horse and giant tortoise coming at him and decided to leave. It bounded away into the darkness.

The commotion in the Rows had stopped. The creatures with the long fingers had ceased their attack. Thunder and Radise stood over the prone Boschina as raindrops fell on them. They stood motionless, listening to her breathing and sniffing—and then Radise nudged Boschina with her nose. Boschina moaned and rolled her head on the ground. The knife was still in her hand and she held it up.

Thunder clicked his jaws.

"Thunder, is that you?"

He clicked again and Radise snorted.

Boschina let her arm with the knife relax and drop to the ground. "Am I glad to hear you two," she said and tried to sit up. Thunder took the hood of her coat in his jaws and helped pull her to a sitting position. The animals nuzzled her on each side. "Ow, easy," she groaned. "Help me out of this mud." She grabbed Radise's reins on one side and Thunder's neck on the other and they raised their heads until she stood on her feet. Leaning against Thunder, Boschina crawled onto the giant shell creature's back and collapsed.

* * *

As darkness closed in on the woods, Thalmus ceased his search for Boschina and climbed up into the lower branches of a tree. He laid the spear across the branches in front of him, pulled his sword from its sheath, and held the blade against his shoulder, ready for an upward thrust or a downward slash. Losing contact with Dallion was frustrating, but getting separated from Boschina and Thunder had been a surprise and very upsetting. How could the giant tortoise have moved that quickly? He had only gone three rows away from them. Maybe time and space in these trees was distorted more than he realized.

It had been a long time since he was last here.

The power of the grove had grown stronger, its creatures more brazen. Still, he had picked up Boschina's trail several times, only to lose it because the tracks had been obscured by someone or something. Chorgens were not a concern. Thalmus knew the voracious beasts feared the Woods of Rows because of its symmetry. The pungent aroma, uniformity, and mirror images completely drove them mad, more so than humans. At the moment, Thalmus himself was feeling the confusion and drowsiness. He wanted to sleep, but by doing so he would become vulnerable to falling under the control of the power that lived here.

He thought about Boschina and what she was doing to survive the night. Was she sleeping in her saddle on Radise? Had she encountered the tree creatures? What did he call them? Tricksters? Treesters? Kairstays? He could not remember.

Why couldn't he remember?

Whatever he had called them, the persistent climbing characters took advantage of people whenever they could. Thalmus hoped Thunder was with Boschina. The giant tortoise was not fooled by any of this. Maybe Boschina was secure, resting safely on his back. And where was Ekala? It was very likely that she was still lost in this grove, as well as Maz. Perhaps they had found one another and were trying to find their way out.

Thalmus realized his thoughts were muddled, his mind was fading into sleep. The tree swayed softly in the wind and the rain dripped steadily. Hoping the storm would be over in the morning, Thalmus gripped the handle of the sword in his right hand, the spear with his left hand, and closed his eyes. Within moments, he felt himself floating in a black cavern with no understanding or sense, just a creeping numbness slowly taking over his body. The feeling was pleasant, comforting, and welcome; it was the deep rest he had desired. It felt good.

Thalmus had just about given in to its control when he was struck with a stabbing pain in his shoulder. He jerked. His hand tightened on the sword, but he did not open his eyes or come awake. The pain dug deeper and he was drawn up, out of the pleasant cavern, out of the numbness. He let go of the spear and grabbed at the pain. Feathers? His hand felt feathers over talons gripping his shoulder. Thalmus opened his eyes and looked right into the bright discs of Bubo. He was struck instantly with a strength of will coursing through him and a rising clarity.

The Great Horned owl snapped his beak and clenched tighter with his talons.

Thalmus winced. "I am awake, Bubo."

His mind was clearing, the pleasant numbness fading into the trees.

Bubo studied him, chortled, and then spread his wing behind Thalmus' head and batted him several times.

"I am alright, Bubo. You brought me out of it," Thalmus replied with his hand still on the owl's claws grasping his shoulder. "Please lighten up on your grip."

Bubo bobbed his head from side to side, studying Thalmus, and then slowly relaxed his hold on his friend's shoulder.

"Thank you," Thalmus said, feeling the pain subside. "Where have you been?"

Bubo settled his wings, bobbed his head, hooted, and clacked his beak.

"Ekala is still in the grove? What about Maz and Camp?"

Bubo bobbed his head and clacked.

"Boschina, do you know where she is?"

Bubo looked away, and then back.

"We must find her in the morning, Bubo." Thalmus rubbed the owl's breast feathers. "With you here, I feel safe to sleep."

Thalmus closed his eyes and this time did not drift into a cavern of numbness. Instead, he felt light with silent feathers surrounding him. During the night, the storm passed on from the grove. In the morning, the rain was gone and sun rays filtered through the canopy of trees. Bubo hopped from his friend's shoulder to a branch and Thalmus climbed down from his perch onto the soggy bed of rotting leaves. He leaned the spear against the tree trunk, removed his frog-skin coat, and shook it out. He adjusted his shirt, pants, and sword and then put the coat back on. Grasping the spear, he looked up at Bubo.

Owl had been watching Thalmus, waiting for him to be ready. Now, he lifted off and winged silently under the canopy between two rows of trees. Thalmus jogged after him, slogging through the mucky leaves. When Bubo wanted to turn out of the row they were in, he would wait on a low branch for Thalmus to catch up. Then he would take off in a new direction, moving carefully from one row to another. Several times, Thalmus waited while Bubo flew up through a hole in the canopy to scout above the trees. When he returned, they would head in a direction Owl had determined from his search.

It was during one of these pauses that Thalmus saw someone in the distance who looked like Boschina staring at him and then ducking behind a tree.

He did not fall for the deception. The imposter's movements were not anything like Boschina's.

Often, he heard rustling in the trees. Although he did not see anything, he could tell the creatures were trying to follow him.

Thalmus had been following Bubo diagonally through rows of trees when Bubo suddenly hooted and made a sharp turn. Grasping his spear with both hands, Thalmus turned into the lane between rows and was relieved to see Radise and Thunder with Boschina sprawled across his shell.

Thunder was happy to see his friends. He clicked and lifted his head higher. Radise nickered and threw her head. Bubo glided softly onto the giant tortoise's shell, landing next to Boschina. When Thalmus reached them, he rubbed Thunder's head and patted Radise's shoulder.

"Boschina?"

Bubo was bobbing his head, turning his head from side to side as he looked at her. Suddenly, he opened his wings and jumped onto her back near the neck. She moaned and lifted her head. "Bubo?"

"Whoo," he blurted and walked down her back and gripped her hip with his talons.

"Oh, ow, that hurts," she complained.

"Bear it. You will be better, Boschina," Thalmus told her.

After a few minutes, Bubo released his grip, flapped his wings on her, and lifted off, flying into the tree overhead. Boschina rubbed her hip and lower back, and then sat up. She turned her head and looked at him watching her from the tree. "Thanks, Bubo. Now I've got owl claw marks on my butt. I do feel better."

Thalmus leaned over to examine the scrapes and bruises on her head. "Were you attacked in the night?"

"I'm sorry, Thalmus. I didn't stay close to you. We saw Ekala and went after her, but she kept moving away. We kept following her and got lost. It got dark and I climbed into the tree to sleep. I wasn't bothering anybody, just trying to get out of the mud and get comfortable. Then I was attacked by I don't know what. There were two or three, maybe four, of them. They tried to pull me through the tree, but I fought them. They tried to get Radise, too. The short tool worked, Thalmus; they couldn't take it from me. But they got my sword."

"It will turn up. These swords always do," Thalmus said. "Can you continue? Maybe ride on Thunder? We have to find Ekala and Maz."

"Yes, I can do that," Boschina said.

Satisfied that his friend was okay, Bubo began hopping and flitting from branch to branch where Boschina had slept. He worked his way higher until finally disappearing through the leaves. Thalmus climbed onto Radise where Boschina's quiver hung, and her bow was strapped along the horse's side. He sat in the saddle, looked around, and waited for Bubo to return.

The great owl silently appeared, flying at them from another row. He clacked his beak twice as he winged by. Thalmus did not have to direct Radise because she instantly turned and followed. Thunder was already plodding after Bubo with Boschina on his back. There was no zigzagging or changing direction this time. Bubo flew in a direct line through the rows, leading them deeper into the grove. The trees never changed, one after the other looking exactly alike, and the rotting, cushy leaf bed of the floor spread underneath them; the humid, sweet aroma filled the air. When the perfume of the grove began to dull his mind, the hunter felt the sharp pain of Bubo's claws on his shoulder and his senses cleared, refocusing his attention on the moment.

Bubo's pausing and waiting kept them connected as they continued toward the center of the grove. Down a row of trees or jumping out from behind a distant trunk, they saw what appeared to be Ekala or Maz waving. Once, Lander stepped out and shot an arrow at Thalmus. It whizzed by well behind him as the archer did not allow for their movement. It was obviously not the real Lander. Radise kept blowing her nostrils out as she trotted determinedly after Bubo, while Thunder tramped along, his powerful legs driving him to where he knew he would be needed to fight alongside his friends. The sweet perfume of the trees became stronger the closer they got to the bowels of the woods. Not knowing what to expect, Thalmus prepared himself for the worst. He prayed that Ekala and Maz were still alive, and if so, that he would be able to free them and find a way out of the grove. Bubo would be essential for their escape.

And where was Dallion? He could not leave him behind.

Thalmus saw Bubo change direction. Owl had turned around and was flying right back at them. Pulling up, almost hovering, he landed on Thalmus' shoulder. They stopped as Bubo hissed and clicked, bobbing his head; he then dropped onto Thunder's shell by Boschina. Thalmus dismounted from Radise and motioned to be quiet. He walked carefully forward as Bubo winged passed him. Thunder and Radise stepped through the wet leaves behind him.

The rows appeared to have ended.

The branches of the last trees of each row hung to the ground creating a curtain so thick that they could not see through. Poking the wall of foliage with his spear to make sure it was not clinging vines or a trap of some sort, Thalmus pushed aside the branches and saw a large circular clearing. He stepped into the hanging branches enough to get a better look. In the center of the clearing were three large trees twice the size of the trees in the grove. They stood in a triangular formation approximately fifteen meters apart. All three were manicured, trimmed to perfection to create a domed look—like giant mushrooms. The tips of their longest branches touched one another, except in the center of the triangle where a round, columned structure stood. The columns were made of stone; and like the trees of the Rows, they were perfectly lined up around the perimeter and through the interior of the building. The pillars stretched ten meters to the ceiling where they shared the weight of an intricate roof made of log beams. It was a majestic stone building that appeared out of place here in the trees.

Around the circle of open ground, between the triangle and curtain of branches, were vegetable gardens and miniature fruit trees; all perfectly groomed and maintained.

Scanning the gardens, the foliage of the three trees, and the unique building, Thalmus saw no activity or movement. Oddly, there were no leaves on the ground, either in the clearing or under the trees. The dirt was raked clean. The sun shone bright in the clearing and created long shadows in the building that had no walls. A suffocating, unnatural silence filled the area, not even the leaves of all the surrounding trees dared to make a sound. The place appeared to be deserted.

However, Thalmus knew that wasn't true. He could feel a presence, a feeling of life pulsating softly.

Where and what was it?

Bubo had brought him here to find Ekala, and hopefully, Maz and Camp. So, where were they? And where had Bubo gone? He felt a hand on his back as Boschina stepped beside him to see. Radise grunted and stuck her head over his shoulder, sniffing the scents floating in the clearing. Raising her head, she snorted softly. Radise smelled something that Thalmus could not. Thunder pushed his head through on Thalmus' other side. He sniffed and gazed at the building. Then he clicked his jaws once. The tortoise was also detecting something. The hunter looked again and realized there were horses lying in the shade of the trees. There were six to eight on their side with their heads and legs stretched out on the ground, appearing as big lumps in the shadows. One of them clearly had white patches.

Bubo flew out of the building and landed on the rooftop. He held his outstretched wings open for a moment before tucking them in and then swiveling his head around, searching the area. That was the signal: Ekala or Maz, and maybe both, were in the building and the way was clear.

Thalmus whispered to Boschina, "Are you ready?"

She nodded and they stepped the rest of the way through the hanging branches. Watching the trees and keeping an eye on Bubo, Thalmus moved at a steady pace across the open, muddy ground—not running, but walking quickly. Boschina was right behind him. Thunder and Radise pushed through the curtain and followed after them.

When they reached the shaded area under the first tree, Dallion was lying there among the other horses. Thalmus knelt beside him, stroking his neck and listening to the big Paint's heart. Thunder nuzzled Dallion with his snout, but the stallion did not move. He was slumbering deep under a spell. Thalmus patted Dallion's shoulder and glanced around; there was still no movement in the clearing.

Bubo remained like a watch dog on the roof.

The eerie silence continued. *The soul of the Woods, the cause of the spell lives in that building amongst those columns,* Thalmus thought. It was time to confront it, to find his friends and to leave this place. He motioned to Boschina. They stood, and under the watchful eyes of Bubo, they passed between the slumbering horses to the foundation of the building. Radise stayed, standing guard over her motionless friends.

As Thalmus stepped up to the columns, he was struck by the sweet, pungent aroma oozing from the building. Inside, pots smoldered with leaves from the floor of the grove. The burning leaves emitted a thick incense that filled the structure and wafted through the stone pillars.

Thalmus stepped back, covering his nose and mouth with the crook of his arm. However, Thunder charged forward between the first line of pillars snapping his jaws as a warning to whomever or whatever he might encounter. Boschina followed right after him.

Hesitating outside, Thalmus took several deep breaths of air before running into the fumes and jumping onto Thunder's shell.

The pads and clicking nails of Thunder's feet echoed off the large slabs of rough stone floor that sloped toward the inside of the building. The pillars were made from the same kind of stone. Large round blocks had been shaved, etched, and cut to fit and stacked on top of one another to support the high-beamed ceiling. The surface of the stone had been carved to look like the bark of a tree. At the base of each pillar, roots appeared to be growing, breaking through the surface and snaking across the floor. They looked so real that Thalmus slid off Thunder and knelt to feel them to confirm the roots were truly made of stone. Boschina was doing the same; although, she lingered longer to study the intricacies of the detail.

There were no engravings or depictions to indicate who the builder was or to praise a monarch or deity. Thalmus thought that was unusual as he searched the interior. Thunder continued down the sloping floor until reaching the center. There, the pillars stood in a circle around a giant statue of a woman turning into a tree. Her backside and lower half were all trunk and tree; whereas, the front from the waist up was still partially human form. She did not have a look of pain or agony on her face, rather one of ecstasy—as if the transition was a great joy. Her face, neck, and shoulders were changing into bark with small branches sprouting here and there.

Boschina walked with her mouth open, staring at the statue in awe. "What is this? Who is this?"

"It is the goddess Arborina," Thalmus said, looking up at the statue. "Stories of old tell of a woman who lived in trees most of her life. She loved them so much that she came to be one. This is the first depiction of her that I have seen."

"The work of the sculptor is exquisite," Boschina said. "Who could have carved this? It's so perfect. Look how smooth her skin is and the hair gradually growing into twigs and leaves. Her outstretched arms, as if she is welcoming someone, are turning into branches. And her eyes, looking so adoringly up the corridor to the tree outside the building."

The detail made the stone image appear lifelike. What did not appear lifelike were the bodies lying amongst the roots around the foot of the statue.

Placed in a perfect circle around the base of the statue, and lying perpendicular like the numbers of a clock, were the bodies of Ekala, Maz, Camp, Lander, and the two Oleen soldiers.

Chapter Fifteen
Arborina and the Kairtaykars

The Queen of Ameram lay on the floor between two large stone roots growing from the base of the statue. Her head rested against the trunk with her face turned up as if in honor to the tree goddess. Ekala Oleen's hair had been combed, her arms rested placidly along her sides, and her blouse, vest, and trousers neatly straightened. To the right of Ekala, on the other side of the bulging root, laid the archer, Lander. Ricken and Karl rested between roots on Ekala's left, as if they were still guarding their queen. Continuing clockwise around the statue were Maz and Camp, and then two unknown men with bloody tunics. All of them had been carefully placed on their backs, equal distance apart in an orderly manner circling the statue. Each one had been cleaned up as much as was possible and appeared to be waiting for a blessing from Arborina.

Thalmus knelt beside Ekala and placed his hand on her neck. There was a pulse. He sighed with relief and checked Maz and then Camp. They were all alive, floating in that comfortable black cavern of sleep Thalmus had experienced until being pulled back to consciousness by Bubo's talons. Thunder nudged Ekala with his snout, pushing her, trying to wake her. But she did not stir or open her eyes.

"They must be under a spell," Boschina said. "What are we going to do? How are we going to get them out of here? The horses are useless."

Looking at Ekala and the others, Thalmus was asking himself the same questions. How were they going to wake them or carry them out through the Rows? Six people and their horses? The Kairtaykars would not allow it. Thunder could handle two, maybe three on his shell, but what about the rest? The horses would be impossible to move.

The odor of the incense was strong, seeping smoothly and gently around him. He could feel a murmur of a presence in the silence of this place. Something besides them was alive here. Glancing around, he saw nothing but the rows of stone pillars and the beam ceiling high above. The statue stood motionless, towering over them, the goddess' face fixed in the joy of her transition. Thalmus gently placed his hand on the rough trunk of the statue that had once been her leg.

"Thalmus, what are we going to do?" Boschina asked again.

"What ancient sculptor created this work of art?" he said softly, examining the sculpture. "And was too humble to put his mark on it? It is as powerful as one of your father's creations."

Boschina looked up at the statue, at the outstretched arms, the angelic face, and once again was stunned by its perfection. "What makes you think a man or a woman created it? Look at the detail and sensitivity of the stone. It's so pure...faultless."

The image held their attention and drew them into her story, into the power of her mystery. Could this be true? That a love so deep and strong could change you into what you desired?

"Great hunter," Thalmus heard her whisper, "man who lives with animals, first intruder to enter my home free of my power, why have you come?"

Thalmus studied the stone face turning to bark. "I have come for my friends," he answered, though he did not speak it.

"And you, Stone Cutter's Daughter, bruised and damaged, what is your desire?"

Boschina put both hands on the statue. "I have come for my sister and my friends. I want to take them home."

Thunder grunted and pushed his head into Thalmus' hip. Thalmus staggered and realized that he had been mesmerized for a moment. The incense was affecting him. Glancing up, he saw the goddess now as lifeless stone. He smiled at the tortoise and patted his head.

Boschina was still staring at the goddess, her hands pressed on the stone trunk.

"Please release them from your power so that we may take them."

Thunder raised his head and clicked his jaws. Turning to look through the columns, Thalmus saw Bubo winging toward him. The owl landed on Thunder's shell, hooted and swiveled his head to look behind him. Thalmus knew what that meant—someone was coming. Stepping around a pillar, he could see people in the distance coming through the curtain of branches and walking in single file around the edge of the clearing.

It was the Kairtaykars.

The first three Kairtaykars carried a limp body over their shoulders and chanted a low monotone song. Thalmus watched the procession for a moment and realized they would be heading into the building. Glancing around for a place to hide, he noticed through the corridor of columns to the outside that Radise still stood near the sleeping Dallion. He looked back to see if the Kairtaykars had seen her. They had not. Thalmus motioned at her to lie down, and the roan responded by kneeling and then rolling onto her side.

"Boschina, we need to hide."

The chanting Kairtaykars had passed the first tree in the triangle and were heading to the second one. A group of them had stayed at the first tree, while the others moved on to the next. Thalmus slid by several stone pillars to watch their march and suddenly realized the angle of the passageways through the pillars lined up with the three trees outside and looked directly in at Arborina. He pointed to Thunder to move into the next row, away from the statue. Thalmus pulled Boschina from the goddess and followed Thunder as they hurried from the center and the visual line of the trees. As they got to the outer pillars, they discovered weapons—bows, swords, spears, and axes—hanging on the columns. There were hundreds of them.

Some were very old, and some were quite new. The hunter's sword began to vibrate. He slid the blade from its scabbard and held it before him. Moving at its will, he walked around several columns and found Boschina's and Ekala's swords hanging on hooks, humming. He pulled the blades halfway out of their sheaths and touched the engraved animals on the blades before slipping the swords back into the covers and taking them down.

"My sword," Boschina whispered, strapping it onto her waist. "I didn't think I'd see it again."

"I told you: they find a way to return."

The chanting of the Kairtaykars was getting louder. Their voices blended in a sad lament, "Kair – tay – kar – mar – bon – ta – kair – tay - kar," as they filed in separate columns from all three trees toward the domed building. Thalmus counted fifty of the tree worshipers as they tramped forward. Thunder lowered himself to the ground and partially pulled his legs and head down in an effort to lessen his profile. Bubo had been riding on Thunder's shell, but now he lifted off and flew up toward the round domed ceiling. Circling between the pillars and around Arborina's head, he looked down at his friends and the strange statue until he landed on a beam from where he could watch. Thalmus and Boschina stood against a column near Thunder. It wasn't much cover. They just hoped that the Kairtaykars would be too distracted to notice them.

Carrying the body of one of their comrades, the vanguard of the Kairtaykars entered the passage between the stone pillars and trudged toward the tree goddess. "Kair – tay –kar – mar – bon – ta – kair – tay - kar." The mournful words echoed through the building. The marchers added new leaves to the incense pots, causing them to smoke and emit more of the suffocating perfume.

Thalmus pulled the neck of his shirt over his nose. He did not want to succumb to the mind-numbing power of the incense. Boschina did the same, holding the shirt in her cupped hand over her nose and mouth. Thunder watched them and prepared himself to stand and fight.

The Kairtaykar's body was dressed in a new gray-green uniform of trousers that his feet protruded from and a long-sleeved shirt to the wrists. The hands and long clinging fingers dangled limp from the cuffs. Thalmus was surprised to recognize him as the one he had knocked down in the grove, the one who had stared at him and then run off. The blow Thalmus dealt him could not have been the cause of his death. Thunder stretched his neck and nudged Thalmus. This was the attacker that Thunder had pulled off Radise the night before. Thunder's jaws must have crushed his insides.

Reaching the statue, the bearers carefully laid their comrade on the floor between Ekala and Lander, in front of the goddess, as the chanters filed in amongst the pillars in rows around Arborina. They kneeled, held their hands palms up before them, and continued to chant: "Kair – tay – kar – mar – bon – ta – kair – tay - kar." Now the mourners sprinkled white tree flowers into the smoldering pots. The air became thick with a burnt sweet perfume. The chanters sang louder, the words echoing off the stone floors and pillars. "Kair – tay – kar – mar – bon – ta – kair – tay - kar."

To Thalmus, Arborina's face suddenly appeared to look down at the dead Kairtaykar, her arms reaching for him. He shook his head. He felt lightheaded, dizzy. His eyes were heavy and he fought to keep them open, to keep the darkness away. He leaned against Boschina.

Bubo had been watching from high above. He saw Thalmus falter. Dropping from his perch, he glided silently down and landed on Thalmus' shoulder. The hunter snapped awake, his vision clearing, light returning. The chanting continued at a higher pitch as the mourners pleaded with their goddess. When he looked again at Arborina, she was motionless, standing in the same frozen position as always; except she was looking at him, holding his gaze, asking what he was going to do. He saw now the peaceful transition of Arborina from human to tree and he understood the innocence and hope of the Kairtaykars. Larma's message throbbed to their rhythm.

Feeling the power of Bubo on his shoulder, Thalmus knew what he had to do. He removed his sword and knife from his belt and laid them with the spear alongside the other weapons on the floor. He motioned to Boschina to do the same. Tapping Thunder's shell, they walked around him toward the center, toward the chanters and the great statue. The giant tortoise stood up and followed behind them.

One by one, as the Kairtaykars saw the strangers walking toward them with the great owl on the man's shoulder, they stopped chanting and stood in shock. Strangers had never entered the Temple of Arborina. No one but the Kairtaykars had ever been conscious or under their own authority in the heart of the grove. Here was this man with a glaring, fierce-looking owl. He must be powerful; and walking beside him, the young warrior woman who fought them in the trees and commanded the shell creature who had killed their friend.

Thalmus and Boschina held their hands out with open palms, showing they had no weapons. Nevertheless, the sight of these invaders caused the Kairtaykars to back up.

"He will not hurt you. He is my friend," Thalmus said, patting Thunder's head. "We have come for our friends." Thalmus pointed at the slumbering bodies on the floor. "But first, your friend needs help, yes?"

The Kairtaykars stared at him. No one moved or spoke as the smoke and incense curled around them. Then one of the men slowly said, "Friend."

He sounded identical to Thalmus.

"Yes, that is right, *friend*. We mean no harm," Thalmus said.

"No harm," the man repeated, exactly as Thalmus had said it.

When Thalmus heard his words repeated, as if from his own voice, he turned to the man and saw that his weathered features had changed. The man now looked like him. Glancing around, he saw in the Kairtaykars the faces of Boschina, Ekala, Maz, Camp, and the others. Their long hands and fingers, though, maintained their original form.

The Thalmus look-a-like pointed at the Kairtaykar on the floor. "Friend," he said in Thalmus' voice.

Thalmus nodded. "Yes, let us help your friend."

Bubo lowered his head, moving side to side, focusing on the lifeless Kairtaykar. He spread his wings and dropped from Thalmus' shoulder onto the body. The Kairtaykars gasped and stepped back with fear and confusion at what this raptor was doing. Covering the unconscious changeling's chest with his wings, Bubo chortled and rocked back and forth. Suddenly, stone leaves dropped from Arborina's branches and drifted like real leaves, softly floating onto the prone Kairtaykar and the Great Horned owl, where they began to glow, pulsating with the bright green color of Spring. Thalmus looked up at the marble face of Arborina and saw tears wetting her cheeks. Bubo caught the leaves in his beak and placed one on the changeling's forehead and another on his chest; then continued chortling and pressing his outstretched wings over him. The lifeless Kairtaykar suddenly inhaled, his chest rising and settling. Bubo hooted, staring into his eyes, listening to his breathing. Bubo tucked his wings in and looked at Thalmus, who reached down so the bird could step onto his hand. Lifting Owl up, Thalmus placed the big bird on his shoulder, where he promptly shook and hooted.

The Kairtaykars gathered around their friend, touching and feeling him to confirm he was alive. A woman with a smooth, marble-like face and white pearl eyes stepped from the mourners and turned to Thalmus. "Friend," she said softly in the voice he had heard from the statue. "You may take your friends. They must stay asleep until you reach the outer rows of the woods. There, they can awaken."

"Thank you," Thalmus replied. He looked up at Arborina, still motionless as the marble she was carved in. Yet, he knew the directions were coming from her. This was the goddess of living trees and the abundant life of the Woods of Rows. She understood the world from the sensitivity of rooted stability, of serene steady growth and solitude. Disruption in the peace of her environment had to be smothered by the essence of the trees themselves. The changeling Kairtaykars were not only her followers, but the guardians and voices of her world.

Returning his attention to the woman, he said, "The horses are also our friends. I need them to carry these human friends out of the grove. Will you bring the horses to life?"

The woman hesitated and looked up the corridor between the pillars to the ground outside where the horses slept; except Radise, who was pretending to sleep. The woman tilted her head back and listened as if someone was speaking to her. Then she slowly turned her white gaze on Thalmus.

"You and your animal friends are different. Are you sure you're completely human?"

Thalmus smiled. "Some may think not." He glanced up at Arborina and then back at the pearl-eyed woman. "My life source flows from one far greater than I. My animal friends and I are united and guided by that gracious power—as, I believe, are you."

Staring with interest while the others waited, the woman's eyes flicked from Thalmus to Boschina to Bubo, and then to Thunder— examining each one fully. She reached out slowly with the long root-like fingers and felt the giant tortoise's head. Then, even more carefully, touched Bubo's feathered feet where his talons griped Thalmus' shoulder. Bubo watched her intently, letting her touch him, and hooted once, softly. She tenderly touched the scrapes and bruises on Boschina's face and said, "Skin is not stone, is it?" She paused and leaned her head back before speaking again.

"Your human friends are fortunate to have such caring, powerful friends as you," she said to all four of them. "The horses will be lifted from slumber to carry you all away. When your friends wake, they will not remember this place, only the confusion of the Woods of Rows."

Thalmus nodded. "Thank you."

"What about you, Stone Cutter's Daughter, do you want to stay?" the woman asked, tilting her head to look at Boschina.

Boschina looked back at her thoughtfully. "Thank you. I'm sure I would learn much, but I want to leave with my friends."

The woman nodded slowly. "Pity, you would find healing here." Then changing her mood, she said, "You must never speak of this place to anyone."

"This grove will always be in my mind, but not on my tongue," Boschina replied.

"What about these other men?" Thalmus asked, looking at the soldiers lying amongst the stone roots of the floor.

"They are passing into the life of our Rows, as many before them have. We will plant them accordingly. You must go now."

"I will gather our weapons and take them with us," Thalmus told her. "I know that you do not approve, but we need them in our world."

"Yes, you will need your tools," the woman agreed. "We know of the evil that lives outside our trees."

She turned to the waiting Kairtaykars and spoke to them in a language Thalmus did not understand. They immediately began lifting the slumbering bodies and carrying them carefully through the corridor to the outside. The white-eyed woman walked into the garden and picked several large leaves from different plants. She rolled them together into a long tube between her hands as she moved to the prone horses. Kneeling down before each horse, the woman blew through the tube of leaves into the animal's nostrils. Rolling slowly, the horses lifted their heads, and then tucked their legs under their bodies and stood up. Dallion, Shadahn, and the others stood calmly, still under the spell, while the Kairtaykars laid their master's bodies over their backs. The Kairtaykars then led the horses, in a single file, across the clearing and into the grove.

Bubo left Thalmus' shoulder and flew out to follow the caravan. The hunter and Boschina gathered the weapons and placed them on Thunder's back, who trudged out to join the others. At the last row of pillars to the outside, Thalmus stopped and turned back to look down the corridor at Arborina. Shafts of light shone between the pillars, illuminating the white marble statue. *Were her eyes watching us?*

"May you and your Kairtaykars live in peace," he whispered.

"And to you, Hunter," the voice said, "though I doubt it will be."

Thalmus joined Thunder and Boschina following the Kairtaykars guiding the horses, weaving through the grove. To Thalmus, the route seemed to be circuitous and unnecessarily long. However, they finally emerged from the depths and stopped between the last two rows of trees. The open plain was visible beyond the final row of trunks. Bubo landed on his shoulder and settled his wings. The Kairtaykars lifted the bodies from the horses' backs and laid them on the soft leafy carpet. Then they released the placid horses and each touched Thalmus and Boschina as they went by them on their way back into the grove.

The last to leave was the pearl-eyed woman. She stood watching the sleeping bodies, and then walked to Boschina and gently touched her face. "Be careful, Stone Daughter. Strength is not found in the flesh." Then she turned to Thalmus. "Your friends will wake soon and the horses will be strong again."

"Thank you," Thalmus replied.

The woman stroked Thunder's head, touched Bubo's feathered feet again, and then Thalmus' arm with her long fingers. She smiled. "One day, you will return to stay." Then she ran into the grove and disappeared through the rows of trees.

Thalmus smiled. *I hope not*, he thought. He looked at his friends, lying in the leaves.

Boschina leaned against Thunder's shell and rubbed her head. "My head's fuzzy. I feel faint."

Thalmus looked closely at Boschina's battered face and head. "All that touching, I thought she might have healed you."

"That would have been nice."

"You should rest," Thalmus told her and motioned at the bodies on the ground. "They will not wake for a while."

Boschina sighed and looked at her sleeping friends. "Alright, but only for a little bit." She climbed onto Thunder's back and laid down.

Thalmus looked through the last row of trees at the open plain beyond. He and his companions had found the queen and rescued her just in time—and in the process, almost lost Boschina. That would have been devastating. *I must be more careful*, he thought. *She is not invincible.* With one hand, he reached up and smoothed Bubo's feathers; with the other, he stroked Thunder's head. "Thank you," he said to his friends. "Now, how do we get back to Ameram without being caught by the Toulon army?"

Chapter Sixteen
Swords At the South Ford

Currad sat on his horse near the South Ford of the Camotop River observing the horses and wagons splashing through the shallow, muddy water. Some travelers were going south, while others headed west toward Castle Ambermal and beyond. It was the usual flow of people and goods in and out of Ameram. All appeared normal, almost picturesque. Yet, the King's Honored Soldier, always watchful, sensed something that made him suspicious of the calm normality. What piqued his interest? An unusual wagon? The way some of the drivers looked at him? Perhaps it was the higher flow of the river for this time of year that caused him to wonder what was happening in Rainland, the source of the Camotop. There had been rain in the East Range, but not enough to account for such a rise in the water. The depth was now above his knee.

In the far distance, toward the land of Zinkila, clouds of smoke blew across the horizon. The smoke had been there for days, caused by fires burning freely across the landscape. That should not be a concern; there were often grass fires in that dry southern terrain. Still, for Currad, it was one more thing adding to the uneasy feeling that all was not right. He could not define the warning he sensed. Call it a soldier's intuition for danger. Having survived a lifetime as a warrior, he had learned to pay attention to the little things and to never, ever, feel comfortable.

Overlooking the river crossing, on the higher ground behind him, on the very end of the Laundo Hills, construction on the old redoubt continued with workers rebuilding walls of the barracks that would become accommodations for two hundred soldiers. It couldn't be done soon enough for Currad. He was anxious to fill it with troops and armaments to defend the ford against whatever or whoever may attack from the south. This was the weak point in the southern defense of Ameram. For many peaceful years it had not been a concern. But now, with a new queen? He shook his head, unconsciously grasping the handle of his sword strapped on his horse's side. The bay mare, feeling her master pull on the sword, raised her head from nibbling grass.

"It's alright," Currad said, removing his hand from the sword and patting her neck. "Sorry to alarm you." He turned her to face Castle Ambermal standing tall and powerful in the distance on the edge of Cold Canyon. Despite the castle's strength, he worried that with King Ahmbin fading and Queen Ekala absent, the courage and resolve of the people was weak. He gripped the handle of his sword again and looked west, at the road leading to Barrunda. Dysaan had been gone too long in his search for the queen. The last he had heard from his friend and fellow soldier was a messenger describing how some beast had ravaged Thalmus' cabin and terrorized the people of Tamar. He had sent a small force to investigate. Since then, scouts reported no sign of Dysaan, his troops, or the queen, which added to his frustration. *What could be delaying them?* If he could leave, Currad would go find her himself. But his first responsibility was caring for King Ahmbin, and the reorganizing and training of the army that was far from complete.

That was critical for the defense of the kingdom.

His most effective and dependable force was the Oleens who had not accompanied Queen Ekala. He had come to depend on the unusual blend of warriors, women and men, who were fiercely dedicated to the queen. He could count on them for training others, fulfilling their duties promptly, standing firm in the face of danger, and, most importantly, for their loyalty to the crown.

A loud splash and angry shouts spun Currad's attention back to the ford. The wheel of a wagon had broken mid-river. The carriage slumped to the side, spilling some of its content. Two men had jumped into the knee-deep water and were quickly pulling wet items out of the water and handing them up to two other men on the wagon. *That will be a mess, causing delays across the ford,* Currad thought. He urged his horse forward, down the bank to the edge of the river. "Do you want help?" he called.

"No," the driver shouted. "We can do it." He was a large man, as were the two in the water and the one on the rear of the wagon reorganizing the load.

They look like they can handle it, Currad thought. There was another heavily laden wagon behind them; both were heading south. "Move your wagon out of the ford as quick as you can," Currad shouted to the men.

The driver frowned at him and waved that he understood.

Currad started to turn away when something caught his attention. One of the men in the river was lifting a long, thin shiny object out of the water. A sword? The soldier in Currad took command and pushed his horse into the river, trotting quickly to the wagon.

"What have you got there?" Currad demanded.

The man in the water looked up at Currad on the snorting horse. In the man's hand was a sword, sheathed in a metal scabbard, water still trickling down its length and dripping from the tip.

"Tha's mine," the driver said from the wagon's bench. "It slid inta th' water when th' wheel broke."

Looking into the muddy current at the man's feet, Currad could see glimpses of more metal objects. "How many swords do you own?"

The driver bristled. "There's no law against makin' and sellin' swords. It's part of our trade. Besides, we need 'em to protect ourselves an' goods from highway thieves."

Currad looked at the snarling driver. "I asked how many swords you own."

"Half dozen, maybe."

"Half dozen, maybe," Currad repeated. "Your wagon looks overloaded. What else are you carrying?"

"Who are you?" The man snapped. "You got no right ta inspec' our load."

Currad stiffened and his voice got louder. "I am Currad, the King's Honored Soldier and commander of the armies of Queen Ekala Oleen. And you, from the make of your wagon and your tongue, are from Toulon or, worse, Banyon."

"We gotta right ta trade in your country," the man atop the load said.

"That you do," Currad answered the big bearded man, "depending on what it is you're selling. Uncover the wagon's load so I can see it."

"It's nothin' more than blankets an' winter clothin'," the driver said.

"What's the hold-up!" shouted the driver from the wagon behind them.

Currad glanced that way and noticed two men on the driver's bench and two more on horseback riding alongside. Turning back to the driver he said, "You're holding up passage."

"We'll fix it an' move on ta Zinkila," the driver said, turning away from Currad.

"Uncover the load now," Currad demanded, "then replace your wheel."

The driver hesitated while the other men watched and waited nervously. One of the men standing in the river still held the sword he'd retrieved from the bottom. The other man stood by the broken wheel.

"I can ride up the hill to the fort there and have fifty soldiers here before you're across the ford," Currad said. "One way or another you will show me the contents of your wagon."

The driver shook his head with disgust. "See it if ya must," he said. Nodding to the other men, he motioned for them to uncover the wagon.

"Here, come look." the man on the rear of the wagon said and started pulling back the canvas.

As Currad moved his horse toward the rear of the wagon, he heard behind him the faint whisper of a metal blade slipping from its scabbard. He grabbed his sword and pulled it out as he turned to swing at the man in the water raising the wet sword. The other man on Currad's left jumped up on the side of the horse, grabbed hold of Currad's vest, and tried to pull him off. The horse, a veteran of many battles, quickly reacted, stepping sideways and smashing the man into the wagon, knocking the breath out of him until he let go and slumped into the water. Currad deflected the thrust of the man on his right, and then sliced his arm with a quick back swing.

The swordsman screamed and dropped away.

A sudden blow to his ribs almost knocked Currad from the saddle. The horse stepped with him and he righted himself as he looked to see the man on the wagon swinging a long pole. He tried to duck, but it caught him again; this time in the back, sending shock waves of pain through his body.

His horse began backing away from the wagon.

Now Currad saw two riders from the other wagon coming toward him in a splashing charge, their swords raised. He spurred the horse to cut to the side of one of the riders, but he couldn't lift the sword above his shoulder—the pain was too great. Switching the sword to his left hand just in time, he deflected a thrust and swiped back, catching the man with a glancing blow. His horse maneuvered deftly around and through the other horses as he battled the two swordsmen. These were not merchants nor common folk, Currad realized, but trained soldiers.

They knew how to fight.

Still, even though Currad was half-crippled and using his weaker arm, the two of them could not take him down. How long he would last was another matter. He stole glances toward the fort on the hill, hoping they would hear or see the fight and come to his aid. Each time, though, Currad was disappointed to see no one charging down the hill to his rescue. *How odd,* he thought, *that the fort being built to protect the kingdom would sit silent while I succumb alone in the ford.*

The two riders slashed and pushed relentlessly, not allowing him rest. In his exhaustion, Currad did not realize they had maneuvered him close to the wagon until he felt a blow in the back. He jolted upright in pain and then a great weight, a big body, fell on him, forcing him from the saddle into the water. The heavy body rolled over, smashing him into the sandy bottom. He twisted in the current of the river to get up, expecting horse hooves to step on him or a blade to stab him at any moment.

His body was in agony, his vision blurred.

His sword had been knocked from his hand, but the short blade was still on his side. Grasping it, Currad got to his knees, the river flowing against his stomach. Blinking and clearing his vision, he saw the big man lunging at him with a sword. Deflecting the blade with his arm and feeling it cut into his skin, he pushed into the man with his knife, feeling it go deep into his opponent's flesh before a blow to his head knocked him face down into the water. The last thing Currad remembered was hands grabbing him.

* * *

Veracitas, Captain Kali, and her force of Oleens had left the cold Stone Hills of Marbala after the stone cutter recovered from the strange spell that had struck him in the quarry. Led by the confident Kali, the wary soldiers followed her and their charge east on the muddy road that skirted the pungent Escat Marshes. Their horses were nervous as they camped as far from the edge of the marsh as they could. However, the flopping, splashing, croaking, and stench of the frogs kept the troops awake and on edge most of the night. The guards changed frequently until morning when they saddled up and hurried on, riding all day to get beyond the marshes before stopping at the Zinkila and South Ford crossroads. The intersection was busy with merchants and migrants traveling in all directions. They were pleased to greet the queen's troops, but disappointed Ekala Oleen was not with them. Still, the people were happy to meet the famous sculptor who had created the statue of the king that saved the kingdom from Metro. Rising early in the morning, the Oleens ate a light meal, mounted up, and took the road north to the Camotop River. A feeling of joy rode with them in their anticipation to reach Castle Ambermal before nightfall. There they could finally relax, replenish their supplies, be with family and friends, and visit Queen Ekala Oleen before continuing on to Ello.

The force had been traveling with and guarding Veracitas for five weeks; and in all that time, they had encountered only welcome and celebration for the sculptor of Stone Truth. Not once had anyone threatened him. Still, he was often troubled, restless, or moody—staring for long periods of time in silence. However, after his awakening at Marbala he had changed. As they approached the busy South Ford, Veracitas brightened, smiling at Kali riding beside him.

"It won't be long now," the tall sinewy man declared. "We'll be at Ambermal tonight."

Kali smiled back at him. "I'm glad to see your mood has changed."

"What do you mean?"

"I've been worried about you."

"Why?"

"Ever since Ello, when the stone broke, you've been confused, unsure of yourself. You haven't been the same man I know."

Veracitas reached over and grasped her arm. "I'm better now. I know what I have to do. And I know that it involves you."

"I hope so," Kali replied. "You know, I'm not here just because Oleen ordered us to protect you."

"Yes, I know. And I hope you know how I feel about you."

Kali suddenly remembered they weren't alone. Glancing back, she saw the first several rows of Oleens watching them.

"It will be good to be at Ambermal tonight," she said loudly. "I'm looking forward to seeing Oleen, as well as Boschina."

Veracitas smiled and withdrew his hand. "Yes, I don't get to be with my daughter very often." He looked down the road. Beyond, a wagon and some people pulled small carts. "She has become so...independent," he said thoughtfully.

"Isn't that how you raised her? To be strong and choose her own road."

Veracitas nodded. "Yes. I just didn't expect her to grow up and take a different road than mine."

"Fathers," Kali replied. "You can't hang onto your little girl forever."

"No, I can't. But I can still worry about her."

"I bet she worries about you more than you worry about her."

"I don't know about that," Veracitas replied. "I'll have to ask her. I do miss her working with me. What about your father? He left long ago, when you were young, didn't he? Do you still miss him?"

"What do you think?"

"I think," he said turning to Kali, "that I'm looking forward to Culinary's food."

Kali laughed. "What? You don't like our road fare?"

Before Veracitas could answer, Kali perked her head up, listening. The distinctive sound of metal striking metal was faint in the wind.

"What is it?" Veracitas asked.

"I hear swords," she replied and stood in the stirrups to look ahead. "There's a fight at the ford!" She spurred her horse into a gallop, dodging pedestrians and veering off the road for the river.

Robon, Veracitas' horse, bolted after her and the Oleens followed. Pounding down to the water, Veracitas saw his friend Currad in the middle of the river, leaning awkwardly on his horse as he battled with two swordsmen, their horses splashing, kicking up water. Two bodies floated in the current. And then a man leapt off a wagon, knocking Currad into the river. They rose out of the water, the man swinging a sword and Currad lunging into him.

Veracitas charged forward and jumped from Robon onto the man, striking him with both feet as he came down. The man grunted in pain and rolled over in the water. The two swordsmen on horseback started for Veracitas, but Kali and the first line of Oleens slammed into the men, knocking them back—cutting one and pounding the other into submission. The driver, still on the wagon, swung a sword wildly as he tried to slash Kali. Two Oleen arrows thumped into his chest and he flipped backward onto the wagon.

Currad was floating face down, the current pulling him downstream. Veracitas splashed after him, grasping at his collar and pulling his head up. Then Kali was there with two other Oleens, grabbing Currad's legs and arms and lifting him from the water. They carried Currad onto shore. He wasn't breathing. Blood streaked his face as water drained from his hair. Veracitas rolled the big soldier onto his stomach and pressed his torso.

"Breathe, Currad, breathe!"

The driver and guard of the second wagon jumped onto horses and were galloping out of the ford, south toward Zinkila.

"After them," Kali ordered. "Bring them back alive!"

Four Oleens charged after the two men.

"Hold those wagons," Captain Kali shouted to her troops. "Nobody crosses the ford."

"Come on, breathe," Veracitas demanded as he pumped on Currad. "This is not how you leave us."

"This can't be," Kali whispered, looking over Veracitas as he worked on the King's Honored Soldier. "This can't be."

"You didn't save me to die this way," the stone cutter hissed through his gritted teeth as he rolled Currad onto his side.

Finally, Currad choked and water spurt from his mouth. He took short breaths while the river gurgled out of him. Veracitas kept rubbing his back as Currad slowly returned to life.

Captain Kali straightened and looked around. Her soldiers had the two surviving men on the bank with rope tied around their feet, hands, and neck. The bodies of the other men were half out of the water on the shore; the river tugged at their legs, wanting them back.

"What happened here?" Kali said. "What did Currad get into?" She swung up onto her horse and plodded through the water to the wagon with the broken wheel. Climbing onto the back of it, she rolled the driver's body into the river and pulled away the cover to find layers of swords wrapped in canvas between blankets. Grabbing a handle, she pulled out a blade and examined it. It was rather cheaply made, she thought, and not very sharp. But what caught her eye was an emblem engraved in the steel at the hilt—a serpentine "S" with cross-hatches in the middle.

Chapter Seventeen
Ekala's Awakening

Ekala, Maz, Camp, and the three Oleen soldiers were sprawled on the leafy ground where the Kairtaykars had placed them under the first row of trees in the grove. The horses, including Dallion and Shadahn, were standing dopily nearby. Radise, who had not been under the spell, waited patiently alongside Thunder and Boschina. Bubo sat next to the sleeping Boschina on Thunder's broad shell, his eyes watching the open plain beyond the trees. Thalmus sat with his back leaning against a tree trunk as he, too, looked out over the plain, calmly waiting for the next step in their journey. In his breast pocket, Larma's message beat softly against his chest. He stood and stepped out from beneath the trees, showing himself to the high clouds drifting overhead on a light breeze. He felt the gentle wind on his face and knew it was friendly; that it was not the malicious wind driven by a devious force, like Metro. Thalmus studied the darkening clouds and listened to their banter about where they had been and what they had seen: desperate people with their belongings trudging toward the North Ford, the Toulon army making an encampment near the ford and patrolling the river and woods, and Glasrauss and his troops riding hither across the plain. Thalmus felt the clouds waiting, listening for him. He slowly spread his arms with his palms turned up. "They are with me," he said softly. "I will bring them back." The hunter paused, inhaled deeply, and slowly exhaled. "Prepare the way."

Pushed by the wind, the clouds continued to roll, puff, and thin––and then tumble together again, moving south toward Table Top and the woman waiting to hear Thalmus' message.

Boschina's eyes blinked, opened, closed, and then opened again. She lifted a hand and carefully rubbed her face. She grimaced, held her hand above her head, stared at it, and wiggled her fingers. Radise nudged her. Boschina felt the wet nose on her cheek and pushed her palm against the horse's nostrils. "Lady." She smiled as she stroked the mare's nose.

Bubo watched Boschina with interest. Then his head swiveled to look at Thalmus beyond the trees, talking to the clouds. The Great Horned owl's head swiveled back to Boschina. "Whoo – whooo!"

"Bubo?"

Boschina rolled over, groaned, and sat up. She gently touched her side and then her head. "Oh Bubo, I'm sore; my body aches." She scooted off Thunder, stood up, and then leaned against him.

Thunder grunted. He was standing guard over the Queen's head. Ekala Oleen blinked and stared into the woods. She twisted to her side and looked up at Thunder's big head and black eyes. She rubbed her own eyes and looked again. "Thunder? Thunder, where am I?"

The giant tortoise clicked his jaws as Maz lifted his head off the damp leaves. "Wha...uh," he muttered, resting his head back on the leaves and staring up at the branches, trying to focus his sight. Camp suddenly tried to sit up, but he was dazed and unbalanced. His head rolled like a pumpkin and he flopped over onto the ground. The old warrior felt for his sword that was not on his side. Confused, he began to look for it while blinking and shading his eyes.

Then the three Oleen warriors—Lander, Karl, and Ricken—came to life, groggily looking about and trying to stand, before stumbling and dropping down or settling to their knees.

"Where's my bow?" Lander mumbled.

"Do not stand up," Thalmus said, walking toward them. "Stay seated until your minds clear and your senses become your own again." He patted Dallion's shoulder and stroked his neck. The big Paint nickered and nuzzled into Thalmus' chest.

Ekala Oleen turned to see Thalmus for the first time. "Thalmus?" She looked at the others and then tried to focus on Thalmus. "What…where…what happened?"

"You are returning from the roots of the Woods of Rows."

Ekala looked at her fingers, rubbed her hands, and felt her boot-covered feet. "What strange tingling under my skin."

"You were all in danger of drifting away," Thalmus said, stepping away from Dallion and standing beside Thunder. "Another day or two and you would have been gone. You would have become part of this grove."

"You mean dead?" Ekala stammered.

"Not dead, just a different form of living. Your life would have been calm and sedate, as you slowly grew into mature trees." Thalmus paused. "Now you must face the consequences of your actions."

Maz slowly sat up, rubbing his eyes. "I remember chasing the raiders into the trees," he said groggily, "and fighting through the rows in the dark, and then…nothing."

"And I followed you here, only to become confused," Ekala said, rising to her knees and rubbing her arms and hands, trying to bring warmth to them. "I thought I saw you and Camp. We chased after you, and those raiders, around and around, deeper into the rows until…until we were lost…and then darkness."

Boschina moved closer to Ekala. "And I thought you called me. Thalmus was looking for Dallion and I saw you in the distance, waving. I followed through the trees, trying to find you. Then night came and the hands grabbed me."

Ekala grasped Boschina's hand. "My sister, you came to rescue me." She blinked and squinted, looking at Boschina's scraped and bruised face. "What happened to you?"

"I got beat up and fell out of a tree."

"What? Who beat you?"

"The Kairtaykars. They tried to nab me like they did you."

"Kairtaykars? I'm confused," Ekala said and glanced around at the Rows. "What is this place?"

"You trespassed into the realm and fell under the spell of Arborina, the goddess of trees," Thalmus said. He looked at Prince Bolimaz. "You could not have made a worse decision. Surely, you knew this was a place to be avoided."

Maz rubbed his head. "We gave chase in the dark. I was intent on catching the scoundrels. I didn't realize we were in the Woods of Rows until it was too late. What happened to the raiders?"

"They are still under her spell. A few are already fodder of the grove."

"Can we find out who they are?"

Thalmus shook his head. "We must return to Ameram as soon as you all are recovered enough to travel."

"No," Maz said. "Camp and I must fight to save my country."

"That is your choice, Prince Bolimaz," Thalmus replied. "Ekala Oleen, however, is needed in *her* kingdom."

The queen's head rolled up to gaze at Thalmus. "Maz fought with me to save our kingdom. I must help him fight to save his."

Thalmus saw the power between the two and felt the intensity of their devotion. He also knew their thinking was muddled—that they were still under the spell of the Rows. He glanced at Bubo, who puffed and chortled. "The time is coming to redeem Toulon, but that time is not now," Thalmus told them. "You have seen the weapons and contraband at the North Ford?"

"Of course, my Oleens are watching it," Ekala replied.

"That is not enough, Ekala. Outside forces are threatening; but more so, you must prepare for an uprising in your own land."

"An uprising," Ekala questioned. "How do you know this?"

Thalmus reached into his pocket, removed Larma's message, and offered it to her. Ekala stared at the cloth, felt its rhythm, and knew immediately who it was from. Boschina watched her lift it from Thalmus' hand and her reaction to its weight. Unfolding the cloth,

Ekala saw the printing, but could not read the words; however, she understood the message, as it spoke to her. It slapped her cold in the face—treachery, betrayal, and merciless evil.

Queen Ekala Oleen carefully folded the cloth and held it out to Thalmus, who took it with both hands and returned it to his vest pocket.

Standing beside Thunder, Thalmus said, "We were sent to find you, bring you back, and to fight at your side."

Dallion raised his head, whinnied, and stomped.

Ekala grasped Maz's hand. "I'm sorry, Maz. I must get back."

"Of course," the crown prince of Toulon said. "There is no doubt. I would do the same."

Boschina had not been under Arborina's spell; she was bruised, sore, and tired, but not muddled like the others. She had been watching, listening, and learning Arborina's meaning, as well as the power of Larma's message and the importance of their mission. It was not just to find the queen and keep her safe from enemies, but to save their country. She wondered what she could do and what would come next. "Thalmus, you said we have to face the consequences of our actions. What does that mean?"

Thalmus turned to Camp and the Oleens. "The weapons are there by that second tree. Can you gather them? I am sure they will be needed soon."

Camp, Lander, Karl, and Ricken rose slowly and meandered to the pile of swords, bows, and arrows.

When the group walked away, Thalmus returned his attention to Boschina. "In this case, Boschina, it means that due to certain people's actions, we and the Queen of Ameram, are in a dangerous place, far from home, and far from a safe way to return home."

Ekala carefully stood up. "I realize what I've done. I was foolish, but I did it to help Maz. And without the knowledge of that message," she said pointing at Thalmus' chest, "I would probably do it again." She turned and helped the prince to his feet.

Thalmus smiled. That was the Ekala he knew: strong and determined, but still a bit reckless.

"Alright," the queen said. "I'm ready to head back."

"It is not that simple," Thalmus replied. "Lord Glasrauss and his soldiers are patrolling this region looking for you two. The Toulon army is setting up a camp on the road to the North Ford. We will have to find another way to, and across, the Sol Linden River—and we have little time to delay."

"Did you say *Glasrauss?*" Camp said, returning with their weapons and handing Maz his sword. "It's him and his family who are after the throne. He convinced the prince's brothers to turn against Maz. Glasrauss' army hunted us, determined to capture the prince, but we escaped to Table Top. That man's a cutthroat."

"How could he know we're here?" Maz asked.

"He does not know you are here in the Woods," Thalmus replied. "But he knows you have crossed the border."

"How could that be?"

"You were recognized at the ford. Those night raiders were sent to draw you across the river and into Toulon to be captured. Their mistake was entering the Woods of Rows."

"Must have been someone at the refugee camp that reported you," Ekala said.

"I don't want to believe that," Maz said. "Those people need me."

"They're also desperate," Ekala replied. "And willing to take food or money to spy for Glasrauss."

"Does Glasrauss know Ekala is here too?" Boschina asked.

"He knows some Oleens followed after the prince. When I spoke with him two days gone, he did not know who. By now, he may have gotten your name from his spies. You were fortunate, Ekala, not to run into him before reaching the Rows."

"We've got to get you back before Glasrauss finds us," Maz said to Ekala. "Camp and I know a route. It's not easy; it's through the Wilderness. Unfortunately, the first leg's across that plain."

"We have fast horses," Ekala said. "If they see us, we can outrun them to the other side."

Thalmus leaned against Thunder's shell. He could see that Ekala and Maz were not thinking clearly. They were still muddled by the spell. "That would expose you too soon. The way to the ford is blocked by the Toulon army. You would be trapped and hunted in the wilderness."

"We could cross the plain at night," Camp said. "At least then they can't see us in the open."

"That is not a wise choice," Thalmus replied. "Ekala and Boschina are being hunted by the night beasts. Out in the open, in the dark, they could be easy prey."

"Night beasts?" Ekala questioned.

"Chorgens," Boschina blurted. "The beast tried to get me on the trail to the Great Water and then again on the way to the ford."

"That must be the animal that came into our camp at the ford," Ekala said. "It got close to me with no one hearing or seeing it." She straightened her shoulders and let out a sigh. "What would have happened to me if Bubo had not been there?"

"They are quiet, quick, and tireless killers," Thalmus said.

"Well, I'm glad Bubo was watching over me. Thank you, Bubo."

Bubo chortled and bobbed his head.

No one spoke as they each considered their situation and what to do next. Ekala Oleen studied Thalmus as he pet Thunder's head. She glanced at Boschina, who was also watching Thalmus. Bubo's head was turned, watching the plain. Dallion paced, as if he knew they were about to move. "Thalmus, you know another way, don't you?"

"I do, your Majesty."

"Well, are you going to tell us?"

Thalmus smiled. "We will travel east, staying on the edge of the grove. Glasrauss is afraid to come in here, so we are safe to a point where a drainage gully crosses the plain. It is just deep enough to hide in. You all will enter that trough and quietly follow it to its end—at the Wilderness. Wait for us there, just inside the cover of the forest."

"Where are you going?" Ekala asked.

Thalmus patted Thunder's shell. "We are too slow to keep up with you. We will go across the open plain to draw attention away from you."

Ekala bristled. "Thalmus, no—"

Thalmus interrupted her. "Your Majesty, I appreciate your concern. Lord Glasrauss is no threat to me. He will confront me, I am sure of that, and that is what we want: that he be so worried about what I am doing, that you and Maz will slip through his grasp."

"He is unpredictable, Thalmus," Maz said. "He may take you just out of spite."

"No, Prince Bolimaz. He may harass me, but he does not have the strength to capture or kill me. Now, let us get started. We still have some daylight left. Stay well back of the first line of trees; if anyone appears on the plain, move back another row."

Dallion snorted and shook his head.

Radise answered with a whinny, nodding her head.

"Yes, alright, Dal," Thalmus said to the stallion and turned to the others. "We will walk the horses until their senses have fully returned."

"What about the Kairtaykars?" Boschina asked.

"They will not bother us as long as we do not go deep into the grove."

"I'll take point, if you wish, Oleen," Lander said, grabbing the reins of her horse in one hand and her bow in the other.

"Yes, keep a sharp eye," Queen Ekala Oleen said.

Bubo spread his wide wings and lifted off Thunder, flapping just a few times to fly under the branches and out onto the plain, where he rose into the sky.

"Thunder and I will follow as the rear guard," Thalmus said.

Ekala put her hand on his arm, "I can't tell you how glad I am that you're here. Thank you, Thalmus."

Thalmus nodded. "At your service, Your Majesty."

Ekala gave him a disgusted look. "Stop it." Then turning to Boschina, she said, "Walk with me and Maz and tell us about this Chorgen."

Chapter Eighteen
The Gulley

At dusk, the column of weary horses and humans gathered into the second row of trees where they could not be seen from the plain. There, they ate a supper of vegetables from the Kairtaykar's garden: carrots, chard, broccoli, tomatoes and beans, and a dessert of cherries and apples.

"I'd sure like some meat," Camp commented.

"You will not get that here," Thalmus replied. "Perhaps you can kill something in the Wilderness."

Camp grunted. "Oh, we'll have to kill something in the Wilderness. You can count on it."

Fires for warmth or cooking were not allowed for fear of revealing themselves to the searchers on the plain. Guards were posted. Conversations were kept quiet as they milled around trying to get comfortable for the night. All but Thalmus and Boschina were still trying to shake the influence of the spell they had been under. The constant aroma from the trees continued to muddle their senses, preventing clarity from returning to their minds and bodies. More than that, the fear of being pulled back into that unconscious abyss from which they may not return kept them awake.

"I can't sleep," Boschina whispered. "I'm afraid the Kairtaykars will come back."

"I'm not ready to trust them either," Ekala said. "A goddess that wants to turn me into a tree? Have you ever heard of such a thing?"

"Do not worry about them," Thalmus said, pulling his blanket from the pack on the giant shell creature. "They are watching, but they will not bother us." He glanced around at the overhanging branches. "It may take a few days after we leave here for your minds to be free of the scent and spell of Arborina's world."

"What about the Chorgens?" Boschina asked.

"The Woods of Rows is one of the few places the Chorgens will not enter. The power of Arborina's message is too strong and the endless uniformity of the trees is confusing for them. Besides, we have our Oleen guards, Thunder is right here, and Bubo is watching and listening." Thalmus tilted his head back and called to his friend. "Who– whooo."

From the darkness came the deep-throated response, "Whoo–who-who–whooo."

The hunter smiled as he spread his blanket on the ground and rolled up in it. "I am going to sleep now; tomorrow will be a long day."

The Stone Cutter's Daughter, prince, queen, and the wary soldiers watched Thalmus for a moment, wrapped in his cover like a cocoon, falling into sleep as if he had no worries in the world. They glanced around at the straight rows of trees fading into the darkness, and then at each other before slowly settling into their own blankets; all the while, they hoped for a restful night—with swords and bows held close by their sides.

Ekala settled near Boschina and Thunder with Maz on the other side. The close proximity of the giant shell creature and the owl made her feel secure. She knew they could sense danger, even in their sleep, and were a threat to any attacker. She relaxed and drifted into sleep that quickly turned to confusing dreams and frightful images. Faces hidden by darkness, sword-wielding soldiers, archers flinging arrows at her, branches and leaves slapping her face, people running, horses stomping and snorting, blood dripping from the trees, and Maz—the only face she could see—waving to her to follow him.

When Ekala awoke, the morning light filtered through the leaf canopy. Lander knelt by a tree on the outer row, her bow in her hand and her eyes on the brightening plain. Camp knelt by an inner tree with his sword ready as he looked into the woods. Shadahn and the other horses waited calmly, flipping their tails, brushing away flies. Dallion was gone; so was Thalmus.

Queen Ekala Oleen stood up, rubbing the back of her head. "Where's Thalmus?" she asked Lander.

"He and Dallion left before sunrise—said he was scouting ahead."

"Did Bubo go with him?"

"Haven't heard a peep from Owl," Camp replied.

Ekala looked through the trees to the open ground beyond. "See anybody or anything on the plain?"

Lander shook her head. "It's as still as a frog pond."

Ekala shuddered. "Until one breaks the surface and its tongue snaps you into its jaws," she said, remembering the frog that almost ate her.

Lander glanced at her. "Bad memory?"

"Could have been my end, but Boschina saved me."

"Boschina? It's a good thing she was there," Lander said and returned her gaze to the plain.

Maz stood up and stretched. "I feel like I'm still sleeping."

"Don't let Thalmus hear that," Boschina said, handing him a carrot. "Have some breakfast."

Looking at the carrot, Maz sneezed and then rubbed the back of his neck. "I feel lousy." He tossed the carrot back to Boschina. "We've got to get out of here today."

Ekala slowly rolled up her blanket. "We better get the horses packed and be ready to move when Thalmus gets back."

"We're ready, except you and Maz," Boschina replied.

Ekala chuckled. "Alright, sister, one of the few times you've risen before me. I guess I'm still under *her* influence."

Hooves pounded in the grove and they turned to see Dallion galloping toward them between the rows of trees. Thalmus rode tight on Dallion's shoulders, leaning forward and low against his neck. The big Paint slowed to a stop as the other horses neighed and threw their heads. Thalmus smiled and slid down from Dallion's back.

"Glad to see you are all up and ready. It is time to go. Your escape route is close." He paused, looking at Ekala. "You look tired." He stepped closer, staring into her eyes. "You are still blurred. And Maz, you look the same."

"We'll be all right," Maz said. "We just woke."

"I just need some action to snap me out of this," Ekala said.

"You may get it, if you are not alert today," Thalmus replied. "This is where we part. Thunder, Dallion, and I will leave from here to cross the plain. The rest of you ride ahead and get into the gully. Once you are in it, move quickly but quietly, no galloping—it can be heard on the plain. You may have to dismount and walk in places where it is too shallow. The sides are sloped, so you can get out if you have to. The deep center might be muddy, as it is drainage for the Toulon Wilderness. When you get across, wait for us there in the cover of that forest."

"How long will it take to get to the Wilderness?" Boschina asked.

"You should be across by noon. Keep a sharp eye, not just toward me, but in all directions—especially eastward. Lander, Karl, and Ricken, have your bows ready."

"What if we're discovered?" Boschina asked.

"Then we ride as fast as we can to that awful forest," Maz said. "At least we can hide there."

Thalmus studied the prince before turning to Queen Ekala Oleen. "Do not be too eager to abandon the cover of the gully." He paused and looked again at Prince Bolimaz. "The Wilderness will give us little comfort, as you know. But traveling in another direction will only complicate our escape and delay the queen's return to Ameram."

Prince Bolimaz nodded. "I know the Wilderness will not be easy. I just want to get us across this open ground."

"Then let's go," Ekala said, patting Maz on the shoulder and moving to Shadahn. "Be careful, Thalmus. We'll see you on the other side."

"Don't worry about us," Bolimaz said to Thalmus. "You just watch out for Glasrauss," he added as he climbed onto Mendu.

Thalmus recognized the handle of a sword sticking out of a leather case strapped onto the horse's saddlebags. It was Corsair's blade. *Why is the prince carrying the sword that almost killed him?* Thalmus wondered.

Lander led off with Ricken, followed by Ekala and Maz, and then Camp and Karl guarding the rear. Boschina held back as the others rode away. She stroked Thunder's head. "Take care of Thalmus," she told him. The giant tortoise clicked his jaws and pushed into her.

"How are you feeling, Boschina?" Thalmus asked, looking at the scabs, scrapes and bruises on her head.

"I'm better today, but I still hurt."

"Of course, you do. You had quite a fight. Ekala needs you now. You were not under the spell like the others. Despite how you look and feel, your mind is clear, but their's are not. Keep an eye on them. They may be prone to bad decisions. Speak up—be strong for them. Can you do that?"

"I will, Thalmus."

Radise neighed and rubbed Boschina's shoulder with her nose. "I know, Lady, we need to go." She swung up onto her horse's back.

Thalmus stroked Radise's shoulder. "Take care of her, Radise."

Radise bobbed her head and then turned to follow the others.

Thalmus was watching them fade between the rows of trees when Thunder snapped a warning and turned his head to look into the grove. A voice from the trees whispered, "Good fortune be with you, Hunter." At first, Thalmus saw only the hazy lines of trees and the quiet dark canopy of branches and leaves, and then a tree trunk moved and the pearl-eyed woman appeared. She smiled at him. He felt her saying goodbye. Then her face frowned. She did not speak, but he heard her voice. "Beware, Hunter, one in your party cannot be trusted."

Surprised, Thalmus waited for more, a name perhaps. When nothing came but the stare of her eyes, he asked, "How do you know this? And of whom do you speak?"

The woman slowly shook her head. "There is one whose heart is confused." She raised an open hand toward him. "Beware." Then the pearl-eyed woman stepped back and disappeared into the Woods of Rows.

Thalmus turned and looked after his friends, who had disappeared into the distance.

Which one could possibly be a traitor? Should he believe the warning from Arborina? Should he go after them, stay with Ekala and Boschina? He patted Thunder's shell. "What do you think?"

The giant shell creature blinked, grunted, and started trudging through the last row of trees and out onto the plain. "I guess you do not believe her," Thalmus said. Dallion blew his nose with a rolling snort and followed Thunder. He was glad to be leaving the perfume and confines of the grove for the open terrain. The hunter took one last look at the trees before stepping out into the open under the passing clouds. The Toulon Wilderness looked small and far away. A pair of large brown birds flew crossing patterns in and out of the clouds across the open ground. Thalmus recognized them as Alton hawks, the largest and deadliest raptors in Toulon. "That is not a good sign," he said to himself.

* * *

The narrow, shallow trough, which Thalmus called the gully, snaked across the flat plain like a rut made from the weight of a monstrous wagon wheel. It was obvious to the searchers as soon as they saw the sinking mouth at the edge of the trees. Lander waited for Ekala's approval and then led the group into the depression. The lowest point in the center was soft and muddy, but riding on firmer ground along the sloping sides exposed their heads and shoulders to searching eyes on the plain. The horses plopped through the muck while their riders nervously watched the higher ground to their left and right.

"This is slow going," Maz grumbled. "I'd rather race across and be done with it."

"We're moving as slow as Thunder," Ekala said. "I feel trapped in here. I can't see if anyone's approaching."

"That's good, right? If we can't see anyone, no one can see us," Boschina said.

Maz turned to Ekala. "It'll take us all day at this pace."

"Lander," Ekala called.

The archer turned immediately to look back at her, "Yes, Oleen?"

"Move faster."

Lander nodded. "As you wish," and urged her horse into a trot.

"Not too fast," Boschina warned. "Remember what Thalmus said about being heard on the plain."

"He also said to not waste time," Ekala replied. "Why don't you and Radise take a peek over the top once in a while? Let us know if anyone is approaching."

"That's risky," Boschina replied.

"I'd rather take that chance than be caught by surprise. Go ahead, just be careful."

Radise stepped carefully up the side of the gully until Boschina's head was just below the top. "Enough, go straight," she instructed the horse. Then Boschina rose in the saddle, scanned the grassy terrain in all directions, and then sat down. "All clear," she reported.

"Can you see Thalmus?" Ekala asked.

Boschina rose again and searched the western ground. "Yes, they're far off, almost beyond sight."

The horses' trotting hooves splattered mud onto the legs and bodies of animals and humans alike. Smelling of decayed plants and stagnant water, the muck was slimy and sticky. Only Radise and Boschina were clear of it as they rode on the side slope.

"Spread apart!" Ekala called. "Get more space between us."

The riders spread out, lengthening the distance between one another. Still, their individual horses kicked up enough mud to continue the splattering mess. The normally steady steeds did not like the sloppy feel and smell of the trench. They snorted and pulled at their reins, wanting to be free from the muddy path. It wasn't long before each rider began edging up the slopes to avoid the slop. As each successive horse followed in the slippery tracks, they began to rise farther, exposing their heads and shoulders.

"Stay down!" Boschina called. "Camp, I can see you bobbing above the plain."

"Do you see anybody?" Ekala said.

"No," Boschina answered, her head swiveling and her eyes searching.

"Then why stay down here?" Maz grumbled and guided Mendu up the slope to take a look for himself. "There's nobody in sight."

Ekala rode up on the other side near Boschina. Lander was so far ahead that she had disappeared around a curve.

"This is much better," Ekala said.

"We should stay down," Boschina said to her. "Like Thalmus said."

"You weren't riding in that muck down there. Look how clean you are compared to me."

"But we could be seen."

"We'll drop down as soon as we see someone."

"What if they see us first?"

"We're only half-exposed," Maz said. "We'll see them first. Just keep a steady watch."

"There could be someone hiding out there that we can't see," Boschina replied. "That's why Thalmus said for us to stay down."

"Calm yourself," Ekala answered. "We're alright. We have as good or better eyes than anyone looking for us."

Boschina shook her head, frustrated. "We should at least slow to a trot. The horses are making a lot of noise."

"Stop it, Boschina," Ekala snapped. "We're doing fine. You just watch the plain."

"Boschina's right," Camp spoke up. "We don't know who's out there. I'm sure Thalmus had a reason for telling us to stay low."

"You can ride in that muck, if you want. I'm not," Maz replied.

"We don't have to stay in the center. Just a little off it and we'll still be below the top," Camp continued.

"I want to see where I'm going," Maz replied.

"We know where we're going," Camp answered. "To that awful forest. If staying down in this trench means we'll get there without a fight, then I'm for it—and you should be too. You know Glasrauss is out there looking for you." He guided his horse lower on the bank.

"Please, Ekala, for your safety, and Maz's, let's drop down," Boschina pleaded. "I'll ride with you."

Ekala glared at Boschina for a moment, and then said, "Alright, for a little while." She patted Shadahn. "We can't run yet, Girl." She guided her horse lower as Boschina and Radise followed.

"Maz," Ekala called to the prince, "drop down with us."

Maz shook his head with frustration, but led Mendu back down the slope.

Bouncing along the sides of the gully, not one of them noticed the hawks drifting high overhead, soaring on the wind just below the clouds. The raptors' sharp eyes followed them, judging their sizes, number, and speed as they circled, around and around, sending a signal. The birds had already seen the hunter with the giant shell creature and the striking brown and white horse walking on the plain. And now, they had found his friends—the ones they had been sent to find. The birds separated, wings beating faster; one flew west toward the ford and the other northeast.

Chapter Nineteen
Betrayal

Thunder clicked his jaws and turned to look at Thalmus. The hunter knew what he was signaling. The shell creature heard and felt a distant vibration—a stressful pounding of hooves on the earth. Thalmus climbed onto Thunder's shell and looked toward the gully. He scanned the flat plain and was relieved he could not see his friends. They were staying low as he had asked. He wondered if Boschina was the reason for that. Cupping his hands around his ears, he listened for unnatural sounds.

There was only the wind, blowing gently in his face.

Inhaling deeply, he searched for any presence of danger, any hint of an odor that could be a warning. Yes, yes, there was: wet horsehair, decayed plants, and the odd scent of feathers, not Bubo's aroma, but a stench caked with death. However, the wide terrain in front of him appeared deserted. Then he noticed the hawks were back, silhouetted high against the clouds. Circling in ever-wider rings, they moved gradually toward the Wilderness as they followed something on the ground.

"The Altons are marking Ekala," he said. "They must belong to Glasrauss."

Dallion threw his head and whinnied. Thunder clicked his jaws again. Thalmus returned his gaze to the plain. To the west, riders had appeared from the direction of the ford, galloping along the edge of the Wilderness, heading toward the end of the trench where it met the forest. Far to the northeast, beyond the thick foliage of the Woods of Rows, he saw more mounted troops turning at an angle to cross the plain, their flag snapping above the front riders. Both columns of soldiers were aimed to converge under the hawks.

"We must hurry," Thalmus said, jumping off Thunder's back. "We are not fooling anyone at this pace." He turned to the big Paint. "Dal, warn the queen." Then he pointed at the troops riding from the west. "And slow those troops until we join her."

Dallion threw his head and bolted into a full gallop toward the gully. Thunder began driving his thick legs forward as fast as he could move.

"We are heading for a clash," Thalmus said, running beside the thumping feet of Thunder. The giant shell creature did not need to be told, he could feel the tension in the air and understood the dire need to join their friends as quickly as possible.

* * *

Shadahn and Radise dutifully plopped along the slimy bank on one side of the gully while Mendu and Camp's horse traversed the other side as their masters and mistresses slumped on their backs. Tired and settling into a rhythm with the motion of the horses, they relaxed, giving themselves up to the long ride. No one had raised up to peek over the edge to check on their progress or to see if anyone was on the plain. They had become mesmerized in the sunken drainage trench: focused on staying low, being quiet, and finally losing track of time and distance all together.

Ekala rubbed her neck, trying to remember what had happened in the Woods, how she had become confused in the fading light. She recalled a fight with faceless soldiers, back and forth through the dark rows of trees: horses charging, swords clashing, hands nocking arrows, fingers pulling bowstrings, and arrows zipping. Maz stepped behind a tree, a blow to the back of her head, and then nothing until waking to see Thunder standing over her. *I was knocked out,* she thought.

"We must be getting close by now," Maz said wearily.

Ekala looked at him as if waking from a dream. *Were you hiding?*

"We've been riding for a long time," he said.

"It has been a while," Boschina said, stretching her back.

Ekala rubbed her neck and glanced back at Ricken and Karl strung out behind them, and then ahead again looking for Lander, who they had not seen for some time. "This ditch curves too much. I can't tell how far we've gone or how close we are to the Wilderness."

"Maybe we'll see it around the next bend," Boschina said.

Camp looked over. "I'll ride ahead, find Lander, and see how far we have to go."

"I suppose so," Ekala replied. "At least find out where we are."

"I don't think that's a good idea," Boschina said. "We should stay together."

Suddenly, they heard a thudding rumble behind them. Turning in alarm, Boschina and the Oleens pulled up their bows and nocked arrows; Ekala, Maz, and Camp drew their swords. They waited anxiously, looking up at the crest.

Dallion appeared on the rim.

"It's Dallion," Boschina shouted.

He turned and galloped along the edge until he caught up with them. That's when he reared, thrashing the air with his front hooves and snorting a warning that sent a chill through them. His hooves landed on the ground and he charged down into the gully, ran between them, and raced ahead—gathering them up with him as if they had been waiting to be awakened. The horses reacted, chasing after him; their riders held on.

"Thalmus must have sent him," Boschina yelled.

"We must have been seen," Maz shouted.

"Where's Thalmus?" Ekala asked. She turned Shadahn up the bank to the brink. "I see him heading our way with Thunder." Her head swiveled, looking over the plain. "Troops coming up behind us," she shouted, "and more on our right."

"How did they know where to find us?" Boschina asked as Radise ran up alongside Shadahn.

Dallion was well ahead of them and was now out of the ditch running with long gliding strides toward the column of troops approaching from the west. They saw the Wilderness of Toulon growing larger before them, but could they reach the forest before the troops overtook them? Either one of the long columns of Toulon soldiers would overwhelm their small number. Their only chance was to beat both of them to the cover of the forest.

Ekala glanced back over her shoulder, counting the riders and judging their speed. *Our horses are faster. We can outrun them,* she thought confidently. Turning to the front, disappointment struck her as she realized the other column coming from the west was much closer and would be waiting for them at the Wilderness—unless Dallion delayed them.

The big Paint was blazing toward the line of soldiers like a battering ram.

"Knock 'em down, Dal," Ekala hollered and turned to look for Thalmus.

Despite his effort, Thunder could not keep up the pace of a long run. It was beyond his physical ability: he was a plodder, not a sprinter. The giant shell creature was slowing and Thalmus did the same to stay alongside him. They would not reach the Wilderness in time to beat the troops.

Ekala realized that immediately. The excitement of the chase was clearing her mind of Arborina's spell. Her ability to discern, judge, and decide had returned. She was filled with the flush of confidence. "Ride to Thalmus," she called to the others. "They're not going to make it!"

This was a decision with which Boschina could not disagree. Leaving Thalmus and Thunder to face the enemy alone was not an option. She turned Radise. "Go, Lady!"

Maz hesitated, looking toward Thalmus, and then at the troops along the edge of the Wilderness and the ones coming from behind, before Camp rode past him after Boschina. Maz turned Mendu to follow. Ricken and Karl waited for Ekala, who was stopped, looking for Lander.

"Find Lander," she told them. "And ride to us as soon as you can."

"We can't leave you, Oleen," Karl said.

"We gave our word to protect you," Ricken said.

"And I can't leave Lander out here by herself. You go get her—now."

"As you wish," they replied and galloped toward where the gully met the Wilderness.

Thalmus saw Boschina and the others riding toward him. It was not what he wanted. He preferred they find protection in the tangle of the forest. Still, he appreciated their concern for him and Thunder. This is how it should be: the power of their fellowship, as it had done before, would stand against the tide of the soldiers bearing down on them.

In the distance, he saw Dallion gallop into the path of the mounted soldiers and their long, neat line suddenly turn into a scramble of rearing, bolting horses with men ranting and fighting for control. The Paint stallion circled round and round as the men tried to shoot arrows at him, while their horses bucked and jerked trying to chase after Dallion.

"Careful, Dal," Thalmus said quietly.

Boschina and Radise arrived, breathing heavily, the Stone Cutter's Daughter waving her arm. "We're here."

"So you are," Thalmus replied, patting Radise's shoulder as the mare came alongside him.

Camp and Maz rode up and slowed their horses to a walk.

"At your service, Thalmus," Camp said.

"Look at Dal," Boschina shouted. "He's got 'em in a mess."

Ekala arrived on Shadahn; the mud-splattered black warhorse circling around all of them, bobbing her head and snorting.

"Your Majesty," Thalmus said, "how good of you to join me."

"You looked lonely out here, Hunter," Ekala replied.

Thalmus smiled. "Thunder and I were doing just fine."

"We've got to move faster," Maz said impatiently. "Those troops will be on top of us soon."

"Where are your archers?" Thalmus asked.

"They should be on their way," Ekala replied, looking for her soldiers.

"I don't see them anywhere," Maz said. "They're not going to get here in time."

The hawks were now directly overhead, drifting in ever-tighter circles. One of them swooped down and screamed its high-pitched call as it flew over them.

"Altons," Maz shouted.

Now the second one dove with a piercing screech, passing closer to their heads.

"Watch out!" Maz called. He swung his sword to strike the hawk, but it turned quickly and winged up to its partner.

"They're leading the troops to us," Camp yelled. "We're not going to make it."

"Keep moving," Thalmus replied. "Dallion has the other column stopped."

The hawks dropped on them again. This time, they came from different directions. Shrieking, and wings beating at full speed, they dodged the swords and tried to gash bodies with their sharp talons. Boschina nocked, pulled back, aimed, and shot an arrow—narrowly missing the menacing red head of the one flying toward her. It banked and circled overhead.

She clenched her bow. "Almost got 'em."

The column of soldiers crossing the plain from the north snaked down into, and then up out of, the gully like a giant centipede with hundreds of legs stomping after them.

"They're going to be on us before we reach the Wilderness," Ekala called to Thalmus.

Walking in front of Thunder, who was going as fast as he could, Thalmus glanced at the soldiers coming up on their left from the north and estimated how soon the galloping column would overtake them. Dallion continued to harass the western column on the right.

Thalmus could see that those frustrated troops would not get free in time to block them from the Wilderness. However, the troops on his left would—and very soon.

"They're not taking me alive," Ekala proclaimed.

"I'm with you," Maz declared.

Boschina looked at Thalmus. "Thalmus, what are we going to do?"

Thalmus kept walking, looking straight ahead at the treetops of the thick forest.

"Where are my archers?" Ekala asked, looking for Lander, Karl, and Ricken.

The troops were very near now. The black banner with the three *S*s flapped from a pole carried by one of the first riders. Swords hung from both sides of their large, lumbering horses. The animal's wide eyes and pointed ears protruded through protective leather sheathing over their heads and necks. The hawks, side by side, circled around and flew out in front of the soldiers, leading them toward the small band of royalty from two countries and their guardians.

Queen Ekala Oleen looked at Thalmus, whose attention was still on the Wilderness. It was as if he was not aware of the impending assault. "Thalmus," she said, "it's time to turn and prepare to fight."

Boschina watched, confused by Thalmus' behavior.

"Thalmus," Ekala repeated. "We must prepare to fight."

He pointed at the trees. "Look."

A shimmering brown cloud was rising out of the tangled forest, shifting and changing shape as it rolled toward them. They stared at it in wonder because the strange force was not smoke from a fire, nor dust pushed by wind, but rather a thousand fluttering parts whirling together in one massive form. The cloud was alive with the crushing sound of clacking, chirping, and countless beating wings as thousands of birds flew tightly together in an undulating, seething storm.

"What the..." Maz said, stopping to stare.

Ekala stopped Shadahn beside Maz. "Where did that come from?"

"Keep moving forward," Thalmus called.

The troops were almost on them, the men raising their swords to attack.

The ominous cloud of birds rolled forward at Thalmus. Then, right in front of him, it suddenly shifted, going round and round, before passing over them and slamming into the column of troops. Blinded and battered by wings and beaks, the soldiers crumbled from formation—the horses panicked, squealing and bolting. The angry, screeching Altons dove into the mass of smaller birds, grabbing with their deadly talons as they tried to break them apart.

A large brown bird with feather horns flew out from behind the cloud.

"Bubo," Boschina shouted.

Thalmus waved at the Great Horned owl as Thunder clicked his jaws. To their right, some of the soldiers were getting free from the melee caused by Dallion and were riding to cut them off from the Wilderness. Thalmus knew it was only a matter of time before other troops would get clear of the birds and come after them.

He turned to the others. "Hurry to the forest!"

One of the Altons spotted Bubo and dove. Just as he was about to hit him with his spread talons, Bubo flipped over with his own talons up in defense. The two great birds locked their sharp claws for a moment in mid-air, glaring at one another—eye to eye, wings spread wide—before the Alton let go and flew to his mate. Bubo rolled over and climbed above the storm of birds. The Altons now swooped, one following the other, toward Bubo. He sensed his attackers' approach, turned, and met the first one as it tried to grab him. Deflecting the hawk's hooks, he swung under its body and came up free behind it with his talons forward to meet the second one that was already there crashing into him. They flipped over, tumbling in the air, clinging to one another in a desperate fight as the first Alton circled and dove again, aiming to strike Bubo in the back while he was tied to his partner. Before he could reach him, the swarm of birds engulfed Bubo and the Alton, pecking and attacking the hawk.

Toulon soldiers broke free of the swarm. They were battered and confused, yet angry and seeking their prey. Some of the men had been thrown from their horses. Others were calming their steeds while moving away from the birds. When the men spotted the giant shell creature and his surrounding friends, they gave chase, hurrying to catch them before reaching the Wilderness.

Suddenly, arrows flew at the soldiers from out of the forest. Ricken and Karl were standing at the edge of the trees shooting at the oncoming Toulon troops. The soldiers slowed as several were hit and went down. Encouraged by seeing their comrades coming from the west, they surged forward again despite the deadly arrows.

"There are my archers," Ekala shouted. "Camp, Thalmus, stop those men on the left!" she ordered, pointing at the soldiers running toward them. "Boschina, stay with Thunder. Use your bow to support Thalmus and Camp. Maz and I will hold off the troops on the right until you and Thunder get to the trees." She slapped Maz's shoulder and drew her sword. It vibrated and hummed in her hand. The engraved blade had not pulsated with such intensity since the Battle for Ambermal. The queen smiled as Prince Bolimaz drew his sword, returned her smile, and urged Mendu forward.

Boschina dropped from Radise and took aim at the soldiers Camp was rushing to engage. She fired off two arrows before running to catch up with Thunder, and then stopped to steady, aim, and shoot again at the moving targets. Each arrow hit its mark as the men jerked and crumpled to the ground.

The cloud of birds split into smaller swarms and spread apart. Bubo and the Alton tumbled out of the turmoil and separated. The hawk was wounded, but could still fly. Its long wings struggled as the big bird staggered away. Bubo let it go as he looked for its mate, and then turned his attention to his friends.

Queen Ekala Oleen and Prince Bolimaz battled the first soldiers coming from the west as Thalmus and Camp dueled with soldiers reforming from the north. The numbers of these Toulon men were few, but growing. Arrows from the Oleen archers in the trees had stopped, allowing more of the green clad troops to move forward.

What happened? Ekala wondered. *Have they run out of arrows?*

But she didn't have time to look as she fought the men coming at her. As Ekala ducked under a sword from an attacker, an arrow whizzed by her shoulder. *That was close,* she thought. *Their archers must have arrived on the field.*

Shadahn battled the enemy horses, pushing, stomping, and biting as Ekala fought their riders. The queen and prince kept moving forward toward the forest, fighting and adjusting their position to make sure they covered each other's backside.

Shadahn suddenly lurched forward to bump another horse coming on the left, causing Ekala to jerk back and the other rider forward. An arrow whistled by her stomach and stuck deep into the man's side. He dropped his sword and slumped forward onto his horse's neck. Surprised, Ekala glanced around, searching for the archer. "That would have hit me," she said angrily.

Thunder was almost to the trees, plodding between Thalmus and Camp fighting on the left and Ekala and Maz on the right. Boschina continued picking targets that were an immediate threat to her friends, switching back and forth across the field to shoot the most threatening attackers. But now, the quiver on her back and those on Radise were empty. Her last arrow was ready on her bow.

She kept stealing glances for Ricken and Karl to see why they had stopped shooting. She expected to see them at the tree line, but they weren't there. Movement in the brush caught her eye. Someone had released an arrow from behind the low branches of a tree. As she looked on, the half-hidden figure shot another arrow. This time Boschina followed its flight to see it hit a Toulon soldier lurching in front of Ekala.

"Only Lander could make that shot," she muttered with admiration and looked back to the woods for the archer. Then she saw Ricken's and Karl's horses standing amongst the trees and a body lying nearby with an arrow protruding from its back.

It was Ricken.

Farther on laid Karl, an arrow through his neck. How could that be? None of the Toulon soldiers with bows had come to the fight yet. Boschina felt her sword begin to vibrate in its sheath against her hip and she suddenly realized the two fallen Oleens had been shot from behind. She saw the archer in the trees moving into a clearing and nocking an arrow.

It was Lander!

The famous archer was watching Ekala, following her with the bow. Boschina shook with horror. Lander wasn't trying to protect Ekala—she was trying to kill her. There was no time to warn Ekala, nor to call to Thalmus. Lander could release at any moment. Boschina lifted her bow and drew back her last arrow. Looking down the shaft, finding Lander at the end of the point, Boschina saw the archer aiming back at her. Surprised, Boschina held for a moment. *Is she really going to shoot me?* She focused on Lander's hand, pulling the string to her chin, while lowering her own visual target to the button on Lander's chest. In an instant, she saw Lander's fingers release the string, the fletching twirl. Boschina let her arrow fly, and then jumped to the side. A searing pain stabbed her shoulder. She grabbed the pain with her hand, rolled over, and bounced up to yell a warning to Ekala—to point out the traitor.

But Lander was gone.

Chapter Twenty
Into the Wilderness

Boschina snatched up her bow and ran to the bodies of the Oleens, shouting the whole way, "Ekala! Maz! Watch out! Lander's shooting at you. Thalmus, Camp, Lander's shooting at us!"

She reached Ricken, grabbed the arrows from her quiver, and put them in her own. She nocked an arrow and searched the woods for Lander, while continuing to shout the warning to her friends. Thunder finally plodded off the plain and stopped to rest by Ricken.

They all reached the woods and only a few weary soldiers still confronted them. Out on the plain, many more troops still gathered from both directions. Thalmus sheathed his sword and picked up Karl's bow and arrows. He began shooting the last Toulon men fighting Ekala and Maz, forcing them to retreat.

The immediate danger over, Queen Ekala Oleen raced to the bodies of her two soldiers sprawled on the ground. Swinging off the huffing Shadahn, she knelt beside Ricken. She put her ear to the lifeless soldier's mouth, listening for a breath. There was none. She stepped over to Karl and did the same.

"No, this can't be." she said. Sweat ran down her face, confusion filled her eyes.

Thalmus, Camp, and Maz quickly formed a protective circle around Ekala. Boschina stayed close, an arrow ready in her bow, watching the forest for Lander.

Thalmus dropped the bow and turned to help Ekala. She looked up at him, her sadness turning to anger. "We can't leave them here."

"They will come with us," Thalmus said. "Thunder can carry them, but we must hurry." He grabbed the arrow protruding from Karl's neck and broke it off, and then lifted his limp body and placed it across Thunder's broad back.

Ekala snapped off the arrow in Ricken's back, and then grabbed her under the arms while Thalmus picked up her legs. Thunder stepped to them and they laid the dead archer on his shell next to Karl. Thunder clicked his jaws and trudged into the trees and underbrush. Dallion galloped in from the plain huffing and bobbing his head, sweat glistening on his coat.

"Thank you, Dal," Thalmus said, patting his shoulder. Knowing that the big stallion was very pleased with himself and ready to do more, Thalmus pointed toward Thunder plowing into the forest. "Follow Thunder, take the others with you." Dallion lifted his head, whinnied, and started after the shell creature with Shadahn, and all the other horses trailed after them.

"Where's Lander?" Ekala asked.

"She was there," Boschina said, pointing at the spot where she had last seen Lander releasing an arrow at her. "That's where I shot at her."

"She's not there now," Ekala said, her eyes searching the foliage.

"No, and we do not have time to look for her," Thalmus said, watching the Toulon soldiers gathering on the plain. Glasrauss was among them, sitting on his horse, pointing as he shouted orders. Behind him rode the standard bearer with the black flag flapping over their heads. One of the Altons circled above, screeching its angry call. Its wounded mate rested on a tall T-shaped wooden perch supported by a brown-clothed man wearing long-sleeved leather gloves.

"We must move into the forest where we have an advantage against their numbers," Thalmus said calmly.

"And cover from Lander," Ekala said. "Everybody stay low."

"This is going to be a mess," Maz said. "Fighting in this tangle."

"It's better than out in the open," Camp replied. "We got no chance out here."

Filing in together, they followed Thunder's trail of crushed foliage, all the time expecting the soldiers to surge after them or Lander's arrows to strike. Even as the thick wilderness closed in around them, and the distance from the plain grew, the troops did not charge.

"What are they waiting for?" Boschina asked, looking back over her shoulder.

"Good question," Ekala replied. "They still have time to overwhelm us."

"They're not in a hurry, that's for sure," Camp said.

"Maybe Glasrauss thinks Lander will finish us," Ekala said.

"Maybe they're afraid of Chorgens in here," Boschina added.

"Chorgens hunt at night," Thalmus responded.

"Then why aren't they coming after us?"

Thalmus glanced at her and around at the trees. "Everybody stop," he said, catching up to Thunder and tapping his shell. "Whoa. Everyone stop, kneel down."

It took a few moments for quiet to take control and settle around them. "Listen," Thalmus whispered, holding his open hand up. Stillness confronted them: no breeze or movement in the branches, no fluttering of birds or scurrying of animals could be heard. All was silent, except a low murmur, a barely audible rhythmic hum.

"What is that?" Boschina asked quietly.

"Sounds like the breath of someone sleeping," Ekala said.

"Or some animal," Maz replied.

"It sounds like the whole forest is breathing," Camp said.

"This place is alive with many creatures," Thalmus whispered. "Some we should not wake; others are missing."

The stillness was suddenly shattered by the clamoring cloud of birds swarming over them and into the trees. Landing and resting for a moment, and then chirping and fluttering, the birds rose up again, gathering into a mass, swirling round and round before flying away over the forest.

Watching the birds fade into the distance, Ekala said, "They're trying to tell us something." She turned to Boschina. "You said that you shot an arrow at Lander, did you hit her?"

"No...I don't think so. I was dodging her arrow," Boschina said, pointing at her shoulder.

"Let me see," Thalmus said. He gently pulled back the torn material of Boschina's blood-soaked sleeve and examined the wound. Lander's arrow had ripped through the fabric and cut the skin of the upper arm. Thalmus smiled at her. "This is at the same level as your heart. She missed her target—or you were too quick."

"I saw her down the shaft of my arrow as she released her arrow at me. I couldn't believe it. But I had no time to think; I let go and jumped to the side."

"This is not deep. You are fortunate, Boschina," Thalmus said, though he knew it was more than good fortune. How many times now had she sidestepped death? What had Larma said about her? She is destined to live a bigger story. "The bleeding has stopped," he said. "We can patch this later. Where did you last see Lander?"

"By a large tree back there with vines hanging all around it."

"She could be anywhere by now," Maz said. "She could pick us off one at a time and we'd never see her."

Camp grunted. "Well, she's missing an opportunity now, the way we're just sittin' here."

"There is a reason Lander is not shooting at us," Thalmus replied.

"What would that be?"

"That is what we need to find out."

Ekala was looking at the bodies of Karl and Ricken on Thunder's shell. "Lander shot them and tried to kill me. She's been an Oleen since the beginning at Table Top and through the battle for Ambermal. She always protected me."

"It is hard for us to understand," Thalmus said. "Treachery has no loyalty, except to the betrayer."

"We need to find her before she kills anymore of us," Ekala said.

Maz was gazing through the trees, watching the Toulon soldiers standing at ease in the plain. Lord Glasrauss had dismounted and was talking to his wounded men. "They're not coming," Maz said. "But, they're not leaving either. They're starting to form a battle line along the edge of the Wilderness."

Thalmus looked at the sky through the canopy of trees. An Alton drifted overhead. The sun was on its downward path in the west. "We need to find Lander before dark." He tapped Thunder's shell. "Go ahead." The giant shell creature with the limp Oleens on his back started forward again with the horses. Turning to Ekala, he said, "Your Majesty, come with me. Boschina, I want you to show us where you last saw the archer. Maz and Camp, if you would stay with Thunder and the horses, Bubo will lead you to a camping spot, a cave where we can hide and rest tonight."

Maz looked around. "Bubo, he's here?"

"In that tree," Thalmus replied, motioning at the thickly leafed branches of a nearby tree.

"I don't see him."

"You will."

"Alright," Maz replied. "We'll watch for him."

"You better catch up to us before dark," Camp warned.

Thalmus smiled. "We will find you."

Maz grasped Ekala's hand. "Be careful."

She smiled at the prince. "The same to you."

As Thalmus had predicted, the Great Horned owl flew silently out of the tree and led Thunder, Maz, Camp, and the horses to a cave they could not see until Bubo guided them through a maze of boulders and trees to the opening. The owl had already been inside to ensure it was not inhabited. He convinced the skeptical Camp by flying in and out again, and then emitting a few all-clear hoots.

The mouth of the cave was a little wider than Thunder and just high enough for horses to pass through. It stayed that size for about thirty steps and then opened into a large domed room with a high ceiling. To one side was a spring with a small pool that overflowed and trickled through a worn rock channel that disappeared down a black hole of a tunnel. Lining the walls all around the room were etchings and faded paintings of people dancing and running. Their faces glowed with joy and innocence.

Once inside the cave, Dallion stood guard at the opening while Maz and Camp carefully pulled Ricken's and Karl's bodies from Thunder's shell and laid them to the side, covering them with blankets. After the horses and Thunder had drunk from the spring, the men drank and washed their faces and arms. Leaving the horses saddled, Maz and Camp removed the bags of food they had been given by the Kairtaykars. They chose some carrots and went out to wait for the others, sitting down where they could watch the passageway leading to the cave.

"There's something strange in there," Camp said. "It gives me the shivers. Did you feel it?"

"Yes, I did—made me feel like an intruder." Maz glanced at the cave. "Where's Bubo? Have you seen Bubo?"

"I think he's off lookin' for 'em."

"I hope they're back before night," Maz said, rolling a carrot in his hand. "This place is bad enough in the day."

"Stop worrying. Thalmus and Bubo will get 'em here," Camp said, snapping a bite of carrot and lying back. "I'm about worn out."

Maz glanced at his companion, and then turned his gaze back to the trail. "It *has* been a long day. At least my head feels better. That chase and fight woke me up."

Camp nodded. "Me too. You know, we wouldn't be sitting here now if it wasn't for Thalmus gettin' us out of the Rows, and then Dallion and Bubo puttin' the fix on those troops."

"And Boschina spotting Lander's treachery," Maz said.

"Lander, do you believe her turning on the Queen?"

"No, I never would have guessed it. She was so protective of Ekala, even against me. Then she up and tries to kill Ekala. That's hard for me to think about." Maz stared down the path, holding his carrot like a sword. Daylight faded and a cool air settled in the forest.

"I should have gone with her. She came to get me when we chased after those raiders. Now here I sit."

Camp hesitated, finishing his carrot before speaking. "If anybody can find Lander, Thalmus can. I got no worries about the three of them in a battle."

"That's for sure. There's no one like Thalmus. Boschina's fearless, and Ekala, well, she's a warrior, and can out fight me. But this is different. Lander's the best archer I've ever seen. She could pick them off and they'd never even see her. I should be with Ekala."

"A lot of good that'd do," Camp replied. "If what you say is true, then you being with her wouldn't make a difference. You'd be dead, too. Then there'd be no chance of saving our country from your brothers."

"You know what I mean," Maz said, pointing the carrot at him.

"I suppose I do. I just want to live and return to our home one day."

Maz nodded. "Me too, and we will."

"I'm glad to hear you say that, Prince Bolimaz. And that you haven't forgotten who you are."

"Oh, I haven't forgotten who I am."

"Good. Now, if you're not going to eat that carrot, can I have it?"

* * *

Thalmus circled back through the tangled trees and vines, staying out of sight of the soldiers setting up camp on the plain. Some Toulon scouts were starting to probe into the trees, moving carefully as they followed Thunder's tracks. Boschina guided Thalmus with hand signals while she kept her bow at the ready. Ekala followed, sword in her hand, watching for any sign of Lander. When they reached the spot where the archer had been, they examined the area and found broken branches tossed aside where Lander had cleared an opening in the tree to shoot her arrows. Footprints in the dust showed where she had stood, and then turned and moved away.

"She stumbled before leaving and fell down here," Thalmus said, glancing at Boschina. "You may have hit her." He carefully followed the tracks through brush, under dangling limbs and down a ravine to a fallen tree. Thalmus pointed at fresh spots of blood on the thick trunk of the downed tree and on the ground in front of it. All three of them hesitated, looking around, scanning the trees and moss-covered rock formations. Here and there, jagged beams of sunlight filtered through the canopy, cutting bright spots in the shadows. An odor of decay filled the still air.

Thalmus spoke quietly. "Lander sat here, resting and..." He stopped and picked up part of an arrow from the other side of the log and showed it to them. It was the fletching end of the arrow's shaft. "She sat here, Boschina, and snapped off your arrow. The other half is still in her."

Boschina stared at the broken arrow. "I didn't think I hit her."

"You did," Ekala said. "But where did your arrow hit her and how badly is she wounded?"

Moving carefully, they followed the marks and blood spots out of the ravine and through the darkening forest. Gradually, the footprints became longer and easier to follow.

"She's dragging her feet," Ekala said.

Thalmus nodded and kept moving as he pulled his sword from its sheath. They walked another twenty meters before he stopped, staring ahead at a small hill thick with brush. *Of course, Lander, you would pick this spot to rest and defend—high ground with good cover,* Thalmus thought. He motioned to Ekala and Boschina that Lander was there.

"Lander," Ekala called. "I'm here. Do you still want to kill me?"

No response.

"Lander," Ekala called again.

Thalmus motioned for them to spread apart. Ekala moved ten paces to the left and Boschina the same to the right as they began walking slowly up the hill. The brush before them rattled slightly; something was moving behind it. Thalmus rushed forward, slashing the branches with his sword; breaking through, he saw Lander on her knees awkwardly raising her bow. The end of a broken arrow protruded from the right side of her chest. She was hunched to her right, trying to lift her arm and hand to pull back on the bow string. Swinging his sword, Thalmus knocked the bow from her hand and she slumped against a tree as Boschina came in from the side, her bow drawn with an arrow ready to release. Ekala came through with her sword forward, ready to fight. She froze upon seeing Lander against the tree. The famed archer looked at her with defiance, but said nothing. Boschina relaxed her bow and placed the arrow into its quiver.

Lander's lips curled into a half smile. "I told you," she said to Boschina.

"What did you tell me?" Boschina asked.

Lander swallowed hard and whispered: "One day you'd best me."

"It's good that she did," Ekala said, kneeling in front of Lander and grasping her good arm so that she couldn't grab the knife on her hip. "Why did you want to kill me?"

Closing her eyes, Lander coughed; her head rolled back. Ekala grabbed Lander's forehead and steadied her.

"What happened to you, Lander? Why did you turn against me?"

Lander's eyes blinked and fluttered open. "It's getting dark. Leave me to the night creatures...I'm done."

"You're not done and I'm not leaving you." Ekala turned to Thalmus. "Let's carry her."

"She killed Karl and Ricken, and tried to shoot you," Boschina said. "Why do you want to save her?"

"I know, Boschina, but I'm not ready to give up on her. Something happened to Lander and I want to know what. I can't believe she did this on her own. She's been so loyal, and then to turn like this: she deserves a chance to explain. And I'm going to give it to her."

"She may not last," Thalmus said, removing Lander's knife from her belt. "But if you wish, I will carry her."

"I do wish it," the queen said. "And thank you."

"Alright," Boschina said, accepting Ekala's decision. "Maybe we can find some Marantac for Lander's wound and my arm."

"We can watch for a plant on the way, but we must hurry to find the others before nightfall," Thalmus said, kneeling to pick up Lander.

Boschina and Ekala helped fold Lander over Thalmus' shoulder. Boschina picked up the archer's loose quiver of arrows and they started off as the light began to fade.

Chapter Twenty-One
Kali's Frustration

"Where is Currad?" King Ahmbin demanded as he rushed down the hallway to the kitchen.

"He is here, Your Majesty," Veracitas answered, motioning the anxious king through the door and into the messy, smoky, and fragrant realm of Culinary. King Ahmbin stopped and peered into the long stone room. Spits loaded with the evening entre hung above fires that flamed and crackled in one of the open fireplaces. Pots of bubbling liquid simmered over coals, bunches of herbs and strands of leafy plants hung from the ceiling, and loaves of bread sat cooling on racks. Colored crocks and bowls of odd sizes filled the shelves. Large knives, long-handled forks, and tongs dangled from hooks on the walls. And on a long, worn, and stained wood plank table rested the man the king was looking for, his honored soldier.

Culinary had insisted Currad be brought to the kitchen where he could heal the soldier's wounds with the salves he had created from various herbs, spices, and odd plants. Now the cook was smearing a yellow paste with his large, powerful hands on the soldier's side and back, where his skin was turning purple and blue from the blows he received in the fight. Bands of gauze with spots of blood were wrapped in various locations on Currad's arms, legs, and his head, which he cradled awkwardly in his left hand.

"Easy," Currad winced. "I'm not a slab of beef." "This must be rubbed into your skin or you will never heal," the cook explained. "I know, you are broken inside and it must hurt, but you are used to pain, yes?" He spread more of the ointment with the palm of his hand.

Currad coughed and grabbed his side. "Aaaah! That hurt. I can hardly breathe," he whispered, taking short breaths.

King Ahmbin ducked under the hanging plants. "My Honored Soldier," he said as he hurried to the table. "I was told you were badly injured—that you almost drowned. Is this true?"

Currad tried to sit up quickly and howled in pain.

"No, no, stay there," the king insisted. "Lie down. You are hurt. Yet, I see very little blood."

"He was prodded and beaten with a pole," Veracitas said. "But he was able to deflect the swords...mostly."

"And the drowning in the ford?" the king asked. "Is that true?"

Currad coughed and winced again. "I would've been part of the Camotop, washed into Cold Canyon, if Veracitas and Captain Kali hadn't pulled me out."

"You saved Veracitas and now he has saved you," Culinary said, slapping on a new handful of paste from a pot.

"Ow," Currad muttered, recoiling from the cook's stern hand.

The king nodded to Veracitas. "You returned at just the right time. We are all grateful for that."

"It was Captain Kali who heard the fight and ordered a charge to the river, Your Majesty," the stone carver replied. "If not for her, we may have been too late. She also helped me pull Currad from the water."

"I'm thankful to both of you," Currad said, glancing around the room. "Where is the captain?"

"Taking care of her duties," Veracitas answered.

The king turned again to Currad. "Who were these men that dared to attack you?"

Currad tried to adjust himself. "Some from Banyon, others were from Toulon." He took several short breaths. "They had two wagons full of swords and clothing, and were on their way to Zinkila."

"Zinkila," the king repeated. "That's odd. Why would King Dieten be amassing weapons?" He paused, bringing his hand to his chin. "Unless his sons, who have always been foolish and ambitious, have taken control. The eldest boy was here for Ekala's coronation. I remember him telling me he was surprised how I let my daughter take over the kingdom. I didn't think much of it at the time. But now...."

Currad shifted on the table. "We would've heard if there'd been a change."

"Send some men to find out," the king said. "We can't wait for Ekala to return."

"When will the queen be back?" Veracitas asked. "My daughter will be with her and I look forward to seeing them both."

King Ahmbin glanced around the room, settling his gaze on a pot hanging from a grate over one of the cooking fires. The soup in the pot was bubbling with a delicious aroma. "Soon, I hope," he said slowly. "Lord Rundall will not last much longer. And now this smuggling and Currad's injury...I fear that something dreadful is upon us."

"Don't worry, Your Majesty," Currad said. "We will be ready and Queen Ekala will return."

Captain Kali suddenly burst into the room and froze when she saw King Ahmbin. She quickly pulled off her hat, freeing a bush of frizzy red hair. "Your Majesty," she said, bowing her head.

"No need for that, Captain," the king said. "Although I appreciate your respect, I'm just your queen's father now."

"Yes, and more, that's why I honor you," Kali replied. She turned to Currad. "We locked the men in the cells and secured the wagons at the barracks."

"Good. Make sure both the men and the weapons are guarded constantly." Currad tried to sit up and groaned, grabbing his side.

"Currad," the king said. "You are in no condition to be up and about. I want you to rest."

"I can't. There's too much to be done."

"King Ahmbin's right," Culinary chimed in as he washed his hands in a bucket. "You, my dear friend, will not heal—and will likely hurt yourself more—if you don't rest."

Currad groaned. "Alright, since I can hardly get off this table, I have to agree." He turned to the red-headed woman. "Captain Kali, I'm glad you're back. I want you to take command of the army until I'm able."

Kali was surprised and very uncomfortable with this promotion. "Sir, you have other captains who have been in service to the king's army much longer than I. Wouldn't one of them—"

"You are an Oleen and one of the Queen's Captains," Currad said, interrupting her. He took short breaths and continued. "You're dependable and determined. Besides, you're a smarter fighter than any of them. The redoubt at the ford must be completed and manned. The training of the troops has to continue; so many of them are new, inexperienced."

Kali glanced at the stone carver. "Ekala Oleen assigned me to guard Veracitas in his travel to make a new statue. I would be abandoning her order."

"Then Veracitas needs to stay and do his work here at the castle," Currad replied, looking at the stone carver for support.

Veracitas hesitated while the others waited. Then he spoke softly, his callused hands spread on the table. "When we were in the quarry, I saw a vision—a warning in the stone—that Metro's evil was not dead. It frightened me. I did not know what to do, until I saw Boschina in a dream, carving stone. I knew then that I had to join her. I thought that it would be at Ello, but now it appears that our work is to be done here at Castle Ambermal."

Kali turned to him. "Why didn't you tell me about this vision?"

Before Veracitas could answer, Currad spoke. "There you are, Captain. You won't be going against the queen's order. No excuse now. We need you."

Captain Kali continued staring at Veracitas, waiting for an answer to her question. Finally, her eyes moved to Currad. After a long pause, while she pondered his request, she said, "If she were here, I think Ekala Oleen would approve. But you are still in command because you should be. You are the King's Honored Soldier; you have the history of authority and everyone knows that. With yours, and the king's permission, I will oversee the work and training in the field with my force of Oleens."

"So be it," Currad said, satisfied. "I will write the notice and announce it immediately. "My first order for you is to post a dozen troops at the ford and inspect any wagons coming from or going to Toulon and Banyon."

"There are two Oleens watching it now," Kali said. "I will replace them with twelve soldiers from the castle guard and rotate them in eight-hour shifts."

Currad smiled. "I knew you were the right one for this job."

"I'm glad you're stepping in for Currad," the king commented. "Ekala has always spoken highly of you, as a natural leader and fearless warrior."

"I had the best teachers," Kali replied. "The daughter of King Ahmbin and, of course, Larma and Thalmus."

"There are none better," the proud king said.

"I agree," Kali said and turned to Currad. "Tell me about the work on the fort."

"The King's Builder can explain the work schedule and materials. His office is with the quartermaster. You must push everyone to get it done as soon as they can. If you need anything, I'll be in my chambers—if I can get off Culinary's butcher table."

Culinary slapped his big hand on the table, startling everyone. "Butcher table! Let me tell you somethin'; this *butcher table*, as you call it, that you lay on now is the very wood on which Thalmus and I bandaged Ekala's leg during the battle for the castle. If it was good enough for Queen Ekala Oleen, then it's good enough for you."

"I just meant that I need help getting to my room," Currad explained.

"Why didn't you say that then," Culinary snapped. "Of course we'll have soldiers carry you. But if you're expectin' food brought to your bedside, then you better be restin'.."

Currad smiled. "Yes, *Lord* Culinary," he said sarcastically.

"Well, I have a lot to do," Kali said, backing away from the table. "I'd better get busy." She turned to the king. "Your Majesty, thank you for your kind words."

"I have confidence you will do a good job," Ahmbin said.

She bowed, reset her hat, and headed for the door.

"If you don't need me, Currad, I'll help Captain Kali," Veracitas said.

"Go," the wounded soldier said. "And Veracitas, your workshop is still there, you know, waiting for you. Nobody has used it; I wouldn't let 'em."

The stone carver nodded. "Yes, thank you, Currad. I might...stop by there." He bowed to King Ahmbin and left.

Veracitas caught up with Kali as she hurried down the stone steps into the street heading to the barracks and the quartermaster's office.

"Currad seems to be recovering," he said, smiling. When Kali kept walking with no response, Veracitas continued. "Between the blows he took and how long he was face down in the water, I thought we'd lost him." Still no comment came from the captain as she trudged forward, eyes straight ahead. "He's strong, maybe the strongest man I know."

"Why don't you make a statue of him?" Kali grumbled, still not looking at Veracitas.

"I did. It's in the Barrier Forest," the sculptor replied. "But I could sculpt one here. I have some good images of him in mind. Did you see his scars and muscles, the lines of his shoulders and back? I just need to find the right stone."

Kali waved her arm in the direction of Marbala. "We were just at the quarry. You could have...." She suddenly stopped and turned to him. "Why didn't you tell me what you saw in the stone at the quarry?"

Confronted, Veracitas wasn't sure what to say. "I...I didn't know how to explain it."

"You don't think I would have understood?"

"I did not want you to think I was crazed."

"Crazed! Crazed?" Kali repeated angrily. "It would have helped me to know why you acted the way you did. I didn't know what was wrong with you."

Veracitas shrugged. "I came out of it."

"Not for several days. I am not one of your statues, Veracitas. I'm not made of stone; I was worried about you the whole time."

Veracitas did not know what to say. "I..."

Angry, Kali shook her head, turned, and headed to the barracks. Veracitas watched her; he started to go after her, and then decided he did not know what else to say.

He slowly made his way to the studio, his thoughts crowded with images and words from Larma, Ekala, Thalmus, King Ahmbin, Currad, and finally his daughter, Boschina: walking with him beside the old horse pulling their wagon full of carving tools and stone figures. Reaching the studio, he slid the large plank door open and stepped into the dusty stone room. He had not been in the workshop since finishing the king's statue, and now the memory of that carving, of Lord Rundall's kind visits and of Metro's glaring eyes and warnings, came flooding out. He leaned against the wall, breathing slowly, trying to block the bad images. He wanted to leave, to run out, but he felt a pull, a desire to stay, to create something beyond himself. It was in this place, this studio, where he must confront his fears and treat them as a vanquished enemy.

A square block of marble rested on a pedestal near a workbench. The stone was waiting for him—calling to him. As he walked to the bench, where tools were laid in a neat row, he felt a tension closing in around him, as if someone was watching. But his fingers were curving inward, gripping chisel and hammer. His mind calmed as the anticipation of action spread through his body and he began tapping the hammer to the chisel, causing flakes of stone to fly. The sculptor smiled as his hands and arms fell into a rhythmic flow of carving.

This is what he knew, what he loved and understood. This is who he was—a carver of stone. Truth, his truth, hid in the work and deep in the stone that would slowly be revealed by his steady hands and his vision of life.

Chapter Twenty-Two
Ahmautahmin

Bubo glided silently between tree branches in the darkening forest, his eyes searching the ground below. Landing on a broken tree trunk, talons grasping tight on the dead wood, he folded his wings and listened. His head swiveled from one side to the other, almost in a complete circle, as his large eyes scanned the forest, finding the sounds he heard and eliminating them one by one. Birds adjusting in their nests, squabbling raccoons digging for grubs, small, furry, four-legged predators sneaking through the brush, scurrying mice and rats that normally would be a meal for him, but not now.

He was searching for his friends.

Sounds of something larger in the distance spun his head in that direction to hear better, to determine the noise. He hooted, deep and resonating: Who – Whooo. Hearing a new voice in their midst, the animals froze, trying not to make a sound. Quieter now, Bubo listened and waited until he heard the noise again, faint and far off through the trees. He knew what it was—footfalls of two-legged creatures, two or more of them, moving slowly. Were those his friends or something else stalking them? The Great Horned owl spread his wings and flew toward the noise.

Thalmus shifted Lander on his shoulder, checked her breathing to see that she was still alive, and started forward again, stepping carefully so he wouldn't stumble in the darkness. It was difficult, slow going; he could barely make out enough shapes and shadows to feel his way along. "Oh, for Bubo's eyes," he muttered to himself.

Ekala was moving closely behind Thalmus, hanging onto the end of Lander's bow. The other end was hooked onto Thalmus' sword handle at his belt so they wouldn't get separated. In her left hand Ekala held the end of Boschina's bow as the Stone Cutter's Daughter struggled along behind, grasping the other end. This was a use for the tool Boschina had never imagined. Her mind wandered, visualizing a statue of the three of them at this moment, in the darkness, held together by the strength of the wooden limbs of weapons intended for death. *How large a stone or how many would it take?* she wondered. How would she carve it? What kind of stone would be best? Her toe caught something hard and she tripped, stopping her fall by placing a hand on the ground.

Ekala felt the tug on the bow and heard the stumble. "Are you alright?"

"Yes," Boschina said, embarrassed. "I just have to pick up my feet." A sound in the darkness stopped her breath—an animal sniffing. It was the quick, wet sniffs she'd heard the night on the way to the Great Water. The engraved sword on her side began to hum. Dropping the end of the bow, she withdrew the blade and pointed it into the darkness. "Stop," she called. "There's a Chorgen following us."

Thalmus spun around, laying Lander down and drawing his sword in one motion.

"How do you know?"

"I heard him sniffing."

Ekala dropped both ends of the bows that she had been holding and slid her sword from its scabbard. It vibrated in her hand. "I can't see a thing," she said. "This is not good."

"Remember what I showed you, Boschina," Thalmus said.

"Duck under and thrust into the underbelly," Boschina answered. "But it will be on us before I can see it."

The sound of snorting and claws scraping the ground came from their right. Crouching and searching the darkness in that direction, they heard a roar and clawing coming from their left.

"There are two of them," Thalmus said. "I'll watch the left; you two take the right."

Suddenly, a vicious fight erupted with snapping jaws, gnashing teeth, howls, thumping bodies, and branches breaking. Blind to what was happening, they listened and waited, expecting to be pounced upon at any time. The savage battle continued with frightening intensity until, finally, the creatures bounded away, crashing through the woods.

"Whatever that was, I'm glad we weren't part of it," Ekala said.

"We had better keep moving," Thalmus said, lifting Lander onto his shoulder once more. "Whoever wins that fight may come back for us."

Thalmus knew they had been making too much noise and were attracting attention from dangerous creatures—animals and humans. But it couldn't be helped in this darkness; they had to keep moving to find the cave. He just hoped the others had gotten there safely, that he was heading in the right direction, and that the Chorgen would not be back. Then he heard a familiar call and stopped to listen. Suddenly, a weight landed on his free shoulder, a wing flapped the back of his head and claws gripped his coat. The hunter reached up with his free hand and stroked Bubo's breast feathers. The owl pulled at his friend's hair with his beak.

"Guide me on," Thalmus whispered.

Maz and Camp had gathered wood nearby. Camp had returned to the cave to start a fire while Maz kept watch outside. The prince rubbed his arms and legs as he peered into the night and listened. With the darkness had come the cold, damp air drifting in from the river and a foggy mist rising from the wet ground of the Wilderness. He loathed this place, had vowed to never come here again. But here he was, hiding once again from soldiers who should be fighting alongside him, not hunting him. Tomorrow, those men out on the plain would come searching to capture him or to carry his head back to his brothers. His life was at the mercy of this tangled forest, its creatures and…his friends.

"I have my friends," he heard himself say aloud.

Ekala Oleen, the Queen of Ameram; the great hunter, Thalmus; his powerful companions and Boschina: He and Camp did not have these friends the first time they escaped from Toulon. Loyal friends and excellent fighters, too; he had witnessed their skill and endurance at the great battle for Castle Ambermal and in the running fight across the plain today. More importantly, Bubo and Thalmus had saved his life when he was cut through by Corsair. And Ekala, she gave him hope. "Yes," he whispered, "these are great friends I can trust." The Prince of Toulon straightened up; he felt better, especially thinking of Ekala.

Movement in the brush caught his attention. Something large was coming his way.

Maz picked up his sword. He waited, listening, ready to yell a warning to Camp in the cave. Raising his sword chest-high, he was ready to thrust as he peered into the darkness. The noises were getting closer, coming right up the passage to him and the cave. He leaned forward, ready to attack, and then heard: "Whoo – who – who."

"Bubo?"

"It's us, Maz," Ekala's voice called from the darkness.

"All of you are with Bubo?" he replied.

"Yes, we're coming in."

Maz backed up and in a few moments, Thalmus appeared, carrying a body over one shoulder and Bubo guiding from his other. Maz caught his breath for a moment looking at the body and then smiled as Ekala and Boschina stepped forward. Turning, he led them into the cave.

Bubo left Thalmus' shoulder and flew through the opening, circled the domed room several times, and landed on Thunder's shell, who clicked his jaws several times with joy to see his feathered friend and to have him resting on his back. Dallion snorted a welcome as Camp helped Thalmus lay Lander down near the small fire he had started on the side of the cave. It was in a shallow pit where the wall was blackened from many fires burned there before.

Maz hugged Ekala. "I'm glad you're alright."

Ekala hugged him back, holding on tightly. "I am too. Are you alright?"

"Yes, now."

She patted him on the shoulder and turned to Thalmus kneeling over Lander. "How is she?"

"Barely alive," Thalmus said.

"What can we do for her?"

"Not much—the arrow's shaft is too deep. She has lost a lot of blood."

"I wish she could talk," Ekala said.

"If we keep her warm and feed her some hot broth, she might come around enough to speak," Thalmus said.

Maz glanced at Boschina, still holding her bow, staring down at Lander. "You did hit her," he said. "Good shooting."

Boschina shrugged, rubbed her wounded shoulder, and turned away to check on Radise.

Ekala followed her to the horses near the back of the cave. She patted Shadahn's neck while watching Boschina lean her forehead against Radise's shoulder. Stepping around the horses, Ekala moved close to Boschina. "You did right," she said softly. "You saved me. That's what sisters do, protect one another."

Boschina looked at Ekala. "I had to. She killed Ricken and Karl, tried to kill you, and almost got me, too," Boschina said. "I don't understand why you want to save her."

"Because I want to know what evil has got hold of her—why she turned against me."

"Does it matter now?" Boschina asked. "She'll be dead by morning."

"It does, Boschina. It matters to me. And it should to you, too." Then Ekala turned and walked to the fire, where Maz and Camp were heating some soup they had made with vegetables in their tin cups placed amongst hot coals they had pulled to the side.

Thalmus was with his three animal companions, thanking each one for their part in the fight on the plain and getting everyone to the cave. Bubo's feathers were ruffled and there was blood on his feet between the talons. He had fared well in his fight with the Altons, giving more than he received. The great owl chortled as Thalmus smoothed his feathers.

Boschina rested her head on Radise's neck. The mare made a soft rumbling noise in her throat. "Oh, Lady," she whispered and glanced across the room to the blanket-covered bodies of the Oleen soldiers. She shook her head and walked to the fire. "What about Ricken and Karl, don't they matter?" she said to Ekala, who was checking on Lander. "They were loyal. They didn't turn against you."

"Of course they matter, Boschina. I didn't leave them lying out in the forest, did I? Lander is different. She's the one that holds the answers, and she's still alive."

Thalmus had been listening and now came alongside Boschina. "Let me have a look at your shoulder," he said. "Sit over here by the fire so I can see it better."

Still looking at Ekala, Boschina said, "Alright, Thalmus." She sat down on the other side of the fire pit from Lander. She removed her coat and pulled up her shirt sleeve, grimacing as the material pulled away from the wound.

Thalmus went to the worn bags on Thunder and pulled out a small wooden flask and a hand-sized pouch. He dipped a cup in the pool and poured some water out, measuring just how much he wanted. Then, he added a few drops from the flask before removing several brown leaves from the pouch, crushed them in his hand, and sprinkled the pieces into the cup. He nestled the cup in the coals of the fire to heat while he took from his pocket the Marantac stalks they had picked in the forest; cutting off two pieces with his knife, he dropped them into the mixture. Stirring the contents with the blade of his knife, he said, "This will take away some of the pain and help mend the torn skin. It might help to relieve Lander's suffering, too."

Camp had taken his hot cup of soup and sat near the entrance tunnel to keep watch. Maz, who had been listening and watching the conversation, handed a cup to Ekala, who gladly accepted it. Lifting it to her lips, she carefully sipped the hot broth.

"Pardon me for asking," Camp said. "But what are we going to do to get out of here, to get back across the river? Glasrauss will be sending his troops after us in the morning; you can count on that."

"It's too dark to go anywhere right now," Ekala said. "If it wasn't for Bubo, we wouldn't have gotten here. And there are Chorgens running wild. Maybe Thunder can lead us to the river in the morning. He can always find water."

"And then what?" Maz asked. "Glasrauss' men will be waiting at the ford."

"Don't you know a way? I thought you came through here when you escaped from your brothers."

"We were farther west," Maz replied. "We wandered until we came out at the river and followed it to the ford, where we crossed at night. It was not guarded then."

"What are we going to do with her?" Camp said, pointing at Lander. "And the other two? We can't move very fast carrying them."

Ekala took a deep breath and exhaled. She knelt beside Lander and stroked her forehead. "She's warmer. Lander, Lander, wake up."

Lander moaned and rolled her head, but did not open her eyes.

Ekala lifted Lander's head and brought the cup to her mouth. "Drink this," she said.

Again, she did not open her eyes or her mouth.

Thalmus took his cup from the coals and dipped his knife into the mixture that had turned to a paste. He scooped a little of the brownish goo onto the blade and brought it up to Boschina's shoulder. "Be prepared, this will be hot and will sting," he told her. Then he carefully spread the mixture onto the wound with the flat of the blade. She winced, but did not pull away.

"Good," Thalmus said, acknowledging her strength. "Let it cool and dry before you cover your shoulder."

"This is supposed to make me feel better?" Boschina said through clenched teeth.

Thalmus smiled. "Yes, the pain will fade and the wound will heal, but your arm will be sore longer than you wish."

"Don't know how steady my arm will be with a bow," Boschina said.

"Rest your shoulder and the bow for now," Thalmus replied.

He moved to Lander, pulled the clothing away from the arrow shaft, and smeared some of the paste on the wound that was black and festering. The archer moaned and tried to lift her hand to the agony in her chest. A chain slid from under her shirt into the opening against the arrow. Dangling on the end of the silver links was an S-shaped piece of bronze. Thalmus hooked the chain with his finger and lifted the curved bronze emblem twisting like a snake above her shirt so Ekala could see it.

The Queen of Ameram stared at it for a moment and shook her head. "No, no, Lander, what...." She took Lander's head in both hands and shook her. "Wake up. What have you done?"

Lander stirred, opened her eyes, and gripped Ekala's arm. "Oleen," she whispered through a dry throat. "Why did you give in?"

"Give in? What do you mean?" Ekala asked, confused.

"You...became one of them."

"One of them?"

Lander's eyes rolled back and her eyelids closed.

"No, Lander, talk to me," Ekala said, shaking Lander's head.

The archer's eyes did not open, but her mouth did—her breathing short and shallow. Swallowing hard, she slowly spoke again. "You are not a queen. You are Oleen...one of us...not a queen." Her breathing stopped and her mouth gaped open—her hand still holding Ekala's arm.

Thalmus snapped the bronze snake from its link and tossed it into the fire.

Ekala let go of the archer's head and looked at the hand gripping her arm. "What does she mean, I'm not a queen?" She grasped the dead hand and pried the fingers loose. Dropping it on the ground, she stepped back. "One of them? She thinks I betrayed her."

"Maz, will you help me move Lander?" Thalmus asked.

The prince and Thalmus picked up Lander's limp body by the arms and legs, and then laid her beside the other Oleen soldiers. Ekala sat by the fire, staring into the flames.

Thalmus knelt beside her. "Do not let her, or anyone, make you doubt yourself. You are a queen. You are Ekala Oleen, daughter of King Ahmbin, and great-granddaughter of the great King Ahmbin the First. Royalty flows in your blood. It is your destiny. You *are* the Queen of Ameram."

"I will fight anyone who says different," Boschina said.

"As will I," Maz said.

"And I," Camp said from his seat at the cave entrance.

"Thank you," Ekala replied, looking around at them. "I do not doubt myself or my destiny. I know who I am. But I did not realize how determined my enemies were to destroy me. Do you think Glasrauss knew about Lander?"

"I think so," Maz said. "But he doesn't know that she no longer lives and that he can't count on her to kill you or me."

"What do you think, Thalmus?" Boschina asked. "Did he know about Lander?"

"Glasrauss did not corrupt her," Thalmus answered. "He is too distant. It was someone much closer. Someone we would not expect. We will all have to be very careful from now on. For tonight, it is safe for us to stay here, and then we must move. As Camp said, Lord Glasrauss will be pushing his troops after us in the morning. I doubt the soldiers will find this cave. Even if they do, we will be gone by then."

"I've been wondering since we got here: What is this place, Thalmus?" Maz asked. "All these etchings and paintings on the walls?"

"This room was dug out in the old days by the natives of this Wilderness," Thalmus said as he went to Thunder and untied his blankets from the pack saddles. "It had a very important purpose, as you can see from the drawings and writings on the walls."

"I can't understand them," Maz replied. "But I get an eerie feeling in here."

"So do I," Ekala said. "Almost like someone's watching us."

Thalmus spread his blanket on the ground toward the cave entrance, and then stood and looked around the room. The flames of the fire lit the walls and dome with a dancing amber glow of light that chased the shadows and caused the characters on the stone walls to appear as if they had come alive—running, singing, and playing with one another. "This is a sacred place," he said. "The people who made this room and painted these wonderful images over the time of many, many lives called it Ahmautahmin."

Boschina had been watching the characters and forming an idea as Thalmus spoke.

"What does that name mean?" she asked.

"Meeting place of the souls," Thalmus replied.

"So, this was a meeting room for their clan," Maz said, "with their history laid out on the walls."

"It is more than that," Boschina said thoughtfully. "I think I understand the images. They brought their dead here, didn't they? To somehow connect with them."

"Yes," Thalmus replied, "and to bury them."

"Here?" Ekala said, a little startled. "This is a tomb?"

"Not this room. Deeper into the cave there are tunnels where they carved niches to lay the bodies of their family, friends, and leaders. This room is where they met and celebrated with the souls of the ones who passed into the next life."

"I know the old stories about a people who once lived in this forest," Maz said. "The common belief is that they are ghosts; that they kill whoever dares to enter. That's why the Wilderness is so feared. This is the first that I've seen any sign of them, that they were living people. How did you know of this place, Thalmus?"

"Larma, she knows of the ancient tribes and of their ways." Thalmus paused, still appreciating the sense of the cave. "I was here once, a long time ago. There is nothing to fear here," he said reassuringly and turned to Ekala. "We can honor Ricken and Karl by leaving them amongst these people."

Ekala nodded slowly. "That would be fitting," she said. "And Lander as well. She was once good and fought valiantly as an Oleen. We will wrap them in their own blankets and leave their bows with them."

Boschina stood up. "I will help you."

"May I help?" Maz asked.

"Yes, thank you."

They carefully rolled each Oleen in a blanket, folded the top and bottom over, and pinned the flaps with arrows.

"How is your shoulder, Boschina?" Ekala asked. "Can you help me carry them?"

Boschina nodded. "I am honored to do so."

Camp kept watch at the cave opening while Thalmus pulled two burning sticks from the fire. He gave one to Maz and led the queen and the Stone Cutter's Daughter, carrying Karl first, down through a slim entrance of the tunnel with a little water trough and into the depths of the cavern as Maz followed with his torch. Walking slowly, they searched for a spot to lay their comrade. They passed many remains; mostly deteriorated wrappings and dusty bones in neat carved-out compartments just large enough for a body. The resting places were stacked three to four high along each side of the passageway and down side caves curving into the darkness. The display of the ancient bones and the stillness of the catacombs surrounded them as they inched along through the narrow tunnels. Long had the tomb been silent; now it was disturbed by the sounds of their breathing and shuffling steps. Finally, they arrived at a room that was lined with niches, half of which were empty. The sisters gently laid Karl into one of the openings, placed his bow at his side, and rested their hands on his body. Queen Ekala Oleen whispered, "Rest in peace, Karl, soldier of the Oleens, loyal son of Ameram and warrior for truth."

They stepped back, bowed, and then turned and started the climb out to retrieve the next fallen soldier. After repeating the ceremony for Ricken, they carried Lander through the maze to the room and placed her in a bottom niche. Boschina laid the archer's bow on top of her and they stood back, silently waiting for someone to speak.

Finally, Ekala spoke. "Lander, you were once loyal and good and fought as a true Oleen. You betrayed us, but I have to believe that it was not your fault. You were tricked by the voices of evil. I forgive you for what you have done. Rest in peace, Archer of the Oleens."

The funeral party filed back through the narrow passages of the catacombs and rested silently around the fire, where they watched the images on the walls dancing in the flickering light of the flames, envisioning their friends amongst the revelers.

Thalmus looked around at his companions. Thunder, Dallion, and the horses were sleeping, resting from the trek and battle across the plain. Bubo's eyes were closed, but he knew the owl was listening, ready to respond at any warning sound. If it had not been for him gathering the swarm of birds and his fight with the Altons, they would not have reached the Wilderness. Ekala, Boschina, and Maz appeared to be in a trance, staring at the many frolicking characters. "We must get some sleep," he said. "We must be moving before sun-up."

"I'll take the first watch," Camp said. "But I can't sleep if we don't know how we're gettin' out of here in the morning."

"You can rest, Camp, knowing we will find our way back," Thalmus replied assuredly.

Boschina had been watching and listening to Thalmus. She knew him well enough to be able to tell when he wasn't sharing everything, which was normal. However, she was sure he had a plan, probably had it thought out long before they'd crossed the plain. "So how do we get out of here, Thalmus?" she asked.

He smiled at her as he rolled into his blanket. "Through the Wilderness, of course."

Chapter Twenty-Three
Surprise at the River

While the forest was still dark and the fire burning low in the cavern, Thalmus roused the others to rise and prepare to leave. He had the last watch of the night and spent the quiet hours alone, feeling the essence of the cave and the depth of the people resting in the catacombs waiting for life to rise again. His last visit to Ahmautahmin had been with Larma, long ago, when they gathered with the Order of Servants to mourn the death of an Ancient who had succumbed after a long life of service. The great guide and teacher had decided to be placed here, amongst the old souls of the native people: a common grave for a common person, as she claimed herself to be. Since then, others of the Order had passed on and Thalmus had visited with them at their graves, paying honor to their loyal service.

Where would my final resting place be? Thalmus wondered. If he had a choice, it would be on a bluff overlooking the Great Water. But this was a distant decision that may not be his. For now, he had a job to do and it was difficult enough without wondering about his mortality. His thoughts turned to Lander. Who had corrupted the once loyal archer and how many more like her were influenced to turn against Ekala? It was hard to believe any of the original Oleen soldiers would do so. Yet, Lander did.

Opposition to Ekala ruling the kingdom was to be expected, but not by someone so close to her. Evil was running rampant in Toulon; in Ameram, it was hiding under the surface. Glancing at Prince Bolimaz's horse with Corsair's sword sheathed along the saddle, he questioned again why the prince kept it with him. It should have been destroyed with the other weapons of Metro's army after the Battle for Ambermal.

Larma's message began to beat in his chest pocket. He removed it and carefully opened the folded cloth. The cryptic letters glowed in the dusky cavern, expanding the words and meaning, speaking to him in the mystic's voice: "Due west, through the Wilderness to the river. Help is waiting." Then the words dimmed and became static once again. Quietly folding the message, he placed it back in his pocket as the others rolled their blankets and packed the horses. Thunder had moved closer to him during the night and had been watching as Thalmus read the message. He extended his big head and pushed into the hunter's chest. Thalmus smiled and pet the shell creature's bald head. Dallion walked over and nickered to Thalmus. "Yes, Dal," he said, patting the stallion's shoulder, "we are getting out of here."

"Where's Bubo?" Boschina asked as she led Radise to the cave opening. Her sword was fastened on her belt, her unstrung bow in its cover on Radise.

"He went out, looking for dinner—or breakfast," Thalmus replied.

Ekala walked up with Shadahn following her. "We're ready." As always, her sword hung from the belt on her left side and the short blade on her right.

Maz and Camp were also ready. "Well," Maz said. "Where are we going?"

"Due west to the river," Thalmus said. "Try to keep close. If anyone gets separated, keep moving. The sun will be up soon and probably hard to see through the trees, but it will be at our backs all morning, casting shadows to the west."

"What happens at the river?" Camp asked. "We can't get across it."

"We'll find out when we get there, right?" Boschina said, smiling at Thalmus.

Thalmus smiled back at her and nodded.

"Let's keep an eye out for the Toulon troops," Ekala said. "They'll be coming after us—as well as those pesky Altons."

"You can count on that," Maz said. "Why don't Camp and I take the lead?"

"It is better we stay in a battle line formation so we can all see one another, with Thunder and me in the middle," Thalmus said. "The horses can follow behind us."

Filing out of the cavern through the small opening and into the cold dampness of the forest, they followed Thunder into the snarl of the Wilderness. Fanning out on either side of the giant shell creature, they formed a line with Thalmus, Ekala, and Maz on the right side of Thunder, and Boschina and Camp on his left. Pushing and cutting through tangled vines, brush, and tree branches, they moved forward with the horses following them.

Bubo was resting in a tree after feasting during the night. Sounds in the distance caused his head to turn in that direction and his eyes opened. He listened for a moment, spread his wings, and then quietly flew to the noises. Landing on a branch against the gnarled trunk of a tree, he blended with the bark and waited. The crashing sounds of swords through branches and stomping feet approached him. Finally, Toulon soldiers with swords and axes in hand emerged into the owl's view. There were many green-clad men in all directions, chopping and working their way through the forest.

The Great Horned owl turned and flew away from the approaching horde.

Coming to a sunken area in the ground, Camp and Boschina separated from the others, finding an animal path around the wide hole.

"How come it's always a mystery with Thalmus?" Camp asked Boschina.

Boschina chuckled. "You don't know him, do you? You haven't traveled with him like I have."

"No. This is the first time."

"Do you trust him?"

"Sure…I mean, he's The Hunter, right? He's been around a long time and he's survived when most haven't. I just don't like not knowing what's next."

"I understand," Boschina replied. "But Thalmus and Larma live and think and move differently than we do."

"Oh, I get that," Camp said.

"I liken it to when I'm carving stone with my father," Boschina said, pushing branches out of her way. "You must be patient, allowing the character and heart of the image to reveal itself, and then you learn more than you ever thought. Thalmus is like that. He has the wisdom of the Ancients and a long life buried deep within him. If you wait and listen, and carefully chip at the stone, that knowledge is revealed."

"Guess I'll never be a sculptor," Camp replied. "Patience has never been a virtue of mine, but I'll give it a try."

Boschina held up the sword that she had been using to clear her path. The engraved images of Dallion, Thunder, and Bubo stared back, filling her with a sense of strength and confidence. "Trust in his way," she said. "You'll be better for it."

They had circled the obstacle and rejoined with Thunder and the others when Bubo drifted by and landed on Thunder's broad shell. Stopping to listen, they all watched Owl as he hooted and chortled, and then lifted off and flew east.

"The Toulons are coming up behind us, aren't they?" Ekala said.

"Yes, we must move faster," Thalmus replied, motioning to Thunder to speed up.

"How far are we from the river?" Boschina asked.

"We must be getting close," Maz said.

With a new sense of urgency, they moved faster. Thalmus did not know what to expect when they reached the river. However, Larma's message was clear: help would be there. Whatever it was, he counted on it now.

Bubo came back hooting and flew past them, before disappearing again into the forest. While the others kept moving, Thalmus dropped back and waited in a thicket of trees. He could hear the excited clamor of the Toulon soldiers who had found their trail and were forging after them. Listening, judging distances, he could tell there were many pursuers spread out through the forest.

Glasrauss must have sent most of his army into the woods, he thought.

Then the hunter sensed the presence of something else—something more dangerous than the soldiers—moving unseen in the forest. He sniffed the air, trying to pick up a scent. Was it the creatures they had heard last night? A flash of movement in the distant trees caught his eye. It was an Alton flying between the branches. The large bird was searching for them. Thalmus scanned the woods looking for movement. He inhaled the scents of the woods for animals. Finding nothing, he moved back carefully through the cover of the brush and caught up with Thunder.

"The Toulons may be ahead of us on our right," Thalmus told Ekala and Maz.

"We're ready for 'em," the queen answered gripping her sword.

Thunder clicked several times. Thalmus tapped his shell and motioned to the others. In a few moments, their struggle through the brush and trees abruptly ended as they emerged from the forest and stood looking at the bare gravel bank, the wide, turbulent river and the green plain on the other side. Standing still now, searching for the presence of help, they could hear their pursuers crunching toward them.

"What now?" Ekala asked. "Do we go west to the ford?"

"We wait," Thalmus replied, scanning the opposite shore.

Camp glanced at Boschina, who appeared confident as she looked across the river. He took a deep breath, let it out, and waited as he, too, looked anxiously up and down at the empty shoreline and rushing water.

"Those troops will be on us soon," Maz said. "What are we waiting for?"

"Our help," Thalmus replied calmly.

Upriver, Bubo appeared flying along the bank on the other side. Riding after him was an Oleen soldier. The maroon-clad rider stopped directly across from them and held up her right arm with an open hand high over her head. Ekala Oleen responded, returning the salute with her up stretched hand. The rider dropped her arm, made the motion to stay, and then pointed at Bubo, who was starting across the river toward them. The great owl was carrying the end of a rope in his talons. The line, trailing behind him, drooped and tugged in the current, causing him to struggle and flap his wings harder and faster. The closer he got to them, more of the line sank into the river and dragged him down toward the roiling surface.

Thalmus saw his friend struggling, fighting to stay in the air, and realized he would not make it all the way and would have to let go of the rope to survive. He ran to Ricken's horse and untied a coiled rope that was used for the horses' security line. It was not very long, but it would have to be enough. Un-belting his sword, he handed it to Boschina.

"Ekala, Maz, hold the end of this rope," he said. "I am going to help Bubo."

Tying the other end around his waist, he moved to the water's edge. Bubo was just several hands width above the water now, his wingtips dipping into the current with each flap; his talons were still clamped onto the rope and his yellow eyes focused across the distance on Thalmus. The rushing water was pulling the rope and Bubo downstream, farther away.

Thunder had moved next to Ekala and Maz, right behind Thalmus. The hunter leapt out as far as he could and was immediately swept up in the churning water. Swimming with driving rapid strokes and kicking hard, he closed the distance and reached Bubo, grasped the rope, and lifted him up just as he was about to be pulled into the river. Bubo dropped the rope into Thalmus' hand and winged upward enough to fly to shore, landing exhausted on a low branch. At that moment, the rope tied around Thalmus' waist came to its end and he was suddenly pulled under the surface. At the other end of the rope, Ekala and Maz were almost yanked into the river, but Thunder clamped onto the line with his powerful jaws and dug in his feet. The giant shell creature instinctively started moving along the shore with the flow of the water.

Thalmus came up for air and quickly tied the rope from across the river around his waist. Then he started swimming through the current toward shore. His friends on the rope moved along the bank, pulling Thalmus and the drag of the other rope gradually to them at the edge. Camp and Maz grabbed hold of Thalmus and helped him onto land as the river rope tried to pull him back in. Thunder released the horse rope from his jaws, clamped onto the river rope, and began plodding up the bank to the trees. They all joined in, lined up along the rope from the water's edge to the trees, and, like a tug of war, yanked the long, wet rope from the current and wrapped it around the largest trees they could find.

The Oleen soldier on the opposite bank clasped her hands in joy above her head and again motioned for them to stay where they were. She turned her horse and galloped east along the river.

They were happy with their success at getting the rope out of the water and tied to the trees, but looking upriver, they began to wonder what the other end of the rope was attached to. What purpose did it serve?

"Now what?" Maz asked. "What good is this rope?"

Camp chimed in. "We surely can't pull ourselves and the horses across with that."

Ekala glanced up the river and then at Thalmus who was untying the line around his waist. "Larma's at the end of that rope, isn't she?"

Rolling up the horse line, Thalmus nodded. "I believe so."

Then he saw the Alton circling overhead.

The slashing sounds of their pursuers turned their attention to the Wilderness once again. Suddenly, four Toulon soldiers stumbled from the forest, not thirty meters upriver from the rope line.

"Here we go," Camp said, pulling his sword from its scabbard.

Maz jumped beside him. "We'll handle those troops."

Boschina handed Thalmus his sword and quickly drew her own. Dallion and the horses reared, stomped, and snorted, ready for a fight. Two more soldiers stepped out of the woods behind them downriver from the line, followed by six more farther down the bank.

"Thalmus and I will take these," Ekala said as they started moving to each side of Thunder. "Guard the horses, Boschina. Make sure no one gets behind us."

"As you wish, Oleen," Boschina responded.

Upriver, four wooden rafts appeared bobbing along the rope line. An Oleen soldier piloted each flat barge, pushed and buffeted by the current down the rope. The barges were fastened together in a row. Boschina saw the rafts and hollered at Camp. "Help is on the rope!"

"I'll be—it's a guide rope for the rafts," Camp said.

"I am Prince Bolimaz," Maz shouted at the Toulon soldiers. "Surrender and fight with me against my brothers."

"That's him," one of the men said. "Let's get him!"

"You fools," Camp hollered as they clashed swords.

The soldiers facing Ekala and Thalmus moved slowly up the narrow spit of land that was the riverbank, eyeing the giant shell creature as he snapped his jaws and hissed. Two men suddenly broke through the brush next to Ekala and thrust at her. She quickly deflected the first man's sword, pushing him aside, and swung to face the second attacker. To her surprise, he was slammed to the earth by a large hairy animal ripping at his throat. The first man recovered and swiped again at Ekala, who blocked his sword and shoved him back. The beast left the dead man on the ground and pounced on the soldier, growling and rolling with him to the water's edge where the soldier, bloody and screaming, jerked free, fell into the current, and was swept away. The beast raised its head toward the sky and howled, and then turned toward Ekala, crouched down, and glared at her.

The approaching Toulon soldiers stopped. The surprise appearance and vicious attack by the Chorgen startled them and they stared with astonishment at the crouched creature and Ekala standing before it. "She commands a Chorgen," one of the men said in disbelief.

Thalmus jumped between Ekala and the Chorgen. With his short blade in one hand and his sword in the other, he stared into the eyes of the beast, waiting for him to leap.

"Thalmus step aside," Ekala said.

"This beast knows you," Thalmus said, his eyes never leaving the Chorgen. "He was protecting you."

"Yes," she said, realizing who the creature was and what it had just done for her.

"We had a little race, didn't we," she said to the beast. "I guess you enjoyed it."

The beast's yellow eyes watched her with anticipation. Its blood-covered, hairy snout snorted and snarled, revealing pointed fangs. It smelled foul, like a long-dead animal.

"It's a Chorgen," Boschina said. "You can't trust it."

More soldiers were tumbling out of the woods and gathering to attack. "Look out!" A soldier hollered. "She commands a Chorgen." The soldiers hesitated, grouping together. Then another called out, "There's Bolimaz behind them." And they surged forward—right into a storm of arrows knocking many of them to the ground.

Looking over their shoulders to see where the arrows came from, Ekala and Thalmus saw the first two rafts coming downstream toward them with Oleen archers reloading their bows and firing again. Then came a chorus of voices shouting, "Oleen! Oleen!"

The Chorgen howled in response and bounded toward Ekala. Thalmus dove under to stab the beast in its belly, but it veered to the side, brushed against Ekala, and disappeared into the forest. Ekala stumbled away from the Chorgen and turned ready to fight it or another attacker.

The lead barge on the rope bumped onto the shore and the Oleen soldiers jumped onto the bank. Some of the archers formed a line behind Thunder while others stood in front of the horses, facing upriver with Maz and Camp. The Oleen archers kept up a steady fire in both directions, driving the Toulon men back into the woods.

"Boschina," Thalmus shouted, "Get the horses loaded. Dal," he called to the Paint and pointed at the now-empty barge, "go!"

The big stallion reared and jumped onto the barge and then trotted across the next two to the fourth bobbing platform. Shadahn and the other horses followed him, but Radise stopped to check with Boschina, who patted her shoulder and ran with her onto the barges.

"Come on, Maz," Ekala called, waving him to the barges.

The Prince of Toulon grabbed Camp's arm, tugging at him to leave, and they joined the queen climbing onto the barge. Then came Thunder, lifting himself onto the jerking, bouncing barge with the help of Ekala, Maz, and Camp pulling on his shell. The Oleen soldiers retreated in formation, supporting each other with alternating lines shooting and then moving. The archers continued shooting as they spread out on the floating platforms, their deadly arrows holding back the Toulon soldiers.

Thalmus surveyed the bank to make sure no one was left behind. The sun reflected on something in the shadows. He thought it might be more soldiers, but then saw the Chorgen hiding in the brush at the edge of the trees, his glaring eyes watching Ekala. The hunter swung his sword, slicing through the rope tying the barges to the tree, and jumped aboard the raft. The current pushed the line of floats away from the shore and out into the rolling river. Thalmus grabbed the loose end of the rope he had cut and, with Camp's help, tied it around the front log of the barge. Then he checked on the passengers, humans and animals, steadying themselves on the rocking floats. The line of log rafts was pulling to the southern shore and he looked that way to see the willowy mystic sitting on her horse. A long row of mounted Oleen soldiers waited behind her. He felt her smile and returned a grateful "thank you."

Ekala gave Larma an Oleen salute and all the mounted soldiers raised their right hands in response.

Chapter Twenty-Four
Barges on the Water

The Toulon soldiers stood hopelessly scattered along the northern bank watching their prey float away. On the southern side of the river a line of mounted Oleen soldiers sat calmly looking back at them. Their leader, a woman of undetermined age, sitting tall and powerful on a stunning gray horse, was sending a message that their cause was lost—to go home. They heard it in their heads and felt it in their chests, heavy and depressing, like lead coursing through their veins. Frustrated, the men began to help their fallen comrades. For two days they had chased and fought Prince Bolimaz, the Ameram Queen, and their strange friends only to be outsmarted and defeated. The big owl with his minions of flocking birds, the devilish brown and white stallion causing havoc amongst their horses, the snapping giant shell creature, a Chorgen commanded by the warrior queen, the barges that came out of nowhere with the deadly archers, and then the mysterious woman with her army telling them to go home.

How could they beat such things?

The men began to think the magic of these people could help Bolimaz return to power over his brothers. They had failed to capture the prince or the queen. The two had escaped Lord Glasrauss' trap and now the men dreaded facing his anger.

On the rolling barges, joy and relief filled the hearts and minds of humans and animals alike. Queen Ekala and Prince Bolimaz moved amongst the Oleen soldiers, thanking them for their rescue and congratulating them on performing such a dangerous maneuver on the river. Thalmus and Boschina checked on Thunder, who had all four feet planted firmly on the log decking of the raft, and then with Dallion, who was not happy about being confined on the rocking boat.

"It won't be long," Thalmus assured him, patting his shoulder as the big Paint grumbled, spreading his legs wider to maintain his balance.

The great owl was nowhere to be seen. He had let Thalmus know he was leaving during the fight by flying past him just before arrows began filling the air. Radise was settled in for the ride with Shadahn and the other horses. Camp stayed on the bow of the first barge and watched the Toulon Wilderness for more troops. As Thalmus and Boschina moved across the deck of the four flat barges, tied together end to end, he examined their construction. Each raft was made with three large logs, approximately ten meters long, laid parallel to each other and set two meters apart. Similar sized logs at each end of the long logs created a rectangle and completed the main structure. Lashed over the top of this frame were tightly packed branches of various diameters, from the thickness of a man's wrist to the size of a leg, which created a bumpy, uneven surface. The reeds and jute ropes that had been used to tie the logs and branches together were stressed to their limit and beginning to crack and loosen from the bouncing of the current and the weight of the additional cargo. The smaller cross-branches suffered breaks as the heavy horses' hooves settled on them.

Boschina watched Thalmus' inspection, saw what he saw, and knew what he was thinking: How long will the rafts stay together? How much time do we have before the river yanks our escape from under us?

"Your Majesty," Thalmus said to Ekala, "these rafts are slowly breaking apart."

The captain of the archers stood next to Ekala and quickly explained. "Oleen, I'm sorry. We tried to build these rafts to Larma's instructions, but we were short of materials and time. We put them together far up river in the woods on the north side of Table Top and floated them down with ropes and horses to where Larma said you would need them. We've never built such things before. I'm sorry. I've failed you."

Queen Ekala Oleen put her hand on the woman's shoulder. "You have not failed me. You and your force saved us. I am thankful for all you have done. As for these rafts, we will have to work with what we have. Now, do you and Larma have a plan for getting us to the south shore?"

"Yes, but not until we reach a bend at the river that Larma said is near a camp of stragglers."

"Then lash the logs together as best as you can with what you have and we'll pray these trees beneath our feet stay together until we reach the bend," Ekala said.

The mounted Oleen soldiers on the south shore had turned and galloped downriver ahead of the rafts as Larma trotted the majestic gray Eidolon at a steady pace, staying even with the barges.

Thalmus could feel Larma's concern as he worked his way through the animals and people across the wet branches to the front of the first barge. Camp stood there watching the river splash over the logs as they dipped and rose in the current. "You know about the rafts?" Thalmus asked him.

"I heard," the old warrior replied. "I guess you'd say, 'we live with what we got,' right?"

Thalmus smiled. "Yes, we make do with what we have."

"That was a narrow escape," Camp said. "Risky, I'd say, and still is."

"Depends on how you look at it," Thalmus replied.

Camp motioned toward Larma, who kept pace with them on the shore. "You knew she was coming, didn't ya?"

"I knew she was sending help," Thalmus said. "I am glad she came with it."

"How'd she know where to find us?"

Thalmus glanced up at the clouds drifting overhead. "She has her ways."

"When Maz and I joined the Oleens to fight Gorga for control of Table Top," Camp said, "and then marched to Ambermal and fought in that battle, I always had an overwhelming feeling of Larma's authority and confidence. I feel it again now."

"Comforting," Thalmus said. "That is what I feel. There will always be trials, challenges; but in the end, if one believes, truth prevails."

Camp studied the hunter, a man who was a full head and shoulder shorter, yet Camp felt Thalmus' power and saw the strength in his quiet, humble demeanor. "I knew of your reputation before we met at Table Top," Camp said. "I fought alongside you at Ambermal, but these last three days have proved to me that all that is said about you is more than true."

Thalmus looked up at him, and then back to the turbulent water ahead. "That depends on what is being said and who is saying it."

Camp snorted a laugh. "That's true." He rubbed his eyes and neck, stretched his back and massaged his shoulder. "I'm getting old, too many aches and sores. What of you, Thalmus, aren't you tired? How long have you been in this life?"

"Not long enough." Thalmus replied and glanced at the taller man. "Did Boschina tell you to ask me that question?"

"No, why?"

"Just wondering."

"She's been trying to teach me patience."

"Boschina?" Thalmus questioned. "Is it working?"

"I think so," Camp replied. "One stone chip at a time."

Thalmus nodded, understanding Camp's meaning.

Ekala Oleen and Maz joined them, stepping carefully across the slippery logs.

"Isn't that the refugee camp up ahead?" Maz asked, pointing at the scattered tents and wagons on the south shore.

"Just in time," Ekala said. "The logs are starting to come apart."

The people who had fled from Toulon had set up camp where the river made a slight bend, creating a small eddy on the south shore. The Oleen soldiers who had galloped ahead were waiting on the bank upriver from the camp.

Onboard the barges, the archers stepped around holes from broken and loose branches and propped up six heavy, oversized long bows, each with a rope tied to thick-shanked arrows. The ropes were coiled in front of the bows and the ends tied to each barge. Two Oleen soldiers on each big bow nocked the sturdy arrow in the taut string and pulled it back as far as they could, and then released it toward shore. Whirling across the water with their braided tails in tow, the six arrows stuck in the ground at various distances from the water as the ropes dropped into the river. The Oleens on the bank rushed to grab the ropes and tie them to horses, who began to pull the barges out of the main current. By the time the decaying rafts reached the river bend, they had been tugged into the eddy where the circling current pushed the rafts against the bank. It was none too soon, as the last two rafts had started tearing apart, the pieces being pulled back into the swifter main current. Everyone rushed to herd the horses forward and off onto solid ground. Dallion bounded from his confinement onto dry land and ran straight up the nearest hill, disappearing over the top.

Larma was waiting on Eidolon when Queen Ekala Oleen jumped ashore on the back of Shadahn, followed by Maz on Mendu and Boschina riding Radise, to the cheers of the Oleens.

"Thank you, Larma, for coming to rescue us," Ekala Oleen said.

"My dear Queen," the mystic said, "mine was but a small part. It was Boschina who carried the message to Thalmus. She joined him and his companions to bring you back to our soil. They deserve the gratitude, though I doubt that they will acknowledge it."

Ekala looked at Boschina. "No matter the danger, you are always there."

"It is my honor to do so," Boschina said.

Ekala said, "As for Thalmus," she turned to see the hunter and Camp helping Thunder off the barge. "I am always in his debt."

Another cheer went up from the people of the camp who had gathered to welcome Prince Bolimaz and the Queen of Ameram. They considered it a victory that the two had ridden into Toulon, challenged Glasrauss' army, and returned through the Wilderness and across the river unscathed. Little did they know of the near-fatal mistakes, the death of two loyal soldiers, the betrayal of another, and the role of the Stone Cutter's Daughter or Thalmus and his companions. They seemed like minor characters to these forlorn people; all that mattered was that a new leader, one of their own in whom they could believe, had emerged to fight for them. The story grew and soon became known as "The Raid on Glasrauss" with the Crown Prince Bolimaz and Queen Ekala Oleen of Ameram as victors. They fought side by side to confound their common enemy and send the message of his impending demise. Thus, much to the queen's dismay, a new legend was born.

Larma held up her hand to quiet the crowd. "Unfortunately, Oleen, we do not have time for you two to enjoy these accolades. Your presence is required at the North Ford, where Captain Ritzs is battling with persistent troops from the north."

"Prince Bolimaz," Benton the swordsman said, stepping forward and nodding his head to the prince. "My sword and my life are at your service."

A dozen other men from the camp gathered around the big swordsman, pledging their support as well. Their voices rang out:

"Mine too."

"I am with you!"

"I stand with you!"

"We'll fight with you!"

Neb, Benton's son, raised his bow over his head and declared, "Crown Prince of Toulon, my bow and I are at your service."

"I thank you, young Neb, and all of you," Prince Bolimaz said. "I will need you when the time comes to take back our country. For now, you have a responsibility to your families, who need your protection here."

"We want to fight with you now," Benton said, "to show Glasrauss' soldiers that you have Toulon men on your side."

"I like it," Ekala said. "Prince Bolimaz, I would be pleased to have your men fight alongside my Oleens."

"Very well," Maz said, smiling at Ekala. "Swordsman Benton, organize your best men and meet me at the ford."

The Oleen soldiers were already handing the ropes and battered barges over to the refugees, gathering the horses and hustling into formation. Additional mounts had been brought for the archers on the raft—and within moments, the entire force was ready to move. Thunder was taking a direct line toward the ford, plodding through the refugee camp as the people stepped back out of his way.

Walking to the queen, and looking up at her, Thalmus said, "Your Majesty, unless you have other orders for me, Thunder and I will see you at the ford."

Queen Ekala Oleen looked down from Shadahn at the hunter. *Where would I be without him?* "Of course, Thalmus, bring Thunder along as soon as you can."

Larma reached out to Thalmus and he took her hand in his. Standing on the ground beside her on the horse, they looked into each other's eyes, saying nothing, yet communicating with one another, exchanging thanks and peace and knowing. Finally, Thalmus released her hand and turned to catch up with Thunder.

The others had noticed the exchange between the two, but didn't pay much attention as Ekala and Maz moved to organize the forces around them. Boschina, however, watched her two mentors closely, impressed by the obvious messages passing between the two Guardians of the Ancient Order of Servants. She could almost tell what they were saying to one another. She definitely felt the intensity of their contact and the strength shared and empowered in them because her own body tingled with a new confidence and her mind was calm.

Larma turned her gaze on Boschina. "Your senses are improving."

Surprised and embarrassed for being caught eavesdropping, Boschina looked away, patting Radise's neck. She then looked back at Larma. "You can tell what I felt between you and Thalmus?"

"I see it in your posture, in your eyes, and your battered face. What did you learn from the Lady of the Woods?"

"Like you, Larma, she had a power about her. She spoke the stone truth of her faith."

"I want to hear more about your journey there and your feelings on the loss of Lander." Larma smiled softly. "Look at you, tattered and worn, inside and out. These last days have been trying for you."

Boschina touched the bruises on her face and neck. "Do I look bad?"

"Probably no worse than you feel."

"I'm alright, Larma. I'm learning a lot. I understood much of what Arborina spoke, even though she was a statue. Last night, we slept in the cave of Ahmautahmin. We left Karl, Ricken, and Lander there amongst the old bones. I could hear some of the voices of the souls buried in its depths. When we got to the river, I wasn't scared. I knew help was coming."

"You are learning to listen and feel, Boschina. You must be careful to not expect too much and how you interpret what you sense. That can be more difficult than the seeing and hearing. What are your feelings about Lander?"

Boschina rubbed Radise's neck before answering. "I am angry. I don't understand why she turned on Oleen…why she killed Ricken and Karl. It doesn't make sense."

"Trying to make sense of another's reasoning is a quagmire that can pull you into depths you never imagined. You are not ready for that, Boschina."

Boschina did not want to talk about it anymore. "I'd better join Oleen," she said. "They're already moving."

Larma stopped her. "For now, I want you to join Thalmus and Thunder. I am sure they will appreciate your company. I will tell Oleen you are with them. We will meet all of you at the ford.

Boschina nodded. "As you wish, Larma. We'll see you at the ford."

Chapter Twenty-Five
Battle At the North Ford

Boschina caught up with Thunder tramping through the refugee camp and Thalmus walking beside him. She swung her leg over Radise's back and dropped on the other side of the giant shell creature, who clicked a welcome. Radise neighed a greeting, bobbing her head, and then trailed behind Boschina.

"You didn't like that float down the river, did you, big guy?" Boschina said, patting the tortoise's shell.

Thunder snorted, turning his head to look at her for a moment.

"You're right," Boschina said. "It's been a rough trip so far, but I'm sure glad you're here. You're always showing up when I'm in trouble."

Thunder stretched his neck out a little longer and raised his head a notch as he continued his march between the makeshift shelters and wagons.

The downtrodden people of the camp smiled and greeted them, yet were cautious. They stayed clear of the giant tortoise as he plodded along until Thalmus lifted several of the children onto Thunder's back—to the horror of the parents, but to the delight of the kids. A gaiety filled the people, something they had not felt in a long time. The children grinned with wonder at the feel of Thunder's shell and the excitement of riding on the back of such a strange creature. Boschina felt their joy and, at the same time, their plight:

separated from home, surviving in a foreign land, and not knowing what would become of them. She smiled sympathetically at Thalmus, who smiled back. He understood what she was experiencing because he felt it, too.

Thalmus had a reason for walking through the refugee camp. Although bringing some joy to the children and families was a good cause, he was looking for a spy. Someone had betrayed Prince Bolimaz and he was pretty sure that individual would not be joining Benton and his swordsmen in a possible fight at the ford. The men still in the camp were too old to fight or were physically broken. The women had all joined in with the crowd following Thunder and the kids, except one. A long-haired, mournful woman stood beside a man leaning on a stick crutch. They were separate from the others, standing in front of a pushcart laden with household belongings and a canvas lean-to tent tied to the side of it. Both of them looked forlorn and sad watching the children playing on Thunder.

The man closed his eyes. He had seen enough. He turned away, said something to the woman, and then awkwardly laid down under the tent. Crossing her arms on her belly, the woman continued watching until she saw Thalmus looking at her. For a moment, their eyes met and Thalmus saw pain and regret before her hands came up to cover her face and she sat down beside the man under the lean-to.

Thalmus took a deep breath and let it out. He felt sorry for the couple. Evil was holding them hostage. They had no control under the thrall of a wicked master. She had so much as told him.

Two children jumped off Thunder in front of Boschina and she helped another one climb onto his shell as he continued trudging forward.

"May I walk with you?" a gentle voice said.

Boschina turned to see Neb walking at an arm's length beside her. He was carrying his bow, a quiver of arrows slung across his back. "It appears you already are," she said.

The tall boy looked down, embarrassed. "Just wanted to talk with you."

"Of course, you can walk with us," Boschina replied. "I thought you were going with your father and the other men to join Prince Bolimaz."

"He only wanted to take swordsmen. I guess he figured an archer wasn't needed."

"Or, he thought the Oleen archers were enough," Boschina said.

"Maybe...either way, I'm still here." He paused, looking at her shoulder. "Your shirt's bloody and your face...did you get hurt?"

"A little," Boschina replied, realizing how she must look. "We were in several fights."

"I'm glad you're okay," Neb said.

Radise nickered and Boschina glanced over her shoulder at the mare. Neb moved a little closer as they walked, watching the children riding on Thunder.

"I didn't know the shell creature was friendly."

"He can be," Boschina replied. "Unless we're attacked—then he'd take your head off with one snap."

Neb straightened up. "He's okay now, right?"

"Of course, Thunder loves kids."

Neb was a head taller than Boschina. He had a lanky frame with a fluid gait.

"Did you want to ask me something?" Boschina said.

"Oh, yes, well...you said you could teach me...help me with shooting." He raised the bow as if she hadn't seen it.

"I remember," Boschina said. "But it wasn't me. You told me Queen Ekala Oleen offered Lander's help."

"But Lander isn't here, is she?"

Boschina looked ahead. They were nearing the end of the camp. An image of Lander's body wrapped in a blanket with her bow resting on top of her appeared from the depths of the catacombs. "No, she isn't here," Boschina said. And then in a whisper to herself, "Nor will she ever be."

"Then, can you help me?"

She looked up at the boy's eager face and thought, *Who will teach him if I do not? How can I say no?* "Alright, Neb, son of Benton, let's do what we can on our way to the ford. String your bow."

"It is."

"Do you always keep your bow strung?"

"Yes, so it's ready. Is that wrong?"

"Neb, the bow should remain unstrung until you're ready to shoot. See my bow on Radise? The string is looped loosely on the limbs. Let me see your bow."

Neb handed the bow to Boschina and she lifted it to a shooting position and pulled back the string. "It's too loose. By keeping it strung all the time you've stressed the string," she said, running a hand over the limbs. "It's weathered and starting to splinter." She looked up at his worried face. "You need a new bow and string, Neb. But for now, we'll have to use it."

"I didn't know—"

"It's alright," Boschina said. "We'll have our bowyer make one to fit you."

They had reached the last tents of the camp and the children jumped off Thunder as Thalmus encouraged them and said goodbye. The refugees waved as Thunder trudged on, flanked by Thalmus, Boschina, and Neb.

"Let's pick a target," Boschina said, handing the bow back to Neb. "You see that tall clump of grass ahead, the one to the left of the wagon ruts?"

"Yes."

"Hit it with an arrow." She stopped while Neb pulled an arrow from the quiver on his back and nocked it in the bow string. "Don't worry about Thunder; he'll keep going." Neb straightened his left arm and hand holding the bow and pulled the arrow back with the fingers of his right hand. He sighted down the arrow, elevated, and released. The arrow arched across the distance and landed three meters beyond the clump.

"Try another one," Boschina said. "This time, don't look down the shaft: focus on a blade of grass in that clump. Narrow your vision to that one blade. And calm your fingers—they're shaking."

The second arrow landed short of the clump by two meters.

"Okay, one more before we catch Thunder and pick up the arrows," Boschina said. "Consistency is the key, Neb. Keep the same nock-point on the string, the same anchor point at your chin or whatever is comfortable, but do the same thing each time."

Neb pulled back the third arrow, hesitated, adjusted, and then released, this time hitting the ground two meters to the left of the clump.

"Good. You've got the distance, but you're off to the left. You need a lot of practice or you'll never survive as an archer. If it takes you three shots to hit your enemy, you'll be dead. Now let's pick another target."

Thalmus watched with approval as Boschina became the instructor. She had learned so much since he first met her. She had always been strong and fearless, willing to attempt anything; traits she'd learned from her father. Now she was confident, growing in wisdom, and was beginning to understand who she could be. The hunter followed along, watching and wondering how much longer it would be, how much more must she experience before she realized her destiny.

* * *

Dysaan and his small force from the King's Guard had ridden into Ello hoping to find the queen, or at least word of her passing through on her way back to Ambermal. Instead, the villagers told him about Oleen troops, with the Stone Cutter's Daughter, who had hurried through on their way to the Great Water; and then returned with Thalmus, Thunder, and Dallion before heading to the North Ford. Upon hearing this, the veteran soldier knew for sure something was wrong. Thalmus would not have been called back for a friendly visit to the gateway to Toulon and the countries north. When the people told him about the broken statue, and Veracitas' departure with the other force of Oleens, his hopes sank lower. He had wanted to rest in the friendly village for a day, thinking the queen would be there or would have already passed through on her way home; but now, there was no time to delay. Something bad was happening. The queen may be in danger and he needed to find her. They watered the horses, purchased food for the days ahead, and mounted up to rush toward the North Ford.

After several hours on the road, Dysaan's concern grew. The Western Road was always busy with traffic. It was a main trade route. However, they had not met one traveler or wagon coming from the north. Finally, they came to a broken-down wagon alone in the road. The driver sat on the ground in the shade, leaning against the back wheel. The front wheel was sticking out at an angle, almost off the axle.

Dysaan stopped his horse in front of the man. "Looks like you need some help."

"The pin slid out," the man said. "I don't have the strength to lift the box to reset it."

Dysaan dismounted and motioned to his men to help lift the wagon. "We'll help you get it set up again," he said. "Did you come from the ford?"

"Yes," the man said. "Are you goin' there to open it? I got turned back. I got vegetables to sell."

"Turned back?" Dysaan said, "By whom?"

"The Toulons. They got it shut down."

"Is Queen Ekala Oleen there?"

"There's some Oleen soldiers facin' off with the Toulons," the man said. "I didn't see no queen. Wish I had."

"What about the Frog Hunter and the giant shell creature? Did you see them?"

The man shook his head. "Didn't see 'em."

The soldiers lifted the front of the wagon and reset the wheel as the man pushed a metal wedge into the shaft of the axle, smacked it with a hammer to hold it in place, and tied a rope around it through the spokes of the wheel.

"I sure thank you for this," the man said.

"Is there a fight going on at the ford?" Dysaan asked.

"Naw, they just ain't lettin' anybody through, north or south."

"Keep an eye on that pin," Dysaan said as he swung up onto the saddle. He urged his horse into a trot as he thought about what could possibly be happening. Oleens were at the North Ford, but not the queen or Thalmus—and the Toulons were stopping transit. Whatever it was, he needed to get there quickly and get in the middle of it.

They rode through the night, only stopping twice to rest the horses and eat a snack from the bread and cheese they had bought from the merchants at Ello. In the morning, Dysaan and his men crested the small hill above the North Ford. They were surprised to see Captains Ritzs and Susa and their Oleens fighting green-uniformed soldiers on horseback. There were twice as many of the enemy as Oleens, though the women warriors were holding their ground. Waiting on the hillside across the river were hundreds more of the green-clad soldiers.

Dysaan reacted immediately, drawing his sword. "Sabers!" he ordered.

His men pulled their swords and held them up at the ready. His small company would be a drop in the bucket against the Toulon numbers if they all came across the river, but he was not going to let the Oleens fight alone.

"Let's chase those people back across the river," he shouted. "Charge!"

Dysaan and his men slammed into the fight alongside the Oleens, slashing the enemy and pushing them back into the water. The sudden appearance of new troops and their bold attack surprised the Toulon men and flipped the momentum to the Oleens. After a brief fight, the green-uniformed men who were still on their horses turned and galloped across the shallow ford to the safety of their comrades. The Oleens gathered the wounded and helped them up the hill to their camp. On the opposite bank, the Toulon army gathered into formation.

"I'm glad to see you, Dysaan," Ritzs said as they watched the green uniforms preparing to march down to the river crossing.

"I bet you are, Captain," Dysaan said. "You are greatly

outnumbered. What is going on here? Why are they attacking? Where is the queen?"

"Oleen and Prince Bolimaz crossed the river days ago," Captain Susa said.

Dysaan wasn't sure he'd heard correctly. "Did you say she crossed the river?"

"Yes, six days past. The prince and Camp chased after some night raiders. When they didn't come back, Oleen went looking for him with Lander and two archers."

"The queen went into Toulon with just three Oleens? You let her go, and you don't know what's happened to her?"

"She told me to wait here and guard the ford," Captain Susa said.

"You know how she is, Dysaan," Ritzs tried to explain. "Ekala Oleen has always done what she wants to do. And now she's queen. You can't argue with her."

Dysaan took a deep breath and let it out. "Yeah," he said, turning to look at the soldiers on the opposite bank. "She and Maz are probably captured or dead. That's why they're coming; they think the door is open."

"I don't think so," Ritzs said. "Thalmus and Boschina went after her three days ago."

Dysaan looked at her with a change of attitude. "Well, maybe there's a chance. You brought the hunter back from the Great Water, didn't you?"

"Yes, and he's going to bring Oleen back."

"And Boschina," Dysaan said, smiling. "In the meantime, we've got a fight on our hands."

"Our numbers are diminished," Susa said. "But we're ready with bows and swords."

Studying the width and depth of the crossing, Dysaan said, "We've got to use the river to our advantage. Slogging through the water will slow their infantry down, making them easy targets. We'll need every bow, shooting as much as they can. We have to stop them in the water. If they get across, their numbers will overwhelm us."

"We can pull the wagons down to the bank and block the shallows," Ritzs said. "They'll have to step into the deeper water to get around them."

"And the wagons will give us cover from their archers," Susa added.

Dysaan nodded. "Good idea, Captain. We'd better hurry; there isn't much time." Dysaan turned and called his men to action.

The Oleens and the King's Guard rushed to hook up the horses to the wagons and pull them down to the water's edge. Then the horse teams were unhooked and led away while everyone pushed and rolled the wagons into a line, end to end, in front of the shallow water of the ford.

The Toulon infantry marched into the current of the ford in a column formation, four abreast, with their shields held high for protection from arrows. These were not the same troops who had chased Ekala and Maz across the plain and through the Wilderness. They had been light cavalry, not as well trained or disciplined as these men. Dysaan saw their steady, determined movement and knew right away these soldiers would not give in easily. Ritzs and Susa formed their archers into groups, placing them at each end and at the lower parts of the wagons as soon as they were set into place.

Toulon archers on the north bank began releasing arrows, arching them high into the air so they would fall close behind the wagons to hit the Oleens. Dysaan, his men, and the few Oleen swordsmen waited and huddled against the wagons for cover as arrows dropped from the sky, sticking into the wagons and the ground around them. The Oleen archers aimed their arrows straight ahead at the approaching infantry, trying to penetrate the narrow, shifting spaces between the shields, or under the protective wall, hitting the men's legs in the knee-deep water. A few of the arrows found their mark. Soldiers staggered and dropped into the river, temporarily leaving a large hole in the shields until the men reformed and continued plowing forward. When the column reached the wagons and started spreading apart to go around or climb over the barrier, the Toulon archers had to stop shooting to avoid hitting their own men.

Dysaan ordered his swordsmen up and onto the wagons to fight back the attackers climbing over. The soldiers trying to skirt the barrier of wagons fell into the deeper water and were sucked under or washed down river. The Oleen archers could now shoot into the ranks of the Toulons at close range. Still the bloody, green-clad soldiers kept coming, their numbers overwhelming. One group, protected by a wall of their comrade's shields, grabbed the tongue of one of the wagons and pulled it into the water, opening a hole in the barrier through which the green wave began to surge.

Swinging his sword and thrusting with the short blade, Dysaan rushed to block their charge. Ritzs and several of the King's Guard joined him and, for a moment, they held the ground, preventing a breach. Then another wagon was pulled aside, and the Toulon soldiers flooded through the larger gap, surrounding the Oleen Forces.

With the enemy swarming around them and exhaustion slowing his moves, Dysaan began to feel something he had not felt since the tunnel in the Barranca—panic. Expecting the worst, he glanced around at his comrades, but he saw no fear, no desire to run in the faces of the Oleens or the men of the King's Guard. They fought with a determined confidence and hope. He took a deep breath, gripped tight on the sweaty handles of the bloody tools in his hands, and lashed into the fight again.

In the clamor of shouts, swords clashing, bodies falling, and voices groaning, another sound began to rise—a high-pitched shrill that grew louder, rolling down onto them from the hill. The Oleens in the fight began to echo it, raising their voices to the same piercing pitch. It rose to a penetrating shriek of alarm as the Toulon soldiers began to falter, looking and wondering what was happening. Then the siren slammed into the melee in the form of the Oleen army, screaming their battle cry and thrashing the stunned soldiers into submission. Still, many of the Toulon fighters pushed forward, only to be met by more maroon and gray-clad soldiers, who had been

282

joined by swordsmen they recognized as fellow Toulon men. But these countrymen demanded their surrender in the name of the Ameram Queen. To their further surprise, this ragged bunch of Toulon men was led by the traitors, Camp and Prince Bolimaz, who they had been told were killed in the Wilderness.

Once the hole in the wall of wagons appeared, the Toulon cavalry charged across the ford, coming behind the infantry that faltered before the onslaught of this new gray force sweeping down upon them. The mounted soldiers who had left the north bank with confidence of a victory were now feeling a strange sense of uselessness. Their job was to run down the fleeing enemy once the infantry had broken their line and created panic amongst them. However, they did not see anyone retreating; if anything, their own infantry was in disarray. Still, they galloped through the water into the gap of the wagons and smack against a shower of arrows. Dropping like so many autumn leaves to the ground, the men felt confused and hopeless. What happened to our easy victory over the woman ruler of Ameram? She was supposed to collapse like a straw doll. They saw her now, behind the line of archers, confident and powerful, directing her forces from a black horse; riding back and forth, she pointed with her sword as she shouted orders.

Up the hill, an upright, tall woman sat calmly on a gray horse. Over the din of the fighting, her voice whispered in their ears, telling them not to worry, that they would rest in peace. Their lord's grand plan of conquest had turned in one devastating battle. They had been misled. Prince Bolimaz had joined forces with a powerful leader, the Queen of Ameram.

Dysaan had never been so happy to see Ekala Oleen and the mysterious Larma with the Oleen forces. Not just to turn the battle and save them, but to see that the queen was safe and was showing why she was queen. No one was going to take that crown from her or invade her country.

He grinned with pride. King Ahmbin would be proud.

The battle subsided; the harsh, violent sounds slowly stilled. The remnants of the Toulon army slogged through the shallow water back to their country. The Oleen soldiers stood amongst the fallen, letting the defeated gather their wounded and leave in peace. The Oleens began the same process for their own comrades.

Prince Bolimaz stood at the water's edge with his band of swordsmen, telling the deflated Toulon soldiers he would return to claim the crown and wanted them to join him. Many of the men decided at that moment to change their allegiance, dropping to their knees to declare it so to the prince.

Camp grasped Maz's shoulder. "Look who's watching," he said, motioning toward the ford.

On the hill across the river sat two finely dressed men on horseback who glared at the bloody scene as the remnants of the green army dragged past them. Behind the two men, an escort held a staff flying a black flag with three white "S's." Maz caught his breath. He knew both of the observers: one was Lord Glasrauss; the other, the man who had chased him from his country and stolen the crown, was his own brother, Prince Sharpna. The brothers stared at one another, the water of the Sol Linden River flowing between them—the border separating two countries now at war.

Behind Maz a shout went up from the victors as Queen Ekala Oleen rode Shadahn through the field to stand beside the Crown Prince of Toulon and his small, but growing band of followers. Maz held up an open hand toward his brother as the chant increased and rolled over the North Ford, echoing in the ears of the defeated Toulon soldiers, "Oleen! Oleen! Oleen!"

Chapter Twenty-Six
It Is Not Finished

Half a dozen Oleens and Prince Bolimaz's swordsmen shoved and pushed the displaced wagons at the river edge back into a line to block the shallow crossing. Oleen soldiers from Table Top took over the guard duty behind the battered wooden carriages, keeping watch on the Toulon army. The tired King's Guard and Oleens, along with Maz's new followers, spread out across the battleground, gathering loose horses and picking up discarded weapons, shields, clothing, and bodies. The smell of blood and death was in the air. Queen Ekala designated a formal burial site for the fallen heroes of the Great Victory at the North Ford. The cemetery was on a hillside overlooking the river within walking distance from the Oleen encampment.

When Thalmus and Boschina arrived at the North Ford, with Neb tagging along and Thunder lumbering between them, they were greeted with a cheer from the Oleens who momentarily stopped their gruesome work. Neb was embarrassed, but felt privileged to be with such an honored group.

"I knew you'd bring Oleen back," Ritzs said, hugging Thalmus and Boschina, and then patting Thunder's shell. "And just in time," she added. Then she saw Boschina's face. "You're bruised up, Boschina. What happened?"

"Oh, Captain, I had a night fight with some very determined tree people. Thunder and Radise saved me."

Captain Ritzs gently touched Boschina's face. "It must have been rough. And, your shoulder's bloody. You're wounded?"

"Yes. Thalmus patched it. I'm alright."

Captain Susa, who was more formal than Captain Ritzs, and did not know the trio as well, nodded respectfully. "Thank you. Thank you for saving our queen. I'm glad you returned safely."

"So am I," Boschina replied. "And you all had a great victory here."

"We did," Ritzs said. "But there are many wounded and we lost some good people."

"I am sorry to hear that," Thalmus said, looking at the remains of the fight. Across the river the Toulon army was milling about, trying to reorganize and come to an understanding about what had happened. Lord Glasrauss and Prince Sharpna were gathered with the officers at the top of the hill. Although they were a long distance away, Thalmus could tell that it was not a conversation. Only Prince Sharpna was speaking and gesturing as the others sat mute on their horses.

"We are all exhausted," Ritzs said. "Dysaan and his men haven't slept for two days."

"If it had not been for him and his men, we would've been overwhelmed before Oleen got here," Susa said.

"He has a way of showing up where he is needed," Thalmus said, smiling at Boschina. "Does he not?"

"That he does," Boschina replied, nodding and remembering how Dysaan and Currad had arrived just in time to protect them from the renegade troops of the King's Guard on the outskirts of Rainland.

"Ekala Oleen waits for you on the hill," Ritzs said, pointing up the slope.

Boschina turned to Neb. "We're going to get you a better bow and more practice. But for now, I see Camp and your father at the wagons, why don't you join them."

Neb glanced toward the river and then back. "Thank you, Boschina. I…." He hesitated when he noticed everyone looking at him. "Thank you for helping me." He nodded politely to Thalmus and strode away with a bit more confidence in his gait.

Ritzs smiled at Boschina. "A new admirer?"

Boschina shrugged. "Oleen promised him archery lessons. I'm teaching him."

"I must return to the clean-up duties," Susa said. "But I have to ask: where are Lander, Karl, and Ricken? They did not come back with you."

Boschina heard Susa's question fly into the air and hang there like a spinning arrow, waiting for an answer. This was the inquiry she had been dreading and had not yet decided how to respond. She looked Susa in the eyes, but could not begin to tell her what had happened—what Lander had done.

After a moment, Thalmus deflected the arrow from Boschina. "I am sorry to tell you, Captain Susa," he said softly. "All three fell in the fight in the Wilderness."

Susa nodded slowly. "When I did not see them return with Oleen…I was afraid something had happened to them."

"We were hoping they were with you, Boschina," Ritzs said.

"No," was all that Boschina could say as she turned away, gripping the handle of her sword.

"We are greatly distressed by their loss, the queen especially," Thalmus said. "Know that your Oleen comrades rest in peace in a cavern with the ancients of the Wilderness."

Susa looked at the horses pulling stretchers of lifeless bodies to the hillside burial ground. "We'll post markers for them with the others," she said and patted Boschina on the shoulder. "You did well bringing the queen back. I can see you suffered for it." Susa nodded to Thalmus and returned to her soldiers working in the field.

Captain Ritzs walked with Thalmus, Boschina, and Thunder through the trampled grass and the fading light of the day up to the fires where Ekala, Maz, Larma, and Dysaan sat talking. They all stood to greet the new arrivals. Boschina turned from frustration to joy upon seeing her friend.

Dysaan held his fist against his chest in a salute to the hunter. "It is good to see you, Thalmus. I'm glad you're here." Then he turned to Boschina. "And you, Stone Cutter's Daughter, Soldier of the Oleens, defender of the Queen…"

Boschina gave him a stern look. "Honored Soldier, mighty warrior, and Great Gauk Slayer," she said, nodding politely. And then laughed and hugged the burly, bearded soldier.

"I've been told of your further escapades. Will you never behave?" Dysaan said.

"I will when you do," Boschina replied.

Dysaan held her head in his big hands, examining the scabs and bruises on her face. "If you're not careful, you'll end up looking like me."

"Except I can't grow hair on my face to hide the scars," Boschina replied, tugging his beard.

"Alright, enough," Ekala said. "Let's sit. Thalmus, I'm glad that you're here. You've been a guardian and a teacher, for my father as well as me since I was a child, but you are much more than that. You are my friend."

Thalmus nodded. "And you are mine. I am at your service, Your Majesty."

Ekala smiled broadly. "Thank you, Thalmus." She turned to the others. "We have a lot to discuss and I need your counsel."

Thunder lowered himself to the ground and pulled in his legs for a rest as the others settled in a circle, adjusting swords, legs, and boots in order to be comfortable. Larma seemed to melt into a crossed-legged position as softly as silk floating to the ground. Her presence was gentleness; yet, at the same time, strength and clarity flowed around and through her.

Ekala looked around at her friends before speaking. "I am going to need every one of you in the days ahead, for we are under assault by forces that oppose me. My father sent Dysaan to find me because Lord Rundall is dying and he wants me back for his uncle's passing. I agree. I should be there to honor him. Lord Rundall kept our country from collapsing while my father was sick from Metro's spell. He was at the king's side all his life, a trusted and devoted servant. And he believed in me and the prophecy of my reign since my mother died. But we just fought off an invasion from Toulon, who seems to think Ameram is easy pickings, and they don't appear to be giving up that endeavor. Weapons are being shipped into our country for an uprising or supplies for their invasion. Chorgens have been bred to hunt and kill Boschina and me. Most distressing of all, my own trusted Oleen archer tried to kill me."

"What!" Captain Ritzs said. "Lander? How? What did she do?"

"She shot Karl and Ricken, and then tried to shoot me. If Boschina had not struck her with an arrow, she would have killed me."

"I can't believe it... Lander?" Ritzs said.

"It *is* hard to believe," Ekala said. "She's been with us since the beginning at Table Top. I wanted it to be wrong, that she'd made a mistake, but she confessed before dying. She said I had betrayed myself and the Oleens by becoming queen."

Ritzs looked to Larma. "How can this be?"

"We cannot always understand why someone commits to a path that we thought they would never walk," Larma said. "This should enlighten us all to the warnings of dark trails—lest we find ourselves stumbling down one."

Larma's warning settled on the members of the circle, each one contemplating his or her own weaknesses and promising to stand strong when tempted. The sun was fully down now and its light almost gone. The glow from the fire partially lit the members of the circle, flickering in their faces.

"I don't want Lander's treachery to be known beyond this group," Ekala said, drawing everyone back to the decisions at hand. "There might be others ready to betray me and I don't want them to know we are watching. When asked, we simply say that Lander died along with Karl and Ricken at the fight in the Wilderness."

Boschina glanced at Thalmus, who was leaning against Thunder's shell and watching Ekala. *He knew what to say,* she thought, *how to smother a flame from starting a fire.*

"I told Captains Ritzs and Susa their comrades were buried honorably in the catacombs of the Wilderness Caverns," Thalmus said. "That should finalize concerns about their remains."

Around the fire, people nodded and agreed.

"I have completely trusted my Oleens," Ekala continued. "But now that one of the most dedicated of them has turned on me—I must be cautious. We *all* must be careful. No plans or information will be shared to anyone beyond this circle. Understood? And we need to watch out for each other. I am not the only one who is a target."

Larma inclined her head toward Ekala. "True, but you are the biggest target."

"I was drawn across the border into a trap because I pose a threat to my brother," Maz said, "but you are much more dangerous to them. You represent something new, a change they fear. The rulers of Toulon do not want you and me joining forces."

"This victory over them will make a difference," Dysaan said. "You have shown your power and authority."

"Our enemy was surprised today," Larma said. "You taught them a lesson. Unfortunately, this will only drive them deeper into anger and despair, fortifying their belief that you must be defeated. Their desire for conquest will become an obsession."

"That is why we have to keep an army along this border. Even with the few we have here now, we must hold this ford," Ekala said. "But I'm bound for Ambermal. Therefore, Dysaan, I want you to stay here with the King's Guard, along with Captain Susa and all the forces of Oleens. Captain Ritzs, Boschina, and two Oleens will go with me, as well as Prince Bolimaz, if he so desires. We'll leave before sunrise so they won't know that I'm gone."

"Oleen," Ritzs said, "that's too small a force for your protection."

"We'll be fine, Captain. We need as many soldiers here as possible. What do you think of Ellie and her brother, Fischer, as the two Oleens to go with us?"

"They both are excellent with all the tools," Ritzs said. "Ellie has been with us since the beginning. Fischer, her younger brother, was in the King's Army before joining us. I trust them."

"That's what I thought about Lander," Ekala replied. "I sent a messenger to Currad to have troops sent here to serve with you, Dysaan. She should have gotten there by now. Larma wants to stay several more days to advise you, and to heal the wounded and see to the services of our dead."

"I will serve as long as I am needed," the mystic said. "Then, I will go to Lord Rundall."

"I'm honored that you are staying with us and for your counsel," Dysaan said. "Thank you, Larma."

A quiet moment passed before Maz spoke. "My duty is here. I have a growing force of Toulon men committed to me; I cannot leave now. Our numbers, though small, will add to the defense of the ford."

Ekala nodded, accepting the prince's decision. "It is right that you stay here; close to your country where you can try to subvert the evil that controls it now. But Dysaan will be in command of all forces, not only at the ford, but of this entire northern region from Rainland to the Great Water, except Table Top—which Larma alone rules. Are you alright with that, Prince?"

"Of course, we Toulons live here at your mercy and we serve to maintain that freedom with the hope of returning home one day."

"I knew that, but I had to make it clear for everyone," Ekala said.

Maz smiled and bowed his head to her. "And so you have, Queen of Ameram."

There was an awkward silence before Ekala said, "I wouldn't trust all the people who claim to be refugees. There's at least one of Glasrauss' spies amongst them. How else did he know you were here?"

"I promise you, I will heed all warnings," Maz replied. "Besides, Camp doesn't trust anyone and he's always watching me."

"I'll have a word with Camp about that before I go," she replied, smiling. Then she turned to Dysaan. "Do you have any objections to your command?"

"I serve at your will and look forward to this duty, Your Majesty," Dysaan said calmly, though he was thrilled to be given this responsibility by the queen. To command troops in battle, to protect the country from invaders, was his calling. It is what he lived for, not training green recruits at the castle and supervising the rebuilding of an old fort at the South Ford.

"Good, Dysaan, I know I can count on you, just as my father did." Ekala directed her attention to Thalmus, who had not yet said a word about her plan, which was not unusual. She knew the hunter had strategies of his own and that he only shared them after being prodded, or when the moment required it. "Thalmus, what is your desire?"

Thalmus was impressed by Ekala's command and her plan. She was confident yet thoughtful and considerate of her council—her friends. Watching her, he was reminded of the war councils he'd been in with the king and how very much alike were the father and daughter. He patted Thunder's shell. "We will go to Ambermal. I wish to see Lord Rundall, hopefully before he passes, and to visit with King Ahmbin. Unless you need me here, Dysaan."

"You are always needed, Thalmus. But I agree you must go. You should know that when we passed through Tamra we went by your cabin. Some beasts had knocked the door from its hinges and clawed up the walls and furniture. So you, too, are a target of this evil."

"Were any of the villagers injured?" Thalmus asked.

"No, but they were scared and staying clear of your meadow."

"Thank you for the warning, Dysaan. We will be careful."

"I'm sorry we can't wait for you and Thunder," Ekala said. "We must move fast."

"Shadahn will be glad to hear that," Thalmus replied.

"Oleen, I have an idea," Boschina said, speaking for the first time.

"What is it, sister?"

"These past weeks have been hard on Thunder. It is a long way to Ambermal and they may not get there in time for Lord Rundall. What if we use the Banyon transport wagon—the one full of weapons—to carry Thunder? It's wider than a normal wagon. I think it's big enough for him and he wouldn't have to walk all that way."

"Well, that's an interesting idea," Ekala said. "Captain Ritzs, what did you do with that load?"

"The Banyon wagon is helping to block the ford," Ritzs answered. "I suppose we could replace it with some of the broken-down wagons people have left behind."

Ekala looked at the frog hunter. "What do you think, Thalmus?"

"Thunder has never ridden in a wagon," Thalmus said, smiling at Boschina. "Thank you for thinking of him. If he fits into it, I think he would appreciate the ride."

Thunder appeared to be asleep. His head was pulled in, tucked under the protective shell.

"We'll give it a go," Ekala said. "Captain Ritzs, can you make the exchange tonight? Empty it out and have it ready with a team in the morning."

"As you wish, Oleen," Captain Ritzs said.

"My men will give them a hand with it," Dysaan said.

Ekala stood up and everyone followed suit. "Let's get our duties done and eat," she said. "I've been smelling the aroma of Cook's stew and I'm hungry."

Dysaan, Prince Bolimaz, and Captain Ritzs headed down the hill to work on the wagons and to organize guard positions and strengths for the night.

Ekala put her hand on Boschina's good shoulder. "Are you still upset with me?"

"Not you, no. I guess I'm still mad at Lander."

"You must put it behind you, Boschina. I'm going to need your full attention so I don't do something stupid again."

"You'll have it, as long as you listen to me."

Ekala laughed and patted her shoulder. "Let's get some food and rest. It'll be an early start tomorrow."

Larma knelt beside Thunder. He opened his eyes and stuck out his head a little. "How are you old friend?"

Thunder grunted and lightly clicked his jaws.

"Yes," Larma said, touching his head. "We are all getting older, but not too tired, yes?"

"Larma," Thalmus said. "There is a sad husband and wife in the refugee camp you should talk to. I believe they are Glasrauss' spies."

Larma looked at Thalmus and waited.

"Glasrauss holds power over them; he probably has their children. They have been forced to spy for him. They are in danger from Glasrauss and from the other refugees if Maz or Camp, or even I, were to question them. They are alone and lost. But I think you can help them find a way to be loyal to themselves and to Prince Bolimaz."

"I will visit them tomorrow," Larma said. "As always, Thalmus, you are thoughtful."

"You will be able to tell who they are," Thalmus said. "Their pain is evident." He removed the message from his pocket and held it out to her. "I can return this now."

Larma looked at the folded note she had written, lying still in his open palm. "Not yet," she said. "It is not finished."

Chapter Twenty-Seven
Masquerade

Captain Kali pushed open the worn plank door of Veracitas' studio. The rusted rollers squealed at the effort and she stopped the door half-way open. Sticking her head inside, she saw the sculptor tapping rhythmically with a hammer on a chisel. Flakes of stone popped into the air from an emerald block and fell at his feet. His back was to her, his full concentration on the point of the chisel. He had not heard the squeaky metal of the door, nor would he hear her if she entered the room and walked up behind him. Veracitas' mind was melded with the image emerging from the stone. His body blocked her view of the marble, so she could not tell what it looked like or what the subject might be. Kali watched his shoulders moving as he swung the hammer with short, deliberate strokes—ringing with each impact on the chisel in his hand as it dug into the cold stone. Beyond a workbench, against the far wall, was an old cot with disheveled blankets.

Kali had not seen Veracitas for days and had become worried he had fallen back into the depression that had paralyzed him at the quarry. Now she knew he was on a work binge and had been sleeping in the studio to be close to his creation. Boschina had warned Kali about this behavior: how her father at times became obsessed when trying to carve the image in stone that he saw in his head. When this passion possessed him, he called it "living in the stone." Although Kali had not spoken to Veracitas since their argument, for which she felt guilty, she was happy to see him so enthralled in his work. Closing the door slowly, in case he might be disturbed by its noise, Kali pulled it shut and headed toward the barracks to check the ongoing training of the army's recruits and to talk with the King's Builder.

In an open area beyond the barracks, the archers of the Oleen force were training a hundred new soldiers in the craft and skill of the long bow. These men and women had already worked with the long and short blade tools this morning. Now, they were lined up in front of a row of straw bales with small paper circles attached to each one as a target. The trainees were aimed away from the small rock wall overlooking Cold Canyon so that their errant arrows would not be lost in its deep gorge.

Cold Canyon, Kali remembered, was where she and Veracitas, Boschina, and Larma, along with their battered army, watched Bubo attack Metro in mid-air and send him tumbling to his death on the rocks at the bottom. The image returned to her eyes as clear as if it had just happened. She could still hear the magician's screams. Shaking her head to clear the memory, Kali turned back to the training. On this very ground, the last of Metro's army had surrendered, giving up their weapons. Now she trained troops here, committed to the queen who Metro tried so hard—with all his tricks and magic—to kill. *"The power of truth had prevailed, and must always continue to do so,"* Larma announced to them all. Kali believed it wholeheartedly, living her life in the light of the truth.

The captain stopped to observe her Oleen trainers walking behind the line of recruits, advising and correcting them. Upon taking command of the training, she continued the instruction of the soldiers as Currad had originally organized and started, but found it to be drudgery and empty of inspiration. So, she revised the order and the focus to include the values, compassion, and loyalty of the Oleens inspired by Larma and Ekala Oleen, their namesake. Kali was pleased to see a change of attitude and growing camaraderie among the soldiers in such a short time.

Climbing the stone steps to the office of the King's Builder, she stopped in the covered archway. From this porch, there was a view looking south over Cold Canyon. The day was clear and sunny with barely a breeze. On the edge of the distant horizon was the Escat Marshes. *Nice view, but nothing like the ones at Table Top*, Kali thought. She longed to return to the Top and Larma Hollow. But her duty was here, and this was where she would serve until Oleen returned.

Kali knocked on the door and then swung it open.

The builder was not there. His tattered, padded chair at the drafting table was empty. From the moment Kali entered the builder's messy office, she was fascinated and a bit overwhelmed. It was a world of creation and design that she'd never experienced. The walls were covered with drawings and structural details of various buildings in Ambermal, including the columns of the Great Hall. There was a schematic of the fountains and water flumes that flowed throughout the city, and detailed sketches of cross-sections of block walls, foundations, and roof structures. In one corner of the room a narrow, wood spiral staircase circled to a catwalk that cantilevered one meter from the walls and stretched around the room at a height of four meters above the floor. Cubicles above the walk were stuffed with hundreds of rolls of plans and records. Sunlight flooded through window openings along the north wall. On the floor, side tables were covered with stacks of open plans spread out on top of one another. Iron stands and wall mounts held half-burned candles that waited to be lit.

The room smelled of time and ancient things.

Kali sifted briefly through the stacks of papers on a table, but did not find the plans for the fort at the South Ford. She was disappointed. She'd wanted to talk with the builder about changing the size of the living quarters and cooking area in order to house more troops there. He must have taken the plans with him and was on his way to the fort. As she turned to go, her eye caught sight of a faded corner sticking out from under new plans on a table by the stairs. Something about the discolored, curled edge attracted her.

Had it moved? Waved a feeble edge?

She stepped to the table and rolled back the large sheets on top to reveal the full view of the old plans underneath. The stained drawings seemed to take a breath, lifting slightly off the table and settling down again. The paper was delicate, the ink faded, and the style of printing no longer in use. One end of the sheet was crinkled and washed out with watermarks.

A sudden chill caused Kali to shiver. She smelled rain and mud.

Glancing around the room, no one had entered, sunlight still shown through the windows. She looked back at the sheet. The plan was of a large building with very few interior walls and a high, arched ceiling. Kali was just learning to read the language of building plans, but it was evident to her there were hallways or hidden passages along the exterior walls and under the floor. She had never seen this building and knew it did not exist in Ambermal. The faint description in the lower corner of the plans read: WEST HALL ARMORY – SOL LINDEN.

"Armory?" she said softly. "Sol Linden? There are no buildings along the Sol Linden River."

The sound of voices and footsteps on the stairs outside brought her attention to the door as it swung open and the builder stepped in, followed by the quartermaster. They were an odd-looking pair. Though both were old and worn from years at their jobs, the builder was tall, broad shouldered, plump at the waist, and congenial; whereas, the quartermaster was short, thin, and suspicious of everyone.

"Captain Kali," the builder said, smiling and pulling off his hat and flipping it onto a table of plans. "What are you doing here?" He lifted the strap of his courier pouch over his head and dropped the case on the floor by the drafting table.

"I wanted to talk to you about expanding the barracks at the fort."

"Why? It's not big enough?"

"I think to be able to defend the South Ford we need to station more troops there," Kali replied.

"How many more?"

"Forty...fifty would be better."

"That would bring it to two hundred," the builder said, thinking. "We'd have to enlarge the storage, too."

"There's plenty of room out on that hill to expand as much as you want," Kali said.

The builder sighed. "Well, we're not too far along. We should be able to do that."

"I don't think so," the quartermaster said abruptly. "I'd have to haul in more stone and lumber. We're already behind the schedule that Currad wanted and it has cost more than the queen allowed. I can't spend anymore without approval. She's not here and you, Captain, don't have that authority. Besides, that doesn't even account for the cost of supplying and feeding those people."

"I'll talk with Currad," Kali said.

"Won't do no good," the quartermaster snapped. "He can't approve spending."

"I'll ask the king," Kali replied.

"The king has no authority anymore, Lord Rundall is about dead, and, like I said, the queen is gone."

The builder shrugged his shoulders. "Sorry, Captain, we're stuck with what it is, unless the queen gets back soon. Let's just keep pushing 'em to get it done so I can get Currad off my back."

Kali nodded, but she was eyeing the wiry quartermaster, standing firm, staring back at her like a snarling badger. She wasn't used to dealing with government rules, regulations, and budgets, let alone the people who enforced them. She realized he was just doing his job: doing what he'd been ordered to do and managing the cost. Whereas, she was thinking of the defense of the kingdom and not what it cost—except in lives when the fighting started.

"Let's hope Queen Ekala Oleen returns soon," Kali said and started for the door.

The quartermaster saw the old plans exposed on the desk. "Captain, were you looking at these plans?"

"Yes. What are they? I've never seen that building," Kali said, the faint odor of mud still in her nose.

The King's Builder leaned over the plans. "Nor have I. Where'd these come from?"

The quartermaster stepped in front of the builder and pulled the new sheets over the ancient plans to carefully cover them. Something hushed in the room like a breath catching.

Kali stared at the plans.

"I found them in the archives—very old," the quartermaster said. "Interesting, aren't they?"

Kali nodded. "Where is it?"

"Oh, it was never built," he said casually. "There are no notes or records about it. Just an idea at one time, I guess."

"An armory?" Kali questioned. "Maybe the king would know of it."

"Naw, he wouldn't remember. Like I said, a plan that never got built; it happens all the time. I should know, being in charge of supplying and paying for the materials."

"Odd to name it after a river," Kali said.

"Yeah, well who knows what they did back then."

Larma and Thalmus would know, Kali thought as she looked back at the quartermaster leaning against the table, watching her. *And he probably knows too.*

* * *

Captain Ritzs and Susa had wanted to place a ring of Oleen guards around Ekala Oleen and Boschina during the night for protection from Chorgens. However, the queen refused, insisting the presence of Thunder and Thalmus was enough and everyone needed to rest. When they rose before sunrise to begin the journey to Ambermal, Bubo was sitting on Thunder's shell, watching them.

"Bubo," Boschina said. "Where have you been?"

The owl snapped his beak and swiveled to look at Ekala.

"No wonder I slept so well," Ekala said. "Thanks for watching over us, Bubo."

He snapped his beak again as Thalmus returned from the cooking fire with bowls of hot stew and handed them to Ekala, Boschina, and Ritzs.

"You have long days ahead. You must stay strong and alert," Thalmus said.

"We will," Ekala replied, taking a bowl. "You do not need to worry about us, Thalmus. Have Fischer and Ellie eaten?"

"They have and they are ready. Now I must get Thunder into the wagon."

Larma appeared from the darkness and gathered the three women together. "Trust in one another," she told them. "But question all others. You saw how evil twisted Lander. As you learned, a friend can become a foe in an instant. But you three have the heart of stone truth. Do you believe this to be so?"

"I do," Boschina said.

"Yes, I do," Ritzs said.

"You know I do," Ekala said.

"Then let that truth guide you on this journey—and always."

All three women nodded, feeling her words in their hearts.

A ramp had been made of wood planks scavenged from derelict wagons. The boards were spliced together with straps to hold Thunder's weight. One end of the ramp was propped against the rear bed of the wagon; Thunder backed up the incline into the wagon, nestling between the side boards. The ramp was then placed over the sideboards to create a solid top. A canvas tarp was draped over the entire bed, completely hiding the giant tortoise. Thalmus had helped to put the ramp together and to pick the two horses harnessed to the wagon. They were strong, confident animals. He greeted them and then climbed onto the driver's bench. His tools were lying under the canvas, except his sword, which Thalmus kept beside him on the bench where Bubo perched. Except for the co-driver being a Great

Horned owl, the wagon looked very similar to when the Banyon smugglers crossed the ford.

Thalmus took the reins, shook them gently, and tapped his heel once on the wood floorboard. The horses leaned into their harnesses and stepped forward, pulling the wagon toward the road.

Maz stepped up to Ekala and they hugged, holding onto one another longer than they should have in front of the assembly waiting to see them off. Neither one wanted to let go because they weren't sure when, or if, they'd see each other again.

Finally pulling apart, Ekala whispered, "Be wise. You have followers who are counting on you."

"Does that include you?" Maz asked.

"What do you think?" she answered and slapped him on the shoulder. Looking over at Camp, she said, "Don't let him do anything foolish, like chasing off across the river—again." Then she walked to Shadahn, where the captains and Dysaan were standing. "Honored Soldier, Captains, you have won a great victory; now let's make it last."

"Rest assured, Your Majesty, we will hold this ground," Dysaan said.

"I don't doubt your dedication, Dysaan. It's the numbers you're facing that concern me. The Toulons may attack again before reinforcements can get here."

"I think that lickin' they just suffered will keep 'em at bay for a while."

"Don't count on it," Maz said. "My brother is foolishly stubborn."

"So is Lord Glasrauss," Camp added.

"Ekala Oleen," Larma said, taking her hand, "do not worry about the North Ford. We are here. Set your sight on what lies before you in the days ahead."

Ekala felt calmness come over her. She hugged Larma and then climbed onto the black horse. "Looks like Thunder's on his way. Are you ready, Boschina?"

"Just waiting on you," Boschina replied, sitting on Radise.

"Then let's go."

Fischer and Ellie rode ahead to scout as Ritzs, Boschina, and Queen Ekala Oleen raised their right arms in an Oleen salute to the watching soldiers and the cooks who had just loaded their saddlebags and the wagon with food. There were no cheers or loud goodbyes to announce their leaving; instead, the horses walked quietly to the road and then up the hill from the ford. Boschina looked back across the river at the campfires burning in the darkness along the opposite ridge. There were many more fires than in the Oleen encampment. She hoped it was because they had an abundant supply of wood from the forest and, therefore, could have more fires; but the experience of the last several days told her otherwise.

Once they crested the rise and the fires fell out of sight, Ekala urged Shadahn into a trot until they caught up with Thalmus rolling along in the wagon. The three women rode alongside him, the horses walking at a steady pace. Bubo spread his wings and hopped onto the flat top of the wagon's bed. It was higher than the seat, more stable, and had a view more to his liking. He hooted and Thunder—in the compartment beneath him—clicked his jaws. Ekala swung off Shadahn and stepped over the gap between horse and rolling wagon to settle on the seat beside Thalmus.

"Did you get the clothes?" she quietly asked Thalmus.

"Yes, and I washed them in the river. I would not have worn them otherwise," he said, shaking his head. "They are drying in the back with Thunder."

"What did you give the Banyon men to wear?"

"Maz and Camp's old uniforms."

Ekala smiled. "They were probably happy to be rid of those worn things, and to put them on somebody else to be a target."

The wagon creaked along, the horses moving in rhythm. Thalmus said, "I like your plan, though it is risky. Nothing may come of it, but it is worth a try."

Ekala shrugged. "I thought we might as well make it interesting on the way to Ambermal. At least until we meet our troops coming this way."

Thalmus smiled. "We might catch something with this disguise."

"I'm counting on it," Ekala said.

Bubo announced he was leaving with a short hoot, and then spread his wings and flew into the darkness to watch for unwanted followers.

After the meeting had broken up the night before, Ekala ate separately with Thalmus, Boschina, and Maz to tell them her new plan. Since they were taking the Banyon wagon south, she reasoned, why not use it as bait to catch the receiver of the weapon shipment? Maz and Boschina thought it too dangerous, especially because there were too few of them to protect her. But Ekala, as usual, was confident and wanted to use the opportunity to draw out her enemy. So, the Banyon wagon drivers were forced to trade their trousers and shirts for the Toulon uniforms. Thalmus, and maybe one from the group, would wear the driver's old clothes as a disguise.

Bubo winged by several times, coming and going in the night, hooting that all was clear, no danger in sight. Owl's particular concern was the fast-moving Chorgens who might be trailing Boschina and Ekala. He knew how suddenly they could strike.

The group kept going through the darkness until sunrise when they stopped to rest and drink from their water pouches. The two scouts, Fischer and Ellie, returned to report that the road ahead was deserted.

Ekala listened to the scouts with her hands on her hips. "Good," she replied. "Word has spread of the ford's closure. We won't have innocent people getting into harm's way."

The rumble of hooves from the north caused them all to turn and look. Bubo was flying toward them and right behind him was Dallion, galloping up the road. The horses nickered, lifting their heads. The great owl landed on the back of the wagon where Thalmus stood. He had pulled up the tarp for Thunder to see out and to get the Banyon driver's clothes. Dallion slowed and walked to Thalmus for a pat, and then a rolling snort to Thunder—who clicked—and finally a nose bump to Boschina.

"It's about time you joined us," Boschina said. "I hope you had a good rest."

The stallion nickered and bumped her again.

"Dal and Bubo will have to stay away from you, Thalmus," Ekala said. "They would be recognized right away."

"So will Ellie and Fischer in those uniforms," Thalmus replied.

"We'll keep an eye on you from a distance and meet up north of Ello for the night, as planned," Ekala said. "This ruse will only last a few days, until we meet Currad's troops coming north."

Thalmus watched them go as he changed into the Banyon shirt and trousers. The pants were too long and baggy, so he cut them off and used his belt to cinch them at the waist after tucking in the shirt. He had picked up an old hat from the battlefield and washed it with the other clothes. It was rounded on top with a short bill and hung down on the sides. It fit him well, but looked odd.

Dallion sniffed him and then snorted.

"I know, Dal, it does not smell right."

Bubo just stared at Thalmus before moving in with Thunder under the cover.

The hunter folded his clothes and put them under the tarp. Patting and talking to the two horses hitched to the wagon, he let them smell him and get comfortable with his new aroma before climbing back into the driver's seat. Picking up the reins, he stamped his heel and the horses pulled forward.

Dallion trotted off to the hills, but stayed within sight.

Queen Ekala Oleen and her entourage continued south until pulling off the road onto the trail to the springs where the blind Chorgen had attacked Boschina. Bones and pieces of fur still remained where it died, but its carcass had been eaten. Radise snorted nervously and Boschina patted her neck. "It's alright, Lady," she said, soothing the mare as she dismounted.

"That was a big beast," Ritzs said, kicking the ribcage with her boot. "Looks like other animals have feasted on it."

"It would have eaten me if it hadn't been for Thalmus," Boschina said.

"I've never seen such fangs and jagged teeth on an animal," Ritzs said. She looked at Boschina. "I'm glad the Insurphs took down the one following you. I'd hate to fight one of these."

"This is the one Thalmus says was after me?" Ekala asked, examining the remains.

"This is it. Bubo clawed its eyes the night it tried to get you."

"I wonder how big the Chorgens in the Wilderness were that we couldn't see."

Boschina smiled. "At least as big as the one that likes you."

"You know," Ekala pondered, "that Chorgen probably saved our lives that night. Why did it do that? Why did it protect me?"

"It certainly took a liking to you, that's for sure," Boschina said.

Ekala looked at the foliage encroaching on the spring and how the forest had grown like an arm extending down to grasp the freshwater pool. A dozen birds suddenly burst out of the thicket and flew away, startling the horses drinking at the pool. A sense of danger suddenly rippled through Ekala and she instinctively reached for the sword handle at her side.

Boschina and Ritzs noticed and glanced around. "What's wrong?"

"Don't know…something…for a moment, I sensed something."

"Did you hear—see anything?" Boschina asked, feeling the sword against her hip. It was still.

Ekala looked at the Chorgen's bare bones, yellowish-white in the sunshine with teeth marks where animals had gnawed away the meat and gristle. "Let's water up and move on to Ello."

"Do you want the scouts to go ahead?" Ritzs asked.

"No. I don't want the village to know I'm coming."

Boschina and Ekala watched the brush while Ritzs and the scouts filled the water pouches. Sniffing the air like Thalmus, Boschina tried to pick up a scent, but the wind was blowing west, toward the forest. They mounted up and rode back to the road, found Dallion trailing Thalmus, and spread out. They stayed along the Western Hills high above the road and watched for anyone approaching the wagon. At dusk, they reached the outskirts of Ello.

Gathering together, they made camp for the night. Uncovering the wagon top, Bubo flew out as they set the ramp for Thunder. The tortoise was happy to get on firm ground and to stretch his legs and walk around. Bubo had enjoyed a long rest and was ready to perform guard duty for the night.

"We'll take the horses into the village for water," Ekala said.

"That may not be wise," Thalmus said.

"I know there might be spies. But I'm not going to hide and sneak around my people. They need to see me and I need to see them."

"As it should be," Thalmus replied. "I will stay here to keep our charade from being exposed."

Both Boschina and Ritzs gave Thalmus a glance and nod to say, *we'll watch her.*

In the growing darkness, the villagers thought it was a small force of Oleens entering their square, until someone recognized the queen and then excited pandemonium broke out. They bowed, curtsied, applauded, and cheered. The village elders were sent for and came running as best they could through the growing crowd. Lanterns were lit and in very little time, the square and side streets were packed with people.

"Your Majesty," said a tall, graying man with short hair and a clean face as he pushed his way before her. "We did not know you were coming or we would have prepared a celebration."

"It's alright, Porter. I did not realize I'd be here so soon myself."

"We will prepare a meal and lodging for you and your Oleens right away," he said.

"No need for the lodging, Porter. My force and I are camped nearby."

Porter saw Boschina standing by the queen. "Oh, the Stone Cutter's Daughter is with you; how wonderful that you are both here. As you can tell, we are very happy to see you once again and to have you here amongst us."

"I can see that," Ekala replied. "And I—we," motioning at Boschina, "are very happy to be here in your beautiful village. Though, last time I was here, no one came out to greet me."

Porter and the people around them laughed. "That's because you had not saved us from Safedor yet," the tall elder said. The villagers cheered and began to chant, "Oleen, Oleen!"

Queen Ekala Oleen held up her hands to stop them. "Thank you, thank you all. We are happy to be with you. We have been riding all day to get here and we are tired. Our horses need water and feed. And we are hungry as well."

"And so you shall have it," Porter said, turning to move the crowd out of the way for the queen and Boschina while Ritzs and the scouts took the horses to the water troughs.

"How long will you be with us, Your Majesty?"

"I'm sorry, Porter, this will be a short visit," Ekala replied as they walked through the people, greeting and touching hands. "We must continue on to Ambermal tomorrow."

"Oh, the people will be disappointed, but we understand. You have great responsibilities," Porter said. "Would you like to see your Oleen soldier's grave before you leave?"

Ekala stopped and looked at the elder. "What Oleen soldier?"

"The one who died near the Middle Road junction."

"When was this?" the queen asked.

"Seven, eight days back," Porter replied. "Some merchants coming from Barrunda found her and brought her body here. We took care of her, placed her in our burial site."

Ekala and Boschina exchanged a look of worry.

"Do you know her name?" Boschina asked.

"No. We have her sword and a few things. Will that help?"

"Show us," the queen said.

Porter motioned for them to follow him as he led them through the people.

A man who had been tagging along after them now squeezed out of the crowd and backed into an alley. He watched the queen and Boschina move away surrounded by the throng trailing after Porter.

"They're both here," he whispered to himself. "How did they escape the Wilderness and Lord Glasrauss? But they are here now, and we will get them."

The man grinned, turned into the dark lane, and walked right into large yellow eyes. Startled, he stepped back. It was an owl, glaring at him. The owl was stationary, sitting on someone's shoulder; a shorter man he could not make out in the darkness. *An owl?* And suddenly, the man knew: he was standing before the King's Frog Hunter.

Chapter Twenty-Eight
Ello

The man could not see Thalmus, but he felt his firm presence and his eyes on him—like the owl's glaring eyes, which he could see. He waited for something to be said: to hear a voice, a greeting, or a command. However, both the bird and the hunter were silent. Did the hunter know who he was? What he had been doing? Hoping this was just a chance encounter in a dark alley, the man stepped to the side to go by.

"Pardon me," he said.

The owl and the hunter moved to block his path and he almost bumped into them again. A snap from the great owl's beak, close to his face, let the man know he was in trouble. He reached into his cloak, feeling for his knife. He had to get past them. He had to tell Redan the queen and the Stone Cutter's Daughter were here in Ello, that he could let the Chorgens loose again.

"Let me by," the man said to the shadow of a face beside the owl's eyes.

Only the fading sound of the crowd behind him echoed in the street. Not a word from the silent hunter before him. Then the hunter's short height seemed to rise, spread across the dark space, and press toward him. The man began to feel something he had never felt before—fear—filling his chest, sending trembles through his arms and legs.

The man's fingers grasped the handle of his knife.

Dare he tangle with the Frog Hunter?

In the dark, he could stab first before Thalmus could react. Then again, he had heard Thalmus could hunt in the night as well as in daylight. Besides, Thalmus had the owl for his eyes and he may already have his sword ready. No, no it was not wise to fight him, not here, not now, one-on-one in the dark. He could not take the chance of being caught or killed. *Why doesn't the hunter speak? Say what he wants? He's just standing there, waiting.* Shaking, the man swallowed hard. He knew what Thalmus wanted—the hunter wanted him.

This silent standoff, the waiting for the hunter to grab him or stab him, was unbearable. The man's legs were shaking. He couldn't stand this any longer. He decided to run, to return to the main street and blend in with the crowd. He stepped back and turned to scurry in among the throng, but the street was empty. The people had moved on.

He was alone.

Run! his mind shouted.

His wobbly legs responded, panic forcing them forward. Then the owl was on him, digging its talons into the back of his neck. Pulling his knife, he tried to stab the bird. A hand grabbed his wrist and twisted. Pain shot up his arm and he dropped the knife. Something kicked his feet out from under him and he fell face forward, the piercing claws and sharp beak riding him down to the cobblestones of the street.

* * *

Flickering torchlight danced on the faces of Queen Ekala Oleen and Boschina as they stood looking at Thoe's grave. Large, flat stones, the color of old iron, were fit together like a puzzle over the patch of freshly turned earth. Small, dainty maroon flowers had been planted in the gaps between the stones. The site was the honored final resting place for the villagers of Ello who had fallen at the Battle of Safedor and the Battle for Ambermal.

"Is it satisfactory?" Porter asked, holding a torch to illuminate the memorial.

"I planted the flowers, Your Majesty," a short woman said, stepping out from among the bystanders.

"They're pretty," Boschina said. She was holding Thoe's sword and scarf that the woman had given to them.

Ekala remembered when she had first met Thoe: at the market in Dudoon; a happy wife and husband, along with their children, selling olives and oil from their farm. And the image of her at Larma Hollow, playfully dancing by the fire when recovering from her battle wounds from the fight with renegade troops outside the East Gate. And then, her smile and Oleen salute as she left their camp at the North Ford carrying the message to Currad.

A joyful spirit, gone.

"Yes, this is lovely," Ekala said, gesturing at the intricate layout of the stones and the placement of the flowers. "Thank you."

"We did not know her, but we knew that she had fought for you many times," Porter said. "She was an Oleen soldier, so we wanted to honor her the best we could."

"She was a true Oleen," Ekala said, looking at the sword and scarf that Boschina held. Ekala suddenly realized that her message for help at the North Ford did not get to Currad—that Thoe had been killed on her way to Ambermal. How did they know of her mission? Had someone followed her from the ford? She stared at the grave as if she expected answers to rise out of the earth and speak to her through the solid stones.

"How did she die?"

"We don't know," Porter replied. He paused before speaking again. "She was a mess when she was brought to us, Your Majesty. Her body was broken, her arm and shoulder were...torn and chewed up."

Ekala looked at Porter. "Chewed up? Were there arrows or sword wounds?"

The woman spoke. "No, Your Majesty. I prepared her body. She was not killed by men. It had to be a vicious beast that got her."

Ekala glanced at Boschina, anger filling her chest and mind. She had to move, do something before it burst. Looking at the woman, she said, "Thank you for taking care of her, for honoring her service, and all the Oleens."

Queen Ekala Oleen took Thoe's sword from Boschina and pushed it into the ground at one end of the stones and tied the scarf to the handle. She cleared her throat, and then wiped tears from her eyes.

"Her name is Thoe," Ekala said. "She is a mother, a wife, and a warrior. She lived in the light and now she has died serving our people." Ekala lifted her head and watched the embers and smoke from the torches floating into the night, rising toward the stars. "May you find your family, Thoe, and peace beyond this life."

The queen bowed to the grave, backed away, and then turned to leave the site.

"Let's get back to camp," she said to Boschina.

Boschina delayed, staring at the scarf on the sword, the toes of her boots touching the flat stones of the grave. She could smell the Chorgen as it sniffed the scent on the scarf, heard it running in the night, saw its bared teeth, its yellow eyes, the paws clawing the earth, and, finally, its deathly leap—gaping, drooling jaws appearing suddenly out of the darkness. Boschina shivered, grasped the handle of her sword, and edged back from the grave. She knelt on one knee and touched one of the flat stones. It was cold and lifeless under her fingertips.

"Goodbye, Thoe," Boschina said.

She then rose and followed Ekala back into the village.

Ritzs and the Oleens had fed and watered the horses by the time Ekala and Boschina returned to the square. Saying goodbye to the people and apologizing for such a short stay, they walked the horses to the edge of town, and then mounted up and rode the short distance to where Thalmus waited with his companions.

Bubo was perched on the seat of the wagon, watching and listening to the night. Thunder rested nearby, his head up, his legs pulled under the shell, sensing the vibrations of the ground. Dallion was on the other side of the wagon, sniffing scents drifting in the breeze.

"Thoe's dead," Boschina told Thalmus as she dismounted from Radise. "Killed by a Chorgen."

Thalmus took in Boschina's announcement and what it meant as he helped to secure the horses on a rope line. Shadahn and Radise were left to roam loose, like Dallion, for these two had proven, long ago, their reliability and loyalty to their human friends and would not run in the face of danger.

"No fire?" Ritzs asked. "If we didn't know where you were, we wouldn't have found you."

"Good observation, Captain," Thalmus replied. "Why draw attention when we do not want it? Besides, no fire keeps our eyes better suited to the darkness. Just ask Bubo."

Ritzs glanced up at the Great Horned owl; his head swiveled to look at her.

"You'll hear no argument from me," Ritzs said and turned to Ekala. "With your permission, Oleen, I'll set guard positions now. Ellie and Fischer will take the first watch. Then Boschina and I for the second."

"Good. Any unusual sound at all should be reported immediately," Ekala replied. "And listen to Bubo and Thunder; they will tell us of any danger."

"As you wish, Oleen," Captain Ritzs answered and moved away into the night with the two Oleens.

"I am sorry to hear about the loss of Thoe," Thalmus said.

Ekala let out a deep breath. "We will miss her. Unfortunately, she died before getting my message to Currad."

"She was not on her way back?" Thalmus asked.

"No. When they found her, she was only two days ride from the ford. She was still on her way to Ambermal. My father and Currad don't know about the smuggled weapons or that Toulon has attacked us. And worse, there are no troops on the way to the North Ford. Ellie and Fischer are leaving at first light for Ambermal."

"Some villagers told us that they had seen Thoe in the square before her body was brought back," Boschina said. "We think someone in Ello set the Chorgen on Thoe to keep her from delivering the message to Currad."

"I believe I have that person," Thalmus said.

"What?" Ekala and Boschina said at the same time.

"He is in the wagon."

They looked at him in disbelief.

"He is not in the best condition," Thalmus continued. "But he is alive."

Ekala and Boschina hurried to the back of the wagon to find a man sprawled in the bed, his hands and feet bound and attached to iron rings on the side panels. He moaned occasionally, but his eyes remained shut.

"That looks like the clothing merchant," Boschina said.

"How come he's knocked out?" Ekala asked. "What happened to his face?"

"He tried to run and fell."

"There's blood on the back of his neck and head, too."

"Bubo was a little rough on him," Thalmus said.

"I'm going to be rough on him as well when he wakes up," Ekala said. "How'd you find him and get him back here?"

"After you left with the horses, Bubo, Dallion, and I decided to follow, stay in the shadows, and watch. This man, who I had seen last time we passed through, trailed after you like a hungry animal. When he saw me, he decided to give himself up."

Ekala almost laughed. "*He* decided? Looks to me like it wasn't his decision. Did he tell you anything about the Chorgens or who his master is?"

"No. I am hoping he will regain his senses so we can question him."

"We have to be on the road early tomorrow," Boschina said. "What are we going to do with him?"

"I have a plan for him," Thalmus replied.

"Of course you do," Boschina said.

Despite their visit into the village and the discovery of Chorgens in the area, the night passed quietly, much to their relief. Whether that was a result of Thalmus capturing the merchant was yet to be proven. Before sunrise they ate a quick meal of vegetables, cheese, and bread. They hooked up the team of horses to the wagon and loaded Thunder in the bed, and then covered him. The merchant sat next to Thalmus on the driver's bench. The man was still groggy, confused, and faded in and out of consciousness. Thalmus had tied his waist to the bench and his feet to the footboard. Because he kept slumping like a rag doll, Thalmus had put a board down the back of his coat—so it didn't show—and tied his chest to the back brace of the wagon's bed. His round merchant's cap partially hid his face and helped to complete the appearance of a tired traveler.

Ekala and Boschina sat on their horses and watched as Thalmus, still wearing the Banyon clothing, climbed onto the wagon and sat down next to the propped-up merchant. They both frowned, showing their lack of confidence in the situation.

Thalmus shrugged. "It is a long road. I needed someone to talk to."

Now the two women shook their heads in disbelief. "Right," Ekala said.

Ellie and Fischer rode up for their final instructions from the queen.

Queen Ekala Oleen looked at the two Oleen warriors. They were good soldiers, experienced fighters from the Battle of Ambermal and then the North Ford. However, they had always been within a larger force, with decisions made by a captain. Now they would be on their own. She prayed the Oleen training had prepared them for whatever they may encounter.

"You know what happened to Thoe?" Ekala said.

"We do," the two said.

"Be careful who you talk to and what you say. Travel only by day; find a safe refuge at night. Do not wear out your horses, but ride as fast as you can to Ambermal. Stay on the road that goes through

Barrunda. It's a little longer, but I believe it's safer. Stay together, unless you absolutely have to part to get the message to the castle."

"As you wish, Oleen," the two said.

Ekala Oleen smiled at them. "I want you to return with the army when it marches to the North Ford. Captain Susa will need you there."

"As you wish, Oleen," they both said again.

"Thank you for this honor to serve," Ellie said. Fischer nodded. Then they both turned and galloped south on the Western Road as the sun began to rise over the Middle Hills.

Ritzs watched the two Oleens ride away with worry for them and their mission, and a rising concern that now there were two fewer soldiers to protect the queen and Boschina. Still, Thalmus and his companions were here. And there was this unknown, this traitor Thalmus had corralled, who she was sure would be more trouble than help.

Thalmus tapped his foot on the floorboard and shook the reins. Thunder grunted from under the cover as the horses pulled forward. Bubo lifted off and flew ahead. Dallion neighed, bobbing his head. Thalmus smiled and then motioned to him to move away. The Paint let out a rolling snort and trotted toward the hills.

"We'll be watching," Ekala said.

"I hope so," Thalmus replied as Ekala, Boschina, and Ritzs rode away.

Skirting the village of Ello, Thalmus drove the wagon down the long, dusty road as Ritzs trailed far behind and Ekala and Boschina kept to the higher ground along the hills. Neither the queen nor the Stone Cutter's Daughter wanted to take the chance of riding on the road where they might be recognized. It was safer to stay out of sight. The merchant slept, muttered, occasionally opened his eyes and looked around, and then fell back into his dreams. Thalmus frequently asked him questions, no matter what state he was in. His few clear words would come out in bursts: "They're here…we have them" or "Let 'em loose."

People passing on the road paid little attention to them. Occasional nods or waves from other wagon drivers or merchants were all the communications extended by either party. No one looked closely or asked what they were hauling. Still, Thalmus kept the hat brim turned down, shading his face and identity while his eyes observed each person, their clothes, bags, or the content of their carts and wagons. When there was no one to watch, he turned his attention to the high, thin clouds sailing south on a gentle wind. He knew that a few had passed over the ford, so he listened for news. Throughout the day he heard nothing of importance, not even a word from Larma. He pulled off the road at midday and stopped to rest the horses and check on Thunder. The giant tortoise was restless and wanted out to walk. Thalmus convinced him to wait until they stopped for the night.

The merchant began mumbling again. Thalmus put the water bag to his lips and the man drank. Thalmus pushed bread in his mouth and he chewed it and drank some more. He suddenly opened his eyes and said, "Where's Redan? We have to find Redan."

"Why?" Thalmus asked.

"He has to know. We have to tell him," the man insisted.

"Tell him what?"

"To let 'em loose."

"Let who loose?"

"They're here," he said.

"Who is here?"

The man looked around, but Thalmus could tell that he wasn't really seeing anything. Thalmus slowly crossed his hand in front of the man's face. His eyes never blinked or followed the hand moving back and forth before him.

"It sure is dark," Thalmus said.

"I can't see Redan," the merchant said, his eyes closing.

"Where is he?" Thalmus asked.

The merchant's head dropped to his chest.

Thalmus watched him for a moment, and then picked up the reins and stomped once with his boot on the floorboard. When the horses pulled the wagon back onto the rutted road, he said, "Redan, a new name."

By late afternoon, he had reached the junction for the road to Dudoon and the Middle Hills road. The sun was settling behind darkening clouds over the Barrier Forest. Travelers were beginning to pull off and make camps for the night in the area where the two roads met. Thalmus stopped and watered the horses from the spring at the junction, avoiding people as best as he could. That was until a burly man with muddy trousers, drawing water from the pool with a large bucket in each hand, confronted him. He had a bad odor about him. One that made you want to step away.

"You from Banyon?" the man asked.

"How couldya tell," Thalmus replied, trying to put a Banyon accent on his words.

"Your clothes. And the wagon. That's Banyon-made," the man said.

"That it is," Thalmus said. "Nun betta."

The man hefted his buckets into the back of an open wagon that was packed full of sloshing buckets of water. "Watchya haulin'?" he asked casually.

"Blankets," Thalmus said. "And some treenkets."

The man gave Thalmus a second look. "You don't say."

"I did say," Thalmus replied. "Blankets and treenkets."

"Where you headin'?" he asked.

"Barruunda. Supposeta meeta man there."

The man rubbed his beard and glanced at the merchant sitting on the wagon's bench; his head was slumped forward as if he were dead. "What's wrong with him?"

"He got sick comin' through Toulon. Not sure he gonna make it."

"Those ain't Banyon clothes he's wearing," the man said.

"No," Thalmus said. "Hata get 'im new clothes in Ello. He ruinet tha othas."

The bucket man was studying the merchant. "I seen him before."

"You been in Banyon?" Thalmus asked.

"Yeah, been awhile. I was pickin' up...supplies."

"That musbe where you seen 'im," Thalmus said. "You soun' like a Toulon, t'me."

The man turned his attention to Thalmus and looked him up and down. "You're short for a Banyon man."

Thalmus stared into the eyes of the big, bearded man and decided to take a chance. Why not let this character he was playing loose to find out what this bucket man knew?

"I can kill jus' as fas' as a big man, maybe faster." Thalmus said and drew a sword so quick that the bearded man didn't have time to react. When he did step back, Thalmus was holding up the sword for him to see.

"You seena blade like this?" Thalmus asked him.

The bearded man noticed the "S" engraved near the hilt and nodded.

"Being Toulon, I thought you might," Thalmus said. "This jus one of my treenkets."

The man glanced around to see if anyone had noticed them. "Shouldn't be showin' it off like that, unless you wanta be caught by the Oleens."

"I ain't afraid of 'em," Thalmus said.

"You best be careful on the road," the bucket man said and climbed into his wagon. "You need to get those delivered. You get found out, then you're a dead man." He slapped his horses with the reins and they jolted forward, splashing water from the buckets.

Thalmus watched the man pull onto the road and head north. On the hill in the distance he saw Ekala and Boschina sitting on their horses, watching him. To the east, Dallion was standing on a knoll in the Plain, his brown and white coat looking like paint spots on the shimmering green grass. Ritzs had stopped on the road behind him. She was dismounted and pretending to examine her horse's leg. The bucket man's wagon was just passing her.

Where is he taking all those buckets? Thalmus wondered. *What is he watering?*

Chapter Twenty-Nine
Message Delivered

Thunder clicked his jaws from under the cover of the wagon. Thalmus lifted the flap and placed a bucket of water before the giant tortoise.

"I had to wait until he was gone," Thalmus told him. "There are too many people here for the others to join us." He glanced around. "We will continue on as long as we have light."

Thalmus patted Thunder's head as he drank from the bucket. "Not much farther," he said and dropped the flap over the back end of the wagon, climbed onto the driver's bench, and started the horses forward.

True to his word, when they had gone far enough away from the junction, and daylight was almost gone, Thalmus drove the wagon well off the road and stopped. In a few minutes, Ekala, Boschina, and Ritzs rode up to join him. They set up the ramp for Thunder and then started a small fire. Unhitching the horses, they tied them to rope lines fastened to the wagon so they could graze. Dallion walked into camp, followed by Bubo, who sailed quietly in and landed on top of the wagon. Owl had spent part of the day on the shoulders of Ekala and Boschina, the other half sleeping in a tree. Thalmus unstrapped the merchant and, with Ritzs' help, lifted the unconscious man down from the bench, propped him against a wagon wheel, and tied his arms to the spokes. Ritzs walked to the other side of the wagon, where the horses grazed, to stand for the first watch.

After telling the others about his exchange with the bucket man, Thalmus removed his herb satchel from the saddlebags on Thunder. He picked small leaves from three different pouches, crushed them together in a tin cup, poured in water, and began to heat the mixture in the embers of the fire.

"He didn't give you a name or place? Just a warning?" Ekala asked.

Thalmus stirred the concoction in his cup. "That was it," he replied. "He thought he recognized this man," motioning at the merchant, "though, he was not sure. When they find him missing, he will be sure and we will get some attention."

"Not the kind we want," Ekala said.

"Are you making something to wake him?" Boschina asked.

"Hopefully, this will get some answers," Thalmus said. He lifted the cup toward his nose and carefully smelled it. Quickly pulling his head back from the powerful odor, Thalmus looked at the others over the fire and smiled.

Thalmus knelt beside the merchant, gently lifted his head, and brought the cup to his nose. The man's neck straightened, head rolling up from the aroma as the cup came to his lips, forcing him to drink. Holding the back of his head, Thalmus poured half the cup down his mouth. The merchant gulped hard and then his body shook and his eyes opened. Looking at the fire-lit faces staring at him, the merchant was confused until he recognized the queen.

His expression turned to surprise. "You...got away."

"Got away from what?" Ekala asked, moving closer.

"The Chor...Sharpna, wilderness."

"You thought you could kill me?" Ekala said. "Are you the one releasing the Chorgens? Did you let one loose on Thoe, the Oleen soldier?"

The merchant coughed, trying to clear his throat. Thalmus put the cup to his lips again and poured. The man swallowed and turned his head.

Ekala grabbed the man's shirt by his throat. "Did you send the Chorgen after the Oleen?"

"Not me," he muttered.

"You saw her."

"Yes…my head hurts…my arms can't move."

"Who'd you tell? Who commands the Chorgens?"

"Don't hurt me," he begged.

"Tell me or I will hurt you."

The man coughed again and tried to look away, but Ekala held him tight. Thalmus watched as she pulled her short blade from its sheath. He prepared to grab her arm. Seeing the knife, the man tried to pull back. "Wasn't me. No, it's Redan. It's Redan, I tell you."

"Where is he?"

The merchant's body was shaking, his eyes drooping. "Bogs."

"What bogs?"

"He'll kill you," the man mumbled.

Ekala gripped tighter. "What bogs?"

"Bog? Uh, uh, Dudoon."

"No, he is not there anymore," Thalmus said. "Where is he now?"

The man was fading, his mental state slipping away. "Now…now?" he mumbled. "A bad place…." He looked at Ekala. "They're hungry…let 'em loose."

The merchant's head rolled down, his chin resting on Ekala's hand.

Ekala shook him one more time. When he didn't respond, she let go. Her other hand holding the knife slowly loosened. She stared at him for a moment before sheathing the blade and stepping away.

Boschina, who had watched and listened, understood Ekala's anger, but knew she would not use her knife on the man. The merchant's knowledge scared Boschina more than Ekala's threatening knife.

"This Redan, and the Chorgens, are near," Boschina said.

Ekala turned to her. "What makes you think that?"

Boschina pointed at the merchant. "He is Redan's spy in Ello. He was going to report on us, like he did on Thoe. And that bucket man with the wagon at the junction, he was hauling water for the Chorgens."

Thalmus nodded as he poured water into his cup and rinsed it out. *Her instinct is accurate. She has learned to listen to her senses.* He looked up at her. "Yes, Boschina, the bucket man had the beast's odor about him. The Chorgens are near."

Reaching into his vest pocket, Thalmus pulled out Larma's folded message. He felt its weight and tingling vibration in the palm of his hand as he held it out to Boschina.

"It is time you carry this," Thalmus said.

Boschina stared at the little package in Thalmus' creased, rough hand. She wanted to refuse, but knew she could not. It was already calling her, speaking to her as if the odd script inside spoke a language only her body and senses understood.

The material felt light as she lifted it from Thalmus' hand, not like the heavy object she'd first carried for Larma. Her fingers wrapped around the folded fiber, gently carrying it to her breast pocket. Buttoning the flap of the pocket, she smiled as it began ever so slightly to beat with her heart.

* * *

Captain Kali walked along the new stone walls of the fort overlooking the South Ford. Two meters thick at the base and four meters tall, the perimeter wall was stout. The large stacked stones were fit tightly together and bonded with gray mortar that filled the joints and gaps. Wooden platforms and walkways were being built on the inside around the top of the walls. Log rafters of the roof structure over the barracks, commissary and warehouse were almost complete. Wagon loads of roof tiles sat nearby. The thick gate doors for the only access into the compound were being assembled on a support frame just outside the opening in the wall. The workers and Ameram Army soldiers were making good progress on the construction. The King's Builder was there inspecting the work and instructing the various crews in their tasks.

"Captain Kali," the builder called when he noticed her. He left the men he'd been directing and strolled toward her. "How does it look?"

"Good, it's all coming together," Kali remarked. "It's close to filling up with troops."

"I want to show you something," he said. "Come this way."

He led her to the end of the barracks building. "I was able to stretch the material we had to extend the sleeping quarters and some of the storage rooms. It's not as much as you wanted. Still, we gained room for another eighteen to twenty soldiers. It made the open formation ground smaller, but I thought it a good compromise."

Kali smiled at the tall man and the look of satisfaction on his face. "I hope this doesn't put you in trouble with the quartermaster."

"No. If he doesn't have to pay extra bills, he won't know and he won't care."

"Thanks for doing this," she said. "I think it's important."

The builder shrugged. "It's my job. It's what the king, uh, queen pays me for."

"I'm sure both the king *and* the queen appreciate your dedication," Kali said. "As well as Currad, to whom I have to report now."

"Give Currad my regards, Captain," the builder said. "Tell him we'll be ready for troops soon." He smiled and, with a wave, he walked back to the roofing project.

Captain Kali complimented the laborers on their workmanship and then swung onto her horse. Riding through the gate and out onto the sloping hillside, Kali looked down at the ford. Castle Guard soldiers were inspecting wagons and carts on both sides of the river. No further weapons had been found since Currad's fight with the smugglers. Traffic through the ford was proceeding smoothly. The changes of the guard at the ford and the steady construction had been going well. She was proud about both.

However, she wondered what was brewing beyond the horizon and in the dark places of their own country. Currad wanted to move Oleen forces here as soon as possible. But Kali wasn't convinced this was where their best troops should be stationed. The King's Honored Soldier was recovering from his wounds, but not fast enough for her relief. He would not be returning to horse and field any time soon.

Where was Oleen? she wondered. *When would she return?* For all her confidence, Captain Kali had a creeping sense that the queen was in trouble, and she could not be there to help her. Kali straightened in the saddle, pulled her shoulders back, and stretched her neck. She took several deep breaths, removed her hat, rubbed her head, brushed her hair back, and reset the hat. She leaned forward and patted the horse's neck.

"We'll just take care of things here until Oleen returns," she said to the brown mare. "Let's go report to Currad."

Captain Kali started trotting west toward Ambermal. The castle and city looked like tiny sculptured stones in the distance under the shadow of darkening clouds that blew across Cold Canyon from the Stone Hills.

When Kali finally approached the massive gates of the walled city, darkness was settling on the land. Travelers going in each direction were beginning to move off the road for the night. It had been a long day: leaving the castle before sunrise to ride to the fort, inspecting the work in order to report to Currad, and riding back before night. Still, she stopped to talk with the castle guards, to hear if they had anything unusual to report. It was then that the approaching sound of galloping hooves sent off alarms in Captain Kali's body. She drew her sword from its sheath on her horse, who had already turned to face the road. Several guards nocked arrows and others drew swords. They waited, and then were relieved to see two Oleens appear on the darkening road. When the two riders reached the gate, they pulled their tired horses to a stop before Kali. She knew them both. They were members of Captain Ritzs' force and from the look of them and their horses, they had been riding hard for a long time.

"What's wrong? Is someone chasing you? Is the queen alright?" Kali demanded.

Ellie cleared her throat and tried to hold her horse steady from stepping and shuffling and snorting. "We have an urgent message for the king and Currad from the queen."

"Is she alright?" Kali asked.

"Yes, yes, we left her two days ago at Ello," Ellie said. "Captain Kali, we must deliver this message right away. The queen demands it."

Kali sheathed her sword. "Follow me," she commanded as she charged through the gates into the city toward the castle.

* * *

The village of Barrunda was a thriving industrial community of businesses that made a wide variety of merchandise. Its people were engaged in the production and marketing of candles, utensils, furniture, quilts, saddles, shoes, boots, clothing, and farm tools; other than food, just about whatever necessary or practical item was needed for living. Large quantities of various materials and supplies flowed into the town for this production and finished products were shipped out across Ameram and to countries near and far. Being such a center for trade and opportunity, Barrunda unfortunately attracted a devious and morally offensive element as well.

It was an unusual location for such a center of industry, not easily accessible by a major river or border. However, that is exactly why it was established where it was, away from invading armies or saboteurs. The people of Barrunda also produced most of the weaponry and equipment for the army, as well as the trappings for the royals and lords. Therefore, throughout many years and rulers, the village and its people enjoyed a favored and protected status, almost as much as the capital city and Castle Ambermal. This history and prominence had imbued the lords, elders, merchants, and craftsmen with an attitude that they were not only important, but indispensable to the kingdom, and should be treated as such. Half of the men in the old King's Learned Council were from Barrunda. They were quite influential and often swayed the other members, and the king, to their advantage. But their influence suddenly ended in frustration and anger when Ekala Oleen erased their power by taking the throne and disbanding the council.

The politics and leverage of business in Barrunda had always been permeated with intrigue. Now, with the change of authority, it was doubly so. How were they to deal with this very different ruler, this new queen so loved by the people?

In the bowels of this city was a small office on a back street that belonged to a man who referred to himself as a financier of goods. He was not a public figure or a man looking for attention. On the contrary, he was practically anonymous. Yet, his reputation was such that when someone was in desperate need of funds to save a business or career, they sought him out for help. It was not the poor soul's first choice, but it would be his last.

It was this man—broad shouldered with a large head, curly brown hair, and one eye—who owned the wagon Thalmus was driving. And it was this man, with one burned hand and a limp, who owned the cargo of weapons from the same wagon the Oleens had unloaded at the ford. He had used many names throughout his life, lived in many places. Here in Barrunda, he was known as Baskin.

When the new shipment of arms from the north was late, Baskin sent men to look for it. He had heard from merchants and his own sources that wagons passing through the South Ford were now being inspected. He was pondering what to do about that when there was a knock on his door.

"Who is it?" he asked in a raspy voice.

"It's Savo. I have news," a voice announced from the other side.

Baskin unlocked the door and let a tall man with a moustache and scarred face slide in, and then closed and locked it again.

"There's been a battle at the North Ford," Savo said, taking off leather gloves. "Passage is shut down. The Oleens and some King's

Guard hold the ford. The Toulon army is gathering on the north side."

"Who told you this?" Baskin asked.

"One of our men. He just came in."

Baskin stomped his foot on the floor. "You can't trust those Toulons. Sharpna and Glasrauss are too anxious. They think they will walk in and take this kingdom by themselves? Zinkila isn't ready to attack, nor are we. What about the shipment?"

"It got held up at the ford, I guess due to the fight. Redan's man saw it on the road outside Ello. It should be getting here soon."

"Good, we'll need it," Baskin said. "It can't get through the South Ford now. When it arrives, take the wagon to the crypt and store it there."

"What about the Banyon drivers?"

"Give those fools the same pay the others got," Baskin said. "Just make sure their remains are never found."

"Something else you should know," Savo said, slapping the gloves against his leg. "The frog hunter and his animals were seen with the Stone Cutter's Daughter passing through Ello on their way to the North Ford."

Baskin sat down in a chair at his desk. "He's going to get in our way, he and that Larma," Baskin said, taping the desktop with his burnt fingers. "Maybe he'll stay up there and not come south. Either way, we'll have to fight him at some point. What about the queen?"

"I heard from merchants she and the Stone Cutter's Daughter were in Ello three nights ago."

"Three nights ago. I hope Redan knows that. Was the frog hunter with them?"

"No."

"You just said he was with the Stone Cutter's Daughter."

"That was eight or ten days ago," Savo said. "Nobody saw him in Ello with the queen."

"That's odd." Baskin thought for a moment. "That concerns me. I want to know where he is, what he's doing. You know he's a threat. He is always in the midst of our failures and their victories. He was there for the king and then brought the queen to the crown. The frog hunter is the key. He's their guardian."

"I didn't know," Savo said. "I'll send riders out to find him."

"Tell them to be careful. The hunter appears simple and harmless, but he's not. Where is the queen now?"

"Nobody's seen them. Maybe they went over to the Middle Road. Or maybe Redan's Chorgens got 'em," Savo said with a smile. "Like they did that Oleen messenger."

Baskin's one eye looked up at his tall henchman. Savo was a good soldier, followed orders, and would do the bloody deeds that needed to be done with no guilt. He was almost as coldhearted as himself. However, Savo was too confident in his physical skills and naïve in the mental game of war.

"A Chorgen kill is a pleasant thought," Baskin said. "But we mustn't count on the beasts. Thus far, the queen and the Stone Cutter's Daughter have been surprisingly tough to kill."

* * *

Boschina snapped awake. She, Ekala, and Ritzs were sleeping around the fire. Thalmus was on guard with the horses on the other side of the wagon. Bubo was perched on top of the wagon. He looked asleep, but she knew he was listening. Thunder was about four meters away, facing into the darkness.

All was quiet. What had awakened her?

The small fire crackled and a wisp of smoke rose from the burning wood. The sky was full of the tiny night lights, thousands of them spread across the great, black vastness above them. It was the third night since leaving Ello. Tomorrow, they should enter Barrunda and then another long day or two to reach Ambermal.

Boschina looked around again, carefully checking each person and animal. She was too close to the fire to smell anything but smoke and burning wood.

What was it? What woke me? she wondered.

At first, she'd heard the violent sound of waves breaking against stone and the image of her father turning away from a sculpture to stare at her, a hammer and chisel in his hands. Then darkness, and in that blindness Boschina thought she'd heard sniffing, snorting. Images appeared of drooling jaws, wet noses inhaling; the sound of a door creaking open, claws scraping the bare earth, and then running, tramping paws, and running once more. Yet, everyone around her was calm, sleeping.

Her sword was quiet. Had it all been just a dream?

Boschina felt a throb on her chest—Larma's message was beating.

* * *

King Ahmbin sat at his uncle's bedside. He was leaning back in the chair, not looking at the prone man in the bed. Lord Rundall's breathing was shallow, his eyes closed, his arms lying at his sides.

"I was remembering the battle of Dinausten," the old king said. "How you taught me to not be brash, to consider all possibilities before acting. Do you remember what you said? We were standing on a knoll looking down on the little valley with the shiny creek running through it. The Hypothos were spread out along its banks. We had been chasing them for weeks, skirmishing here and there, but they kept maneuvering around us, their army just out of reach. I was so frustrated and angry. And here they were, finally in our grasp, waiting for us to attack and destroy them. Our officers and soldiers were lined up in formation ready to charge, waiting for my signal. And I was ready to send them. Do you remember?"

The king turned to look at Rundall. The old man's eyes were still closed, his body motionless.

"You said, 'It looks too easy,'" the king continued. "You said, 'I would not brashly commit our entire resources to one course of action. This might be a trap. If it is, they could be the victors, and we the vanquished, leaving the door open to Ameram. If it is not a trap, and they have truly given up, it will be a slaughter. Is either one of those what you want to remember?'"

The king gently grasped his uncle's thin arm. "Oh, you stopped me with that, made me think, as you always did. You were always there, right beside me, in all the years, good and bad. You carried me through the pain of Lady Ahmbin's death and stepped in to help educate Ekala. You fought to save me from Metro when other's left me—and I turned my back on you. I was lost in his darkness, but you never faltered, never stopped believing in me…you were always there."

King Ahbim gripped Rundall's hand. "Thank you, Uncle, for all you have given to me, our family and our country."

Standing, he leaned over, softly kissed Rundall's forehead, and quietly left the room.

Chapter Thirty
Surprise In the Torchlight

"The Chorgens have been released. They're on their way," Boschina told the others as they crouched around the campfire, warming cornmeal and honey for breakfast.

The sky was beginning to brighten, though the sun was still below the horizon. Morning dew lay softly on the earth and would remain until evaporated by the day's warmth. The horses were calm; Thunder was resting and Bubo was scouting. The unconscious merchant was secured in the wagon bed.

Boschina's companions looked at her with questions on their faces and on their tongues. They had started taking her observations seriously.

"Why do you think that?" Ekala asked.

"I heard them last night."

Ritzs stood up. "Around here?"

"No, but they're coming," Boschina said, stirring the meal in her cup.

"You said *they*. There's more than one?" Ritzs asked.

"Yes," Boschina replied. "There's at least three, maybe four."

"Four!" Ritzs looked from Boschina to Ekala.

Ekala glanced at the merchant in the wagon. "Maybe the bucket man remembered who Thalmus' partner was. He told Redan and they let the animals go to come after us."

Thalmus had been watching Boschina. He knew Larma's message was tucked into her pocket. Was this vision Boschina's own determination or Larma's? Taking his last bite of breakfast, Thalmus wiped his cup and packed it into the saddlebags.

Ekala put her hand on Boschina's shoulder. "You're sure about this? I mean, what you saw or heard?"

Boschina looked up from her cup and spoon. Her face was calm and her eyes clear. "Remember what Larma told us when we left the ford?"

"To let the Stone Truth guide us," Ekala answered.

Boschina nodded. "I'm sure what I saw and heard were true."

Thalmus believed her. He knew what it was like when the spirit of truth filled you with knowledge.

"The sun is almost up," Thalmus said. "The beasts will be looking for a dark place to sleep for the day. We need to get on the road and reach Barrunda before night; the Chorgens will be looking for us as soon as it gets dark."

"What if you meet the people waiting for the weapons?" Ritzs asked.

"We'll deal with them and move on," Ekala said.

Thunder climbed up the ramp into the wagon and nestled in alongside the merchant. If the man awoke, he'd be pinned against the side panel and the giant tortoise's shell. Plus, his head was lying even with Thunder's, which for a stranger would be a frightful awakening. Thalmus knew that to continue using the merchant in the seat, as the second Banyon driver, was no longer viable. The ruse had served its purpose. Now the man's presence could expose Thalmus as a fake instead of helping him.

The team of horses were harnessed to the wagon and Thalmus started them off and back onto the road as Ekala, Boschina, and Ritzs took up their trailing positions. Dallion trotted alongside Thalmus and the wagon until people were spotted in the distance. Then the stallion galloped out onto the plain, where it was common to see wild horses. By now, the Western Hills Road was passing through the broad Bushy Plain. The scattered bunches of tall, brown brush, for which the plain was named, provided more cover than the open Great Plain. The last time they had been through this region was the brutal march with their ragtag army from Safedor, struggling through the immense dust storm to finally assail Castle Ambermal.

When the day had half passed, they were still a long way from their destination. Thalmus was pushing the wagon's horses a little faster than usual to try to reach Barrunda before dark. At a safe distance around him, his companions rode to keep pace. Ekala and Boschina were reminiscing about that suffocating, blinding dust storm and how Thunder had guided them, when they noticed riders approaching the wagon. They slowed Shadahn and Radise and prepared to charge if needed. The two horses sensed the change and perked up with anticipation. Boschina pulled her bow from its cover and, placing its tip on her boot in the stirrups, strung the bow. The quiver on her back was full. Her sword waited on her hip. She was ready.

"Now we'll find out who these traitors are," Ekala said, patting Shadahn's neck.

Thalmus saw the four riders approaching and knew from their behavior that they were coming for him. He reached down to the floorboard, unsheathed his sword, and slipped it behind him on the bench. Then Thalmus slouched and once again became a Banyon.

The four men rode up quickly. Slowing their horses, they waved for him to stop. One of the men—with a moustache and scar, and who acted like the leader—moved his horse alongside the wagon.

"You got a shipment for the lizard," the man asked.

"Maybe I do," Thalmus said. "Ya got one?"

"Don't fool with me," the scarred-face man said.

"Lookit," Thalmus said, "I was tol' ta see a sign of a lizard befo handin' this load over ta anybody. Ya got one, show it ta me."

The man glared at him. "You Banyon drivers are all the same." He looked around to see who else was on the road. There was a wagon coming up behind them and a lone rider behind that. They were too close to kill this man now and take the wagon, which is what he wanted to do.

"Why are you alone? Where's the other driver?" The scarred-face man demanded.

"He got sick, died," Thalmus said. "Buried 'im two nights ago. "Lookit, you gotta sign ta sho me, an' my money, you can have this wagon right now for one of ya horses so I can git home."

One of the other men laughed. "You're pretty bold for a short Banyon."

"You boys don't scare me," Thalmus said. "Now thos' Oleens tha' pushed me at the ford, they're scary."

"You talk too much," the scarred-face man said. He glanced back at the oncoming wagon and then quickly pulled up his sleeve to reveal a tattoo. It was an image of a lizard crawling down his forearm from the elbow to his wrist. The beady eyes and open mouth were just above his hand, ready to bite. Under the lizard's sharp nails was the word "Savo."

Thalmus noticed that it was his sword hand.

"Now tha's jus' ugly," Thalmus said. "Ya got my money?"

"You'll get paid when you deliver this load," the man said, putting his sleeve down. He pointed at Thalmus with the arm held by the lizard. "You follow us, and don't slow down."

"I will if this ol' wagon stays together, Savo."

The scarred-face man jerked around. "How'd you know my name?"

"The lizard's got it," Thalmus said motioning at Savo's arm.

Savo stared, and then pointed a finger at him again. "If this wagon breaks down, we're leaving you and you won't get a thing. Now keep up."

Savo rode to the front while two other men rode on each side of the team of horses. The fourth man fell in behind the wagon as it rolled by him and then picked up speed on the road.

Dallion had been watching from the plain. He sensed his friend's danger with riders now on each side of him. The stallion wanted to gallop over and shake the men's horses up, but Boschina and Ekala had not charged in so he knew to wait. Instead, he trotted through the brush, keeping a little back from parallel so he could keep an eye on them. Ekala and Boschina did the same on the other side, holding back enough on the hill so the men would not see them. Ritzs, though, had to speed up to stay with Thalmus—yet not appear to be following them.

Continuing this way for several hours, they caught up with and passed numerous wagons loaded down with materials. Under the noise of the bouncing and creaking of the wagon and clumping hooves, Thalmus could hear the merchant beginning to grumble and scuff about in the back. The riders around him could not hear the merchant over the noises. As long as they didn't stop, his escort would not hear the passenger under the cover. Still, the riders on each side of the wagon's horses kept turning to look at Thalmus with threatening glares and smirks.

The sun was dropping toward the Barrier Forest, the daylight beginning to fade, when the red tile roofs of Barrunda, tucked against the Western Hills, came into view.

"It won't be long now," Ekala said to Boschina. "Let's join Ritzs so we can follow them into Barrunda."

There were two main roads entering the village. One was for horses and foot traffic that weaved into the narrow streets of shops, offices, and neighborhoods. The other road was for shipping: wagons hauling all the necessary supplies into the warehouses on the western outskirts of Barrunda, and then wagons full of finished products being carried out to the world. This road was much wider with two rutted tracks from heavy wheels, one entering the industrial area and the other exiting. It was onto this second road that Savo directed Thalmus to turn the horses.

The darkening of the day was hastened by thick clouds that had drifted from the Great Water through the Barrier Forest before settling over Barrunda. Thalmus slowed the team to a walk as he made the turn and continued on the route into Barrunda. This was a community he rarely visited. The presence of arrogant people, powerful merchants, and wealth insulted his priorities. He had been here numerous times early in King Ahmbin's reign to help inspect the battle tools and armaments for the army and Castle Guard. Since then, he had visited only a few times for various items he could find nowhere else. For his own tools, Thalmus used an old craftswoman hidden away in the Middle Hills. She imbued a spirit into the work which no other blacksmith or forge could duplicate. It was she who made the unique swords that Ekala, Boschina, and he now carried.

Ekala, Boschina, and Ritzs had moved closer to the wagon as they entered Barrunda. In the growing darkness, they tried to blend in amongst the other travelers who were bunched up on the road. Boschina had put her coat on and covered her head with the hood. Ekala pulled the brim of her hat lower in front of her face. Dallion, a lone horse, did not want to be on that road near strangers and curious people. He stayed on the fringe, paralleling his friends.

Thunder clicked several times. Thalmus could hear the merchant moan intermittently as they separated from the other wagons onto a trail by themselves that went beyond the last row of warehouses.

"Keep movin'," Savo ordered.

Trailing blindly in the night behind Thalmus, Ekala whispered, "I can't see them. I can barely hear them."

The three women were staying close together and riding slowly, side by side, with Ekala in the middle. Searching the darkness, they could hear the wagon and horses ahead of them, but couldn't tell exactly from which direction. They had lost the ruts, gotten off the trail.

"We'll lose them if we don't keep going," Ritzs whispered.

Radise bobbed her head. "What is it, Lady?" Boschina said. Then something bumped her shoulder. She jerked to the left to see Dallion coming alongside her. "Dal."

Ekala and Ritzs were suddenly surprised by wings behind their heads and then claws grasping Ekala's shoulder. She flinched and realized who it was. Bubo pulled his wings in and looked at her. He snapped his beak once, and then his head swiveled and looked ahead into the darkness. That's when they heard Thalmus.

"Can't see a thing out here," Thalmus said loudly. "Ya kno where you boys are goin'?"

"Quiet," the man on his left said.

"Makes me nervous," Thalmus said and started singing. "If I'd been born an owlll, I'd be nothin' but a fowlll, driftin' on my wings thru ta nighttt, seein' everyting that I might bite—"

"Shut up and keep movin'," the man on his right said.

"Well now, I can't drive if I can't see," Thalmus yelled. "It's them clouds covern' the night lights."

The man on the left moved back to Thalmus on the wagon. "We're guiding your horses. Now shut up!"

"Why you yellin' at me?"

"I'm goin' to run you through, little man," he said and started to pull his sword.

"Leave it!" Savo called from ahead. "We're almost there."

The man dropped his half-drawn sword back into its scabbard. "You don't got much longer."

Ahead, several torches appeared in the darkness, creating a reddish umbrella glow and revealing human silhouettes in front of a gaping mouth of a cavern in a rock wall of the hillside. Thalmus counted four to six silhouettes. If they were all armed, there was a total of eight to ten men he would have to overcome. Thalmus hoped his support was not too far back because the confrontation was near.

"Turn it right here," Savo called.

Thalmus pulled the reins, turning the horses and the wagon into the light in front of the cave opening. There were four torches, two on each side, burning on iron stands that were taller than the waiting men. He could see the horses were worn out. It had been a long day for them with no rest or water. Abusing their endurance and loyalty bothered him; he would have to apologize. When the wagon stopped, Thalmus heard Thunder click his jaws twice. It had been a long, rough ride for him, too. Now, the giant tortoise was letting Thalmus know he sensed trouble and was ready. Thalmus lightly knocked twice on the wall behind him.

"Let's get this unloaded," Savo commanded the men from his horse. "You," he said, pointing at Thalmus, "Get down here and help."

"I'mma driver," Thalmus said, "notta loaderr."

"I said get down here."

Thalmus grunted and shrugged disgustedly. He grabbed his sword and jumped onto the flat top of the wagon and walked to the rear.

"What are you doing? I said get down here!"

"I gotta cut the ropes," Thalmus said.

"Get him down," Savo ordered the man who had threatened Thalmus. "And get rid of him."

The man smiled and walked to the back of the wagon while he pulled his sword.

"That sword'll do you no good, little man. Your job's done and so are you."

"I want you to meet Thunder." Thalmus said in his own voice and pulled the canvas off the back end. The man found himself staring into the black eyes and the giant head of a shell creature. There was a moment when the man was confused in the flickering light. *What's this? Where are the weapons?* Then the head lunged at him, the crushing jaws clamping over his head and neck. The sword dropped to the ground as the man's lifeless body slumped against the wagon and Thunder spit him out.

The other men were stunned at what they had just witnessed.

"It's the frog hunter and his shell creature," one of them said.

Thalmus jumped down from the wagon and knocked the sword from the closest man, and then struck him in the head with the butt of the sword handle, crumpling him to the ground.

The other men started to back away, until one man yelled, "His shell creature can't get out of the wagon. He's all alone. We can take 'im."

Keeping a distance from Thunder, they began to encircle Thalmus, thrusting and swinging their swords at him.

Savo couldn't believe it. It's the frog hunter? He's been driving a wagon with the shell creature behind me all day and I didn't know it? And I led him to our cache. Baskin will kill me...unless I kill the hunter now—then I will be honored. The hunter's back was to him as he fought the men on foot. Savo drew his sword and charged his horse forward.

Thalmus heard the horse coming behind him and prepared to dodge into the men he fought when Bubo sailed over his head at the rider.

Savo was about to swing his sword down on Thalmus when Bubo flew into his face and grabbed Savo's head with his talons. Jerking the reins, Savo's horse pulled to the side and galloped past as Bubo let go of the shrieking man and flew off.

Another man picked up a loose sword and ran up behind Thalmus. Before he could thrust into the hunter's back, an arrow thumped into his chest. The man staggered to the ground, grasping at the shaft.

Outnumbered by six, Thalmus jumped onto the wagon where Thunder could protect his backside and he could protect Thunder's head from the top while he fought with the men trying to climb on from the other three sides. One of them grabbed a torch and started to jab it at Thunder. Thalmus knelt on the back end of the wagon and swung his sword low to knock away the flaming stick at the same time an arrow zipped into the man's belly.

Into the torch light galloped Thalmus' companions: Dallion rearing and stomping at men; Ekala thrashing with her sword from atop a snorting, squealing Shadahn; Boschina firing arrows from the back of Radise; and Ritzs jumping from her horse onto the wagon to duel with the men still fighting there.

By the time Savo recovered from the shock of Bubo's attack—wiping the blood from his head and face, and from the fear of being attacked again—he had lost the advantage. His men were falling now before these new fighters.

Who were they? Where did they come from?

He watched from the darkness as the battle was fought in the torchlights. These fighters were skilled warriors and their mounts trained warhorses. Then he realized the three with Thalmus were women. *Oleens!* He thought. No, more than just Oleens. *The one on the big black horse is the queen. And the archer is the Stone Cutter's Daughter.*

How did they go unnoticed? They must have followed the hunter here.

How did he not see them?

Savo held his head in his hands. It hurt as if the owl's claws were still grabbing him. The wagon was a trap from the beginning, and he fell into it. He needed to run, get away before morning. But where would he go that Baskin couldn't find him? That vicious man had spies everywhere. Toulon, Banyon, and Zinkila were under his influence. He could not hide for long before being discovered. Savo rubbed his head and tried to think, come up with a plan.

It was hopeless. He was a dead man.

Then other sounds in the night caught Savo's attention—something coming closer, sniffing, a snort. The animal wasn't approaching him, but was sniffing and pawing its way toward the torchlight, toward the queen. Savo knew what it was. *Maybe I have another chance*, he thought.

The fight around the wagon was ending. Only one of Savo's men still stood. When the man realized he was alone, he dropped to his knees, surrendered, and begged for mercy. The horses were still stomping and huffing, even though Ekala and Boschina had dismounted. Ritzs helped Thalmus set the wagon top down for Thunder's ramp. The giant tortoise tramped down and immediately joined Dallion and Shadahn as they checked the bodies on the ground. When this was done, he began lumbering toward the cave. They were all relieved, but still keyed up. Thalmus checked the fallen fighters and found Savo had gotten away.

"Their leader is not here."

"We'll find him," Ekala said. "We know who he is now." Gesturing toward the cave, she said, "This must be where they're hiding the weapons."

The three engraved swords had been humming throughout the fight. Ekala still held her sword as she walked around. Thalmus had set his down to move the ramp. Boschina had never pulled hers from the scabbard. Yet all three continued to vibrate. Ekala thought hers was still in motion from the battle. Boschina now felt her blade against her hip. Just as Thalmus noticed his sword was still humming and picked it up, Boschina felt the presence of Larma's script in her vest pocket. She didn't have to open it to read the message. The word came to her—Chorgens.

Thalmus looked at Boschina and knew. "Ekala!"

The queen, still excited from the fight, looked over at him, saw the look on his face, and turned to Boschina, who was drawing her sword.

"They're here," Boschina said, backing toward the wagon.

Behind them a horse suddenly charged out of the darkness toward the cavern. Glancing over his shoulder, Thalmus saw Savo riding the horse and kicking the torch standards down as he rode by each one. Thalmus turned and ran after him. Dallion was already chasing him and got to Savo just as he knocked over the last light. Savo, sword in hand, was ready to slash Dallion, but the big Paint stopped and reared up on his hind legs. Savo's stallion did the same, rearing suddenly to face Dallion. When the horse's front legs thumped down, Savo was barely hanging on. He'd dropped his sword and was grasping the saddle with both hands. Dallion charged into him and the horse bolted with his rider dangling on the side. Snorting and stomping, Dallion chased after him, disappearing from the fluttering light into the great darkness. The wagon's team of horses shuffled and whinnied during the fight, but had held. Now they too panicked and bolted, pulling the wagon away with them. The one survivor who had surrendered saw his chance to escape and ran after the wagon.

The torches, broken apart on the ground, their embers scattered, were almost out when Thalmus gathered the remnants and reset the standards. Ritzs called their horses to join them. Radise moved behind Boschina and Shadahn followed Ekala as they kept backing toward the dim light near the cavern, their swords at the ready. They gathered near the torch standards, the queen and Boschina in the middle with Thalmus and Ritzs on the ends.

Savo climbed and crawled back into the saddle of his frantically galloping horse as Dallion ran beside them, bumping and biting.

Having dropped his sword at the cavern, Savo could only try to kick Dallion when he came near, but the Paint would move away into the darkness and then suddenly attack again. The other stallion ran instinctively through the dark night for the shelter of the stable in the village, where he could escape the powerful Paint stallion. When they finally entered the cobble lanes, their hooves clacking on the stones, Dallion slowed and followed them through several turns to a door. Then he retreated and headed back to search for the horses pulling the wagon.

A pounding on his door woke Baskin from a comfortable sleep. He did not like being disturbed late at night. It made him angry.

"It's Savo," a voice called. "I have important news you need to hear."

There was panic in the man's voice.

Baskin rose, put on a robe, and opened the door.

Savo rushed in and closed the door himself, latching the bolt before turning to Baskin. "The queen, the Stone Cutter's Daughter, and the hunter are here," he blurted out.

Baskin was surprised. "Here? In Barrunda?"

"At the crypt," Savo explained. "They must have followed us there. We were unloading and they attacked us—killed our men. The owl clawed me. Look at my head. The giant shell creature and—"

"Stop!" Baskin ordered. "They followed you to the crypt? How many Oleens? How did you not see them?"

"It was dark; they must have been hiding somewhere. But they didn't go inside; no, they didn't get that far because the Chorgens got 'em. I knocked down the torches as the beasts were coming in."

"Chorgens are here?"

"Yeah, they were chasing the queen."

"Did you see the Chorgens kill the queen and the others?"

"Well, no. The Paint stallion and owl chased me. I barely got away to come here and tell you."

"And our men?" Baskin asked.

"I think they're all dead."

"How many Oleens were there?"

"I don't know, not many; it was dark. They took us by surprise. But the beasts came; they had to have gotten them."

Baskin sat down at his desk to think. This is what he had planned: to execute the queen so that the kingdom would be leaderless. And with the hunter and the Stone Cutter's Daughter gone too, the spirit of the queen's prophecy would be dead. He and his followers could easily conquer the rest and rule Ameram. However, if the queen wasn't dead, or one of the other two survived, then his victory was in doubt, at least for the present. Their sudden appearance at the crypt baffled him.

"How did they know about it?"

Baskin's eye studied Savo. His stalwart lieutenant was nervous, shifting his feet, clearing his throat and swallowing frequently. *He's not telling me all he knows.* "Go back to the crypt and make sure they're all dead," Baskin ordered.

Savo hesitated. "Chorgens are roaming loose out there."

"If they made their kills, they won't be wanting you," Baskin said. "Now go quickly and report back right away. I have plans to make."

Chapter Thirty-One
Duty Fulfilled

Bubo winged out of the cavern, hooting that the cave inside was safe. With the owl's clearance, they sent the horses into the cavern to join Thunder, and then turned to wait for the beasts. Darkness prevailed all around them save for the small circle of fading light from the flickering torches.

"At least we have a little light to see by," Ekala said.

"For how much longer though?" Ritzs said.

"Shh," Thalmus whispered softly.

The gentle breeze had stopped. The air was still, as if it, too, was waiting. Smoke wisps rose straight up from the torches that crackled and hissed. The darkness was quiet.

Quiet, and then sniffing on the left; on the right, claws scraped the ground.

"One, two," Boschina counted. "Where's the third one?"

There was more scraping and sniffing, closer this time.

"They are moving in, teaming together," Thalmus said. "The torches may be confusing them. Be sure to look up because they will come down on us. You have to stab them in the bellies, use their own weight to kill them."

"Whoo – who," Bubo called.

Thalmus smiled. Owl was watching, waiting to attack.

One of the torches sputtered and went out, leaving three still burning.

Claws scraped the ground. Bubo squawked. Grunts rumbled as a beast leapt from the darkness at Boschina and Ritzs. Boschina lunged forward and tried to thrust her sword up into its belly, but the blade barely penetrated its skin. The beast growled as it landed on the captain, chomping her shoulder in its jaws. Gritting her teeth from the pain, Ritzs tried to stab it under the neck, but the animal rolled over tossing Ritzs to the side and flipping Boschina and her sword away. The beast came to its feet, snorting and sniffing, its lips curling up. It smelled Boschina and turned to look at her.

Boschina's sword was out of reach. The animal would be on her before she could grab it. She pulled her short blade and held it ready, breathing heavily through her mouth and staring into the eyes of the beast.

Ritzs had scrambled up to her knees and stopped. She was dizzy; blood ran down her face, neck and arm. But the Oleen warrior wasn't done. She glanced around, searching for her sword.

A moment after the first beast attacked and they had all turned to it, a second one appeared into the light with its drooling jaws aiming for Ekala.

"Ekala!" Thalmus shouted. Shoving her to the side, he struck the beast on the nose with his sword. Ekala reacted quickly, falling with the momentum of the push; she ducked under the beast as it flew over her. But its back legs collided with her head and it stumbled to the ground on the other side. Thalmus pulled Ekala to her feet, her eyes blurry—the vibrating sword still in her hand.

"Can you see?" Thalmus asked.

Ekala lifted her sword to the ready, pointing at the Chorgen. "Everything's blurry," she mumbled.

Rolling up to its feet, blood oozing from the cut on its snout, the animal raised its head and roared. Bubo squawked wildly and Thalmus turned in time to see a third Chorgen almost on top of him. Bubo, with his wings flapping, clawed at its head. Thalmus dove under the animal, thrusting his sword into its belly and held onto the handle as the beast came down on the blade, driving it to the ground and deep into its body. Thalmus rolled away, jumped to his feet, and pulled his short blade as the Chorgen tossed and wailed, pawing at the blade in its gut.

The hunter didn't dare try to retrieve it.

The snarling Chorgen in front of Boschina crouched, preparing to leap.

The Stone Cutter's Daughter held her knife ready, knowing it would not be enough to kill the beast. Yet she felt oddly at peace and was not afraid of the outcome of this moment. She looked into the animal's eyes and saw death glaring back at her.

Boschina stared into the yellow eyes. "Iech ma ta," she said coldly.

The beast hesitated, tilted its head, and stared at her. Boschina thought she heard the words repeated back to her. Then its eyes turned mean again; its snarl returned and it pounced.

There was a sudden snap and the beast flopped face down in the dirt. Thunder had clamped onto the Chorgen's rear leg and yanked it away from Boschina. The Chorgen groaned in pain and flipped around to bite Thunder's head. Bubo dropped into the light, his wings spread; his legs stretched forward with the black talons spread apart like fingers of hooked blades, and gouged the beast's eyes before its jaws could reach Thunder's neck.

The animal screamed in agony, threw its head back, and flailed with its front paws trying to claw its attacker. It was too late, Bubo had already flown away and was clear.

Boschina ran and picked up the swords. Ritzs was still on her knees, leaning against the rock opening of the cavern. Boschina placed the captain's sword into her hand.

Ritzs looked up at Boschina. "Help me to my feet."

Taking Ritzs' good arm, Boschina lifted the captain up.

"I'll finish it," Ritzs said.

"You're too weak, Captain," Boschina told her. "I'll do it." Boschina turned away, her arm and hand covered in Ritzs' blood. "I'll be back for you."

Ritzs tried to stop her. "No, Boschina!"

Standing near the flailing beast, Boschina raised her sword with both hands above her head and the blade pointing downward, poised for the right moment to plunge into the animal's belly.

The Chorgen flopped to its side and tried to turn back on Thunder, who was still clamped onto its leg. Boschina saw a chance; she rushed in and drove the blade straight down through its soft underbelly. The beast roared and doubled over, kicking Boschina on the side and knocking her across its body. It snapped blindly at her as she dodged, scrambling to get away, but its jaws found her lower leg. Pain shot through her. Grabbing her short blade from its sheath, Boschina tried to jab it into the beast's neck, but couldn't get the right angle to penetrate its tough skin.

Thalmus saw Boschina's peril and wanted to run to her, to kill the beast, but he could not leave Ekala. The Chorgen before the queen was crouching to pounce, its eyes fixed on her. The hunter sidestepped the dying Chorgen and rushed to defend Ekala, but the beast was already springing at her. Thalmus would not reach Ekala in time to save her. At that moment, a large brown blur ran by him, jumped, and collided with the Chorgen in mid-air. The two animals tumbled to the wall in a cloud of dust.

It was another Chorgen—Ekala's Chorgen.

The two beasts separated, snarling and snapping at one another— —and then slammed together in a vicious battle of gnashing teeth.

"Hurry," Thalmus said as he took Ekala's sword and pulled her away. "We have to save Boschina!"

They turned to see Captain Ritzs falling onto the Chorgen attacking Boschina, driving her sword through its heart. The beast jerked and went limp. Ekala and Thalmus lifted the half-conscious Ritzs off the Chorgen and laid her down. They kept glancing at the two fighting Chorgens as Thalmus worked his fingers between the dead animal's fangs and pried it's jaws apart while Ekala slipped Boschina's leg out through the teeth and helped her lie next to Ritzs. Putting his foot on the dead beast, Thalmus yanked Boschina's sword free. Now, he had two vibrating blades with which to fight the winner of the dueling Chorgens.

Thunder plodded over to look at, and to sniff, Boschina's leg. Radise was right behind him. Ekala untied the water pouch on Radise and began washing Boschina's wound. Thalmus had started to do the same with Ritzs when the clamor of the fighting beasts changed tone. The smaller Chorgen's jaws were locked on the other one's throat, choking it to death. The brawny victor gave the larger beast a final shake, let go, and then lifted its head. The bloody snout rose to the sky and howled, long and deep.

Grabbing the swords, Thalmus and Ekala moved away from their wounded comrades and toward the Chorgen.

"Are you ready for this?" Thalmus asked.

"I have to be," Ekala replied, blinking and rubbing her eyes.

The beast lowered its head and glared at them. It sniffed toward them and snorted. Then it raised its head and howled again, sending its victorious voice bouncing off the hill and echoing through the night. The hunter and the queen watched and waited for it to finish and come after them. Lowering its head again, the beast looked at Ekala, growled softly, and then snorted. To their surprise, the Chorgen walked away to the shadowy edge of the light and sat down with a satisfied, calm appearance.

"Well," Ekala said, "I guess you still like me."

The Chorgen grunted and faced them, resting its bloody head and drooling jaws on its front paws as it laid down.

Three dead Chorgens sprawled in the dirt around them and a fourth one lay nearby, watching. The swords had stopped vibrating.

"I guess we won?" Ekala said incredulously.

Thalmus shook his head in wonder. "This Chorgen has adopted you, Ekala."

"I'm glad of it," Ekala replied, sheathing her sword. "Otherwise I'd be dead."

"Even though it has protected you several times, it is still a wild Chorgen; you cannot trust it."

Ekala agreed. "It seems content right now, but I'll watch it while you help Boschina and Ritzs."

"Holler if it moves," Thalmus said, stepping back to the dead Chorgen he'd stabbed and retrieving his sword. Then he knelt beside Boschina, who grimaced with pain while she tried to wash the teeth punctures in her calf.

"See to Ritzs first," Boschina said, "she's worse."

Thalmus checked Boschina's leg. "Your leg is straight; I do not feel a break. The bite is deep, but it can wait, a little." He moved to Ritzs lying still on her back, her right hand holding the left side of her neck as blood trickled through her fingers. "Let me see, Captain," Thalmus told her.

Captain Ritzs shirt was torn apart at the shoulder and covered in blood. Thalmus carefully pulled the material away and washed the gashes in her skin. The Chorgen's teeth had ripped deep into her, severing blood vessels. She was fading rapidly. There was nothing he could do save her. Still, Thalmus retrieved his herb pouch and cup. He mixed the contents from one of the bags with water and put the cup to her lips.

"Drink this, Captain." He helped her until it was finished and laid her head down. Then he unstrapped the blanket from Ritzs' horse, who was standing nearby watching, unrolled it, and covered her body up to her neck.

"Thank you, Thalmus," Captain Ritzs whispered.

"Ekala Oleen," Thalmus called, "Captain Ritzs needs you."

The queen backed away from the Chorgen. It watched her, but stayed put. Thalmus kept an eye on the Chorgen as he shook his head sorrowfully to Queen Ekala Oleen. She knelt beside Captain Ritzs and picked up her bloody hand.

"Oleen," Ritzs said, smiling. "We killed the beast."

"You killed it," Ekala Oleen said. "And you saved Boschina."

Ritzs' breathing was shallow. She spoke slowly. "Tell Larma, I fulfilled my duty."

"I will, Captain," Ekala promised.

"In the morning…we'll go to Ambermal?" Ritzs asked.

"Yes, Captain, we're all going to the castle," Ekala replied, tears welling in her eyes.

"Please bury me there...on the hill...with my fellow Oleens."

Ekala Oleen tightened her grip on the captain's hand and nodded. "You were my first Captain of Oleens, Ritzs. You are a great warrior. You will always be honored at Larma Hollow, amongst the Oleens, at Castle Ambermal, and in my heart."

Ritzs' eyes closed, her breathing slow and faint.

"Ritzs?" Boschina said, touching the captain's face. "Thank you for protecting me."

The captain's eyes opened. "Boschina, Oleen...can you hear me?"

"Yes, we're here," they said.

"I believe..." Her eyes closed and her breath stopped.

Ekala Oleen slowly laid Ritzs' arm down beside her body. She reached up and brushed Captain Ritzs' hair back. "She's been an Oleen from the beginning, always dedicated and fearless. She fought with us at Safedor and then at Ambermal, where we lost so many friends. Did you know that her father and husband died fighting for my father? And now, this daughter and widow of soldiers has died for her country and queen."

The captain's horse sniffed her mistress' body and stood over her. Ekala patted the horse's neck and then pulled the blanket over Captain Ritzs' head.

Queen Ekala Oleen wiped the tears from her face and eyes. With a weary heart, she turned to Boschina. "You're not leaving too, are you?"

"Boschina is not going anywhere," Thalmus said. "Unless I do not get that Chorgen saliva cleaned out."

"Is your leg crushed?" Ekala asked, sitting beside Boschina, but watching the Chorgen.

"It really hurts, but Thalmus says no."

"Bite on this," Thalmus told Boschina, handing her an arrow from her quiver on Radise.

Bubo landed beside her, tucked in his wings, and swiveled his head to gaze at her.

"Bubo, you gonna help me?"

The owl chortled, Thunder clicked his jaws, and Radise neighed.

Boschina looked at her friends, smiled, and then grasped the arrow and put the shaft between her teeth. Thalmus had set his knife in the torch-stand to get the blade hot. Now he removed it, knelt, and pulled Boschina's torn pant leg up to fully expose the wound that was still oozing. Holding the blade over the punctured skin, he looked at Boschina.

"Ready?"

She took a breath in through her nose and nodded.

"Do not jerk your leg," he told her and touched the hot tip of the knife to the first puncture.

Boschina stiffened, groaned, and bit hard on the wood shaft, but didn't move her leg. She closed her eyes and thought of the waterfall pouring from the rocks in the little cove at the Great Water, of the cold surf that rolled up on the sand with flying fish skimming along its foamy edge, and of her father's carvings in the craggy rocks of the cliff wall. The little folded message pulsated in her vest pocket. Larma was standing with her on the edge of Table Top Mountain listening to the clouds drifting overhead. "Can you hear them, Boschina? They're calling your name...'Stone Daughter...Stone Daughter.'"

The Stone Cutter's Daughter had slipped into a warm, safe sleep.

Thalmus continued to burn the flesh around each tear and hole in her skin. Then he made a paste from the leaves in his pouches and dabbed it on the burns and cuts. When he was done, Ekala rolled the pant leg down and they wrapped and bound Boschina's leg with strips cut from her Oleen shirt in her saddlebags. When they had finished, Bubo hopped onto Boschina and spread his wings over her.

"Will that do it? Is she going to live?" Ekala asked.

"Yes, though the wound will take time to heal." Thalmus replied. "She is exhausted. She has not slept much since she left Table Top. And then this fight tonight, and the Chorgens—maybe she can rest now, despite the pain from that bite."

Ekala watched Boschina for a moment and said, "She's endured a lot of abuse and pain in these recent days. But nothing seems to stop her. She's very strong."

Thalmus nodded. "I saw that the first day I met her, before I knew who she was."

"And now, she's learning Larma's wisdom," Ekala added. "We have to take better care of her, Thalmus."

The hunter looked at the Queen of Ameram, battered and dirty in blood-stained clothes. "Yes, and we need to take better care of you."

Ekala stood and looked at the Chorgen lying at the edge of darkness. "I must admit, this trip has not been the pleasant tour I anticipated. And it's not over yet." She swiveled back to look at Boschina and Ritzs lying on the ground. "We're under attack, Thalmus. I don't know who or where the leaders are, but I'm going to find them. We're going to carve out this evil and burn it. There has to be justice."

"There is, Ekala, as long as you believe in the truth and keep fighting for it."

"You know I do, Thalmus. It's just hard when I keep seeing its wicked power hurt good people and kill my friends. I thought we had destroyed it when Metro died." Ekala glanced around at the dead Chorgens. "Whew, they stink. I hope we're done with those beasts at least."

"I do, too," Thalmus said. "But I doubt we are. You should sleep, Ekala. Tomorrow will be another long day and you need to have your senses about you. Bubo and Thunder will keep watch. Besides, your Chorgen guardian is right over there."

"Yeah, my pet Chorgen. What am I going to do with him?"

Thunder clicked and Bubo lifted off Boschina. The horses raised their heads, ears turned forward. The Chorgen sat up, listened, and raised his snout to the breeze. The beast sniffed, and then lowering its head, it slipped into the darkness.

"What now?" Ekala said wearily.

They heard the sound of horses' hooves and the creak of wagon wheels. Then came a horse's whinny Thalmus knew well: Dallion appeared leading the team of horses pulling the Banyon wagon. He trotted up to Thalmus, bobbing his head and nickering. Thalmus held his palm up to Dallion's nose and then stroked his neck. The Paint hung his head over Thalmus' shoulder and then his nostrils flared; he snorted, curled his upper lip, and backed away.

"I know, Dal, I smell like a Chorgen."

Dallion blew out his nose and walked to sniff Boschina. He nudged her, checked the bandaged leg, and then shook his head and blew out his nose again. Looking at Ritzs' horse and then down at the blanket-covered body, Dallion grunted and rubbed his head on the side of the mare's head. Then he rubbed noses with Shadahn and Radise.

Thalmus and Ekala unhooked the team of horses from the wagon. The merchant was still lying in the back. He was awake and looked curiously at them.

"Are you hungry?" Thalmus asked him while he checked the ropes on the merchant's wrists and legs.

The man stared blankly at him and then looked around at the wagon.

"Here, you better eat something," Ekala said, putting a chunk of bread in his hand.

Out in the darkness, Savo walked his horse slowly toward the glow of the torches he thought he had extinguished. *Somebody was alive.* He could see the horses, the giant shell creature, bodies on the ground, and someone moving at the back of the wagon. In the dim light, he couldn't tell who it was. Beyond them were…three Chorgens lying down? Their posture looked unnatural. His horse resisted, but Savo tugged it forward with the reins. He wasn't about to let it go. Stepping as quietly as he could, Savo finally realized the shorter figure was the frog hunter and the other was the queen. *How did they live? They must have killed the Chorgens.* Now he knew he had failed and would have to tell Baskin. He turned to mount his horse and saw yellow eyes and fangs flying at him.

A man's painful scream suddenly erupted from the dark. A snarling, snapping sound and the panic of a horse running away came with it. Ekala and Thalmus pulled their swords and waited. The horses whinnied, snorted, and stirred. Bubo flew past Thalmus toward the sound as a Chorgen's howl reverberated in the night.

In a few moments, Bubo came back hooting.

"Your Chorgen just took down someone he did not like," Thalmus said.

Ekala shook her head. "I guess I should feel protected."

Thalmus looked at Ekala and smiled. "I will take the watch, so you can try to sleep."

"If I wasn't so tired, I'd say no," she replied. "But I know you've got Bubo, Thunder, and all the horses to help when you fall asleep."

When the sun rose, breaking through the clouds and bringing a new day, Thalmus and Ekala saw the aftermath of the fight from the night before. Swords, men's bodies, and three large humps of Chorgens were sprawled and scattered about. Dark pools of blood stained the earth. One torch still smoldered; the other two had burned out during the night. Thunder was still resting near Boschina, so was Radise; Ritzs' horse stood by her mistress' body. Bubo was perched on a ledge over the opening to the cavern. Dallion and Shadahn were with the team of horses near the wagon. Ekala's Chorgen was nowhere in sight. And the red-roofed buildings of Barrunda stood but a short distance away.

"Boschina," Thalmus said softly, checking her leg.

"Time to get up, Sister," Ekala said.

Boschina came up from the depth of sleep, her eyes trying to focus on the two faces looking at her. "Thalmus, Oleen? Oh, I ache—my back, my shoulder, my head, and my leg."

Ekala smiled. "Are you going to lie there and whine or get up and live?"

Boschina blinked. "What do you think?" she replied and struggled into a sitting position.

"Whoa, careful," Ekala said. "I was kidding."

Radise nudged Boschina with her nose.

"Easy, Lady," Boschina said and rubbed her head.

"I've got some bread and the last of the grapes for you. And here's your water skin," Ekala said. "Thalmus is going to look in that cavern while we keep watch, and then we're riding into Barrunda."

Boschina nodded. "I'll be ready."

From the outside, the cave appeared dark and ominous. However, upon stepping inside, the passageway turned abruptly to the left where candles burned in niches along the walls. Thalmus had been able to light a candle from the embers of the last torch and then use it to ignite the others. After the first turn, the tunnel curved to the right. He carried a candle and lit more candles on the wall down a long passageway. Portions of the wall had openings filled in with blocks and mortar. In the candles' small flickering light he could see family crests and insignias of stone imbedded over or beside these areas. Thalmus recognized the emblems as belonging to the families of the lords and merchants.

This cave was a crypt for the villagers of Barrunda.

"Whoo," Bubo called.

He continued down the passage, following Bubo's call, until finding an opening with a pair of new wooden doors. Both doors were standing open and Bubo sat on top of one. He hooted again as Thalmus stepped through, holding the candle before him, into a large room half full of crates, barrels, and boxes replete with spears, swords, shields, axes, bows, and arrows.

Thalmus lifted an axe with a crude wood handle and a heavy iron head etched with an "S." The bows were made of northern wood and had an "S" burnt into the limb above the grip. One crate full of wooden shields was the most disturbing. Each one had the vicious looking lizard, like Savo's tattoo, painted on it.

Counting the containers and the tools in them, Thalmus estimated a total amount of each tool. They were not very well made; still, there were enough weapons to supply a small army. And the Banyon wagon he drove had been bringing another load. *So, where is the army that's waiting for these weapons?* Taking one of each tool,

Thalmus walked back up the tunnel, extinguishing the candles as he went.

Chapter Thirty-Two
The Lords of Barrunda

Bubo flew out of the cavern and circled over his friends. From high above, he inspected the scene: the dead men and Chorgens still lay where they had fallen; Boschina was rising; Ritzs' body, wrapped in a blanket, rested near the snuffling waiting horses; and Thalmus with Ekala looking at the tools. Owl saw no movement in the surrounding landscape and was satisfied there were no threats. He snapped his beak and hooted several times, and then winged east toward Castle Ambermal.

Thalmus waved and watched Bubo fly away. He could not count the number of times over the years he had depended on the owl. The hunter had always been thankful and confident of Bubo's help. However, lately, whenever Bubo left, he wondered if it would be the last time he would see his friend.

"These are not Ameram-made tools," Ekala said, examining the weapons Thalmus had brought out of the crypt. "They're like the ones we captured at the North Ford. Were they all like this?"

"Yes," Thalmus said as he harnessed the horses to the wagon. "There are enough different tools to outfit three hundred soldiers."

"Three hundred?" Ekala questioned.

"As you see, they are not well made. But they would last a battle or two, which could be long enough to conquer another force."

"Well, I'm glad to see that our people—our factories are not making tools to use against me," Ekala replied, dropping an axe on the pile of weapons.

They set the ramp for Thunder to climb into the wagon. Thalmus pulled the merchant out and laid him aside. Boschina and Ekala had wrapped Ritzs in her blanket. Now, Thalmus and Ekala carefully placed her in the wagon alongside Thunder, and then they picked up the wooden ramp and set it on top. Thalmus hefted the merchant and strapped him on the top along with the weapons.

He stopped to check on Thunder in the back.

The tortoise lifted his head from looking at the wrapped body beside him. Sadness filled his eyes.

Thalmus nodded with understanding. "Ritzs was a good friend. We will miss her." He reached up and patted Thunder's shell. "She was a warrior of truth and cared for everyone, including us old warriors. We are taking Ritzs to her Ahmautahmin."

Thunder grunted, pulled in his head, and tucked his legs. He had saved Boschina from the Chorgen's leap and she had tried to protect him from its jaws. But it was Ritzs who paid the ultimate price for saving her friends.

The tarp was ready to be drawn over the back. Instead, Thalmus pulled the canvas up and away. "We can leave it open. No sense in hiding you now, is there?" Thalmus said as he tied the cover so that Thunder could see out.

Boschina stood up next to Radise, strapped on her sword, and put her foot into the stirrup. The arrow wound in her shoulder was sore and her body ached from the Chorgen rolling on her. The bandaged leg hurt to stand on. She tried to jump and push herself up onto the saddle, but her wounded leg was too weak.

"Whoa," Ekala said, coming to help Boschina. "You should sit in the wagon. Riding will be too hard on your leg."

"I can ride," Boschina said. "Just help me onto Radise."

"No, I'm helping you onto the wagon. We don't want that leg to start bleeding. Thalmus would have to stick you with the hot knife again."

Boschina stroked Radise's neck and glanced at Thalmus. "Okay, I don't want to put him through that again."

Thalmus smiled at Boschina. "Thank you for thinking of me."

"Of course," Boschina replied as they helped her onto the wagon's bench seat and Radise stood alongside her.

"Keep an eye on her, Lady," Ekala said and patted Radise's shoulder. "Let's go ask some questions of the lords of Barrunda," she said, swinging onto Shadahn. "I'm sure they will be glad to see us."

"Well, I'm glad you changed your clothes," Boschina said. "You weren't looking very queenly in those filthy, bloody garments."

"You're one to talk," the queen replied. "Look at you."

"I have nothing else," Boschina said. "My Oleen shirt is in pieces wrapped around my leg."

Despite the clean clothes, the queen's attire was still not the elegant and colorful fashion of royalty that people expected. Then again, she was Ekala Oleen, and her reputation was not one of fanciful style. She wore her usual boots, brown pants, and shirt with threaded drawstrings at the neck. A broad-brimmed hat covered her head.

Thalmus had also changed from the scratchy Banyon clothes into his own comfortable trousers and shirt. He climbed onto the wagon's seat next to Boschina, picked up the reins, and tapped his heel on the footboard and the horses pulled forward. Humans and animals alike were relieved to be leaving behind the ugly mess in front of the cavern and the odor of the Chorgens. The team of horses turned onto the tracks heading into Barrunda with the queen riding in front. Dallion walked beside the wagon next to Thalmus and Radise stayed by Boschina on the other side. Ritzs' horse followed behind.

A short way down the trail, they passed the remains of a man who had been chewed on. Thalmus recognized the lizard tattoo on one of the arms. The body reminded Ekala and Boschina how pain and death could come so quickly from the teeth of a Chorgen.

Few people gave them a second look as they entered the busy streets. The villagers were accustomed to odd-looking strangers and merchant wagons. It was when the three left the warehouses, workshops, and factories behind and drove the wagon to the steps of the Hall of Business that they received attention. The three-story stone building with a portico supported by four fluted columns stood proudly on the square in the very center of town. This edifice housed the meeting hall on the main floor and offices of the various businesses, elders, and lords on the upper floors. At the entrance was a pair of arched iron doors that stood four meters high and were decorated with the shields of the families and businessmen who controlled the community's economy. The white marble steps across the entire front of the building announced the structure's importance. Outside of Ambermal, the Hall of Business was the grandest official structure in Ameram.

As the threesome approached the building, some folks had started gesturing and talking when they spotted the giant shell creature, recognized the Paint stallion, and realized the man driving the wagon was the frog hunter. A small crowd started to trail after them. Finely dressed men on the steps to the hall looked at the rider and the drivers indignantly, as if to say: how dare these workers drag a battered wagon in front of the Hall of Business.

"Move that wagon away," one of the men called. "You can't stop here."

Ekala turned a snorting Shadahn to face the men. Thalmus pulled on the reins and stopped the wagon. "My apologies, Lord Huston, if I have offended your delicate manner," Ekala Oleen said loudly, "but I have something to show you."

Lord Huston stared at the rider on the black horse. How did she know his name? The voice was familiar. He glanced at Boschina and then at the driver. "Oh my," he said.

One of the other men stammered, "It...it's the queen."

"And the hunter and the Stone Cutter's Daughter," another said.

There was a moment of stunned realization. Then the men dropped to a knee and bowed their heads. Ekala Oleen did not tell them to get up right away as she usually did when people knelt before her. Instead, she stayed on Shadahn and looked them over. Several of the men, including Lord Huston and Lord Clarks, had been counselors for her father, members of the Learned Men.

Finally, Ekala said, "You may rise and tell the other lords, elders, and merchants inside to come out."

"Yes, Your Majesty," one of the men said and hurried inside.

Lord Huston, a tall man with wavy brown hair and a close-trimmed beard, left the group and started down the steps toward the queen. He wore calf-high boots and a long, tight-fitting coat that accentuated his height. "I apologize for not noticing you, Your Majesty. I was not aware you were coming to visit us," he said, still recovering from the shock as he clicked down the stone steps and people began to pour out of the iron doors behind him.

"I hope my arrival has not interrupted your business," Ekala Oleen said.

"Why, no, it's just, well, we have not had a royal visit in years. We are a bit surprised."

"Surprised?" Ekala Oleen said. "Did you not receive the letter saying I would be stopping here on my tour of the kingdom?"

"Uh, yes, Elder Amble informed us of your travels. It's just...well, we heard about the fighting at the North Ford and thought you...would still be there."

"Did you not hear I was at Ello?"

"Um—" Lord Huston mumbled.

An older, shorter, and heavier man with a thick neck spoke. "Only rumors you were there, Your Majesty. We were discussing it when you appeared. May I say we are pleased you are here now?"

"Thank you, Lord Clarks. I wish I could say the same."

The square and steps were filling with excited people as word spread of the queen and the Frog Hunter's arrival. Dallion snorted, shuffled, and grunted to keep the crowd away from him. Hiding amid the back fringe of people on the steps was a quiet, watching, and listening Baskin. Standing beside him was Lord Onus of Dudoon.

"I don't understand. The people are happy to see you," Lord Clarks said, motioning at the gathering crowd.

"I am glad of that," Ekala Oleen replied. "But I believe there are some here who are *not* happy to see me, nor the Stone Cutter's Daughter and Thalmus."

"Frankly, I am shocked to hear that," Lord Clarks said. The men around him agreed, nodding and expressing their surprise.

"And so you should be," Ekala said, "As I was when I followed this Banyon wagon here last night and discovered a stockpile of tools for war hidden in your crypt."

Stunned silence struck the crowd. The men on the steps looked at one another, confused and whispering: "What is she talking about? What tools? Where in the crypt?"

Thalmus began lifting up the various tools and showing them to the lords and merchants.

"We are baffled, Your Majesty." Lord Huston said. "These weapons were not made in our forge or factories."

"I am aware of that, Lord Huston. The quality of these tools does not meet your standards," Ekala said and turned to the crowd. "Our people would never make something so inferior."

The people in the square and on the steps agreed and cheered. Ekala Oleen raised her hand for silence and then looked again at the leaders assembled on the steps.

"Someone in this town is bringing those weapons here. I want to know who it is."

"I find this hard to believe," Lord Clarks said. "Imported weapons hidden in our crypt?"

Ekala Oleen glared at him. "Do you think I made this up? Do you think I'm lying? Before you answer, Lord Clarks, ride out to your crypt. You will find ten dead men who attacked us last night. And if you dare to enter the cavern, you will see the weapons."

"Well, I—"

"Do you know what a Chorgen is? Any of you?" Ekala Oleen asked.

Lord Huston spoke. "Yes, Your Majesty, it's a hunting—fighting animal which no longer exists."

"Oh, they exist, Lord Huston," Ekala Oleen said. "The beasts have been after Boschina and me for weeks. Last night at *your* crypt, three of them attacked us. One of them killed Captain Ritzs, who lies in this wagon, and it almost chewed off Boschina's leg. Someone is training these beasts and I believe the same people are smuggling the weapons." She paused and looked around at the gathered host. "I know you all want to catch the traitors and stop a war. We just lived through a terrible struggle with an enemy who tried to take our kingdom from us. We don't want that to happen again."

Shouts of support rose up from the crowd and melded into: "Oleen! Oleen!"

She pointed at the unconscious merchant on the wagon. "This delirious man is one of them. He was spying on us in Ello."

The people looked at the merchant, who groaned and rolled on top of the wagon.

"Lord Clarks," Ekala continued, "your primary business is making clothing, yes? You have made many uniforms for our soldiers."

"That's right."

"Perhaps you know this man? He was selling clothing and fabric in Ello."

"No," Lord Clarks said, shaking his head, "I have not seen him before."

"Then from whom was he getting the merchandise he was selling?"

Lord Clarks shrugged and said, "Certainly not from me. He must have purchased it from someone else."

Ekala Oleen pointed at the unconscious merchant again. "Look at him. This man needs new clothes and food. He is in a poor way. Since you are both clothing merchants, I want you take care of him, keep him safe until the Castle Guard comes to get him. I believe when this sick man comes to his senses he will tell us who he works for."

"I don't run a hostel," Lord Clarks said, indignantly.

"You do now, by my command," Ekala replied. "And I will hold you responsible if any harm comes to him."

Lord Clarks pinched his lips and then bowed his head slightly.

"Lord Huston," Ekala Oleen said, "You are a long-time maker of tools of war."

"Yes, Your Majesty. Those are some of the things my forges and craftsmen make."

"I want your workers to remove every tool from the crypt and keep them under guard in your warehouse. I want a complete inventory sent to me. And have it checked every two days."

"That will be an added cost to me," Lord Huston said.

Ekala Oleen nodded. "I imagine it will be. I thought you would be eager to do this for no fee as a loyal and concerned citizen of Ameram. Am I wrong?"

Everyone was looking at Lord Huston, waiting for his answer. He heard murmuring in the crowd. "No, Your Majesty, you are not wrong. It will be my honor to keep those tools from getting into the wrong hands."

"That is generous, Lord Huston, thank you."

Boschina had become aware of hostile eyes. She felt an evil presence in the crowd and began searching for the source.

"In the back, next to the third column," Thalmus said softly to her.

She saw a familiar face moving and rising to look over a man's shoulder in front of him. A shiver went through Boschina as she recognized Lord Onus of Dudoon. But he was not the worst. No, the real evil came from the man near him, who she could not see hiding behind others.

"Queen Oleen," Boschina said, "Lord Onus is here."

"Lord Onus?" Ekala Oleen said and scanned the tightly packed people on the steps. "Lord Onus, where are you?" she called. "Boschina tells me you are here."

People looked around, searching for the man Queen Ekala Oleen was calling. Unable to hide, Lord Onus cleared his throat, puffed his chest, and stepped through the crowd.

"You called me, Your Majesty?"

Shadahn turned her head toward Onus, laid her ears back, and snorted.

Ekala Oleen patted her horse's neck. "Ah, Lord Onus, there you are. A long way from Dudoon, are you not?"

"Yes, Your Majesty. I'm negotiating contracts for my village's produce."

"Are you getting good prices for them?"

"Of course, Your Majesty."

"What a fascinating business," Ekala Oleen said. "I would like to learn more about what you do for your village and how the farmers fare. Unfortunately, I don't have time now, but I will be checking in with you and the people of Dudoon. Oh, and I must apologize for not delivering your message to my father yet. I have been busy."

Lord Onus could feel Baskin's eyes on him. "Of course, I understand, you've...been traveling."

Ekala pointed her finger at Onus. "You know, you were the first one to warn me about the Chorgens."

"I don't remember," Onus said.

"You were—and I thank you, Lord Onus." Ekala waved her finger at him. "But you were wrong about one thing."

Lord Onus did not like the attention he was getting, not only from the queen, but the other lords and merchants as well. He cleared his throat again. "What would that be, Your Majesty?"

"You said we would never meet again. And I told *you* to not be so sure. Well, here we are, talking like old friends, as if nothing had ever happened when so much has. Do you not find this interesting?"

"Well, I suppose," Lord Onus said, glancing around to see the reaction on the faces in the crowd.

Ekala Oleen smiled mischievously at Lord Onus. "It is good to see you." She turned in the saddle and raised her arms. "It is good to be amongst all of you. But I have to go, we must move on to the castle. I will return and stay longer. However, I want to thank you for helping to fight the evil that's trying to infest our kingdom."

The people cheered and shouted: "We're with you! We'll find them! Oleen! Oleen!"

Thalmus untied the merchant and handed him to Lord Clarks' men, who carried him away. Getting back on the driver's bench, Thalmus was glad to be rid of the merchant and wondered if he would ever see or hear of him again. The hunter tapped his boot and the horses moved slowly through the throng of people following Ekala Oleen. The crowd walked with them out of the village all the way to the main road, where Thalmus turned the team south. As they started the last leg of the journey to Castle Ambermal, Queen Ekala Oleen and Boschina waved goodbye to the villagers of Barrunda.

Baskin watched them go and searched the terrain for the queen's Oleen guard. There was no Oleen force—Savo had lied to him. It was just the three of them: the queen, the hunter, and the wounded Stone Cutter's Daughter. If he had known, he could have destroyed them last night. Anger rose in his chest and boiled into his head like the molten metal in the blacksmith's forge.

How did he not see it? He had lost the perfect opportunity.

Now the conquest would take much longer. His archer had failed to kill them. The Chorgens had failed. His own men had them in hand and failed. He cursed at the wagon bumping along with the queen riding beside it. *What is it that protects them?* Baskin gritted his teeth.

The clouds had cleared. The sun was mid-sky. Baskin suddenly realized the queen could not reach Ambermal before night and would have to camp. The hot metal in his veins subsided. There was one more chance to kill them before they reached the safety of the castle and its surrounding forces.

* * *

Captain Kali was leading a force of mounted Oleens followed by a long column of foot soldiers heading north on the Western Hills Road when she saw the owl. It was unusual to see an owl at mid-day and this one was flying right at her. The large bird was determined; its wings fully extended, it flapped in a steady rhythm. As it got closer, she could see the feather tuft horns and knew it was Bubo.

When Ellie and Fischer had ridden into the castle with Oleen's message about the smuggled Banyon weapons, the battle at the ford, and an order for troops to be sent north to confront the Toulon army, it caused a shockwave that snapped King Ahmbin from his depression and Currad from his convalescence. After a discussion with Currad and the military officers, as he had done so many times in the past, the king laid out a plan. He insisted Captain Kali lead the force to the North Ford and Currad rise from his recovery to take active command again at the castle and prepare for an assault from the south.

Captain Kali went to work choosing forces from the army and Oleens, gathering supplies and getting them ready for the long road. The column of troops had left the castle at sunup and marched at a steady pace with only two rest stops. They would still be short of Barrunda by night. Kali had hoped for all the troops to be mounted in order to move faster, but there weren't enough trained horses. So, here they were, tramping along—until Bubo flew into them. He circled over Kali and the Oleens, hooting and clacking his beak, and then flew north.

Captain Kali turned to Infantry Captain Tyno riding beside her. "I'm taking twenty of the Oleens and following the owl. You know the orders: keep moving to the North Ford. I'll be back as soon as we find the queen."

"Yes, I know the urgency. Good luck, Captain," the infantry captain replied.

"Ellie! Fischer!" Kali called. "Bring the first twenty and follow me." She spun her horse around and galloped after Bubo.

Chapter Thirty-Three
Lord Rundall and the Message

Lord Rundall opened his eyes. The room was blurry. Someone dabbed his face with a cool damp cloth. His body seemed detached, separate from his head. Breathing was a struggle. A voice said his name. He knew this voice—strong yet gentle. Was that stone dust he smelled? Veracitas? Did he say the name or think it? Swallowing, his throat was dry. "Stone Cutter?"

"Yes, Lord Rundall?"

"You've been carving."

"I have. How did you know?"

"The hammer…heard it striking chisel, stone chips falling, and your eyes—focused."

Veracitas workshop was too far away for Lord Rundall to be able to hear him working. Still, he did not discount the counselor's vision. He was one of the Ancients, a member of the Order of Servants, like Thalmus and Larma. He had a sensitivity far different from others. Veracitas studied the white-haired, gaunt man lying on his back under maroon blankets. His arms rested alongside his body on top of the cover; under his head was a soft pillow. Even in bed he looked tall. Rundall had suffered under Metro, been put into a cell—the same prison cell in which Veracitas had been tortured.

"Would you like some water?" Veracitas asked.

"Yes. Would you mind washing my eyes, Veracitas?"

Veracitas put his hand under Lord Rundall's head and carefully lifted, putting the cup to his lips. When he was finished drinking, Veracitas dipped a towel in a pan of water and gently rinsed Lord Rundall's eyelids and cheeks. The once clear blue eyes were now cloudy, though they were still friendly. Drying his face with another towel, Veracitas laid the old counselor's head on the pillow.

Lord Rundall glanced around the room and chuckled. "I'd thought, just maybe, the magic touch you have with stone would clear my sight."

Smiling, Veracitas said, "That would be remarkable."

"It would," Lord Rundall said, closing his eyes, his breathing slowing. "I can still see you working on the king's statue and how perfect it was."

"It sure caused us all a lot of trouble and pain."

"Ah, but in the end, the stone served its purpose." His breathing was very shallow. Veracitas thought he had fallen asleep. Then Lord Rundall's lips moved and he said softly, "Change can be that way. Never stop believing in your stone messages, Veracitas." There was another long pause before he spoke again. "Ekala and Boschina are on their way here."

He did not ask—he knew, Veracitas thought. "Yes, Lord Rundall, a messenger brought word. They're coming down the Western Hills Road."

"I will wait for them," Lord Rundall said quietly and dropped into sleep.

* * *

Captain Kali was prepared to follow Bubo as long as the great owl kept flying. She was sure Bubo had been sent because the queen was in trouble and needed help. The Chorgens Ellie and Fischer had described were horrifying, but to think Prince Bolimaz's brother attacked at the North Ford signaled something much worse—a war with the northern kingdoms. And what about the weapons Currad stopped at the South Ford? Was Zinkila planning to attack as well?

For Kali, however, the worse feeling was not the other countries starting a war, but the wrenching knowledge that the source of the evil may very well live in Ameram.

A blanket of gray clouds drifting over from the Barrier Forest blocked the light of the setting sun. Off to the left of the road was the last stretch of the Bushy Plain before it ended abruptly on the edge of Cold Canyon. At the bottom rushed the Camotop River. The narrowing canyon held the river in its grip and squeezed the current all the way to the Stones of Anset and out into the Great Water.

Night was coming. The Oleens were still following Bubo as the road began its long bend to the north when Kali spotted the riders coming out of the Bushy Plain on their right. In the dusk, she couldn't tell how many or who they were. They rode in a bunch instead of a formation, which told her they were not military. The group was riding hard toward the road ahead of the Oleens, where a camp fire glowed. She knew some of the lords of Barrunda had their own small forces to protect their shipments and wealth. It was also a matter of prestige for a merchant to be able to afford his own security guard. But the sense Kali had of these riders was that they were hostile and were on a determined and deadly mission. Why else would they be coming out of the brush of the deserted plain in the shadows of early night?

Bubo also saw the clump of riders. He had been flying steady, resting, letting the Oleens keep up with him. Now, he sped up, beating faster to get ahead of the threat. In the gathering gloom, Bubo saw the white spots of Dallion gliding across the road at the riders, and then the galloping bunch suddenly jerking about and breaking into chaos.

Captain Kali ordered her column of Oleens into a battle line. "Archers to the front," she shouted. "Arrows ready! Second line, swords! Forward we go!"

The riders in the Bushy Plain were separating. Kali could see their numbers were twice her Oleens. No matter, she was used to being outnumbered and she had confidence in her soldiers. The plain riders had seen her force; and as they reassembled, many of them raised swords and charged toward the Oleens. Kali halted her line to let the attackers come to them.

"Archers, hold," she called. "Wait." When the charging force was nearly on them and could be seen clearly, she pointed with her sword and ordered, "Shoot! Swords forward!"

Every arrow hit its target and the enemy fell into disarray as the Oleen swordswomen rode out between the archers' horses and into the remainder of the attackers.

The other riders from the plain had continued up the road toward the camp fire.

"Stay together! Ride to the campfire," Kali shouted. She was sure Oleen and Boschina were there—that they were the target of these raiders. She wanted to let them know the Oleens were coming. And what better way than with the Oleen battle cry?

In the camp, Thunder and Dallion had warned of the approaching raiders. Dallion had galloped out to meet the attackers as Boschina gathered her bow and arrows from Radise and Thalmus unsheathed his bow from the back of the wagon. Ekala Oleen was ready with her sword and Shadahn was nearby if she needed to fight from horseback. They stood behind the wagon, waiting. In the fading light, they could hear pounding hooves, shouting, and fighting. They could barely make out the melee on the road. Then the hooves thundered toward them and they readied their arrows.

"Sounds like there's a lot of them," Ekala said calmly.

"How is your shoulder?" Thalmus asked Boschina.

"Ready," she replied.

Bubo winged over them, hooting.

"Help is on the way," Thalmus interpreted.

A crack in the clouds slid open and, for a brief moment, a shaft of moonlight shown on the white shield of Dallion's neck and chest as he galloped in front of the approaching horses. Then the light was gone, and a new sound rose in the night—a high-pitched shrill of Oleen voices bearing down on them.

Ekala, Boschina, and Thalmus did not relax, but now they knew they weren't alone. However, they would have to pick their targets carefully. The first four attackers appeared with swords in hand, but were struggling to control their horses, who were throwing their heads and snorting. Arrows quickly dropped two of the men. The other two jumped from their wild horses onto the wagon as three others rode into the firelight. Boschina hit two of these men with quick shots and Ekala went after the third man on the horse, while Thalmus drew his sword and deflected the men slashing down at them from on top of the wagon. One of the men jumped at Boschina, but Thalmus pushed him away in mid-air and knocked him out. The other man jumped down behind Thalmus, but landed right in front of Thunder, who took him out with one snap. Shadahn reared at the horse of the man Ekala was fighting; it jerked back, stumbling, and the rider fell off. Before Ekala could get to him, another rider charged in at her. Out of the night came the shape of the beast, the Chorgen, as it leapt on the man, knocking him from his horse and driving him to the ground.

At that moment, the Oleens rode in around the wagon, their horses snorting, sweating, and stomping. Captain Kali was shouting orders to set up a perimeter, smiling at Ekala Oleen and Boschina until she saw the Chorgen. It had thrown the first man aside and pounced on the other one. Stunned, the Oleens stared at the beast mauling the man until it stopped and turned to look at Ekala. Eight archers drew arrows and prepared to shoot the wild animal.

Ekala threw up her hands to stop them. "Don't shoot! He's defending me."

The archers were tense, aiming at the beast and holding their release, while their horses shuffled with fright.

The Chorgen kept his eyes on Ekala—blood dripped from its snout and fangs.

Ekala faced the beast and looked into its eyes. "Enough, I'm safe," she said and pointed with her sword into the darkness. "Go."

The Chorgen hesitated, sniffing at the horses, riders, and the bodies on the ground. Then, it lifted its snout into the air and howled its victory cry. It lowered its head, went into a crouch, and fixed its eyes on Ekala again, its nostrils flaring and sniffing.

Boschina's sword hummed on her hip. The folded message beat in her vest pocket. The glow of the fire's flames turned the Chorgen burnt orange and its eyes blood red. The beast had changed. The playful look was gone. *Ekala doesn't see it.* Boschina dropped her bow, pulled her sword, and ran. She was only steps away, but her wounded leg crumpled and she stumbled forward, falling to the ground.

The Chorgen jerked its head to look at Boschina sprawled in the dirt next to Ekala. It growled, opened its jaws to expose its long fangs, and then leapt.

"No!" Ekala dove in front of Boschina and under the beast, thrusting her sword up into its belly and trying to push it away. Boschina started to roll to the side and was suddenly yanked away by Thalmus. The archers started to shoot, but stopped for fear of hitting Oleen. The leaping animal came down on the sword and screamed in agony, jerking and snapping. Ekala jumped back and arrows thumped into the Chorgen's fur and thick skin. It was still kicking when Ekala Oleen waved off the archers, picked up Boschina's sword, and finished its death.

Except for the exhausted breathing of wary humans and horses, the camp was still as they all stared at the motionless beast. Nearby, in the dark, the Oleen swordswomen could be heard forming a circle around the camp. The archers still had arrows nocked and aimed at the beast in case it came back to life.

Queen Ekala Oleen motioned for her archers to relax and then knelt beside Boschina. "Are you alright?"

"Yes," Boschina replied. "I didn't think you saw the Chorgen change."

"You're right. I didn't see it. I thought the creature was just worked up from killing. Thank you for saving me, once again."

Boschina smiled. "It was *you* who saved *me*."

"Well, I owe you a few more," Ekala said and helped Boschina to her feet. Thalmus was there. He put Boschina's arm over his shoulder and walked her to the fire, where he sat her down to check the wounded leg.

Queen Ekala Oleen turned to face Captain Kali. "We're glad to see you, Captain."

"Oh, we're happier to see you, Oleen," Captain Kali said.

"Is my father with you?" Boschina asked.

"No, he's at Ambermal now, working on a new statue."

"And my father?" Ekala asked.

"He anxiously awaits your arrival, as does Lord Rundall."

Ekala nodded. "How many troops do you have with you?"

"Twenty-two. We're checking now on any wounded. We have a full army, horse and foot, on the road. They will be in Barrunda tomorrow."

"I'll have instructions for them. Who's in command?"

Captain Kali smiled. "Me."

Ekala looked surprised.

"It's a long story," Kali explained. "I'll tell you everything when you're ready."

Ekala watched the Oleen soldiers carrying the dead men away into the dark. She picked up a loose sword and saw it was the same as the others with the "S" and hatch mark. She motioned to Boschina and Thalmus, who nodded. He'd already seen it. Queen Ekala Oleen dropped the blade on a pile of others being gathered. She glanced at the wagon, at Ritzs' wrapped body barely visible from the light of the fire. She looked at the dead Chorgen, arrows stuck out of its body in all directions, its bloody jaw propped open in the dirt.

She suddenly felt very tired.

Could she relax now that Captain Kali and the Oleens were here?

"We lost Ritzs," she said to no one in particular.

Kali had seen the bundle in the wagon. She had been watching Ekala, waiting for an explanation or orders. "How?"

"To one of these," Ekala responded, as she put her foot on the beast and pulled her sword from its body. "They're wild animals, Captain." She paused and looked at her bloody sword. "You can't trust them." Then she turned to the Chorgen again. "Get it out of here. It's fouling our camp. In the morning, drag it the rest of the way to the canyon."

Kali was staring at Ritzs' body in the wagon, remembering her friend's face and earnest demeanor. She wanted to know more about Ritz's death—how it happened, and why. She looked at Ekala, whose tired eyes were still fixed on the Chorgen, and said, "As you wish, Oleen."

For the first time in many nights, the three travelers had a good night's sleep. In the morning, by the time they were ready to start on the road for the castle, they and Kali had shared all that had gone on in the north and in the south. Only three of Captain Kali's Oleens had been wounded in the fight—shoulder and arm cuts from swords. However, in the morning's light, the riders from the Bushy Plain littered the road and terrain around the camp. The dead men all wore black pants and shirts, and head caps with a narrow bill over the eyes and flaps that hung down the back, covering the neck. Neither Thalmus nor Ekala had seen this style of uniform. They examined the material and stitching and decided the clothing had not been made in Ameram. Dallion had gathered the loose horses and stood waiting while they grazed. The Oleens loaded the bodies onto the dead men's horses and led them, along with the Chorgen they dragged, to Cold Canyon.

Thunder climbed up the ramp into the wagon and Boschina sat on the driver's bench with Thalmus. Captain Kali divided her force of Oleens with half in front of the wagon and the other half riding behind with the extra horses. She posted outriders to each side and scouts far ahead and in the rear. Queen Ekala Oleen rode Shadahn wherever she wanted: at the head of the column, in front of the wagon, or behind. Mostly, she rode alongside the wagon by Boschina. They frequently encountered merchants and travelers who were thrilled to see the queen, the hunter, and the Stone Cutter's Daughter. The queen paused to talk with the people as Thalmus kept the wagon rolling and the Oleens waited patiently until Ekala was ready to move on.

Boschina and Thalmus could see Ekala was restless and troubled; they were concerned for her. When Ekala joined them again and rode next to Boschina, Thalmus said, "It has been a hard journey."

Ekala knew the hunter's comment wasn't idle talk. He didn't do idle talk. He was giving her the opportunity to speak about her feelings, if she wanted to. "Hard on all of us," she finally said.

"So much death," Boschina said, staring at the road ahead.

"It's not over," Ekala replied. "Now we face Lord Rundall's end. And I fear my father's is not far away. And there will be battles..." She stopped speaking and rode, looking straight ahead as Shadahn kept pace with the wagon's team. "It's the deceit I can't grasp, and the evil that comes with it." Ekala continued. "It has killed our friends and good people. It has shaken me." She sighed. "I even started to trust a Chorgen. I've been surprised by those who I thought I knew, but turned out to be someone else."

"Like Lander?" Boschina asked.

"Yes. That was the worst. Her betrayal hurt, but it opened my eyes. There were spies in Dudoon, on the river, in Ello and Barrunda. Except for you two, I'm not sure about anyone."

"What about Maz? Why did he go across the border? Why does he carry Corsair's sword?"

Ekala glanced at Boschina and looked away.

"I'm sorry, Oleen," Boschina said. "I shouldn't have asked."

"You don't need to be sorry. Unfortunately, I've asked myself the same questions. I want to believe in him, but..." She shook her head. "Larma was right when she said a friend can become a foe in an instant."

Boschina looked over at Ekala. "Larma also said to trust one another and to believe in the heart of Stone Truth."

When they met up with the army, a great cheer erupted from the soldiers and melded into the chant of "Oleen! Oleen!" Thalmus and Boschina waved and kept the wagon moving while Queen Ekala Oleen stopped to greet the troops and talk with the commanders. There were three infantry captains and one Oleen cavalry captain.

"Captains," Queen Ekala Oleen said after she had gathered them to the side of the road as the army marched on. She dismounted from Shadahn and stood with Ellie, Fischer, Captain Kali, and the other officers. "Ellie, Fischer, I am so glad you made it through to the castle. Thank you. I want you to continue north with this force and join Captain Susa. I am going to keep Captain Kali and her original force with me"

"As you wish, Oleen," the siblings said.

"Captain Tyno, I want you to leave a small force of trustworthy soldiers in Barrunda to keep an eye on activity there and to guard a large cache of contraband weapons Lord Huston should have—also, a strange merchant who is under Lord Clarks' protection. I will send troops from the Castle Guard to gather them as soon as possible. You must all be aware there are forces rising against us. I believe some of the leaders of these rebels are in Barrunda. Tell your men to be watchful. The lords and elders can be sneaky and intimidating. We were attacked last night by raiders coming out of the Bushy Plain. If it had not been for Captain Kali's arrival, I might not be with you today. Stay alert. Trust no one, but believe in the truth that you know."

"Yes, Your Majesty," the captains all said.

"The situation at the North Ford is desperate. Dysaan and Captain Susa are greatly outnumbered by the Toulon Army. You must get there as fast as you can. You will be under the command of Dysaan. Is that clear?"

"Yes, Your Majesty."

She looked into each face before saying, "I trust in you all, and know this: we will defeat our enemies from whatever direction they come."

"And we trust in you, Oleen," Ellie said.

Queen Ekala Oleen smiled. "That's right, Ellie. If we hold fast to trust and faith in one another, who could possibly defeat us?" She turned, climbed onto Shadahn, and looked down at the captains. "Hold onto that truth and we will be victorious." Ekala swung Shadahn around and trotted to catch up with Thalmus and Boschina.

It was late afternoon when they finally approached Castle Ambermal. The Oleen scouts had ridden ahead and reported the queen's imminent arrival. Colorful flags with the queen's emblem of "EO" had been raised all along the walls and parapets. The Castle Guard's honor guard stood in formation on each side of the entrance gate. People lined the streets, waiting to see the queen.

Before they reached the gates to the castle, Captain Kali rode alongside Ekala and asked, "Do you want the Oleens to take the wagon and Captain Ritzs through the east gate instead of here?"

"Thank you, Captain, but no. I want the people to see part of the cost of the fight with our enemy."

"As you wish, Oleen," Kali replied and rode to the back of the column for the queen to be alone at the front.

The procession passed into and through the cobbled streets of Ambermal. The people cheered and shouted "Oleen!" and then quieted as Thalmus and Boschina bounced by in the wagon—and they saw Thunder in the back guarding a wrapped body. The queen was warmed by the applause and cheers, but she smiled little. She looked like she had just come from a fight, which she had—a long, four-week fight. Ekala stopped the column at the base of the wide, stone steps rising to the Great Hall. King Ahmbin, Currad, and Veracitas were waiting there on the first step. Ekala dropped down from Shadahn and her father wrapped his arms around her. He held her at arm's length, smiling and looking at her, and then hugged her again. "I'm so happy you are back," he whispered. "Lord Rundall has been waiting for you."

The crowd in the plaza cheered and watched with anticipation. The people had heard about the battle at the North Ford and seen the activity throughout Ambermal—the gathering of the army and then it marching away. They were glad to see the queen return, even as weary as she appeared, because they believed in her strength.

Captain Kali and nine of the Oleen soldiers dismounted. Kali and three of the soldiers helped Thalmus set the ramp for Thunder, who plodded down onto the stones of the plaza. The captain directed the three Oleens to help her as they lifted Ritzs' body; carrying her on their shoulders, they walked down the ramp. The other six Oleens joined the bearers as an escort and together they climbed up the stone steps to the portico at the top.

Veracitas smiled at Boschina as he helped her down from the wagon. She hugged him as best she could with both arms. He looked at her wrapped leg, the blood-stained dirty clothes, and then at her face, which still had some scabs and bruises. But there was a broad smile on her face and an age and wisdom in her eyes which had not been there before.

Queen Ekala Oleen walked halfway up the steps and turned to look at the people, who were quiet and waiting to hear what she had to say.

"Thank you for this welcome. It is good to be home."

There was some cheering and responses of, "Welcome home" and "We're glad you're back."

"As you have heard," Ekala Oleen continued, "we are preparing to defend ourselves against an enemy who wants to rule us. It is not just from outside where this enemy comes, but also from within our own kingdom." She raised her hand toward the Oleens holding Captain Ritzs. "This is Captain Ritzs of the Oleens, wrapped in her own blanket. She died defending me and Boschina and Ameram. Already, we have lost dedicated and loyal people like her—and just like you. This fight will not be easy. We must all rise together and support and believe in one another. I am counting on you and all of Ameram to dig out the roots of this evil and destroy it once and for all."

The people, packed into the plaza, cheered, voicing their support. Queen Ekala Oleen waved as she waited for her father, being helped by Currad, to slowly climb the steps. Then they continued up the rest of the way together. Veracitas assisted Boschina with his arm around her waist, as they followed the king. Thalmus walked with Thunder through the plaza around to the side entrance of Culinary's kitchen, where the cook greeted them at the door. Ritzs was carried into the Great Hall and laid before the throne. Four Oleens stayed with her while the others returned to their force.

The queen, king, and others continued through the passageways and buildings to Lord Rundall's room.

Ekala Oleen went to one side of Rundall's bed and the king to the other. Currad stood at the end like the guard he was. Veracitas and Boschina stayed back against the wall.

Lord Rundall's eyes were open, but they were cloudy and staring at the ceiling. "You are here," he said slowly. His hands, lying beside him, rose off the maroon bedspread. Ekala grasped one and the king took the other.

"Ekala Oleen," Rundall said, his voice raspy and weak. His hand squeezed hers. "You have many trials ahead of you. Do not be discouraged. I have watched you since you were a baby. You are so much like your mother, independent and strong. Yet, your faith in this world suffers. Like your father, you are now the strength of our people. We waited and believed in your prophecy, and you fulfilled it. But if you live and rule by your head only, you will not survive." He paused, swallowing. "You must remember—strength is more than body and mind. True power lives in and comes from your heart. Truth must dwell in both, and then in your words and deeds."

"I will remember your wisdom, Great Uncle Rundall," Ekala said. "Thank you for being our family's guardian and teacher. You have protected and taught us well."

Lord Rundall closed his eyes and rested. Thalmus quietly entered and stood with Currad. Even quieter than the hunter, Bubo landed on the sill of the open window and tucked in his wings. His head pivoted, looking at the people in the room. His eyes then focused on the white-haired man in the bed. A small, knowing smile curled on Rundall's lips. "Thank you for coming," he said softly.

"Boschina, Stone Cutter's Daughter," Lord Rundall whispered. "Come to me."

The king stood and stepped aside as Veracitas helped Boschina kneel beside the bed. She gently held Rundall's beckoning hand. "Yes, Lord Rundall?" she said softly.

His eyelids opened, the hazy blue eyes stared at the ceiling and his grip tightened on her hand. "You are a gift, an open door, for those of us who are blind to our journey. Your strength inspires us all. You have your own destiny to discover, Stone Cutter's Daughter." Lord Rundall paused, listening. "You have a message for me from Larma?"

Boschina had been so enthralled with Lord Rundall she had not noticed Larma's message beating in her chest pocket. Perhaps she had become accustomed to the rhythm of the small package. She unbuttoned the pocket, pinched the folded material with her fingertips, and pulled it out in front of Rundall.

"I'm sorry, Lord Rundall. I don't know how to read the language in Larma's message."

"One day you will understand, Boschina," Rundall said. "Open it and lay the words on my chest."

She let go of his hand and unfolded the cloth. The text appeared to move as if it were breathing. Her fingers tingled as she gently spread the material with the message face down on Lord Rundall. Then she held his hand again.

Lord Rundall's chest lifted with deep breaths. He closed his eyes as a smile spread on his face. As if completing a conversation, he whispered, "Thank you. It has been my honor to serve." The cloth pumped slowly with his heart, the beats coming farther and farther apart—until it stopped.

Silence filled the room. No one moved. They stood waiting, watching the cloth with frayed edges and ancient script lying motionless on Rundall's chest. Was it finished? Had the message expired along with the humble servant's life?

Bubo bobbed his head, focusing on Lord Rundall. The great owl spread his wings, and then lifted off from the window sill. He sailed past Currad and landed gently on Lord Rundall's chest. He stretched his wings over the lifeless man, gripped the corner of Larma's cloth in his talons, and then, with one soft hoot and a silent beating of wings, flew toward the ceiling. A soft flow of air rose with him. Bubo circled the room, and then winged out the window, with the message dangling in his grasp.

PROFILES

Characters

Ahmbin (Ahhm-bin): aging king of the land of Ameram. Andus Ahmbin III, grandson of the great King Ahmbin the First, was the last male in a long and continuous line of his family to rule the kingdom. His wife, and true love, died while their only child was still young and he never remarried.

Arborina (Are-bore-eena): the goddess of trees. "A woman who loved trees so much and lived in them most of her life that she came to be one." Her statue and essence stood in a stone temple at the center of the Woods of Rows. Her intoxicating power ruled the woods and was enforced by the Kairtaykars. Researchers think she contributed to Boschina's development as a mystic. Recently, it was revealed that archeologists believe they located and unearthed the foundation stones of the columns and statue of the temple.

Baskin (Bass-kin): a devious, malicious, and highly manipulative man who lived in the fringes and shadows of society and people's lives. He was disfigured both physically and mentally from his battles with Truth. Many researchers believe he was the ultimate evil power behind the public faces and voices who fought for control of the kingdom.

Benton: Born in Northern Toulon to a family of farmer merchants, he became a swordsman with a reputation for skill, power, and integrity. He fled Toulon with his family to avoid conscription into the army under the oppressive rule of Prince Sharpna. Living in a refugee camp in Ameram, he met Prince Bolimaz and joined him to save their country from Sharpna and Glasrauss.

Blayon (Blay-yon or Blah-yon; depending if you lived in the north or south): a famous mercenary soldier whose loyalty was devoted to the highest bidder. He was well traveled, experienced in all weaponry and tactics, and considered himself homeless.

Boschina (Bah-sheen-uh; archers referred to her as Bow-sheen-uh): some scholars think it was Bosch-in-uh; either way, she was definitely known as "Stone Cutter's Daughter." Her story is long and intertwined with the makers of history in this kingdom. Most importantly, she is recognized as the spark that ignited the flames of the ancient prophecy for Princess Ekala.

Camp: A veteran soldier exiled from Toulon. He is Maz's companion. Together, they join the Oleen forces to fight for Princess Ekala. His history and purpose is revealed through the battles and Maz's relationship with Ekala.

Cartridge (Cart-ridge): a member of the Council of Learned Men from a wealthy family with a long heritage as farmers and merchants. His ancestors started by building the carts and driving the horses that carried the farmer's produce to markets. Then, they expanded into farming. Their original home, and cart factory, sat on a central ridge overlooking the growing fields; hence, they took the name, Cartridge. This was the third generation of Cartridge to advise the royal family. This Cartridge took over from his ailing uncle at the age of 33 and had only been in office for six months when Metro's coup occurred.

Corsair (Core-sair – a pirate): the vicious Captain of Rainland's castle guard and troops. He forced his way to the high command and to be Lord Luminous favorite by devious and malicious means. It is unknown how he fell under the influence of Metro. Some historians believe that Metro had promised Corsair a lordship when he became king. It was also believed, that Corsair's sword held a deadly curse.

Culinary (Kyoo-le-nair-ee): a renowned and creative cook. He managed such a unique kitchen (some might say, experimental food laboratory) that so many others imitated him to the extent that his name became synonymous with the art of cooking and kitchenware. Even today, in our world, the word is widely used.

Currad (Cure-add): was designated by King Ahmbin as the King's Honored Soldier for his many years of dedication, loyalty, and his strategic combat ability. Though an independent soldier, this title gave him leadership of the army, as directed by the king or queen. His strong belief in justice led him to risk his life and position for truth. Currad was a friend of Veracitas, Boschina, and Thalmus and joined their journey to fulfill Ekala's prophecy. Currad's recently discovered journals reveal his study of the Ancient Servants faith, and has helped to fill in events during this period of Ameram's history

Dysaan (Die-sen): a career soldier, good friend of Currad, and dependable and loyal to the Ahmbin Throne of Ameram. Along with Currad, he was a King's Honored Soldier, and helped train and command the armies. He was a friend of Veracitas, Boschina, and Thalmus and fought to fulfill Ekala's prophecy. Records show that Dysaan was a descendant of a long line of soldiers. A formidable warrior, he fought in many battles defending Ameram—and had the scars to prove it.

Ekala (E-kay-la; or if you lived in the south, E-kaw-law): King Ahmbin chose the name for his daughter after his wife, Lady Ahmbin, had died because it meant the "beauty of strength." She was his only child.

Kali (Caw-lee): a tall, strong-shouldered woman with bushy, frizzy, red hair and freckles. She had met Veracitas when Boschina was a very young child and he carved a statue of her village elder. Kali was a struggling potter and he had admired her work, as she did his. They had a friendship that bordered on romance, but neither one pursued a deeper relationship because of Boschina's missing mother. When the statue was complete, Veracitas sadly left with his little Boschina in search of another job. Oleen met Kali at an artisan's fair and asked her to join the community at Larma Hollow to teach others the art of pottery. Once under Larma's tutelage and Oleen's training, she quickly gained confidence and became a leader.

Kairtaykar (Care-tay-cr): a race of short, wiry tree-climbing people who were also changelings. Their skin was weathered and creased like the bark of a tree. They had long fingers and toes that resembled roots. A resilient and tough people, they protected, maintained, and lived in the mysterious and deadly Woods of Rows. These creatures were rarely seen because they never ventured outside of the Rows.

King Dieten: king of Zinkila, the country immediately south of Ameram. He was about the same age as King Ahmbin; the two of them played together as children when the families visited one another. Unlike Ahmbin, Dieten had four sons, all of whom wanted to succeed him. It was rumored that Dieten and Ahmbin were distant cousins.

King Souma (Sue-mah): He was the third generation Souma to be the king of Toulon. He had a competitive relationship with King Ahmbin of Ameram and teased him about not having any sons. Souma had three sons, Bolimaz, Sharpna, and Tamar; two of which maliciously coveted his throne.

Lander: a fierce, dedicated Oleen warrior. A great archer, she taught archery at Table Top and fought in the battle for the North Gate at Table Top and the Battle for Ambermal with Larma's army of Oleens. She became a Captain of Oleens and one of Queen Ekala Oleen's trusted guards.

Larma (Lar-ma): a mystic woman of undetermined age and authority with a spiritual power of truth that was beyond understanding. Some believe that she had obtained unity with the Deity. Scholars still debate the consequences and the amount of her influence in historical changes of this period.

Lord Clarks of Barrunda: fourth-generation head of the Clarks Family who had a dynasty in the garment and clothing business that expanded beyond the borders of Ameram. Like his father before him, he had been on the King's Council of Learned Men.

Lord Glasrauss (Glaws-ross): first born son of Lord Glasrauss of Middle Field Toulon. Striving for power, he joined with two of the Souma sons to control Toulon. Records show the family raised and fought Chorgens for sport at various times in their history.

Lord Collier Huston of Barrunda: the present lord of the Huston family factories and forges that manufactured just about anything made from metals. The wealthy merchant enjoyed the long-standing contract for all of the kingdom's military weapons. He had been on the King's Council of Learned Men, which afforded him great influence.

Lord Onus of Dudoon (O-nus): an elder of the village of Dudoon and a merchant for the produce grown in his region. He had become wealthy buying out the farms and orchards that had struggled to survive in the time of turmoil during the king's "sickness" and Metro's rule. He had served on the King's Council of Learned Men, which had been beneficial to his success.

Maz: A mysterious young man from Toulon hiding at Table Top. He and his older friend, Camp, join with Larma and the Oleens to fight for Princess Ekala's cause. His secret, and importance in Ekala's life, is revealed in a dramatic dying moment.

Metro (Met-trow): a devious, power-hungry magician of unknown origin. He was able to use his extensive knowledge of alchemy and mind-control methods to fool and manipulate people.

Nattie (Nat-tee): full name Nateen Nadar. A surprisingly durable, short elderly woman. She served in the household of the royal family of Toulon for many years until being released for voicing her opinion about the political shift of King Souma. She sided with Prince Bolimaz and his supporters, and had to flee for her life. She had waited on Ekala as a child when the young princess and King Ahmbin visited Toulon in more congenial days.

Neb: teenage son of Benton. Although he admired his father, he preferred the bow and arrow over the sword. He was earnest about his choice of weapon, but lacked the training needed to be a skillful archer. Like his father, he was compassionate and believed in justice.

Oleens (O-leens): Devoted followers of Ekala Oleen; specifically, her army of warriors. Started by Ekala and trained by her and Larma, they were initially women who had been alone, widowed, abandoned, or had no home or way to survive. Eventually, as Ekala rose in authority and the movement for her grew, men were allowed to join the Oleen Forces as separate units.

Pawndors (Pon-doors): people from the country of Pawndor far to the east who had invaded three generations previous, through Toubor, and controlled part of Ameram for a number of years until King Antell (Ahmbin's grandfather) chased them out and destroyed their army on the fields of Touborna. It is not clear, but many scholars believe that Thalmus fought in this campaign because of praise in the historical records for a "fearless small man with a bloody blade of death and endless strength...."

Redan (Rah-dan): an infamous animal breeder and trainer who worked for any client who would finance his experiments in breeding the most vicious fighting and hunting beasts.

Ritzs (Writ-zz): a dedicated captain in the Oleen Forces. Her father and husband had served as officers in King Ahmbin's army. Her father died in the battle of Tanden and her husband had disappeared.

Ekala found Ritzs teaching archery and horseback riding to children for food and lodging. Ekala invited her to join the growing band of women at Table Top and she became a devoted follower of Oleen.

Savo (Sav-o): a lieutenant for Baskin. Savo was the first son of a poor family who had worked nearly all their lives in Lord Clarks' garment production factory. He trained and served as a soldier in The King's Army, until he fell under the influence of Baskin, who had taken advantage of the young man's anger toward the wealthy class. He joined the renegade troops who had deserted and fought for Metro and anarchy. When Ekala Oleen became queen, he continued his subversive efforts by working for Baskin to overthrow the throne for the promise that he would hold a high-ranking position in the new order.

Sharpna (Sharp-nah): second son of King Souma of Toulon. Always jealous of his older brother, Bolimaz, he conspired constantly to usurp him as crown prince. Ambitious to a fault, Sharpna married Princess Contra of Banyon in order to solidify control of that country and to use its army, along with his own, for conquest of other kingdoms.

Tamar (Ta-mar): third son of King Souma. An impetuous child of an entitled man with an arrogant attitude. His deviousness, fits of anger, and rash behavior have been well documented. His attempted knifing of Bolimaz left the eldest brother with a scared face.

Thalmus (Thall-mus): commonly known as the King's Frog Hunter and guardian of the Prophecy of Ameram. He was a man of mystery to people of his day and continues to be so to researchers because he appears to have been present and influential throughout the history of the kingdom.
Tobazi (Tow-bah-zee; some recent scholars think it was pronounced Tow-bahz-eye): helped Thalmus and Boschina escape from Rainland, where they saved his life; fought with his own small army, and the

Oleens, in the battle for Ambermal and became a devoted ally of Thalmus and Boschina.

Veracitas (Vera-see-tahs; man of truthful and accurate statement): the ancestral name of a long line of sculptors who were renowned for their artistry in making stone statues so accurate and realistic that some believed the "stone cutters" to have magical powers, turning people and animals into stone. This generation, Veracitas was the first to have no sons, only one daughter (Boschina); and he struggled with his talent under the burden of his famous paternal predecessors.

Animals

Bubo (Boo-bow): a Great Horned Owl with a power and spirit to change lives. He was the indomitable friend of Thalmus and steadfastly helped and defended him.

Chorgen (Chore-gn): a nocturnal muscular beast, two-thirds the size of a horse, which historically was bred for fighting and hunting by lords in Banyon and Toulon. The animal had large jaws with long fangs, big round eyes for night vision, an extraordinary ability to follow a scent, was very fast, and could run long distances chasing its prey. A Chorgen never gave up; it stalked its victim until it killed it or was killed. They were very dangerous animals because of their unpredictable viciousness and uncontrolled aggression. People stopped breeding them and they became extinct—until men once again thought they could train them to follow commands.

Dallion (Dal-lee-in): a striking white and brown Paint stallion who had a free spirit that influenced other horses and animals. Saved by Thalmus and Thunder from the quagmire of the Laundo Marsh, he was forever devoted to his new friends.

Eidolon (Eye-doe-len): a silver-gray mare that was also known as Larma's Phantom. It seemed to appear whenever she needed to ride and the two of them together were a formidable presence.

Radise (Raw-dice): related to Shadahn and was from the bloodline of the great warhorse Radisadan. She was a steady, experienced horse that knew how to help a new rider with maneuvering and tactics.

Robon (Row-bon): a tall chestnut mare bred by a farmer as a racehorse to win financial stability, but he had to sell her to the army to feed his family. She understood the military training, but resisted the various soldiers who rode her until she was declared unfit and used as a pack animal. That's when Shadahn and Ekala saw her, recognized her quality and strengths, claimed her, and took her to Larma Hollow. Ultimately, she settled in comfortably as Veracitas' horse.

Shadahn (Shaw-don): from a spirited bloodline of warhorses bred for the royal family. Ekala was the only person to ever ride her. Shadahn became friends with Dallion because of Thalmus' and Ekala's friendship.

Shell creature: a mix between a tortoise and a snapping turtle, but with more dexterity. It had a broad flat shell and webbed feet that gave it the ability to move on dry land and swim in the water. Adults could be two and a half meters in size and carry three times their weight. These unique creatures were wild and already rare in Thalmus' time.

Thunder (see shell creature for description): the giant shell creature that was Thalmus' companion and fellow frog hunter. It is not known when or how the two met, but records are clear as to their loyalty and defense of one another.

Locations

Ahmautahmin: (Ah-maw-tah-men): translates from the native language as "meeting place of the souls." The cavern and catacombs discovered in the Wilderness of Toulon; it was an ancient burial site in which families celebrated with souls of their loved ones who had passed on. The term is also used as a general expression for the final resting place of a body whose soul has passed into the next life. As in, "Where will be *my* Ahmautahmin?"

Ambermal (Amber-mall): the name of the castle and walled city where the king of Ameram lived and conducted the affairs of the country. It was named for King Amberm, who chose the defensive location on the cliffs of Cold Canyon and started the castle's construction.

Banyon (Ban-yen): a kingdom north of Toulon that had always been a troublemaker. It was controlled by a devious, opportunistic family always looking for conquest. They respected no boundaries, agreements, or morals in their drive for land or wealth. The country was known for producing cheaply made and counterfeit products. It was in the Chorga region of Banyon that the vicious beasts called Chorgens were first bred and grown.

Barrunda (Bar-run-da): a wealthy industrial village that was the business center of the kingdom; producing a wide variety of merchandise. Other than food, the craftsmen in the forges and factories made just about whatever necessary or practical item was needed for living. The busy and financially powerful Great Hall of Business stood on the plaza in the center of the village. More than half of the members of King Ahmbin's Council of Learned Men were lords or wealthy business men from Barrunda.

Bevie (bev-ay): a village and its surrounding land named after its owner and noble, Lord Shawnden Bevie, who served the king on the Council of Learned Men. The community was known for growing delicious fruit and abundant vegetables.

Camotop River (Kam-ot-op): a wide and deep channel of water with a strong current that flowed from the rain and a copious spring in Rainland through Cold Canyon, below Ambermal Castle, and on to the Great Water. There were only two places where it could be crossed without a boat; but in a wet season, even these usually shallow fords were impassable. The name is derived from ancient indigenous people. It means: source of life and death.

Dudoon (Duh-doon): a somewhat isolated village at the north end of the Middle Hills Road. It was a hardworking farming community, growing fruit and nuts in the foothills and grain along the Dudoon Run. However, because of its close proximity to the frog-infested Dudoon Bog and no through-road for travelers, it was unfairly labeled as a place to be avoided. Records show a cruel expression used in the rest of the kingdom when telling someone they weren't necessary: "You might as well go to Dudoon."

Ello: a small, but important, village because of its water wells and its central location near a gap in the hills that held one of the few roads to the Great Water. The village enjoyed a relaxed atmosphere of trade and hospitality.

Escat Marsh (S-cat): a series of three large ponds linked together by narrow channels of water that had wooden bridges spanning the channel for travelers. But, over time, the marshes had enlarged, encroaching on the trails to the bridges. This resulted in making the passage more dangerous and, therefore, practically abandoned. The name is derived from the odor of the scat of the frogs.

Laundo Pond (La-un-doe): a great swampy pond in the lowlands of the mid-eastern portion of the kingdom that was named after a prince who disappeared there while hunting frogs. The pond, strangely enough, had its own tide that would rise and ebb with the phases of the moon, creating sticky mud bogs which could become fatal traps to the novice adventurer. The ponds were inhabited by particularly aggressive frogs that were dark brown in color with black spots.

Marbala (Mar-baw-lah): A village west of the Escat Marshes and nestled into the foot of the Stone Hills. Known for its unique white or blue-grey marble that was quarried there in the hills, it was the home of artists, sculptors, and stone cutters. The community enjoyed a good trade in its stone and the artistic wares produced from the famous marble. The people of Marbala had a reputation for durability, independence, and for speaking the truth.

Moxfet: a picturesque and friendly community of farmers and tanners who had built and maintained the first home for orphans. It was named after the land's noble family, Steponus Moxfet.

Safedor: a box canyon in the western hills. It is also known as *Ekala's Surprise at Safedor* and is commonly accepted in the ancient annals as the turning point for the throne of Ahmbin. The princess led her small band of soldiers in a shocking victory over a larger force of renegade and mercenary troops by climbing down the craggy walls of Safedor, a feat never done before or since, to surprise the troops and save the captive villagers of Ello.

Seena (See-nah): a region of the land that had rich faming soil and had been worked by the same families for generations. It was a major food source for the realm and therefore had always been protected; but with a breakdown in authority, unscrupulous soldiers took what they wanted with few repercussions.

Table Top Mountain: a remote flat top mountain with sheer black, craggy walls rising out of the northern Great Plain. There were abundant springs on the surface that created several creeks that flowed through hollows and rocky ravines until pouring off the edge of the Top into ponds at the base of the mountain. There were only two access routes (known as the North and West Gates) from the Plain to the Top. With its inspiring view of the Plain below and its seeming acceptance of those who were lost and searching, the Top became a refuge. It had always been a special place for Ekala who, along with Larma, started the Oleen community there in the hollows and the protected great shelf known as Larma Hollow.

Tamra (Tom-raw): a village that was named after a tasty small fish that flourished in the local ponds. It was so delectable and desired that over time the local people turned it into a profitable fish-farm business. As young children, they learned to swim in the ponds while working the nets and harvesting. Once, a frog moved in and Thalmus endeared himself to the villagers by harvesting it for the king.

Toubar (Too-bar): a mysterious, ancient land many leagues east of Ameram. It was a dry and desolate terrain inhabited by resilient nomadic tribes of people who fought constantly for control of the few water sources in the land.

Toulon (Too-lawn): A kingdom to the north of Ameram, across the Sol Linden River, and beyond the Wilderness of Toulon. Depending on which family was in power, Toulon was either at peace or trying to conquer Ameram. At the time of our story, the two countries had been at peace since Ekala's great-grandfather.

Wilderness of Toulon: a thick, tangled forest that was once the realm of an ancient native tribe, now inhabited by wild animals and undesirables. The Wilderness stretched along the southern end of the Kingdom of Toulon, forming a natural barrier. The forest's stunted trees and underbrush grew to the edge of the Sol Linden River, which was the border between Toulon and Ameram.

Woods of Rows: an ancient and mysterious grove (orchard) of trees with a thick canopy shading and darkening almost the entire woods.

Distance and time was distorted within its seemingly endless symmetrical rows of trees. The Toulon people stayed away from its enchanting appeal because many who entered its rows were never seen again. It was the domain of the Kairtaykars and the goddess Arborina.

Zinkila (Zin-kee-la): a small kingdom to the south of Ameram and a historical ally of doubtless support. Ruled by the same family for generations, the present King Dieten struggled with his four sons, who were competing to rule the country when he died.

Acknowledgements

First and foremost are Cindy and Heather, my wife and daughter, who not only continue to encourage me as I slog through my writing world but help to put all the pieces together for a finished book. Much gratitude to my editor, Dan O'Brien, for his skill, and for this book's title. Of course, a huge thank you to Steve Ferchaud for his beautiful cover; to the readers and "friend editors" who helped to hone the details: the sculptor, Matt Auvinen; Sid Crane, for all things archery; Vicki Bertaina, Kayla Gutierrez, Josh Kerney, Aeon Lem, Claudia Olson, Kathy Wilson and Gerry Young. Without the knowledge, thoughtfulness and honesty of these friends I would be lost in the Woods of Rows.

About the Author

The King's Frog Hunter (Book 1 of the series) is a novel Young created from the ongoing stories he wrote for his daughter throughout her childhood to encourage her to grow strong and own the values of honor, integrity, courage, friendship, loyalty, graciousness and mercy. Book 2 of the series, The Shadows of War, delves deeper into those themes with the plot continuing into the third book, which is scheduled for release in 2019.

Ken Young lives with his wife and family of real and imaginary characters and creatures in the Sierra Nevada Mountains of Northern California.

www.kingsfroghunter.com
Facebook: KenYoung@authorbuilderkenyoung

www.ingramcontent.com/pod-product-compliance
Lightning Source LLC
Chambersburg PA
CBHW030804260626
47169CB00001B/184